The Seafaring Girls

FIVE ISLAND COVE, BOOK 7

JESSIE NEWTON

feel-good fiction

ELANA JOHNSON

Chapter One

Alice Rice got up from her desk when she heard the back door open. The twins were home from school. Or at least one of them was, as Alice glanced at the bright pink sticky note on her computer. *Ginny's working today!* had been scrawled there, in her daughter's handwriting.

She smiled at it and tapped it as she went by the computer on the other side of the desk. "Charlie?" she called as she stepped into the hallway. Down and around the corner into the back of the house showed her that her son had indeed arrived home from school, but he wasn't alone.

His girlfriend, Sariah Page, had come with him, and she currently had her fingers fisted in the collar on his jacket, kissing him.

Alice cleared her throat, and Sariah and Charlie jumped apart. He looked at her, plenty of panic in his eyes. "Hey, Mom." He cleared his throat too, and she dang near rolled her eyes.

"Didn't think I'd be home?" She folded her arms and glared. "Hello, Sariah."

"Hey, Alice." She hovered half a step behind Charlie. "I should go, Charles. I'll see you tomorrow."

"Okay," he said, following her to the garage exit. They didn't kiss again, and the pretty blonde slipped outside. He faced her, his usual devil-may-care expression on his face. "I knew you'd be home."

"You seemed surprised."

"I'm a little surprised. You don't always come out of your office the moment we get home." He sighed and opened the fridge. "I don't know what to do about Sariah."

Alice scented blood, and she moved in for the kill. "What do you mean?" She strode toward him, telling herself to calm down, move slow. Big movements could scare the teenagers away.

"I mean...I like her. She's pretty. She's smart." He closed the fridge and opened the cupboard, obviously trying to do anything he could not to look at Alice. "But she's also going to NYU in the fall, and...I'm not."

"Ah, I see," Alice said. Charlie had never particularly excelled in academics—except for chemistry. He loved the stuff, and he had applied to Boston University. He'd gotten in too. No scholarship. No nothing. He'd have to pay for all of it, and Alice had helped him look into getting grants to help fund it.

Truth be told, he hadn't even decided if he was going to go or not. She knew one of his New Year's goals was to make a decision for the fall, but only a week into January, and he hadn't done it yet.

Alice was trying not to put any pressure on him. A pressured, cornered Charlie usually wasn't a good thing.

"Plus," Charlie said, and he turned his back on her. Alice sat at the bar, ready for anything. Or so she thought.

"Mandie and I have been talking again," he said, and Alice so wasn't ready for that. She almost toppled off her barstool she flinched so hard.

"What?" she asked, her voice mostly made of air. "Mandie Grover?"

"Yes." Charlie pulled down a box of popcorn and turned toward her. "Can I make this?"

"Sure," she said. Arthur wasn't home from the high school yet, but he loved popcorn as much as Charlie did. Alice was just glad they had something in common, though Arthur got along very well with the twins. He was one of those special breeds of human who actually liked and understood teenagers, and they liked and understood that he just wanted them to be the best they could be.

He'd helped Ginny a lot with her college applications, and she'd gotten into NYU, BU, Yale, and Towson. Charlie had only applied to Boston University, and he'd gotten in, so that had spared him from feeling like a failure compared to his sister, something Alice knew he did a lot.

"And?" she prompted. "What about Mandie?"

"I'm thinking...I don't know what I'm thinking."

Alice watched him put the popcorn in the microwave

and start it. Her mind whirred like the appliance, and she drew a breath. "I think I know what you're thinking."

"What's that, Mom?" He finally gave her his full attention, plenty of challenge on his face. He looked so much like his father, but he was much gentler, and much kinder. Alice thanked God for that every day.

"I think you're wishing you didn't have a girlfriend," she said. "Then it wouldn't be so confusing to be friends with Mandie. You might even be able to take her to a dance this spring and hang out with her in the summer."

Charlie didn't make a face and sigh, which meant Alice was right. He'd never admit it right away, and he simply turned to get out a big bowl for his popcorn. The buttery, salty scent of it started to fill the air, and Alice let the silence fill the spaces between what she'd said.

"Maybe," Charlie said as he opened the microwave and shook the bag of popcorn. "And Mom, you were right about girls."

"Which part?" Alice got to her feet and approached her son. She curled her hand down the side of his face and around to the back of his head.

"They're aggressive," he said. He shook salt all over the popcorn and looked at her again. "Sariah wants to, you know. Do it before we graduate. I told her you'd be home this afternoon, and she still sort of attacked me when we walked in."

Alice narrowed her eyes. "She's being aggressive with you?"

"I mean, I think so," Charlie said. "Maybe it's just

because you've talked to me and *talked* to me about sex, and girls, and I don't know." He did the hefty sigh she'd heard before and walked into the living room.

Alice stayed in the kitchen, almost afraid to move. His girlfriend wanted to sleep with him, and he hadn't done it yet? She wasn't sure if she should rejoice or panic. Usually, the guy had to convince the girl that everything would be okay. Not having that barrier would make everything easier for Charlie.

Her stomach churned, and now the popcorn smelled slightly charred instead of delicious and buttery.

She turned as the garage door opened again, and this time, her husband of four months walked in. "Hey, beautiful," he said, a smile curling the ends of his mouth instantly. He took her into his arms, and Alice pulled on Arthur's strength and stability to use in her own life.

"Hey," she whispered into his shoulder.

He pulled back and looked at her. "Everything okay?" His gaze skimmed further into the house, obviously searching for what had upset Alice.

"Yes," she said firmly. "Everything's fine."

Arthur took his briefcase over to the counter that acted as a credenza and said, "Hey, Charlie. How was school?"

"Great, Arthur," Charlie said, flipping through the channels without looking at his step-father.

Arthur turned back to Alice, and she shook her head. Her son was sitting here, bored out of his mind while he tried to find something to watch on TV, when he could be with his girlfriend. It wasn't that hard to find somewhere for two teenagers to go, not if they were both properly motivated.

Charlie obviously wasn't, and Alice didn't want to disrupt something in the cosmic universe by freaking out about nothing.

Yet, she told herself. She didn't have anything to freak out about *yet*.

———

A WEEK LATER, ALICE HUMMED TO HERSELF AS SHE went around the house, picking up socks, shoes, and dishes. No one seemed to be able to get anything where it belonged except for her. She'd needed a break from her case —a nasty dispute between two parents fighting over their kids—so she didn't mind the clutter that had accumulated this week.

She usually made everyone go around on Saturday for a few minutes and help her put the house back together. This week, they'd been busy with Arthur's mother, who didn't have very much time left on this earth. She'd been sick for a while, and Alice would miss her once she finally passed.

The silence in the house filled Alice with peace, where it had once struck her with fear. She knew now that no one was going to ring her doorbell and judge her the way they did in the Hamptons. She had no images to protect or uphold here. No pretenses to live up to.

She was a busy lawyer who worked from home, with two kids who'd graduate from high school in six short months, a new husband to dote on, and plenty of household chores to keep her busy.

Her phone chimed in her back pocket, one notification after the other, telling her that her friends had started a lively conversation while she'd been in a dead zone picking up plates with dried cheese on them from Ginny's nachos last night.

The device continued to sing at Alice until she put all the dirty dishes in the sink and pulled it from her pocket. "My goodness," she said, swiping to see what was so important.

I'm dying, Eloise had sent. *Billie got asked to Sweethearts today. She's fourteen. Aaron's going to go ballistic. I need all the chocolate I can get to sweeten him up.*

Who asked her? Robin had asked immediately. Now that she wasn't swamped with clients, she had more free time to respond to texts quickly. Not that she hadn't before. Her cellphone was practically sewn to her fingers.

Alice's was too, so she wasn't judging. She did so much business with her phone, and it was easy to get absorbed into it for long periods of time and not even know it.

A boy named Luke Howard, Eloise said. *He's a year older than her, and Aaron's not going to like that.*

It'll be okay, AJ had said. *The Howards live right by us, and they're a good family.*

Agree with AJ, Robin said. *The Howards are good people.*

Aaron's looking them up right now, Laurel sent as Alice watched. She sent a winking emoji, but Alice didn't think she was kidding at all. The Chief of Police would probably run a background check, call them in for fingerprinting, and do a deep dive into their past going back generations. He had all the resources to do it.

How wonderful for her, Kristen sent.

Jean chimed in with, *I can help with a dress if she needs one.*

I don't even know if it's formal or not, Eloise said.

It's not formal, Robin said, and she would know. Robin knew everything that happened in the cove, and sometimes she irritated Alice. At the same time, there was no one Alice loved more than Robin Grover. *But it's not casual either,* she said. *It'll be best dress. Not jeans. Not prommy.*

Alice didn't really have anything to add to the conversation, but she tapped out, *It'll be okay, Eloise. He's got a month to get used to the idea, right?*

Good point, Eloise sent. *I just wish they got along better. He's so protective of her.*

There could be worse things, Kelli said. *How exciting for her to be asked. How does she know Luke?*

The conversation went on from there, but Alice had work to do. She rinsed the dishes and put them in the dishwasher. She wiped down all the counters and the stove. She straightened all the pillows in the living room and took the kitchen trash out to the big, black can Charlie towed out to the street on Thursdays.

She started a load of laundry, taking Ginny's clean clothes upstairs to her room. She peeked in the twins' bathroom and frowned. She didn't clean their rooms or do their laundry, but she would come up here to make sure the toilet and tub weren't going to rust through or be stained permanently.

Obviously, no one had cleaned this bathroom for a while, and Alice couldn't even remember whose turn it was. The garbage can lid bulged open, and she stepped into the bathroom to collect that.

She opened the lid, her hand already reaching for the sides of the bag that had been pulled over the can. She froze, her breath wheezing into her lungs, at the sight of the pregnancy test sitting there.

It had been used, and it showed only one line.

Not pregnant.

Her heartbeat sounded like a bass drum as it banged through her whole body. Whose was this?

Her mind raced; Sariah had been over to the house just yesterday, along with the rest of the Academic Olympiad team she was on with Charlie. She'd asked to use the bathroom, and since someone else had been in the half-bath off the kitchen, she'd gone upstairs.

Ginny had a boyfriend, but to Alice's knowledge they hadn't slept together.

She pulled in another breath, and the extra oxygen reminded her of the conversation Charlie had had with her last week about Mandie. They'd been talking and texting again—Alice checked his phone regularly—and Mandie had dropped by two or three days ago. She'd talked to Charlie and Ginny together on the front porch for about a half-hour, left a loaf of chocolate chip banana bread, and gone home.

Alice didn't recall her coming in the house. Charlie couldn't be sleeping with her...could he?

She reached for the pregnancy test, dislodging some used make-up remover wipes. In her mind, teenagers were so very stupid, because whoever had put this in the trashcan should've done a better job of hiding it. Even if it had been under the make-up remover wipes, Alice probably wouldn't have seen it.

With the stick in her hand, Alice felt like she was swimming outside of her body. Nothing made sense, and questions formed her whole world. Her feet felt like they were slipping down a muddy slope, and she couldn't catch herself.

Bottom line, she needed to know who'd used this pregnancy test. No matter who it was, Alice felt like her whole world was about to change.

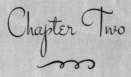

Chapter Two

Jean Shields could not stop crying. Every time she managed it for even a moment, her mind would attack her, and the tears would flow again.

I'm so sorry.

There were so many things those words couldn't make up for. Having a baby taken from her was one of them, and Jean reached for another handful of toilet paper as a fresh set of tears ran down her face.

At least her crying had gone down a notch from the howling sobs she'd dissolved into earlier that morning.

I'm so sorry, Jean.

She was so sorry too. She'd used the same words to cancel her sewing students for that afternoon, and she honestly didn't know how to even leave the bathroom. She had no idea how to tell her husband. Rueben had been as excited and as anxious as Jean to finally have a human baby to take care of.

Outside the bathroom, both of her dogs lay on the carpet, watching her. If she even twitched, they lifted their heads, and Jean had sobbed into Timber's neck for a good twenty minutes right after receiving the horrible text from her adoption case worker.

The birth mom has a relative who said she'd take the baby.

Jean brought her knees to her chest and set her forehead on them. Her own mother had been so excited. She'd come to the cove twice in the past four months to help Jean set up a nursery. Kristen, Rueben's mother, who lived only fifteen minutes away on the other side of Diamond Island, had sat with Jean in the afternoons while she made baby dresses in a variety of sizes.

They'd spent a small fortune on bedding, a crib, diapers, bows, a stroller, and every other baby item on the market.

Jean knew this was her only chance to raise a child, as she'd turned forty-one in December. Rueben would be forty-four in March, and their case worker had already admitted their age might keep a birth mom from selecting them.

She'd had no idea that the adoption could be stolen from her at any moment. Had she known that, she wouldn't have painted the walls a soft pink. She wouldn't have sewn baby giraffe curtains, with the cutest zoo animals in the background. She wouldn't have been shopping online for blessing dresses and scrapbooks and digital picture frames.

Jean wanted to scream. She wanted to shake her fists to the sky and bellow at God for His cruelty in allowing her to love the baby that she'd never even get to see now. She wanted to pound the earth the way hail did, and she wanted to whip her fury against the cliffs the way the wind got to.

As it was, Jean, a woman of only five-feet, three-inches and barely a hundred and twenty pounds, sat on her bathroom floor and sobbed into her arms.

This was hell, and Jean had no idea how to find her way out of it. There was no ladder tall enough to get her to the top. There was no floatation device that could keep her from drowning.

The dogs—she and Rueben had parented several over the years—lifted their heads, both of them looking down the hall and toward the microscopic kitchen on the bottom level of the lighthouse where Jean lived.

It had taken her some months to warm up to the idea of living underground, but Reuben loved the lighthouse, and Jean loved Rueben. They'd had many years on the mainland near her parents, and it was time for him to be here, with his mother.

"There you are," his voice said, and Jean wanted to disappear. She didn't want him to find her like this, but she couldn't get herself to move.

He bent down and patted the dogs. "What are you guys doing—?" He'd spotted her, and Jean didn't have anything to say.

"Honey." He stepped into the tiny bathroom and knelt in front of her. "Are you hurt?"

In so many ways, yes. The kind where she bled? No.

She cried so hard she couldn't answer him, and Rueben ran his hands down her arms, his eyes searching for injuries.

"Hon," he said again. "Talk to me. Calm down a little and talk to me." He wrapped her in strong arms that could pull in heavy, wet ropes from the sea. He smelled like coffee and peanut butter, what he'd likely consumed for his afternoon snack. The man loved a good peanut butter cookie, and Jean had nothing better to do than perfect her recipes and provide food for her husband.

She needed something to *do*. Something to give her purpose in her life.

She clung to him, feeling the soft quality of his cotton shirt against her face and giving him some of the agony that had plagued her for hours. "My phone," she managed to say, and Rueben picked it up from where it sat on the closed toilet seat.

He kept her close, and the awful messages didn't take long to read. "No," whooshed out of his mouth, and Rueben sat down heavily on his knees, no longer trying to kneel up. He probably couldn't, because Jean knew that feeling of suddenly carrying the world on her back.

That was how Miranda's texts had felt. Like she'd tossed Earth, then Mars, then Jupiter onto Jean's back with the words, "I'm so sorry."

She also knew it wasn't Miranda's fault that the birth mom had changed her mind. Jean supposed they'd been warned that birth moms could do that, especially young ones. The one that had chosen them was in her early twen-

14

ties, though, and Jean and Rueben only had five weeks to go until their baby would be born.

Not your baby anymore, she told herself, finally feeling some semblance of peace enter her heart. That came from Rueben, because while the man was tall and a bit bear-like in the breadth of his shoulders, he possessed a marshmallow heart. He was kind, and good, and loyal. He was hard-working and strong, and Jean loved him with everything she had.

"I'm okay," she said, taking a breath. Air felt like cement in her lungs. "You're here. I love you." Tears leaked down her face as she pulled back. "We're okay, and that's all that matters."

Rueben cried too, and she hated seeing the broken, anguished look on his face. "I'm so sorry, Jean. I—I don't even know what to say or do."

"I don't either," she whispered. "Maybe you could help me up? I've been in here for hours."

After crying for those initial twenty minutes, Jean had gone into shock. She'd wandered the lighthouse living levels —there were two—and once she'd realized what was happening again, she'd needed to throw up. Pure devastation could make one nauseous, she supposed.

Rueben stood and lifted Jean easily into his arms. "Do you want to lie in bed?" he asked, his voice low.

She nodded and clung to him. He laid her on her side of the bed after pulling back the blanket, and he tucked her in tightly. Jean started to cry again, and when Reuben slid into bed with her, his boots and jeans off now, they held each other and wept. Both dogs jumped up onto the bed, but Jean didn't find their presence as comforting as she once had.

"I love you," he whispered. "You're enough for me."

"I love you too," she whispered back. "You're enough for me too."

"It still hurts," he said, his arms around her gently, but with plenty of pressure so she'd know how very much he wanted her to be close to him.

"Yes." She closed her eyes and tucked her face right against his chest, where she could hear his heart beating and smell the scent of his skin. "It hurts so much."

***

"I CAN'T CRY ALL DAY TODAY," JEAN SAID THE NEXT morning. Reuben looked at her over the top of his coffee mug. "Can I come up top with you?"

"Of course," he said. "No sewing today either?"

"I canceled all week," she said, looking away now. "That way, my students will still be even." She stirred her coffee absently, and she still hadn't taken a sip. "Did you tell your mother?"

"Yes."

So Kristen would be coming by today. Jean was surprised she hadn't arrived yet, actually, though she supposed it was only five-thirty in the morning, and Kristen was seventy-eight years old now.

She'd probably told all her girls, and Jean's eyes filled

with tears. She didn't want to see anyone. She didn't want to talk about it. She didn't want cards, gifts, food, or sympathy. It would only make her feel weak.

Her phone sat on the table in front of her, and she swiped it on.

"She's going to bring lunch," Rueben said, his voice so quiet. Everything about living underground was so quiet, and Jean found that urge to scream some sound into their living space increasing once more.

"I don't want her to bring lunch," Jean said, plenty of bite to her tone. "I don't want to cry all day today." She met her husband's eyes, and he nodded.

"I'll tell her." He picked up his phone and started typing.

Jean looked at her texts. None of the women she'd spent last summer and fall, then the holidays, with had texted her. The group text had gone quiet after Eloise had told everyone about Billie getting invited to the Sweethearts Dance. Either Kristen hadn't told them, or she'd used a different group text —one with Jean not on it.

That idea made bitterness surge up her throat, and Jean started typing a message to the whole group.

I don't know if you've heard, but Rueben and I lost the baby. I don't want to talk about it right now. It's too raw for me. We don't need any food. I don't want to push you away, but I really don't want to cry all day today, so it'll just be easier for me if everyone just gives me a little space and a little time to process it.

Jean didn't think there was enough space in the universe,

or enough time left in her life, for her to get over this. Her mother had told her she was over-dramatic growing up, and Jean pulled back on the reins of that dramaticism. Perhaps she would find a way through this confusing maze of disappointment and grief.

But right now, she just wanted to be alone.

"I'll bring my eReader up to the top," she said as she finally lifted her coffee mug to her lips. She couldn't remember if she'd eaten yesterday or not, as everything felt hollow and strange inside her. "And I'll just read by you. Is that okay?"

Rueben got up and came around to her side of the table. "It's absolutely okay," he whispered, dropping into a crouch beside her. "I'm worried about you, Jean. Do we need to go see the therapist again?"

She traced her fingers down the side of her husband's face, enjoying the soft quality of his salt-and-pepper beard, and the concern in his dark eyes. She'd seen a mental health professional for years, off and on. She'd had trouble accepting her infertility, and she often suffered from depression.

Moving to the cove permanently had actually been wonderful for her, as she'd learned to rely on herself and on Reuben, instead of her mother and sister in New Haven. Forging a friendship with Kristen had buoyed her up, and when Kristen started bringing her to the Wednesday luncheons with the other ladies, Jean's outlook on life had improved drastically.

Those women cared about her, and she cared about them. She loved being involved in their lives, and she looked down at her text again. It was all still true, and while she knew Robin, Alice, Eloise, AJ, Kelli, and Laurel would be at the lighthouse in two minutes flat if she asked them to be, she *really* didn't want to cry all day today.

She sent the text and focused on her husband again. "Yes," she said. "I think I need to see someone again." She appreciated that he'd said "we" when he'd asked her, but the therapy wasn't for him. Sometimes he did attend her sessions with her, if her doctor wanted him there, or Jean did.

He'd dropped everything for her over the years, and Jean felt like such a failure. She couldn't get pregnant. Couldn't give him the children he wanted. Her body literally couldn't do what it was meant to do, and she'd never felt so broken before.

More tears pressed behind her eyes, especially when her phone vibrated. That was probably Robin or Alice, as they had older children who got up early for high school. Jean suddenly didn't want to see their replies. Even reading how sorry they were about the loss of the baby would make her cry.

"All right." Reuben drew her into a hug. "Leave your phone here, hon. Get your eReader. Let's go up top and watch the sun rise together."

She nodded and left her phone right where it was on the table. She'd have to deal with the messages later. Or maybe she wouldn't. Maybe she'd just delete them all and pray someone else would have something to talk about soon enough.

When she returned from the bedroom with her eReader, Reuben took her hand and raised it to his lips. "What about the Seafaring Girls?" he asked, his voice low and kind. "My mom's been asking you to do it, and you couldn't because the baby was coming."

Jean heard the unspoken words. *Now there's no baby coming, Jean. What are you going to do with your life? Who cares that you're even on this planet?*

She'd resisted becoming the Seafaring Girls leader, because the program was starting the first week of March, and she was supposed to have a baby the second week of February. With that out of the picture, perhaps she could take on the nautical safety and education program.

"I'll think about it," she told Rueben, and he nodded. They started up the steps, and by the time they reached the top of the lighthouse, Jean knew what she wanted to do. "I should do the Seafaring Girls," she said. "Maybe then I'll have a purpose to my life."

"You bring me joy," he said, smiling at her. She marveled how he could be so strong. He had to be suffering too; he was. She could see it in his face. She'd felt it in his pulse last night. She'd heard it as he'd cried with her.

She managed a smile for him too, and his eyes did light up a little more. "If I had someone counting on me for something, it might help," she said. "Doctor Hill has always said to pour myself into service whenever I'm feeling worthless."

"You're not worthless, Jean."

"But I *feel* that way," she said, turning away from him. "I'm okay." She sat down in one of the chairs on the balcony and faced the cool, gray water. The sun had started to light the day, but none of its gold had kissed the earth yet.

Rueben sat beside her, and she slipped her hand into his. Yes, she should take on the Seafaring Girls if the position was still open. That would definitely give her something to focus on, something to do, and something to help her feel like she wasn't perfectly inconsequential.

"Will you text your mom?" she whispered as the first rays of light started to glint over the water. "Maybe they've already filled the leader position."

"I'll text her and find out," he said, reaching into his pocket for his phone.

Jean nodded, because Kristen hadn't mentioned the Seafaring Girls in a while, and she didn't know if she'd found a leader yet or not. She wanted to pray that she hadn't, but Jean's heart felt like a piece of wood in her chest. Praying for a baby had never worked. Praying for this birth mother hadn't either.

She wasn't going to pray to have the Seafaring Girls job, because God didn't listen to her anyway.

Jean didn't know how to hope anymore. That ability felt as cracked and as crumpled as her ability to bear children.

So she simply sat in her chair, her hand in her husband's, and watched the sun come up. *Whatever will be, will be*, she thought.

"She hasn't read it," Rueben said, tucking his phone away. "She's probably still asleep."

"Probably." Jean kept her focus on that moment. The very one in which she lived and breathed. Every inch the sun moved, she saw it, because if she let her attention wander forward or backward, her eyes would fill with tears, and she *really* didn't want to cry all day today.

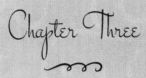

Chapter Three

Eloise Sherman ran toward the ferry, because she could not be left on Sanctuary Island for the night. The inn she ran, The Cliffside Inn, was booked full for the night, and she didn't want to show up on her mother's doorstep again.

Thunder rumbled overhead, and Lawson gestured her forward as if she could run any faster. "Sorry," she said breathlessly as she darted past him. "Thanks for holding it."

"Late again tonight," he said after her, and now that Eloise stood on the ferry, she paused.

"Yes." She sighed and wiped her hair back off her face. "Thank you, Lawson."

The ferry worker gave her a smile and closed the gate behind her. The boat began to move, and Eloise went inside to find a seat. At almost ten p.m., that wasn't hard to do, and she selected a chair away from the few other passengers on the ferry.

She sighed as she sat, her muscles aching, her eyes

burning as if someone had rubbed sand in them, and her emotions quivering on the edge of a knife. She couldn't keep working this much. She had no idea how Aaron, her husband, dealt with this much pressure.

As the Chief of Police for Five Island Cove, Aaron had about fifteen thousand pieces moving at any given time. Eloise was starting to understand how exhausting that was, and she didn't have nearly the personnel Aaron did to help her.

Not only that, but everyone in her family would be in bed by the time she got to their home on Diamond Island, and Eloise's tears pressed against her closed eyelids. She couldn't break down and cry right here on the ferry, so she breathed in and held it in an attempt to control her emotions.

You need more help, she thought, and her mind immediately conjured up an image of Jean Shields. The dark-haired woman could probably use something to distract her from the terrible loss she'd suffered, but Eloise didn't know how to reach out to her.

Jean had asked them not to bring food, not to stop by and offer condolences, but to give her time and space. Eloise understood that, and she'd done her best to respect Jean's wishes. She'd sent her a text off the group string, saying she loved her, she was sorry, and if there was anything she could do to help, she would. All Jean had to do was let her know.

Jean had not responded. Only a couple of days had gone by, and Eloise didn't expect Jean to heal completely in forty-eight hours. Some things required decades of work and wrestling, and Eloise wished she could get in the ring with Jean and help her pin down her struggles and make them dry up.

She opened her eyes and breathed strength into her lungs. She'd wanted The Cliffside Inn with her whole heart, and she wasn't going to complain that only a year after a tsunami and opening the inn found her in the black, operating well, and able to pay all of her business and personal expenses.

Made it on the ferry, she texted to Aaron, right below the picture of her dinner plate, covered in foil, which he'd taken bathed in the yellow light above their stove.

Good, he responded. *See you soon. Be careful on the roads. It's raining here.*

January in Five Island Cove always saw a lot of rain, and Eloise closed her eyes again and listened to the drops intensify on the roof above her head. Before she knew it, the ferry began to slow, and she disembarked to a fury of wind and water.

She shielded her face with her hand and hurried to her car. Her headlights barely cut through the storm, but she made it to the house where she'd been living with Aaron and his girls, Billie and Grace, for eight months now. She loved being married to him and coming home to him, and she hoped she provided the same comfort for him and his daughters.

She knew she did, and as she pulled in beside his police cruiser in the garage, she wasn't surprised to find Billie framed in the doorway leading into the house. The fourteen-year-old was angelic, with white-blonde hair and big, soulful blue eyes. She was thin, with long legs, and just the beginning of womanly curves that made her attractive to teenage boys.

She was the kind of girl Eloise would've envied in her latter junior high and early high school days, but seeing her standing there brought nothing but a smile to Eloise's face.

"What are you doing up?" she asked as she got out of her car, towing along her huge bag that acted as a purse. "It's a school night."

"Jean texted," Billie said, holding up her phone though it stayed dark. "She said she has my dress pieced, and she wanted to know when I could go over to the lighthouse and try it on. Then she can finish it."

Eloise wanted to say they could go tomorrow, of course. She'd cancel everything on her schedule to be there with Billie, not only for her step-daughter, but so she could check on Jean in a non-evasive way. Her heart pounded as she closed the car door behind her and moved toward the few steps that led up to the landing and then the entrance to the house.

She swallowed, her mind racing. "Have you told your dad about the dance?"

"I mentioned it at dinner tonight," Billie said, rolling her eyes. She was a sober child who'd matured a lot in the past couple of years. She'd also been slowly loosening up, and she was really good at dealing with her father now.

They were so much alike that they didn't always get along, and Aaron simply didn't understand what it meant to be a teenage girl in today's world. Eloise had to work hard not to give in to everything the girl wanted, because she wanted to be a united front with Aaron with his daughters. She always deferred to him, as he was their parent and she was not, but she did love Billie with a fierceness she did not understand.

She reached the top of the short flight of steps and pushed Billie's hair over her ear. "What did he say?"

Billie met her eyes, unrest and anxiety swimming in hers. "He asked who I was going with. I told him Luke had asked me, and I'd like to go with him. You know how Dad is. He was all like, 'Luke who? Do I know this Luke character?'"

Eloise gave her a soft smile, but Billie sighed like her father was the most difficult man on the planet. Eloise had definitely experienced moments like this herself, and she wished she could open the pages in the book of life a little wider for Billie. Then she'd be able to see that not everything that happened right now was of the utmost importance. That there was so much more out there, and in ten years, or even only one, this dance wouldn't matter at all.

"Did he look him up?"

"No, thank goodness," Billie said. "I told him Luke's last name, and you could just see the relief on his face. Of course, he replaced it with defiance or something a moment later. He knows the Howards, and he likes them, so there's no reason I can't go with Luke."

Eloise nodded, indicating that Billie should go inside. The January night air held a chill she didn't want to stand in much longer. They went into the kitchen together, Eloise hitting the button to close the garage door behind her. She hefted her purse onto the dining room table, where Grace's homework and backpack sat, along with Aaron's coffee mug.

He took his police business into the office, and if she went in there, she'd find stacks of files, his police vest, a closet with several uniforms hanging inside, and a wall filled with clippings, notes, and pictures. The man was extremely dedicated to his job, but he'd managed to carve out time for his girls—and Eloise—too. She admired him so much for that, and she had a moment of vertigo where she was adrift in a sea of busyness.

The inn could pull her in, suck her under, and refuse to let her go, and Eloise felt like she was drowning for a few seconds.

Billie said, "El? Are you okay?" and Eloise blinked. She wasn't in deep water. It wasn't dark and black around her. She stood in a warm house, with soft lights and a beautiful girl who needed her.

"Yes," she said, her voice telling of her weariness. "Just tired." She pulled in a breath through her nose. "What was the verdict, then? You're going to the dance?"

"Dad said he'd have to 'have a talk' with Luke, but yes, I could go with him." Billie sounded like she'd swallowed lemons as she spoke. "What do you think he'll say to him?"

"He's just worried, because Luke is older than you." Eloise reached for Billie and drew her into a hug. "He said yes, and we can go do your dress fitting tomorrow."

"After school?"

"Yes," Eloise said, deciding on the spot. "I'll leave the inn before check-in, and I'll be home when you and Grace get here."

Billie pulled away, shock in her expression. "Really?"

Eloise nodded, determined to make it so. "Really. I'm working too much, and I need a break. I'll be here, and we can go over to the lighthouse after school." She nodded down to Billie's phone. "You better text her. I know she has sewing students in the afternoon. You should find out when she's available."

"I'll ask her right now." Billie's fingers flew across the screen, as she was already an expert texter despite getting her phone only a year or so ago.

Eloise simply wanted to go to bed, and she noted that Aaron had put her plate in the fridge. She'd grabbed something to eat at the inn as the hour grew later and later, and a twinge of guilt pulled through her. "Come on, sweetie," she said. "Plug in your phone, and let's go to bed."

"She said anytime is fine," Billie said, looking up. "She's not doing her lessons this week."

Eloise pressed her lips together and nodded. Billie went to plug in her phone at the "command center" where Aaron required his girls to put their electronics, and she preceded Eloise down the hall toward the bedrooms.

"Love you, Billie," she whispered into the dark hallway as the girl turned into her room.

"Love you too, El." Those words brought warmth to Eloise's soul, giving her another dose of strength and one of determination to not get stuck at the inn tomorrow, no matter what. She had an on-site manager. She had a full-time cook. She had a maintenance lead. *She* didn't have to be there to do everything.

In the bedroom, Aaron had left a light on in the bathroom for her, and she appreciated that she didn't have to fumble her way through the dark. She changed quickly, switched off the light, and slid between the sheets just as her husband rolled toward her.

"You're home," he said, his voice half drowsy and half awake.

"Yeah, sorry," she whispered. She eased into his arms, because there was nowhere she'd rather be than in the arms of Aaron Sherman. "I'm taking a half-day tomorrow. Would you have time for lunch?"

He pressed his mouth to her forehead, then her cheek, and finally her ear. His lips caught her lobe as he said, "Lunch with my wife? I'm in."

Eloise tipped her head back and kissed her husband, feeling like the luckiest woman in the world. Now, if she could get away from the inn by lunchtime, she'd really be working miracles.

Chapter Four

R obin Grover had arrived at the restaurant first, which happened quite often for her. She didn't mind, because Alice had already texted to say she'd left her house, and Laurel had said she was on the ferry from Sanctuary. They'd be here soon enough.

Her phone buzzed, and she plucked it from her purse, her mind focused on that morning's conversation with Jamie, her youngest daughter. The girl had matured a lot, right before Robin's eyes, when she hadn't been looking. She'd started hanging out with boys more and more, and at some point while Robin was dealing with her husband leaving the cove and fishing in Alaska for the past two summers, her eldest daughter, Mandie, dating and now preparing to go to college, and amping up her event planning business, Jamie had become a teenager too.

Not only that, but she'd made it into the musical theater class for the second semester of school, and her very best friend was in the class, along with her latest crush. Robin had been open and honest with her about boys, despite Jamie's insistence that she'd "heard it all" when Robin had talked to Mandie about the same things.

This text wasn't from either of her daughters, thankfully, but her husband. Duke had sent a picture of a full deck of fish, with the words, *Found those tuna!*

She pulled in a breath at the size of the fish, as well as how many there were. "Thank you, Lord," she murmured. She and Duke had never been the richest of people in Five Island Cove. They lived in her mother's house and paid a nominal amount in rent. They'd always managed to make ends meet so Robin could stay home with the girls—until last year's tsunami had taken Duke's fishing boat and the only way they made a living and turned it into splinters.

They'd had to get a loan to buy a new boat, which was bigger and better, and Robin had taken on dozens more clients last year to help pay that loan, keep their family afloat, and get ahead.

Duke had gone to Alaska again, where the fishing was phenomenal in the summer, and together, they'd gotten back on top of their misfortune. He'd been following this school of fish for over a week now, and Robin couldn't wait to see her husband in the flesh again.

"Hello," Alice chirped, and Robin looked up from her phone as her best friend slid into the seat beside her. Alice placed her designer bag on the floor and looked at Robin, her smile cemented happily in place.

Robin and Alice could bicker like sisters, but Robin

loved her fiercely. "Hey, Alice." She put down her phone and side-hugged her friend. "How's the Thomas case coming?"

"They are never going to agree," Alice said wearily. She hugged Robin back and wiped her hand down the side of her face. "You know, it's actually made me see how easy my divorce was with Frank."

"Easy?" Robin asked. She remembered that summer, two ago now, where Alice had practically disappeared inside herself. She'd stopped eating, stopped sleeping, and at one point, Robin had feared they'd have to hospitalize her.

"Comparatively," Alice said. "As far as divorces go. I don't think they're ever easy."

"They certainly aren't," Robin said, though she hadn't been through one herself. She'd seen others endure the split, and she didn't want to find herself in that position. In Alice's case, the separation had been a good move, and Alice had worked hard to learn, grow, change, and find herself again.

Robin supposed she'd had to do that on some level too over the past couple of years, and she felt stronger and more sure of herself today than she had even last year at this time.

She gave Alice a smile, the gesture wobbling a little on her face. "It's the hard things that make us stronger and better."

"Life lived in fire is better than life not lived," Alice said, something their Seafaring Girls leader used to tell them. Kristen Shields was still one of Robin's very best friends, and she wondered if she could stop by her condo and get an update on Jean.

She reached for her water glass, a tactic she'd used many times over the years to make her question more innocent than it really was. "How's Jean? Have you heard?"

"No," Alice said. "You?"

"I texted her privately, but she didn't respond." It was killing Robin not to go to the lighthouse with a five-course meal in tow. "I'm trying to respect her privacy."

"How many meals do you have in your freezer for her?" Alice asked with a smile.

"None," Robin said, a touch of disgust in her voice. Alice grinned harder, and Robin rolled her eyes. "Fine. Just two, I swear."

Alice laughed, and they both looked up as a policewoman pulled out the chair across from her and sat down.

"Hey," Laurel said, a long sigh accompanying the word. "Sorry I'm late." She reached up and took out her ponytail, which had started to droop a bit. She fixed it up, looking from Robin to Alice. "What did I interrupt?"

"Nothing," Robin said. "Just Alice making fun of me for having food in the freezer." She gave Alice a side-eyed look from the corner of her eye. "Though she has benefitted from such meals in the past, I'll have you know."

Laurel grinned from Robin to Alice. "When does Duke come home?"

"He got a *huge* load of fish today," Robin said. "I'd just gotten a text when Alice arrived." She couldn't help smiling. "He rarely has service, so I'm not sure when he sent it, but with that many fish, he should be on his way back."

"That's great news," Alice said, looking at the picture

Robin pulled up on her phone. The waiter arrived, and they put in their appetizer and drink orders. Laurel buried herself behind the menu, but Robin had eaten at Mimi's so many times, she had their offerings memorized. Alice likewise didn't pick up the menu.

Their eyes met, and a zing of nerves ran through Robin. "What?" she asked.

"I have to tell you something, but I don't want you to freak out."

"I hate it when you start conversations like that."

Laurel put her menu down, her eyes definitely searching for clues. She'd been moved onto the narcotics team several months ago, but after she'd blown open the biggest drug case the cove had ever seen, she'd decided that undercover work and the division wasn't for her. She'd asked Aaron to put her back in a car with a partner, and he'd done according to her request.

Alice threw a look across the table to Laurel, who nodded. "It involves Mandie."

Great, Robin thought. Alice had already run this by Laurel, and she was the last to know. If there was one thing Robin hated, it was being left out of something. Especially something to do with her own daughter.

"Okay," Robin said as carefully as she could. "Go on."

"She came over a few nights ago," Alice said. "With banana bread. She chatted with the twins for a little bit. Came inside for a minute to use the restroom." She cleared her throat.

Surprise darted through Robin. Mandie had made

several loaves of chocolate chip banana bread over the weekend, and she'd gone out to deliver them to a few elderly people in their neighborhood. At least that was what she'd told Robin.

Ginny and Charlie didn't qualify as senior citizens, no matter how anyone sliced their age.

She cleared her throat. "Okay."

"Charlie's been talking to her again," Alice said, her nerves only amplifying Robin's. "I think he still likes her."

Robin would not allow that relationship to pick up again, and her jaw tightened. Mandie had been devastated when the cute boy had broken up with her to go out with someone blonder and skinnier. Mandie still liked Charlie, Robin knew that. He was fun to talk to, and good-looking, and popular.

"Okay," she said again, the two syllables very measured as she let them out of her throat. "And?"

Alice looked at Laurel helplessly.

"And she found a pregnancy test in the twins' bathroom," Laurel said. "It showed not pregnant, so there's nothing to freak out about."

Robin blinked at Laurel, the words she'd said not quite making sense in her head. She floated outside her body for a moment. *Pregnancy test.*

Nothing to freak out about.

Twins' bathroom

Charlie likes her still.

Robin looked between Laurel and Alice. "Why are you telling me this?"

"It could be Mandie's," Alice said. "I thought you should know."

"How could it be Mandie's?" Robin demanded. "She doesn't have a boyfriend." She shook her head. No. None of this made sense. She grabbed her phone and started tapping. Beside her, Alice said something, but the words didn't make it to Robin's consciousness.

Are you dating Charlie again? she sent to Mandie. *You took bread over there on Sunday. Alice found a pregnancy test. She thinks it might be yours. What is going on?*

Her fingers shook, and everything in her life spun. Her daughter was six months away from her high school graduation. They had four campus tours planned in the next few months so Mandie could pick a university and start planning her future.

Nowhere had she mentioned Charlie Kelton, a baby, or anything along those lines.

Her daughter didn't answer, and Robin hurried to pull up the screenshot of her classes so she'd know where Mandie was. Or where she was supposed to be.

Foods.

She was probably elbow-deep in making mashed potatoes, something she already knew how to do. She'd complained about having to take the class at all, and Robin couldn't blame her. Mandie had been wonderful over the past year, stepping in to help Robin on dozens of occasions when she'd had to work outside the home in the evenings.

I'm sorry, she quickly sent. *That sounded so accusatory. We'll talk when you get home.*

She wasn't going to jump to the worst conclusion possible. She put her phone face-down and looked at Alice and then Laurel. "Thank you for telling me," she said. "Has Ginny decided on a college yet?"

ROBIN LOOKED UP FROM HER COMPUTER WHEN THE front door opened. Mandie's and Jamie's voices entered the house, and they both started laughing a moment later. She rose to her feet, as Mandie always checked in here before continuing down the hall and past the steps leading up to the second floor as she went into the kitchen.

Her lovely daughter appeared in the doorway, suddenly sobering. "Hey, Mom."

"Hey." Robin moved out from behind her desk and went to hug Mandie. "I'm sorry about my freak-out texts." She closed her eyes as Mandie hugged her back. Jamie continued down the hall, and Robin would need to talk to her too, as it was the day she had three classes with Damien Robinson, the boy she'd been "hanging out with" a lot since last summer.

She claimed they were just friends, and she did like someone else, but Robin wanted to keep up with both of her daughters on all things related to boys.

"It's not my pregnancy test," Mandie said, pulling away. "Yes, Charlie's been texting me more and more." She stepped past Robin and into the office, dropping her backpack near the double-wide entrance and moving over to the window seat. She sighed as she dropped into it and looked out the front window. "I don't know what to do. It's confusing."

"What is he saying?" Robin perched on the front of her desk, trying to be casual when she was really beyond curious.

"Nothing bad. Just normal stuff. How do I like my new classes. When am I working." She frowned. "He did say he might come by the shop when I'm there, which makes no sense."

Robin didn't say anything affirmative or oppositional. Charlie really had no reason to go into a perfume store, that was true.

"So it sounds a little flirty," Mandie said. "Which makes no sense, because he's still all over Sariah every time I see them together."

"Maybe he's confused too," Robin said.

Mandie shrugged. "I did take him and Ginny some bread, because I had an extra loaf, and I texted *Ginny*, not Charlie. She said she'd love it, and they happened to be sitting on the front steps together when I got there."

"Do you think she was trying to get the two of you back together?" Robin asked.

"No, Mom," Robin said. "Ginny's not like that."

Robin nodded, because she wouldn't classify Ginny to be a matchmaker for her brother either. Besides, Charlie didn't need help getting a girl's attention. "Okay," she said. "I believe you. I trust you. There were just a lot of scary words thrown at me."

Mandie faced her, her expression open. "I'm sure. Does Alice know whose it is?"

"No." Robin shook her head and straightened. "She hasn't said anything to the twins either, so she'd appreciate it if you didn't yet." She extended her hand toward Mandie. "I just don't want there to be secrets between us. I don't want us to be like me and my mother."

That was her greatest fear, actually. That she was too much like her mother, and she'd drive her daughters away from her the way Jennifer Golden had.

"I know, Mom," Mandie said, getting to her feet. "I wasn't trying to hide anything from you."

Robin hugged her again, saying, "Come on, let's go make that Boston cream cake. Your dad sent a picture of a huge haul of fish, and I feel like celebrating."

Mandie pulled away, and her face brightened. "He'll probably be home soon, then."

"I hope so," Robin said as Mandie slipped her hand into Robin's, just the way she'd once done as a little girl when they used to have to cross parking lots or busy roads. Her mother heart squeezed with love for her nearly grown daughter, and they started down the hall.

"Jamie," she called, and her youngest poked her head around the corner. "Come see the picture your dad sent." She showed the girls the fish, and they all talked about how Duke would be home before they knew it while they put together pudding, cake batter, and chocolate ganache.

Robin enjoyed the afternoon, but she was a natural-born worrier, and she couldn't help the vein of unrest that streamed through her. She worried about Duke; she worried about Mandie; she worried about Jamie; she worried about Alice, Charlie, and Ginny.

She worried about Jean and Kristen, and she vowed she would text or call them both tomorrow and make sure they were okay and well taken care of.

And your mother. The thought entered her mind, and it wouldn't let go no matter how hard Robin pushed against it.

Fine, she finally acknowledged to herself. She'd call her mother tomorrow too and see how she was doing and if there was anything Robin could do to help her.

Chapter Five

Kristen Shields stood in front of the navy blue door that led into the lighthouse, an obstacle she'd faced many times in the past. She juggled the plate of mint brownies and the plastic container of soup she'd spent yesterday afternoon making, finally getting the plate to stay securely on top of the round container.

Jean had had a few days to herself now, and when Kristen had texted that morning, her daughter-in-law had said she could come this afternoon. Apparently Billie and Eloise would be there too, because Jean had been working on a dress for Billie's Sweethearts Dance.

The event was still a month away, but Jean couldn't normally whip out a dress from start to finish in less than a week. She'd only been able to do so much in the past few days because she'd canceled her sewing students and holed up in the lighthouse.

Kristen reached for the doorknob, her mind partly on

keeping the food balanced and partly wondering what Jean would do with her sewing students should she truly take on the Seafaring Girls program.

Rueben, Kristen's son, had mentioned that his wife was once again interested in being the Seafaring Girls leader now that the baby they'd been expecting would not be coming. Kristen hadn't heard if another leader had been appointed at the time of her son's text, and she'd immediately called Baron Downing to find out.

Nope. No one had been named as the new leader of the program. The Seafaring Girls should be starting in a few weeks, and even if someone was asked and accepted the position of the leader of the after-school water safety and sea education program today, Kristen didn't think they'd be ready to begin in March as planned.

For one thing, the town of Five Island Cove hadn't even started to advertise that the program would be coming back. No one had the opportunity to sign up yet.

As she stepped inside, she muttered to herself about how she had a meeting with Baron in the morning, and all of that would be worked out. Kristen knew that more got accomplished when she gave opinions and asked respectful questions than with demanding to know when things would happen and why they hadn't yet.

Five Island Cove had just gone through a pretty major governmental shakedown, what with a new mayor unseating the incumbent and the city's manager being responsible for bringing illegal drugs into the cove over the past several years.

Nathan Baldwin's trial would be a huge public spectacle,

and one of Kristen's dearest friends was still in the middle of all of it. She worried constantly about Laurel Baker—Lehye now that she and Paul had been married for a few months. Laurel had requested to be moved out of narcotics, and she currently worked with a partner on Sanctuary, the island where she'd been before her reassignment that had led to cracking open the drug case.

Aaron Sherman had his name cleared, and his father had won the mayorship. That involved Eloise, who Kristen couldn't wait to see. El had been beyond busy at The Cliffside Inn that she hadn't come to any midweek lunches for a couple of months now.

Kristen felt somewhat distant from everyone, in fact. Alice had to support herself now, and she did that by meeting with clients, going to court, filing paperwork, and more. She also had two seniors in high school she was trying to keep alive and get graduated.

Robin had been ultra focused on her family since Duke's return from Alaska. She'd finished out her major events, and she often told Kristen she so enjoyed just "detoxing" during the day. Kristen always smiled at those texts, because Robin sometimes forgot *how* to relax.

"It's just me," Kristen called as she inched down the steps to the lower living levels in the lighthouse. Jean had been living here for almost two years, and while Kristen knew she hated living underground, she'd seemed to thrive. At least until this devastating setback.

Jean loved plants, and she'd brought as many inside as she could. Somehow, even without huge windows that let in a lot of sunshine, her greenery survived. She used lamps and fertilizers, so Kristen shouldn't have been too surprised.

The outside of the lighthouse had also been spruced up, having been whitewashed in the past year or so, and Jean's green thumb had really improved the wide, circular base. She'd planted a lot of bulbs that would bring bright spots of color in the springtime, and her rose bushes had earned her an honorable mention in the yard contest Five Island Cove did every Independence Day.

A sense of nostalgia swept through Kristen as she put the containers of food on the counter and looked around the small kitchen, dining area, and living room.

Jean came bustling down the hall, saying, "I'm coming."

"Just me," Kristen said again, and no one needed to hurry to greet her. She gave Jean a warm smile, her eyes filling with tears. Jean had been terribly close to her own parents in Long Island before moving here, another hard thing for her to give up and leave behind.

Kristen opened her arms, and Jean positively flew into them. Kristen wasn't sure if she was crying or not, but she assumed. They clung to one another, and while Kristen could've said so many things—reassurances, words of comfort, expressions of love—she simply remained silent and let her own sadness, disappointment, and desperation to help stream through her.

She hated feeling helpless, and it sure seemed to happen more and more often the older she became. Finally, when Jean shifted, the two women parted, and Kristen gazed at her beautiful daughter-in-law.

"I made that cabbage patch stew," she said. They'd joked previously about how much it made, so Jean would know Kristen still had plenty at her condo for herself, and she'd even made up a container for AJ and Matt Hymas. She got over to visit them at least once each week, and AJ alone had kept Kristen from drifting away from the civilized world completely.

"We love that," Jean said with a watery smile. "Thank you, Kristen."

She glanced toward the TV cabinet. "Is that the dress?"

Jean turned toward it, her shoulders lifting high as she drew in a long breath. "Yes," she said. "I'm afraid it turned out more pink than I'd like." She took the few steps toward the dress, which wasn't in the realm of prommy, but definitely a step above a casual sundress, and reached for the hem of it. "I guess we'll see what Billie says. I want it to be perfect for her."

A level of perfection existed inside Kristen too, she just didn't normally sew it into precisely straight lines of perfectly matched fabrics. Jean did, however, and she was very good with a sewing machine and her hands.

"I have other fabric I can use," she continued while Kristen went around the end of the peninsula and took the brownies from the top of the soup container.

"I expected Billie and Eloise to be here," she said, causing Jean to turn around and face her.

"They're on the way," she said. "El got caught up at the inn."

Kristen nodded and removed the plastic wrap from the paper plate of dessert. "Brownie?"

"Absolutely."

She held the plate out toward Jean, who actually took two brownies. She sighed as she bit into one. "Thank you for coming." She swallowed quickly, as Jean never took big bites of anything. "I didn't think I wanted anyone to come, but it's...nice. Having you here."

"I'm glad," Kristen said, her own memories flowing thick now. She hadn't wanted anyone to come after Joel's death. She'd wanted to grieve her husband's passing in her own way. And yet, Robin Grover had shown up with that basket boasting a red and white checkered cloth, stuffed with all of Kristen's favorite things.

Chewy Werther's candies, cookies, and a brand-new visor. Kristen reached up to touch the one she wore now, realizing it was the same one Robin had brought her less than twenty-four hours after Joel's death.

So much had changed in the past twenty-one months. So much had renewed. So much had also stayed exactly the same.

"Do you really want to do the Seafaring Girls?" Kristen asked. "You don't have to, Jean."

"Hello," Eloise called, drawing both of their attention back toward the stairs. Jean finished her second brownie and stepped to Kristen's side as Billie appeared first in the doorway, followed by Eloise.

They didn't look like they went together at all, but at the same time, they looked like they belonged to each other. The way Billie glanced to Eloise for support, and the way El smiled at her encouragingly.

Billie could only be described as beautiful, with high cheekbones and that white-blonde hair that fell in ultra-sleek, straight strands to halfway down her back. Her eyes were huge, and bordered between blue and gray, and Kristen could easily see why boys liked her. She was as tall as Eloise already, with most of that in her legs.

"Hello, dear," she said to Billie, enveloping her into a hug first. "How exciting, this Sweethearts Dance." She stepped back and looked at Billie, whose cheeks bore a flush. Oh, so she liked this boy who'd asked her. "Who are you going with again?"

"Luke Howard," Billie said, clearing her throat afterward and cutting a look toward Eloise. But she stood with her eyes closed, her arms clamped around Jean as the two of them embraced.

Kristen was so glad her girls had accepted Jean so readily. It had been exactly what Jean needed—and exactly what Kristen had needed. She wasn't sure why she'd thought they might not, because her core five girls who'd grown up together in the Seafaring Girls program had opened their group to anyone who needed them.

Kristen, Laurel, Jean, even AJ's new step-daughter, Lisa. They'd all been welcomed, as had several new men as they'd come into each woman's life.

"I'm so sorry we're late," Eloise said, moving from Jean to Kristen. "I didn't know you'd be here."

49

"Just crashing the party for a few minutes," Kristen said, giving El a squeeze. "Are you terribly busy at the inn still?"

El gave a huff made of pure frustration. "Yes," she said. "I'm not going to complain about it." She looked at Billie, something unsaid between them. "Things are going well; it's just busy." She drew in a deep breath and focused on Jean again. "We don't want to take much of your time."

"The dress is right here," Jean said, turning and indicating it only a few feet away. "It's too pink."

"Oh, I don't think so," Eloise said slowly, which meant she totally thought so. She was simply far too nice to say so. Kristen watched Billie, and the fourteen-year-old definitely thought the dress was too pink.

"Maybe Jean could work at the inn," Kristen said, and that got Jean and Eloise to throw surprised looks her way. She steeled her breath inside her lungs. She just had to say one thing, and then she'd let it all drop. "You want something to do, Jean. It doesn't have to be the Seafaring Girls. I want you to do what *you* want to do."

Not only that, but she wanted someone at the head of the Seafaring Girls who wanted to be there. Someone who could take the program as it was and make it into something necessary and needed for the teen girls on Five Island Cove today. She believed that everyone should be sea-savvy, knowledgeable about the dangers of the ocean that surrounded them, and able to captain boats of any size.

"I could always use more help at the inn," Eloise said, her voice full of bright, cheery lights. "There are jobs I'm hiring for now that I didn't even know I needed before."

Jean looked back and forth between the two of them. "I...don't know."

"Something to think about." Kristen reached for her hand. "You don't have to do the Seafaring Girls just because I want you to."

"I know," she whispered with a waver of emotion.

Billie turned back to them. "I love the style, Jean," she said. "Thank you so much." She swallowed as she looked at Eloise. "I do think it's too pink."

"It is," Jean said. "I have some other fabric back here. Do you want to come look?" She indicated the hallway, and she and Billie went that way, leaving Eloise and Kristen alone.

"I didn't mean to volunteer her for a job."

"I'd hire her this afternoon," Eloise said. "It's fine." She peered at Kristen. "How have you been doing? I feel so removed from everyone, despite the texts."

"You just need to come to the lunches," Kristen said with a smile. "They've kind of dwindled to me, Robin, and AJ, I'll admit."

"Alice doesn't come?" Eloise let her eyes wander down the hall. "Or Jean?"

"Occasionally," Kristen said. "Kelli's so busy at her health studio on Bell. You're out on Sanctuary. Laurel's back on her patrol. Alice has clients that can sometimes only meet during their lunch hours." She too looked down the hall where Jean and Billie had gone. "Jean...is still trying to find her place here in the cove."

"I know how she feels," Eloise murmured, and that sent a hint of surprise through Kristen.

Before she could ask Eloise what she meant, her phone rang. With the almost cartoony, pop-like song, her heartbeat picked up speed and adrenaline poured through her body.

"That's you," Eloise said, because Kristen had frozen. "Are you okay?"

She spun away from the brunette, wondering what showed on her face. "Fine," she said as she reached the counter and fumbled for her phone. Sure enough, Clara's name sat there. Kristen shouldn't have been so surprised. Her daughter had programmed in this ringtone the last time she'd come to the cove—about twenty-one months ago, for her father's funeral.

Kristen had only heard it a handful of times—on birthdays or Christmas. "It's Clara," she said, not comforted by the haunted quality in her voice.

Jean and Billie's voices reached her ears, somehow penetrating the horrible sugar-coated music still blaring from Kristen's phone.

"Excuse me," she said, rounding the peninsula and lifting her foot to the first step. She swiped on the call as Billie said something about some great silver fabric Jean had that Eloise *must* come see, and said, "Hello, dear," to her daughter in the most controlled voice she could conjure up.

She focused on the stairs as she went up, because they were uneven, and she was getting too old to fly up them. Her pulse ricocheted around inside her chest, throat, and stomach as she waited for Clara to say something.

"Clara?"

"Mom," she said, her voice unlike any Kristen had ever

heard her use. She sounded wounded and weak, and Kristen would've never used those adjectives to describe her daughter. "I need to come home for a few days. Would that be okay?"

Though Kristen and Clara had been up, down, and around over the years, Kristen didn't even have to think. "Of course," she said, hating that her daughter even had to ask. "Anytime."

If Clara *needed* to come home, something serious must be happening, and Kristen wanted to ask what it was. "Is everything okay?"

Why did her daughter *need* to come home?

She reached the top of the stairs and went out the door, only to be greeted by the January wind.

And silence from Clara.

Chapter Six

A J Hymas got out of the shower, the sound of her baby's crying reaching her from wherever her husband had the boy. She sighed, already beyond exhausted. Asher never seemed to stop crying, and AJ simply wanted to get back in the shower so the sound of the spray would drown out the sound of his wails.

Matt managed to quiet the child, and AJ dried off and started brushing her teeth. She'd wanted to be a mother for over a decade, and now that she had the baby, the doting husband, the quaint little beach cottage with emerald green grass surrounding it—at least in the summer months, the grass was green—AJ certainly didn't have anything to complain about.

Her husband's job paid all of their bills. He could golf anytime he wanted. She still had a couple of hours each day during Asher's afternoon nap to work on her freelance writing. So why did she feel like crying almost all the time?

Previous to her marriage to Matthew Hymas and then becoming a mother to their son, AJ simply took care of herself. If she wanted Chinese food for dinner, she stopped at her favorite place and got some. Or she had it delivered. She never had to ask someone what they wanted too.

She went to bed on her own timetable, and she got up when she wanted to, at least for the most part. If she had an early-morning meeting with an athlete or her boss, it was by choice. It was something she wanted or needed in order to further her career.

Now, AJ felt like she didn't do anything for herself. She ate to stay alive. She showered because she had to take care of her body. No one was handing out any awards or accolades for keeping a fussy baby alive for the past six months, and no one cared if she sat on the couch all day or walked Asher in the morning and then planned music and playtime for him.

She dressed and went down the hall toward the kitchen, her hair still damp and making her shoulders shiver. Matt stood in the kitchen with a half a piece of toast in his hand, while Asher had been strapped in his high chair and was currently trying to get his chubby fingers around a chunk of watermelon.

"Hey, beautiful," Matt said, sliding one hand around AJ effortlessly. He leaned down and kissed her, and all of the stress in AJ's life dried up with the taste of his mouth. He'd been drinking coffee, and he liked a ton of sugar and cream in that. AJ smiled against his lips, breaking their kiss.

"Is there coffee left for me?" she asked.

"Barely," he said. "That son of yours is on his third breakfast."

"Maybe he's part hobbit," AJ joked, looking over to their child. Her life could've been taken from one of the lifestyle pages of the famous Eastern Seaboard magazines, something she'd always fantasized about having.

"Matt," she said, stepping out of his arms to get her coffee mug. "Are you happy?"

"Yeah," he said easily. The weight of his eyes on the side of her face landed far too heavily. "Are you not?"

"I don't know," AJ said. She poured the last of the coffee into her mug and opened the drawer to get out a spoon. Anything to keep herself from looking at him. "Don't you ever feel like you're just living life on the surface?"

"I'm not sure I know what that means." His voice tickled her eardrums, as he'd lowered it and added that sober, husky quality to it, the same way he did whenever they talked about something serious.

"It's...do you ever think we just spend our whole lives pursuing things that don't matter?" She turned to face him, her throat clogging with desperation. "And then, that leaves me thinking, well, if the job doesn't matter, and the accolades don't matter, then what does matter? Is it us?"

She gestured between the two of them. "Our relationship? Our family ties? What really matters? What's below the surface?"

She was tired of living on the surface. Tired of making sure the house was clean to entertain Matt's clients, and tired of dressing Asher in the cutest nautical outfits to impress the other moms she ran into at the grocery store or the outdoor mall.

None of that seemed to matter.

She wanted life to be messy again, because then she'd be able to sort through the good, bad, and ugly and pluck out what she should really be focusing on.

"I think our relationship absolutely matters," Matt said. "We work on us, AJ."

She nodded, because he was right. They did work hard to stay in communication with each other, stay on the same page, help one another out if at all possible.

"Maybe you need something more." It wasn't the first time Matt had suggested such a thing. When she'd questioned him as to what the "more" would be, he'd said a steady job, where someone else scheduled her time.

AJ had balked at the idea from the moment he'd said it. She didn't want someone else to care for her son, though she hadn't been able to admit out loud that she didn't find as much joy and accomplishment in doing so. At least not as much as she'd thought she would, or as much as she'd hoped she would.

All of it left AJ feeling like she was still broken somehow, and no matter what amazing, grand things came her way in life, she always would be.

"I don't want something more," she said quietly. "I need to figure out why I feel like I do. Why just being me—as AJ, as your wife, as Asher's mom—isn't good enough."

"It *is* good enough," Matt said. "You always have been."

"But I don't *feel* like I am." So she did laundry twice a week, because it was measurable. The clothes and sheets and towels didn't sit in the basket for longer than an hour before she folded them. She baked bread—homemade bread—and took it down the street to a woman she'd befriended who had a baby a few months older than Asher.

She made cards and mailed them to Matt's kids with twenties or fifties stuck inside. She met her friends for lunch; she texted them all the updates on her life, something only two years ago she would've never even considered.

Tears pressed behind her eyes. Yes, Lisa, Derrick, and Justin always texted or called to thank her for the cards. The act of doing it wasn't enough for AJ. If she didn't get those texts or calls, she still felt like she wasn't doing enough.

Savannah down the street had cried the last time AJ brought bread. If she hadn't, AJ probably wouldn't have felt good about doing it. She hated that she needed the approval and acknowledgement from others.

Asher started to fuss again, and AJ set down her coffee mug and went to collect him. Matt had been up since four-thirty, when Asher had made his first peep. AJ had groaned, and Matt had rolled over, kissed her forehead, and whispered, "I'll get him."

Her husband was a saint; her baby the cutest on the planet. He wasn't well right now, and AJ pulled the tray away from him, though he still had two chunks of fruit to eat. "Hey, baby," she cooed at him. "Did Daddy give you your medicine this morning?"

"Not yet," Matt said, and AJ knew he'd let the conversation drop. He didn't know what she wanted to hear, and she didn't either. She'd let it stew inside her until she couldn't stand it anymore, and then she'd bring it up again.

Matt opened the fridge and got out the violently pink liquid antibiotic. AJ held Asher on her hip and collected the syringe from the towel beside the sink. They'd only been given one, and she washed it every time she administered the medicine to Asher. At least it tasted like candy, and the baby didn't protest taking it.

She got the job done easily and looked up at Matt.

"AvaJane," he said, and that was all he had to vocalize to let her know that he saw her. He cared about her. What she did during the day while he went to the golf course mattered to him.

Did she really need to matter to anyone else?

"I'm fine," she said. "You're going to be late."

"I am working the check-in desk this morning." He looked at the clock on the stove. "What do you need from me?" His kind eyes came back to her, and AJ hated this unrest in her soul. He'd given her everything she'd ever wanted, even if it had come a couple of decades later than she'd have liked.

"Nothing," she said, the word getting stuck in her throat. "I'm doing good." She just kept thinking that if she got outside of her own head, she'd be able to find her true purpose in life. It hadn't been getting the scoop on professional athletes. It hadn't been playing sports professionally.

As she gave her husband a tight smile and let him kiss her

good-bye, AJ allowed her thoughts to roam free. She normally didn't, because she had some anxiety and depression that had always required a tight leash.

Call Jean, she thought, and AJ determined to do that the moment she could get Asher to stop whining.

Matt left to go run his father's golf course, which he would be inheriting in the next couple of years, and looked at her son. "All right, Ashy," she said. "What do you need from me to be happy today?"

The boy cuddled into her, and AJ decided she could rock him in the chair that faced the big picture window for a few minutes. Perhaps then he'd go to sleep, and then AJ would check in on Jean.

***

THE DOORBELL WOKE AJ, AND HER EYES FLEW open. Adrenaline flowed through her, and she looked down at her sleeping infant. Asher slumbered on, and AJ rocked forward to get herself to her feet. She'd always been tall and thin, but her pregnancy had changed the shape of her body. She carried a few extra pounds now, and it was distributed oddly around her hips and in her chest.

"It's us," a woman said, the voice belonging to Kristen Shields. Her footsteps approached, and she appeared in the arched doorway of the living room. "You are here."

Both Alice and Robin crowded in around AJ, and happiness burst through her. "Here I am," she said. "I fell asleep and obviously lost track of time." She was honestly surprised she hadn't dropped her son.

"When you didn't show up for lunch and you didn't answer your phone, we decided to bring lunch to you," Robin said, her smile built of sunshine. She held up a white plastic bag. "It's crab legs; your favorite."

AJ's mouth watered at the possibility of warm butter and salty, smooth crab legs. She grinned at Robin, something inside her settling now that she wasn't alone. AJ had never done very well alone, choosing to surround herself at times with people who weren't even good for her.

"Thank you," she said, moving to give Kristen a hug. She did, then passed Asher to the older woman.

"I'll go lay him down. The poor thing. How is he?" She moved away before AJ could answer, which was okay, because Alice drew her into a hug next.

"I haven't seen you in forever," Alice said.

"Who's fault is that?" AJ teased. "Miss Big-Shot Family Lawyer."

Alice laughed as she stepped away, and it did AJ's heart some good to see her friend so carefree and happy. Something lurked beneath the surface, and the reporter in AJ was very good at sensing it. She said nothing for now and turned to follow Robin into the kitchen.

"Jean's on her way," Alice said. "Kelli said she was bringing lunch to Shad, and once they finish, she might stop by if we're still here."

AJ's emotions swelled up, as if someone had stuffed

them all into a tiny roller coaster car and sent it up a big hill. The chains clicked and clacked, and she'd finally reached the top of the mountain. Down she'd gone, and she should be screaming, but her stomach had lodged somewhere in her throat.

"I haven't seen Kelli in far too long," she said, allowing her emotions to come out in the words. "It's my fault. I said I'd come to the Mommy and Me class, and I haven't." She'd meant to, but life had gotten busy. Then Asher had gotten sick.

"There's always next week," Alice said from behind her. "I find that if I text Kelli, she'll respond, but she's not going to reach out."

"Jean's like that too," Kristen said, coming back into the kitchen. "Thank you, girls, for not letting her pull away from you." She wore such warmth and appreciation on her face. "It means a lot to me. Moving here was very hard for her."

"We love Jean," Robin said, speaking for all of them the way she was apt to do.

AJ wouldn't have said differently about Jean, but she knew Kelli used to reach out to her specifically. They'd been very close growing up, and out of everyone they now divided their time between, Kelli and AJ had always made more time for each other.

While the others chatted about the Seafaring Girls program, Billie's Sweethearts dress, and more, AJ texted Kelli.

I miss you, lady. I hope you can come today.

I miss you so much. I will come by your place whether everyone is there or not. I'm on my way to Shad right now, so it's looking good.

AJ smiled and looked up from her phone. Robin had gotten out the crab legs. Alice handed AJ a Styrofoam cup of sweet tea, and Kristen removed the rewarmed butter from the microwave.

"This is exactly what I needed today," AJ said. "Thank you all for coming."

She wasn't great at expressing her emotions, but it was something she was trying to get better at. She tended to do things instead of say them, but with all of the joy pouring from her friends' faces, AJ could see how important vocalizing things was.

"Of course," Robin said. "Now that I'm not so busy, I need this too." She and Alice exchanged a glance, and AJ volleyed her gaze back and forth between them.

"What's going on?" she asked.

"What?" Alice asked innocently.

"What?" AJ mocked, cocking her hip and putting her hand on the right side. "I saw you two. Always in a conspiracy with each other." She grinned and shook her head, took the plate Kristen handed her, and loaded up with butter and crab legs.

"Oh, Alice just has a mystery to solve," Robin said dismissively. She even waved her hand like the riddle would work itself out. "I'll let her tell it."

"She doesn't want to tell it," Alice practically growled, giving Robin a daggered look.

"She found a pregnancy test in the twins' bathroom," Robin said. "There. Done. Told." She threw a withering look in Alice's direction. "Now she just has to figure out whose it is."

AJ's heart leapt into the back of her throat, because her own experiences with pregnancy tests had trained her pulse to riot when seeing the results of one. She didn't know what to say, and Kristen saved her by saying, "Wow, Alice. Do you really think it's Ginny's or Charlie's?"

"Well, it's not Charlie's, obviously," Robin said. "Though he does seem to get around to a lot of girls."

"I told you about Mandie." Alice whipped the words at her. "I'm doing the best I can."

"Just *ask* them," Robin said as she brought her own plate of food to the table where AJ had retreated. She met AJ's eyes, clearly begging her to join the conversation. Giving advice really was more Robin's style than AJ's.

She dunked her crab leg into the butter and took a bite. "What strategies have you tried, Alice?"

Her baby wailed down the hall, and Kristen practically threw her plate into the sink as she said, "I'll get him. Don't get up, AJ."

AJ hadn't moved yet, and relief painted through her as Kristen turned her back and hustled away. AJ switched her gaze to Alice as the dark-haired woman came to the table. She looked polished and professional, as she usually did. Today, she wore a long pair of gray slacks with a purple sleeveless blouse that showed she clearly spent time with a pair of barbells.

Alice sat down, taking her time to get settled before she met AJ's eyes. "Not much, admittedly," she said. "I've talked to the twins about a lot of things, but for some reason, I'm blocking on this." A sigh accompanied the words, and AJ's heart went out to Alice.

The moment froze, and AJ lived inside it alone as she realized that no matter what a person looked like on the outside, no matter how clean their house was, or how trimmed the grass, they still had struggles. Most people simply kept their struggles and issues contained behind closed doors, or makeup, or perfectly polished professional outfits and classically styled hair.

But life was hard for everyone. AJ suddenly didn't feel so alone, and she breathed, blinked, and beamed at Alice. "You'll think of something," she said. "Maybe you just need more time for it to come to you."

"I'm honestly considering not doing anything," Alice said. "It was a negative test, so it's not like a baby will appear in nine months or anything." She sighed and picked up her fork to start in on her krab salad. "At least I have this delicious salad." Alice looked up and smiled, though it drooped around the edges, her eyes full of weariness. "And you guys."

AJ reached across the space between them and patted Alice's hand, wondering when her maternal instincts had kicked in. "Yes," she said. "All you need is crab and friends."

Kristen returned with a tearful Asher on her hip, and once she came to the table, the conversation turned to lighter things. Everything wasn't right with the world, but some-how, for AJ, that was...all right.

She'd see Jean and Kelli today, and if she set a reminder in her phone, she could text Alice in a few days to get an update or just to check on her. That decided, when a lull in the conversation hit, she asked, "So, how is Jean really? Anything I should avoid in the conversation?"

Chapter Seven

Jean hurried up the steps, the scent of freshly baked bread going with her. She'd already texted Robin to say she'd picked up the rolls and would be at AJ's in ten minutes, so she wasn't surprised when the front door opened as her foot hit the top step.

Robin stood there, and Jean beamed at her. "I'm going to drop this middle one."

Robin lunged forward to take the sliding box, and she caught it just as it gave way. "Whoops."

Jean bobbled the boxes and managed to stabilize them as she came to a stop. Her purse had slid down her arm, and she dropped it on the porch. "I'll come back for that." She stepped past Robin and into AJ's cottage, fully suspecting Robin would get her purse for her.

The other ladies welcomed her in the kitchen, and Jean opened the top box of lobster rolls. She began passing them out, even to Alice who protested that she'd already eaten too much that day.

One of Alice's favorite foods was the lobster roll, and Jean served her a whole one with that knowledge. "What did I miss?" she asked as she took her purse from Robin and looped the strap over the back of an empty chair at the dining room table. "You would not believe Opal today. She was in fine form." She smiled and shook her head.

She normally loved going to the fabric store on Pearl Island, but the owner was getting up in years, and Opal had told two stories today that Jean had heard before. "I got the fabric I needed for the vests though."

She took the last of the crab legs from the plate and spied the butter on the table.

"Who ordered the vests?" Alice asked. "Is it for a wedding?"

"The Murphys," Robin said knowingly. If anyone loved gossip more than Robin, Jean hadn't met them. "Their son is getting married in a few weeks."

Jean knew the Murphys, but only because they'd asked her to put together a half-dozen matching vests for the nuptials. The mother—Daisy—had seemed nice enough, if a little stressed. Jean couldn't imagine trying to put together a wedding on five weeks' notice, and she couldn't judge the woman.

Robin filled them in on the latest gossip surrounding the woman Triston Murphy had met his first year at college, and Jean listened though she didn't care. She knew Robin well enough by now to know that she was simply giving Jean time to acclimate to the situation before she started asking questions.

The woman could be relentless in her quizzing sometimes.

Today, it was AJ who leaned forward in the break during the conversation and said, "So, Jean, you started your sewing students up again?"

"Yes," Jean said, glancing at Kristen. She didn't want anyone walking on eggshells around her, especially AJ. The tall blonde was Jean's opposite in every way. Where Jean was dark, AJ was light. AJ towered; Jean cowered.

She looked at Asher as the baby boy babbled and banged his hands against his tray. "Okay, buddy," AJ said, reaching to remove him from the highchair.

"I'll take him," Jean said, surprising even herself.

The room froze. The women inside it did too. The very air itself seemed to solidify.

"You don't have to hold him while you eat," AJ said, her words warbled and wobbly as they entered Jean's ears.

"I'm not going to break down if I hold a baby," Jean said, more power in her voice than she intended to release. Instant regret shot through her. "Sorry." Her voice returned to its normal mousy level. She had held Asher plenty of times since his birth, and yes, maybe it would be different this time. Jean couldn't just keep living half a life. She didn't want to do that.

"I don't mind," AJ said, and with that, she plopped the six-month-old in Jean's lap. Jean scrambled to hold onto him, breathing in deeply as she did. The scent of milk, powder, and something sweet came with the child, and when he tilted and turned to look at who held him, Jean's whole soul filled with light.

"Hey, bud," she whispered to him. To her great delight, the boy snuggled into her chest, and Jean looked up, sure starlight poured from her eyes.

"I heard El offered you a job," Robin said coolly.

"She did," Jean said, returning her attention to her lobster roll. She pinched off a tiny bite of bread and held it steady for Asher. "I don't think I'm going to take it."

"No?" Alice asked. "It would be really busy. She's drowning up there."

Guilt tore through Jean, because Eloise was very busy at The Cliffside Inn. The job offer had come a week ago, and she needed to tell Eloise yes or no so the woman could staff her inn properly.

"Yeah," Jean said just as Kristen said, "She doesn't mind being busy."

Jean exchanged a glance with her mother-in-law. "No, I don't," she said slowly. "But I don't want to be on the first ferry off Diamond Island, and I can't be late coming back to my sewing students."

A familiar debate—one she'd been teetering back and forth with for the past seven days—began inside her. "If I take the Seafaring Girls job, I'll have to cancel my sewing students."

"Not all of them," Kristen reminded her. She'd done so often enough that Jean had been correcting herself in Kristen's voice for a few days. "And you can set the hours for the Seafaring Girls."

This conversation was like blood in the water for Robin. She scented it, and she was going in for the kill. "Which would you rather do? Sewing or Seafaring Girls?"

Everyone's eyes landed on her, and Jean had never liked such a shiny spotlight. "Both," she said. "I want to do both." She sounded so selfish, and she hated that. For a very dangerous year before she'd moved permanently to Five Island Cove and into the lighthouse, her selfishness had almost cost her her marriage.

She'd been working steadily on thinking about Rueben, as well as others, before herself. She weighed all of her decisions, ran them by her husband, and made the most informed choices she could. She'd changed a lot, and she was grateful for that.

"Is that selfish?"

"Why would it be selfish?" Alice asked. "You love sewing, and you love teaching sewing. You're very good at it, and if you can still do your lessons, you should."

"You'd be very good with the girls," AJ said with a smile. "At least I think you would."

Jean wasn't so sure about that. She often felt meek and like her voice never reached past her own ears. How would teenagers possibly hear her?

"Plus, you have the best Seafaring Girls leader that ever walked the cove to guide you," Robin said, grinning at Kristen.

Kristen smiled back and looked at Jean, sobering.

"Whatever you choose will be fine, dear." Her unspoken words were clear: *It is time to choose, however.*

Jean nodded and took a bite of her lobster roll. The conversation flowed around her, but it switched topics every few sentences, until it paused again.

"I think I want to do both," Jean said, picking up her end of the conversation as if it had never ended. "I can move my Wednesday sewing students to Tuesdays or Thursdays or Saturdays. I can do the Seafaring Girls on Wednesdays after school, and some weekends. Use my mornings for prep for both things."

Robin started nodding about the time Jean finished her first sentence, her approval obvious. "I have some great scheduling software I can show you," she said. "It literally saved me last year."

"Thank you," Jean said. "That sounds great." She met Kristen's eye. "So." She pulled in a breath, held it a beat, and pushed it all out in a big huff. "What do I need to do to be appointed the Seafaring Girls leader?"

Her lungs trembled on her next breath, and Jean wasn't sure if it was from excitement or nerves. Probably both, as Jean was often excited-but-nervous about the things in her life.

"I'll talk to Baron," Kristen said. "We'll get the paperwork drawn up, and once you sign..." She trailed off like that would be that.

"Will they make a big announcement?" Alice asked.

"I hope not," Jean said, giving her a glare. "That's the last thing I need."

"I've been working on an article, actually," Kristen said, and once again the room went mute.

Thankfully, Robin was in the room to go, "An article is a great idea. Let me know if you want me to proofread it. I've been doing that for Mandie's college application essays, and I've gotten quite good at it."

"ALL RIGHT," JEAN SAID, SMOOTHING DOWN THE corner of the comforter. "That's it, unless you need anything else." Vibrations ran through her stomach and down to her toes as she looked up and into Clara Tanner's eyes.

Rueben's sister had stood in the doorway and watched her remake the bed without moving a single muscle or offering to even so much as put a pillow on the bed. Jean tucked her hands in her skirt pockets and waited for Clara to say something.

She had the type of face no one forgot. She screamed good genes, with thick, dark hair that looked amazing even when it was untamed. Her dark skin could hold a lot of sunlight without freckling, and she always seemed to have the right amount of makeup on.

"I don't think so," Clara said, something guarded in her voice. "Thank you for letting me stay here."

"Sure," Jean said, though it wasn't exactly convenient to have Rueben's sister here for an undetermined amount of time. Kristen had a brand-new condo across the island, with a second bedroom Clara could've stayed in.

Jean had had to move her two sewing machines out of this room and into the one a level down in order to accommodate Clara. She'd known the woman for a while, and Clara was used to being catered to, that was for sure.

"Reuben will go get dinner in a little bit," she said, moving to step past Clara in the doorway. "When he comes down from the tower."

Clara said nothing as Jean went into the hall. She continued down the flight of steps to the bottom level in the lighthouse, glad she had some separation from Clara. Jean got along with her, mostly by biting her tongue and keeping her opinions to herself. She'd learned that at the first meeting with the woman.

She wasn't sure why Clara had come back to Five Island Cove, because everything Rueben or Kristen had said indicated that she had not liked it here. She'd left the moment she could after her high school graduation, and she almost hadn't even returned for her father's funeral a couple of years ago.

Jean understood how deep feelings could run, as it had taken her mother over six months to finally return one of Jean's texts after she'd chosen to leave Long Island permanently and move to the cove to live with Reuben in the lighthouse.

Their marriage had been stronger since Jean had put him at the top of her list, and she didn't regret the move. She did regret the times she'd complained to her mom about him or the cove, because her mother hadn't needed to be inside that relationship.

She did regret acting so juvenile about moving here. She'd been working on the things she'd done wrong and making them right.

Timber barked as Jean stepped off the last stair, and she simultaneously giggled and rolled her eyes. "It's just me, you dolt." The black lab quieted, his lips curving into a doggy smile. "Aunt Clara is all settled in, and she doesn't need your loud voice bothering her."

"He doesn't bother me," Clara said as Jean continued past her duo of dogs and into the kitchen. Her heart tried to go north and south at the same time, making her a little lightheaded and definitely surprised Clara had followed her downstairs.

"Do you?" she cooed at the dog, taking his jaw in her palms. "No, you don't." She smiled at Timber, gave him a healthy scrub and then did the same for Rolo. More shock coursed through Jean, because Clara had always been more of a cat person. Or maybe she was so much like a cat that Jean had just assumed.

Snooty, proper, her tail up and her back turned whenever anything went wrong.

Jean instantly recalled her thoughts, because she didn't want to make assumptions or judgments about anyone, least of all her sister-in-law.

"I'm sure you're wondering what I'm doing here," Clara said, releasing Rolo, who looked at her with wide, nearly black eyes, wishing she'd get rubbed a little longer. The Cavalier didn't get nearly the same attention Timber did, because her coat came off in long hairs Jean didn't like to touch.

"Hey, hey," Rueben said before Clara could fully straighten or Jean could wave away her statement. She didn't need to pry. No big deal. They had the room.

One glance over to the hallway, where Jean had lugged her sewing machines told her they didn't really have the room.

"You made it." Reuben grinned at his sister and drew her into a big hug. "How was the flight? The wind was murder today."

"Very bumpy," Clara said without smiling or laughing in return. She did hug Reuben, and they had always gotten along. He definitely carried sunshine in his soul, while Clara possessed the chilly, dull light of the moon. It didn't penetrate as far. It seemed to ice through Jean's veins with a single look, and she turned away as the siblings parted.

"How are things up top?" she asked.

"Good," Reuben said. "Do we want to go out to dinner? Or go pick up and eat here?"

"Let's go out," Jean said at the same time Clara said, "I'd rather eat here."

Whether Clara wanted to battle with Jean or not didn't matter. The war had started. "It's fine," Jean said. "We can eat here." She offered Clara a smile and looked back to Rueben. "Clara was just going to tell me why she's here."

Reuben peeled his gloves from his fingers, though he should be leaving them on so he could leave again. "Oh?" He came into the kitchen and grinned at Jean. "You look good today, hon." He kissed her right on the mouth, and Jean melted into his touch. He seemed to know exactly what she needed from him, and he was always so willing to give it.

She'd been to her therapist yesterday afternoon, and she did feel more grounded today.

"Scott and I are having problems," Clara said. "I just needed a little bit of space to clear my head."

Reuben turned back to his sister. "And you chose the cove? You hate it here." He could say things Jean would never get away with, and she stayed half a step behind him, watching Clara.

Her pulse boomed through her body as Clara pierced her older brother with a sharp glare, but Reuben didn't care at all.

"I don't have money to go stay somewhere nice," Clara said, and Jean actually winced.

Whether Rueben recognized the implication that the lighthouse was not nice or not, Jean would never know. He didn't react to what Clara had said. "I'm sorry about Scott."

"Yes." Clara inhaled deeply through her nose as if going through a great challenge only she could weather. "Lena and I might return to the cove. I just needed some time and space to think." She leaned into her palms on the counter. "So thank you for letting me stay."

Jean gave her a smile and said, "Of course," in a much quieter voice than her husband, who'd uttered the same words.

"No problem," Rueben said as his sister collapsed on the couch and switched on the TV. Jean saw her cozy evenings with her husband dry up right on the spot. She looked at Reuben, who seemed to see this exact scene playing out, night after night, for the next several evenings.

"I'll go pick up from the deli," Reuben said, frowning at Clara.

"I'll go with you," Jean said. She didn't want to be stuck with Clara in the subterranean levels of the lighthouse, wondering what half-veiled insult the woman would throw her way next.

Out in the car, her hands clenched tightly around one another. She'd grown close to Kristen over the past couple of years. She'd want to know how things had gone getting Clara settled in. She'd want to know if she'd said anything about why she was there.

What would Jean tell her?

What *should* Jean tell her?

In the driver's seat next to her, Reuben didn't seem to have a care in the world, and Jean sure did envy him for that. She'd never seen Scott and Clara together where they didn't act like they were blissfully in love, and she wondered what had happened.

It's not your place, she thought, and that settled all of the unrest inside her. Just like she didn't want people talking about her behind her back, she wouldn't do that to Clara.

Kristen would have to get her information from the source. Jean wasn't going to start a gossip session.

Satisfied with her decisions, she leaned her head against the head rest and turned toward her husband. "Let's just hope she really is only here for a few days."

Reuben glanced away from the road and at her. "I'll add it to my prayers, because yeah." He sighed. "She can be a handful, can't she?"

Jean thought that was putting it mildly, but she didn't say a word.

Chapter Eight

Laurel Lehye pulled into the driveway at the house she now called home. She'd managed to list her house and sell it over the holidays, and the weight that had lifted from her shoulders had alleviated a lot of stress. She and Paul had been married for about five months now, and they could afford both house payments, but it wasn't comfortable.

Not only that, but their realtor had done a fabulous job staging Laurel's house to get top dollar for the place, and now she and Paul had some money in a savings account.

Peace and happiness flowed through her as she gazed at the house. She couldn't stand the curtains or blinds being open, especially at night, and the moment she walked in, Paul would pull them closed. They stood open right now, because he liked the natural light pouring in through the windows, especially in the limited daylight they got in the wintertime.

Laurel had thought she was happy before, but Paul had

brought everything to a pinnacle she hadn't even known existed. She started to get out of her police car, and she reached back inside to get her lunchbox and purse. She didn't really carry a purse, but she did have a personal pack with her IDs, credit cards, and a bit of cash. She just didn't like carrying something huge that she couldn't put in her pocket or loop around her waist, and she tucked her pack under her arm as she turned back to the house.

Her husband stood on the front porch, leaning against the railing, his arms folded. He wore a smile with his gray T-shirt and navy basketball shorts, and he'd obviously just gotten home from running. Paul loved to run, and while Laurel thought she was in decent shape, she couldn't keep up with him.

She preferred working out in the mornings anyway, so he ran in the evenings after his shift at the police station, usually before she got home. Her new assignment on Sanctuary Island had allowed their schedules to line up pretty well.

"Hey," he called. "Alice texted and invited us to dinner at their place."

Laurel nodded, her feet suddenly very tired and made of something like cement. Maybe wood. No matter what, every step seemed to require great effort from her, as if she were journeying toward a great cliff, and when she reached it, she'd fling herself from the top of it into the black waters below.

She focused on Paul. She loved Paul. He loved her. He'd handle this news far better than she had, and she couldn't believe she hadn't told him yet.

"You said you had something to talk about," Paul said. "We don't have to go."

"We can," she said, still approaching with the speed of a sloth. "It isn't really something to talk about. It's just..." She started up the steps, everything easier the closer she came to Paul. "Hey."

He grinned down at her as he slid his arms around her. He kissed her, and Laurel stopped worrying about how he'd take the news. They both wanted a baby.

She put a tiny sliver of distance between them and whispered, "Paul, I'm pregnant."

He froze, much the same way Laurel had that morning. She'd done a lot of blinking at the double lines on the pregnancy test too, and she'd texted her husband, who'd already gone into work, that she had something she wanted to talk about that evening.

"Laurel." He said her name with reverence and awe, as if she'd done something phenomenal and he'd only just found out about it. His hands came up and pushed her hair back off her face. "Are you happy?"

She looked at him, seeing the joy streaming from him, and her own doubled. She smiled and nodded. "Yes," she said through a tight throat. "I'm very happy."

He kissed her again, but it landed differently. This wasn't an *I'm-so-glad-you're-home* kiss. It was an *I-love-you-and-we're-a-family* kiss. He moved slowly, and Laurel sank into every stroke, once again marveling that love could feel so completely amazing.

"When?" he asked, stepping back. He looked out over

their front yard, as they lived in a quiet neighborhood with homes lining both sides of the street. "Let's go inside."

Laurel followed him through the front door, saying, "I think probably late September or early October," she said. She kept the fact that they'd have a baby almost within a year of getting married. She wasn't in her twenties, and no one would think anything of it. In fact, her friends would probably throw her a baby shower every month until the infant came.

She smiled just thinking about Alice and Robin and Eloise, then Kristen, Jean, AJ, and Kelli. Paul would likely broadcast the news to the entire world, starting with a blow-up carriage he'd position on the roof of the house. He'd done some amazing things with Santa's sleigh and some inflatable reindeer that had left Laurel slack-jawed and surprised at his level of holiday cheer.

"I don't want to tell everyone right away," she said.

"I can't call my mom?"

"Sure," she said. "You can call your mom. *Just* your mom." Laurel should call hers too, but with a dinner with Alice and Arthur on the immediate horizon, she suddenly felt too tired to have another emotional conversation. "I'll call my parents tomorrow."

They'd want her to come to Nantucket to celebrate, and Laurel could admit she liked riding the steamer across the ocean, especially when Paul came with her. She enjoyed the pop-up restaurants that came to the Point, and if there wasn't one—as often the winter months in Nantucket were slower—she liked the food at The Glass Dolphin a lot.

Paul put one palm over her stomach, which wasn't any different than it had been yesterday. "I love you, Laurel."

"I love you too, Paul."

Their eyes met, and he gifted her with a small smile. "So yes to Alice? Or no? We can just stay home, curl up on the couch, and eat frozen pizza." They'd done that several times since they'd been married, and those were some of Laurel's favorite evenings.

She wasn't a woman who cared much about fancy things, which made her friendship with Alice Rice a little surprising. Alice never wore anything that didn't have a designer label, and she always looked like she belonged in an upscale New England magazine.

She'd been nothing but kind to Laurel, and they had a unique friendship that meant a great deal to Laurel. Robin Grover had accepted Laurel for exactly who she was, and it had been Robin who'd been right at her side once everything had been blown open with the City Manager last fall.

"We can go to dinner with Alice and Arthur," she said.

"I think it's just at their house," Paul said. "Alice texted to say she called you, but it went straight to voicemail. So she texted me. Something about how Arthur brought home a ton of enchiladas from the school."

"Leftovers from the school," Laurel said dryly. "Delicious."

Paul chuckled at her sarcasm. "I guess they had a professional development day, and Enrique's catered."

"Oh, Enrique's is good." Laurel started undoing her

belt. Her hips ached with how much they had to carry. "I'll get changed."

"I'm going to shower," Paul said. "Then we can go." He gave her another smile and leaned in for another kiss. "You could come shower with me. I'll just tell Alice we need a few extra minutes because you had a rough day." His voice turned rougher with every word, and the kiss he offered this time held more urgency and desire inside it.

Laurel kissed him back and moved down the hallway with him toward their master bedroom. "Don't tell her I had a bad day," she whispered as she let her husband finish with her belt. "Then she'll have questions. Just tell her we'll be about an hour."

"Okay." Paul sent the text, threw his phone on the bed, and reached for Laurel again.

ALICE GREETED PAUL AND LAUREL AT THE FRONT door with worry pinched between her eyes. "Hey, you two," she said as pleasantly as ever, but Laurel saw things a normal person didn't. Not only that, but she knew Alice, and she knew something was wrong.

A shout came from somewhere inside the house, drawing all of their attention. Laurel nudged Paul away from her. "Why don't you go see what that's about?"

"Yes, ma'am," he said, all smiles. Paul always seemed to have something to be glad about, and his optimism was one of the things Laurel loved most about him. The moment he disappeared around the corner, Laurel focused on Alice again.

"What's going on?" she asked.

"Nothing," Alice said lightly. "What about you?"

"Yeah, nothing." Laurel stepped past her friend and into Alice's office. Nothing seemed off in here. Papers, folders, a notebook that Alice sketched in while her mind ran in circles. All normal. She turned back to the brunette who'd been letting her hair grow out over the past few months. Silver adorned the dark strands, and Alice wasn't bothering to cover it up anymore. She said it made her feel wiser, more distinguished.

"How are the twins?"

Alice's eyelids fluttered. "Great," she said. "Apparently, the Academic Olympiad season is coming up. Charlie's busy with that. Ginny got made an assistant manager at the ice cream shop, so she's busy with that."

"And her boyfriend," Laurel said, knowing that the worry Alice carried could almost always be attributed to her kids.

Alice sighed and tucked her hair before folding her arms. She'd looked away from Laurel, but her gaze came back. "Yes."

"Tell me what's going on so I don't say something stupid," Laurel whispered.

Alice shook her head. "I'm going to channel Robin." After a deep breath, she exhaled the words, "Remember the pregnancy test I found? I still don't know whose it is."

Laurel's eyes widened. How unlike Alice not to confront the problem head-on.

The longer Alice looked at her, the faster her pulse raced through her body. She knew what Alice's look meant.

"I don't see how I can help."

"You're a cop. You could, I don't know, interrogate them."

Laurel's eyebrows went up. "Interrogate them?" She had another idea, and while she'd told Paul only an hour ago that she didn't want to tell people, she suddenly wanted to tell Alice about her own pregnancy.

Alice shook her head, her lips pressing together as she glanced toward the hallway. "I don't know how to bring it up. You're good at this."

Laurel drew in a long breath, hoping Paul would forgive her. "I have another idea," she said slowly. Alice looked at her, one eyebrow cocked. The two of them laughed, and Laurel rolled her eyes. "I hate it when you do that."

"Start talking," Alice said.

Laurel moved over to the arched doorway that led into the office too. The hallway sat empty. "Okay," she said. "I just found out I'm pregnant. I haven't told anyone—like, Alice, you can't tell *anyone*. Paul barely found out tonight."

Alice put one hand on Laurel's forearm, and that single human connection nearly caused Laurel to burst into tears. "Oh, honey, that's great. Congratulations."

Laurel stepped into Alice and hugged her, her emotions storming through her chest and parading down her spine and arms. "Let's make a big scene out of it," she said, all those things choking her evident in her voice. "And we'll watch Ginny and Charlie and see if either of them react." She stepped back and studied Alice's face. "They'll be nervous if we start talking about pregnancy tests."

Light filled Alice's face, followed quickly by determination. "Okay." She nodded. "Let's get it over with. I'd like to sleep tonight." She looped her arm through Laurel's, and the two of them walked down the hallway toward the kitchen together.

In the big room that took up the back of the house, Laurel found Paul and Arthur laughing in the kitchen, with Ginny and Charlie sitting at the dining room table, both of them focused on their phones.

"So then I had to figure out how to read the pregnancy test," Laurel said loudly. "They're not that easy to read, you know?"

Neither twin looked at her.

"Of course, that was after I found one. Apparently, the holidays are a busy time, and I had to go to three stores to find a *pregnancy test*."

Alice's arm in hers tightened, as Laurel had practically screamed the last two words. Charlie, the closest to her, glanced up, but it was clear he didn't care what she was talking about. "Hey, Laurel," he said.

"Hi," she said.

"So you found a pregnancy test," Alice prompted, and Charlie certainly heard that. He had the look Laurel would expect from a teenage boy listening to his mother talk to her adult friend. He didn't care. And the words *pregnancy test* had zero effect on him.

"Dinner's ready," Arthur said, and Ginny looked up.

She smiled at Laurel, perfectly at-ease. "Did you say you were pregnant?" she asked.

"No," Laurel said, throwing a look toward Paul. Whatever Alice had found didn't belong to Ginny nor Charlie. "How are you, Ginny? Your mom said you got made an assistant manager." She beamed at the pretty teen, who beamed back at her.

"I did."

Alice released Laurel and moved toward the kitchen. "Come eat, guys. Arthur tried to light the house on fire, but he failed."

"Hey," Arthur said good-naturedly. He growled at Alice playfully and swept her into his arms.

"Gross," Charlie practically yelled. "Let's just eat."

Laurel stepped over to Paul's side and put her arm around his waist. "I'll explain later," she murmured.

All Paul did was lean down and press his lips to her temple, a silent testament that he trusted her. Laurel exchanged a glance with Alice as she put a stack of plates on the counter, her nerves still there.

She did have a negative pregnancy test in her trashcan, so if it didn't belong to anyone who lived here, whose was it?

Chapter Nine

K elli Webb followed her son out the door, reaching to close it behind her as it swung away.

"I got it, Kel," Agatha said, jogging over in her black leggings and bright coral-orange tank top. She wore a perpetual smile, and Kelli had struck gold when she'd hired the yoga instructor. Just the fact that the three p.m. class was full testified of that.

Things were going really well at Whole Soul, the yoga, fitness, and wellness center Kelli had been running for the past several months. Their enrollment was up, and she had the freedom to spend afternoons with her son and evenings with her new husband.

"That's the car, Parker," she called as she bustled down the steps in her own pair of black leggings. Kelli loved leggings, and she didn't wear hardly anything else. Maybe a skirt to church every once in a while. A pair of jeans or slacks when she went out alone with Shad.

Her son opened the back passenger door of a dark sedan that had just pulled to a stop in front of the house on Seabreeze Shore. She heard the driver ask, "Kelli?" and Parker affirmed. She slid onto the back seat with him, pulling her bulky tote bag onto her lap before closing the door.

"We're just going to the ferry," she told the RideShare driver, and they set off. She'd lectured Parker many times about being good for Jean. He had to ask before he went down to Seal Beach, and Jean had to know where he was at all times.

The two of them got along so well, and Kelli had been offering for Parker to come since finding out about Rueben and Jean's loss of the baby they'd been planning to adopt. Finally, Jean had said she could bring him.

She'd seen Jean at a lunch last week, at AJ's house. Kelli sighed and wiped one hand across her forehead, though it wasn't hot outside. She was still plenty warm from the aerobics class she'd finished only a few minutes after Parker had arrived. Though he was only ten, he had some friends in his class now that lived on Pearl Island, not far from her and Shad. They rode the ferry to school together in the morning —Shad went with them—and Parker could ride from Diamond to Bell in the afternoons.

He then waited with Kelli until she finished work, and they went to the twinhome on Pearl together. Sometimes they rode back to Diamond to visit Shad or go shopping, and last week, Kelli had taken lunch to her new husband and then gone to see her friends.

She'd removed herself from them slightly, but she told

herself it was necessary if she wanted Whole Soul to succeed. She did, and she'd spent a lot of time in texting conversations with Eloise, actually. She too ran a super busy business, with dozens upon dozens of moving parts. Alice headed up her own law firm. Robin could bring her event planning to a thriving, extremely busy business any time she wanted.

Her friends understood; at least Kelli had been praying that they did.

"Thank you," Kelli said as she tapped her RideShare pass and got out of the car. "Come on, Park. We're already late."

Jean didn't have sewing students on Friday afternoons, but that didn't mean Kelli wanted her waiting around for Parker to arrive. She texted her that they were getting on the ferry, and they'd be at the lighthouse in forty minutes or so.

Almost to the minute, Kelli and Parker got out of another RideShare car and approached the lovely, white lighthouse. Memories assaulted Kelli, most of them making her smile. "You've got the gift card?" she asked Parker, her adrenaline spiking and making her pulse bounce in her veins.

"Yep," her son said, and she smiled at him. His normally blonde hair had started to get some red creeping into it, and she thought he was such a handsome, good boy.

"You tell her thank you," Kelli murmured as the big blue door approached. "She probably has cookies."

"I will," Parker said.

"It's too windy to go to the beach today." Kelli's eyes traveled along the path that went around the lighthouse. "So just stay here, okay?"

"Mom, okay," Parker said, plenty of frustration in his

voice. He'd started thinking he was fifteen-going-on-sixteen, not only ten. Kelli ignored his attitude and reached to knock on the door.

A buzzer sounded, startling Kelli back a couple of steps. The sound rang through the air, completely out of place. She looked around, confused.

"Who is it?" a woman asked, and it wasn't Jean.

"Uh, Kelli Webb?" Kelli didn't like how she'd guessed at her own name. "Parker is here for Jean."

"Jean doesn't have sewing students today," the woman said.

The door swung open while Kelli was trying to figure out how to respond to the buzzer-woman, and Jean filled the doorway with her petite frame. She pulled her jacket tighter around her as she exited.

She wore a disgruntled expression on her face, her eyes almost narrow slits. She pressed the button and said, "I've got it, Clara."

Kelli put her arm around her son's shoulders to keep him at her side. "If you can't take him tonight, it's fine. I can ask AJ."

"He's fine." All of the unrest melted away from Jean's face as she looked at Parker. "Come on, baby."

He went to her, his own smile covering his features. "Hi, Jean." He hugged her, and Kelli's mother heart warmed.

"I have oatmeal cookies in the basement," she said. "Go get a couple and take them up to Reuben. I'll be right up." She kept her eyes on Parker as he stepped away from her and did what she said, pulling open the door and going inside the lighthouse.

Only when the door closed did Jean exhale and look at Kelli. "If she doesn't leave soon..." She pressed her eyes closed and drew in another breath through her nose. "She's been here for ten days."

"Who?" Kelli asked.

Jean's eyes opened, and the darkness had returned. "Clara Shields. Reuben's sister. Kristen's daughter."

Shock swirled through Kelli. "Oh." She couldn't come up with anything else to say. She hadn't known Clara was here, and all she could wonder was *why*.

"Kristen knows she's here," Jean said. "Clara said a few days, but it's been a while. She's claiming that she only has one more appointment, and then she'll go back to Vermont."

"What kind of appointment?"

"Lord only knows," Jean said with a sigh, tipping her head back as if truly petitioning heaven.

"What is she doing here?"

"She and Scott have been having some problems. She said she needed some time and space to think." Jean wrapped her arms around herself again, all traces of angst disappearing from her face. "How are you, Kelli? How's the studio?"

A smile popped onto Kelli's face. "Good," she said. "Really good." She'd never been great at talking to people, especially about hard things. It was far easier to text, but Kelli plowed forward.

"I'm so sorry about the baby, Jean." She lunged forward and took the woman into a hug. They stood about the same height, but Kelli simply had more round bits than Jean did. They clung to one another, as Kelli hadn't been exactly lying on the beach sipping cocktails for the past several years.

"It's okay," Jean whispered. "I'm okay." She stepped back, her smile wobbling and her eyes watery. "At least I will be. I'm seeing my therapist again, and my schedule is getting back to normal, and—"

"Jean," Clara blurted through the intercom, making both women jump. "There's a boy here taking all the cookies."

Jean rolled her whole head, the stress of the situation beyond the navy blue lighthouse door obvious. She didn't reach for the button. She met Kelli's eyes, and the two of them burst out laughing.

"If I can get rid of Clara," Jean said between the giggles. "Things will really start to look up."

Ten days was a long time to stay with someone, and Jean only got elevated another tier in Kelli's opinion. "I'll bring you and Rueben something sweet from the restaurant," she promised. "Okay?"

Jean kept her grin in place and nodded. "Okay, great. He'll be fine here, I promise. Clara's been disappearing into her bedroom at about six." She pulled her phone out and looked at it. "Still got a couple of hours, but we're going to sit on the deck and look for the whales. They've been out every afternoon for three days."

Gratitude filled Kelli. "Thank you for taking him. He loves you guys, and he'll be so excited to see the whales."

Jean nodded, her irritation gone. "We love having him. Thank you for sharing him with us."

"Of course." Kelli cleared her throat. "Are you going to babysit for AJ?"

Surprise lit Jean's eyes. "She hasn't asked me to."

"Oh, okay." Embarrassment flooded Kelli. Her face burned in the cool winter air. "Forget I said anything. She probably just hasn't asked you yet, and I ruined it."

"What's going on with AJ?"

"Nothing," Kelli said, because she'd guard AJ's feelings and secrets to the death. They'd had a great visit last week, but AJ felt a bit trapped by her new role as mother. Kelli had suggested that she take some time for herself. There were plenty of people right here on Diamond Island who'd take Asher—Jean included.

"Once a week," Kelli had said. "Go get your hair done. Your nails. Go to lunch by yourself."

AJ had blinked furiously at the last suggestion, and they'd laughed together. They'd cried together. They'd held onto one another fiercely when it had finally come time for Kelli to leave. She loved AJ as much now as she always had, and she didn't want her yoga studio to come between them. She needed to make sure it didn't.

"Kristen mentioned you had a meeting about the Seafaring Girls coming up," Kelli said, deftly changing the subject. "Are you excited?"

A new round of nerves paraded across Jean's face. "I

think so?" She shrugged inside her jacket. "I don't know. I didn't grow up with the program or anything. I don't know what to expect." Her dark, lovely eyes searched Kelli's. "Maybe you could tell me a little bit about it."

"I'm sure you'll learn all about it," Kelli said with a dismissive wave. "I'm surprised Kristen hasn't detailed it for you."

"Schedules and lessons, yes," Jean said. "How to sail, water safety, certificates." She shook her head. "No, I want to know why this program means so much to her. To you. What it'll mean—or could mean—to the girls who sign up." She wore eagerness in her eyes now, and Kelli couldn't wave that away.

She did look away, far up into the sky, wishing she could find the things that the Seafaring Girls had meant to her and boil it down to one or two sentences. Perhaps Robin or Eloise could do something like that, but Kelli couldn't.

"I..." She struggled to find the right words. How could one put such strong feelings into words? It almost felt like she'd cheapen her experiences here at the lighthouse, on the boats she'd learned to sail, and the way she'd been able to overcome her fear of the water that lapped around Five Island Cove constantly.

"I was always accepted here," she said simply. "No matter what. When my pants were too short, and my shoes had holes and were dirty. No one cared. Kristen folded me into a hug and asked me how I was."

Her hands started to shake, and Kelli didn't try to quell them. "I could just walk through that door, no knocking necessary. I could go up to the deck and watch the water. Kristen would bring me hot chocolate and a sandwich, and she'd sometimes stay and sometimes she wouldn't. It was like she just knew what I needed."

Jean gave her a shy smile and nodded encouragingly.

"My friends didn't care that I was poor, or not pretty enough, or any of that. They accepted me, and they counted on me out on the boat. That mattered." She pressed her lips together and steadied herself for another moment.

"It's okay," Jean said, her own voice small under so much sky. "I get it."

Kelli nodded, glad someone did. She watched the gray sky give way to some blue in the distance as the clouds shifted. She felt the same way—that she was constantly shifting, trying to find the patch of sunlight that would warm her and bring her home.

"I think you'll be amazing with the girls," Kelli said, grinding the words through her throat to clear the emotion. "You love Parker so much, and you always have. They'll come to you broken, and you'll be able to fix them up."

"I hope so," Jean said quietly, obviously worried about it.

"You're amazing," Kelli whispered, stepping into the other woman again. "Don't let anything make you think you're not." She pulled back but kept her hands on Jean's shoulders. "I did that for so long, and it was AJ who reminded me of who I am and how great I am."

"AJ is great," Jean said.

"You're great too," Kelli said. She dropped her hands

and stepped back. The moment intensified until it finally broke. "Okay." She blew out her breath and looked back toward the RideShare car waiting for her. "Let me know if you need something with Parker. Otherwise, Shad and I will be back in the morning to pick him up. You sure you and Rueben can't go to breakfast?"

Jean shook her head. "I wish. Kristen is doing breakfast at her condo before Clara's flight."

Kelli held up her hand, her first two fingers crossed. "I'll keep my fingers crossed she leaves in the morning." She grinned and fell back another step. "See you tomorrow."

"Bye." Jean lifted her hand and waved, and she turned back toward the door as Kelli moved in the direction of the parking lot. She hadn't quite reached the car yet when the blaring buzzing sound filled the air again.

Then Clara's voice chirped into the seaside silence. "Jean? Are you there? *Jean?*"

Kelli giggled to herself as she got in the front passenger seat.

"Ready?" the driver asked.

"Yes," she said, still grinning at the white façade of the lighthouse. "To the county courthouse, please." She had a hot date with her husband that evening, and she couldn't wait another moment to see Shad.

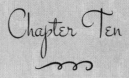

Chapter Ten

Robin shifted the papers on her desk, wishing the colleges didn't use such tiny print. There was no way anyone read this stuff. She pitied the person who'd had to write it.

"I think this one is done," she said, sliding the papers into the folder Mandie had labeled NYU. "They've confirmed for a campus tour?" She peered over the tops of her reading glasses to her daughter.

Mandie sat in the chair opposite the desk, where so many of Robin's clients had perched before. They usually looked more enthusiastic than Mandie currently did. At the moment, she stared blandly at her phone, only looking up after a few seconds, as if she hadn't realized Robin had spoken to her.

"I have the email right here." She didn't seem that enthusiastic about taking a trip to New York, Boston, and Maryland. Robin had been going over the itinerary for a solid week. She loved making travel plans, as she didn't get to do a whole lot of globetrotting. Going with her eldest daughter to college campuses up and down the Eastern Seaboard brought bubbling excitement to her blood Robin usually only got when she pulled off a spectacular event.

Robin took off her glasses and set them next to her laptop. "What's going on?"

"What?" Mandie asked. "Nothing."

She didn't want to go Full Mom on Mandie, but something was definitely going on. "Mandie," she said slowly, and that got her daughter to drop the phone to her lap. "It's a lot of time and money to go to campuses. If you don't want to go…" She let the sentence hang there. She had done her best to stay out of Mandie's college application process, only stepping in when her daughter asked for help.

She'd offered a listening ear when Mandie needed to go through her options out loud. She'd looked up websites and forums for her daughter. She'd helped proofread her application essays. She'd done nothing without first waiting for Mandie to talk to her about it. Even this trip had been a topic of discussion for over two months now.

Mandie had gotten precious little for Christmas, because this trip was on the horizon. Robin and Duke didn't have extra money sitting in cupboards or corners, and time was as valuable as dollars. So what had changed?

"I *do* want to go," Mandie said. "I just…I don't feel like anything in Boston is for me."

"Okay, then we'll cancel that one," Robin said, a trickle of relief filling her. She wanted a vacation from Five Island

Cove as much as her daughter did. She'd never left after high school, as she hadn't known what she wanted to do with her life as an eighteen-year-old. She'd told Mandie she could take all the time she needed to learn what she wanted to do.

Mandie loved children, and she'd spoken of becoming a teacher or running a preschool. Robin secretly hoped her daughter would try college and get away from the cove, at least for a year. Experience something different, as Robin sometimes wished she had.

She tried hard not to dwell on such thoughts, because she loved her life in the seaside town with her husband. They'd carved out a good living, and she didn't want to ever be ungrateful for that.

Speak of the devil, Duke poked his head into the office. "How's it going in here?" He wore a black apron with a bright red lobster on it, as well as a pair of jeans and a smile that kicked Robin's pulse into the back of her throat.

"Good," she said, rising from her chair. "Mandie's thinking about crossing BU off her list." She looked at her daughter for her reaction.

Duke focused on Mandie too. "Yeah? Why's that?"

Mandie stood too. "I don't know, Dad. It just doesn't feel like my city. Not my vibe, you know?"

Robin barely understood what that meant, but Duke nodded along like a pro. "You know what is your vibe, bug?" He lifted his arm, and Mandie moved right into her father's side. They'd always been close, and that was another thing Robin had to be grateful for. "Shucking corn. Come on, I have an earful of things for you to do."

Mandie groaned at the bad corn Dad-joke, but Robin smiled. As Duke threw her a glance that said he'd get the real story from their daughter, Robin could only watch the two of them leave the office. She loved having a partner she could communicate with without having to say anything out loud.

"We have a call with the realtor tomorrow," she called after him.

"I know," he yelled back, though Robin was sure he'd forgotten. She'd have to tell him again that night, and then again in the morning.

She sighed and let her worries run rampant for a moment. Mandie. Looking for a house they owned and didn't rent. It was a good thing she wasn't doing a lot of events this year.

Mandie definitely wasn't telling the whole story about BU, but Robin didn't know how to get it out of her. Duke would put her to work in the kitchen, and they'd laugh and talk, and somehow he'd get her to talk without seeming like he was coming at her with questions. Robin did tend to fire things at the kids to get to the meat of the problem, and she forced herself to stay right where she was so she wouldn't go do that right now.

Both girls opened up more when she wasn't in the room, and she wasn't sure if that made her happy or sad.

"It's neither," she said almost under her breath. "This is why they have a mother and a father." She picked up her phone and went out onto the front porch. Duke had bought her a rocking chair and placed it there over the holiday break.

Robin sank into the chair now and began to toe herself

back and forth. She hadn't yet texted her own mother, and while her husband put together a seafood feast in the middle of winter, she figured now was as good of a time as any.

Hey, Mom, Robin started. She wasn't sure what else to say. She'd told her mother last year that she and Duke were saving to buy a house of their own, as her mom tended to make threats if Robin didn't do exactly what she wanted her to. As they lived in her house and paid very little rent, sometimes Jennifer Golden held that over Robin's head.

How are your puzzles coming? Got any new ones?

Robin sent the text with the benign topic of jigsaw puzzles, something she and her mother had always been able to talk about. Robin didn't enjoy them half as much as her mother did, but she did love making a ton of pieces fit together into a single event, which was very much like putting together a jigsaw puzzle.

I got a new one, her mom answered. *It's of the lighthouse, and it's a commemoration of the two hundredth anniversary of Five Island Cove!*

"Wow," Robin said, smiling at the text. Her mom rarely used exclamation points, and Robin's fingers flew across the screen as she responded.

The talk moved on from puzzles quickly when her mom asked, *How's the house-hunting going?*

Robin looked up then, the darkness around her suddenly there when it hadn't been before. Evening fell quickly in late January, and she hadn't seen it coming. Dusk arrived like a thief in the night in the summer, taking its sweet time and only fully committing when it finally had to let go of the daylight in the west.

But in the winter, the sun sank like a rock, turning everything gray, then blue, then black all in under five minutes.

She got up and went back inside, the lights shining brightly now when they'd barely been noticeable before. She moved down the hallway and past the steps, then the hall that branched to her left, and into the kitchen.

Just as she arrived, Mandie and Jamie burst out laughing, and Robin smiled at their joy before looking at Duke. He held a lobster up to his face as if it were a mustache, and she shook her head. She thought her husband was funny too, but she didn't want to encourage him.

"Almost ready," Duke said with plenty of laughter in his voice too. He put the lobster on a plate and turned to the fridge. "Girls, get the table finished."

Robin watched as they did what he said, putting the plates on the table, then glasses, and finally silverware.

"Sit, sit," Duke said, motioning with a bowl of pasta salad Robin had made earlier that morning. "Thanks for doing this. I could've stopped at the store." He followed her over to the dining room table, where Robin sat while her family continued to bring the food over and spread it down the middle.

Finally, Jamie sat on one side, Mandie on the other, and Duke at the other end. Tears pressed up Robin's throat, but she pushed just as hard against them. "Thank you," she said, taking in the corn on the cob, the lobsters, the garlic bread, and her pasta and spinach salad. "It looks great."

"There's cake too," Duke said. "So don't stuff yourself on dinner alone." He grinned at her and jumped to his feet. "Wait. Presents. Mandie. Jamie." They all bustled away, and Robin wanted to call out to them that they were her gifts. She didn't need anything else.

Jamie returned first with a package wrapped in bright pink paper with white stripes. "Happy birthday, Momma." She gave Robin a side-squeeze and went back to her seat.

Mandie carried in a huge box that had to hold a small kitchen appliance, and Robin's hope soared. She'd wanted an Instant Pot for a while now, and that looked like the right-sized box for one... Mandie's grin gave it all away too. She set the box on the kitchen counter and came back to the table.

Duke returned to the kitchen with an envelope and the biggest bunch of red roses Robin had ever seen. He put the vase at her place, tucked the envelope under her still-empty plate, and leaned down to kiss her.

"Happy birthday, my love," he murmured. Robin could lose herself kissing her husband, but she didn't want to put on a show in front of their kids.

Duke retook his seat and beamed at her. "Food and presents at the same time. Let's eat."

"Thank you," Robin said again. "This is the best birthday ever."

"You say that every year," Jamie said with a smile.

"That's because when you get to be my age," Robin said, reaching first for the pasta salad she liked. She'd eaten it for lunch too, taking it from the bowl before setting it to chill in the fridge for tonight's birthday dinner. "Every year is important. It's another year you've lived on the earth. Another year of experiences and wisdom. Another year of being with the people you love most."

Her voice cracked on the last word, but thankfully, Duke covered for her by saying, "Open Mandie's present first, babe. I think you're really going to like it."

Robin took a bite of the bowtie pasta first, the creamy sauce of mayo and sour cream and dill making a party in her mouth. She then stood and started tearing the pale purple paper from the box, the Instant Pot words coming out really quickly.

"Thank you," she gushed, ripping the paper off like it was Christmastime and she was five years old again. "I've wanted one of these forever."

"Now you can make that sausage soup you've been talking about," Mandie said with a smile. "Dad helped me pay for it."

"She saved for a month," Duke said, clearly proud of his daughter. Robin experienced a powerful dose of pride and love for her oldest daughter, and she leaned down and hugged her.

"Thank you," she whispered in Mandie's ear. Back in her seat with another bite of pasta salad in her mouth, Robin picked up Jamie's present.

"It's not as good as Mandie's," the girl said. "But I don't have a job. Just some babysitting money."

"It's fine," Mandie said at the same time Robin said, "It'll be awesome." She removed the paper to find a three-pack of socks with a friendly alpaca on the cardboard wrap-around.

Joy burst through her. "These are those alpaca buddy socks I've been eying." She jumped to her feet and hugged Jamie on her side of the table. "Thank you so much."

"They're supposed to be the softest socks known to mankind," Jamie said.

"I read that. I can't wait to put them on tonight." Robin hated having cold feet in bed, and she'd been collecting socks for years, trying to find the perfect pair. These weren't cheap either, and she poured sunshine into her smile as she aimed it in Jamie's direction. "Thank you."

"You can open mine later," Duke said, clearing his throat. "Might be best."

Robin met his gaze across the table, shaking her head. "Is that right?"

"Just open it later," he said, and he turned to Mandie. "Tell your mother what we talked about while we made dinner."

Mandie nodded and finished her bite of lobster. She exchanged a glance with Duke and took what Robin would classify as a steeling breath. "Mom," she said. "I only want to tour NYU and U-of-Maryland in College Park."

"That's fine." Robin didn't see the problem with that. "You already told me you didn't want to do Boston."

"I don't know if I want to go to college at all," Mandie blurted out, a wild look in her eyes. "But I still want to do the tours. I don't know if that's responsible or not, and I know we don't have a lot of money." She tossed a look toward Duke, who simply took another bite of his corn on the cob.

"It's fine," Robin said, volleying her gaze around to everyone at the table. "We've saved for this, and I want to do whatever you want."

"Charlie's thinking about NYU," Mandie said. "I didn't tell you that, but he is. He hasn't told his mom." Her words rushed over one another, and this news did cause Robin to slow down in her consumption of the pasta salad.

"I didn't think we were worried about what Charlie was doing."

"We're not," Mandie said. "He just told me a few days ago, and he's not even sure he can get in."

"He got into BU," Duke said. "And she crossed that off her list."

"Which is likely why Charlie is now considering NYU," Robin pointed out.

Duke waved his fork and shrugged, clearly saying, *Maybe. Maybe not.*

"I just wanted you to know." Mandie shook her hair over her shoulder. "I'm not going to start dating him or anything."

Right now, Robin thought, but she had enough sense and tact to keep it to herself. "We'll just cancel in Boston then," she said. "We can still go there if you want to visit. I really do want this trip to be fun for you." She reached over and covered Mandie's hand with hers. "A vacation."

"I know." Mandie gave her a smile. "It'll be awesome."

Robin's phone rang, and she expected it to be her

mother. Her birthday wasn't for a few more days, but Duke had a fishing trip planned and he wouldn't be home for it. Thus, the dinner and presents and cake tonight. But Robin had been texting with her mom earlier, and she thought she might be calling to continue that conversation.

Instead, Kristen's name sat on the screen. She swiped the call away, because this was her family celebration for her birthday.

She'd only taken a single bite of her garlic bread when Kristen called again. "Just answer it," Duke said. "It's Kristen, and we don't care."

Robin swiped on the call and said, "Hey."

"I hope I'm not interrupting," Kristen said, but she didn't leave a breath for Robin to say she could call her back in thirty minutes, once dinner had finished. "I'm driving and wondering if I can stop by. Jean just called."

The urgency in her tone told Robin to change what she'd been about to say. "Sure," she said, the word whooshing out of her mouth. "What did Jean have to say?"

"You'll never believe this," Kristen said, and Robin was able to identify the controlled anger in the older woman's voice. "But Clara has been looking at Friendship Inn."

Confusion puckered Robin's eyebrows. "What does that mean? Looking at it?"

"To buy it," Kristen practically spat. "She's been looking at that inn to buy it, fix it up, and move back here." On her end of the line, a horn sounded, and she added, "I have to go. I'll be there in ten minutes."

The line went dead, and Robin stared at the screen as it

went dark. "Oh, boy," she said as she set the phone down. She looked up and surveyed her family. "Kristen will be here in a few minutes. Can she join us?"

"Of course," Duke said, and the girls nodded.

Robin got up to get another plate, a sense of calmness moving through her she didn't expect.

Chapter Eleven

Kristen pulled up to Robin's house, the sight of her getting-older-by-the-day minivan sitting in the driveway oddly comforting. The bins resting on the shelves in the garage, along with a heap of beach gear, also told Kristen that real people lived here.

She wasn't sure who or what her daughter had become, but Clara was some sort of beast.

Kristen breathed in deeply through her nose. She'd often thought she'd love to see Clara return to the cove. She'd prayed for her daughter daily, especially since Joel's death.

This place needs a good inn.

The words rotated through Kristen's mind, and she vowed she would never repeat them out loud. No one—especially Eloise—needed to know the sharpness of her daughter's tongue. She wouldn't even tell Robin, though she'd been the first person Kristen had thought of once she'd gotten Clara off the phone.

Thankfully, she'd left the cove last week, because Kristen hadn't been sure how much longer Jean could stand to have Clara around. She'd overstayed her welcome, that much had been certain.

Clara had always done what she wanted, and this impromptu, unexpected visit to the cove was no different. As was buying Friendship Inn to fix it up and make it "the premier inn" in Five Island Cove.

A sigh leaked out of her body as a light flipped on over the front porch. Robin probably knew she'd arrived, and Kristen twisted the key to turn off the ignition. She went up the sidewalk, and the moment the front door came into view, she found Robin standing there, her arms wrapped around herself.

"Kristen," she said, hurrying down the few steps to come greet her.

"I'm fine."

Robin rushed into her arms, and Kristen needed the strength and solidity that came from her hug. "Tell me what's going on," she said before she pulled away.

"The same thing that always happens with Clara," Kristen said, her foul mood kicking up the way the breeze did at the beach. "She says rude things, implies untruths, and then acts like I'm the bad guy when I disagree or question her."

Robin searched her face, her bright blue eyes wide. "Is she really going to buy Friendship Inn?"

"I don't know," Kristen said. "I thought they'd condemned that building years ago."

"I don't know about that." Robin turned and started for the front door. "Let's go inside. It's too cold to stand out here and chat."

This was about as far from a chat as Kristen had ever been, besides. She followed Robin inside, getting a noseful of butter and chocolate. She froze. "It's your birthday."

"Not for a few more days." Robin continued to move away from her. She turned back when she reached the stairs. "Come on. We set a plate for you."

"I didn't mean to interrupt."

"You didn't." Robin came back to collect her, a warm smile adorning her face. "If you can't come by here any old time you want, who can?" She took Kristen into the kitchen, where Duke, Jamie, and Mandie all sat at the table. Presents in various stages of being opened sat on the table and counter, and a huge vase of red roses waited at Robin's place.

Kristen wanted to protest again, but she couldn't get herself to do it. She let Robin put her in front of a clean place beside Mandie and kitty corner from Robin. The roses got moved to the counter, and Robin smiled around at everyone as she sat down.

"We were just going over what I should make first in the new Instant Pot," she said.

"I want baked beans," Duke said. "The kind your mom makes, with the tabasco and the ground beef."

"Mm, yes," Robin said, and she met Kristen's eyes, hers moving to the lobster and other food on the table. Her message was clear. *Get eating.*

Kristen picked up a lobster tail and then reached for an

ear of corn. Such a simple act—eating—felt so hard, but she had done plenty of hard things in her life. She could butter a piece of corn and take a bite.

She did, the second one easier, while Jamie said she'd read a blog that said cakes could be made in the Instant Pot.

Soon enough, the darkness that had come with Clara's phone call dissipated, and Kristen joined in the conversation about whether a person should wear socks to bed or not. Apparently Robin did, and Duke thought it was a crime to do so.

"I don't even want my feet under the blankets," he said, his smile wide and white and filling the house with light. Kristen liked him so much, and he complimented Robin so well.

"I make myself a foot bed," Robin said. "Around my socks." She laughed, and Kristen rarely got to see her so relaxed and so free. It was another reminder that what she could see outside people's lives was rarely what went on behind closed doors—both good and bad.

This was definitely a good dinner, and the life, energy, and love here rejuvenated Kristen. Soon enough, Jamie and Mandie got out the cake, loaded it with candles, and the singing started.

Kristen glowed just like the forty-seven candles on Robin's cake, and her gratitude for being included so easily seeped through her as Robin leaned forward and blew out the flames. Duke served the cake, and everyone seemed to move into the living room with their dessert. They clearly had family traditions, and Kristen thought about what she used to do for her children on their birthdays.

They got to choose their favorite foods, and she and Joel usually managed to scrape together enough money to get them a few presents. Clara had expensive tastes, and the older she became, the less Kristen had been able to do to appease her. Even now, she lived beyond her means, and something quieted inside Kristen about Friendship Inn.

Clara would never be able to afford it. She wouldn't sail back to Five Island Cove and put Eloise and The Cliffside Inn out of business.

She dug her fork into her cake and took a bite, needing the chocolate to fix everything in her life that had cracked with a single conversation.

"I thought you might want Clara to move back here," Robin said casually, as if she were asking Kristen if she wore socks to bed. "No?"

"For the right reasons," Kristen said, focusing only on her cake. "She said Scott wants to take a promotion and move to the Midwest. She doesn't want to do that. She loves the sea too much." The last sentence came out in a higher pitched voice, with plenty of sarcasm mixed in.

Kristen's throat constricted with it, the bitterness flowing through her too much for her to handle and take another bite of cake.

"She won't go with him?"

"I don't know," Kristen said. "She said she wants to live on the coast, but it's a great promotion. I asked her if she'd file for divorce over a job. She said she was preparing to do whatever she had to."

"What about Lena?" Robin asked.

Scott and Clara only had one daughter—Lena. She was almost twenty, but she lived at home full-time and always would. She had Down Syndrome, and while she could hold a job and manage a few things herself, she wasn't able to live on her own completely. Clara would always have to be there to help her do things like pay bills and get simple household tasks done. She didn't understand time well, so she relied on alarms to do everything and get to work on time, go to bed on time, and all sorts of other things.

Scott had set all of that up for his daughter, and Clara enforced the timers while he went to work. Kristen had always admired them for how much they loved their daughter, and all the sacrifices they'd made in their own lives to raise her and help her as much as possible.

"She said she'd bring Lena here. She loves the cove." Kristen shook her head and forked up another bite of cake. "I think she's insane. A new, big promotion isn't something to file for divorce over."

Robin said nothing, and Kristen finished her cake without having to explain any more.

"Maybe there's more to it," Kristen finally admitted. "I was just so shocked to hear her say she wanted to buy an inn, move back here, and run it."

"She hated the cove more than AJ," Robin said, and that was the truest thing that had ever been uttered. "And she came back." She lifted one shoulder in a shrug and stood.

She took Kristen's empty plate and went into the kitchen with hers.

She returned to the couch and sank into it right beside Kristen, leaning into her as if Kristen was her mother. "I'm sorry it upset you."

"She just... I swear she knows exactly what to say to push my buttons."

"I'm sure she does." Robin sat up and opened her free right arm so Mandie could sit beside her. "I know how to rile up my mother."

"Just text her," Mandie said, a knowing smile on her face. "And ask about Aunt Anna-Maria."

"I am never doing that again," Robin said, and the two of them laughed together. Kristen smiled at them, a sense of gladness sliding through her that this mother-daughter pair seemed to have a good relationship.

"When is your campus tour trip?" she asked.

"Oh." Robin sighed and took a moment, as if she didn't know down to the minute when the flight to New York was. "Let's see. Ten days?"

"About that," Mandie said. "We're leaving on Thursday so Mom doesn't have to miss her Wednesday lunch."

"That lunch is important to me," Robin said, her voice defensive.

"I know," Mandie said. "But that's why we're leaving on a Thursday."

"Plus, your dad said the currents will change about then," Robin added. "We'll only be gone five days. Mandie's ruled out BU."

"Oh?" Kristen asked. "Isn't that where Charlie is going?" She caught the exchanged glance between mother and daughter, and she regretted bringing up Alice's son.

"For now," Robin said elusively.

Kristen nodded and let Mandie move the topic to what she wanted to do that summer—her last on the cove before she left for college. It was a nice thought—the sand, sea, surf, and sunshine—and Kristen let herself relax fully with the thoughts of summer.

"Tell us about the Seafaring Girls," Robin said, and that brought Kristen back to the present.

"We're putting off the signups for a couple more weeks," Kristen said. "Jean's doing well with it so far, but we're still working on the language and the class description." A new form of anxiety needled at her. "I just want it to go well. I don't want to step on Jean's toes. I want it to be something so amazing for her, the way it was for me."

Robin reached over and covered Kristen's hand with hers. "Me too. It'll be amazing." She gave Kristen a reassuring smile, and she wondered when their roles had changed so completely.

"Jamie would be in the age range," she said.

"I'm already planning to sign her up," Robin said with a grin. "The moment you text me that the registration is open."

Kristen nodded and pushed herself to the edge of the couch. "Thank you for letting me come over. It's past my bedtime." She smiled as she got to her feet, the action much harder than it had once been.

Robin walked with her to the front door, where she pulled her into another hug. Kristen didn't have to vocalize the other things she worried about—that no one but Jamie Grover would sign up, that running the Seafaring Girls would only remind Jean of what she didn't have, that sometimes life threw curveballs she couldn't handle—but Robin heard them all.

She acknowledged them all without saying anything, and Kristen stepped out onto the porch.

"All right," she said as she exhaled. "What else will be thrown my way?" As she went back to her car and then back to her new condo, Kristen strengthened herself. She'd been doing this life thing for seventy-eight years.

Whatever happened next, she'd handle it.

She would.

She stepped into the dark condo and flipped on a light. She hated coming home alone, and she pulled out her phone and saw it wasn't too late to text yet.

I'll take that puppy, she tapped out and sent before she could second-guess herself again. If she had a dog, then she wouldn't be swallowed by the enormous, yawning gulf of loneliness currently threatening to whisk her out into the ocean and never bring her back.

Chapter Twelve

E loise brushed out Billie's hair and started on the braid again. In her opinion, the girl already looked like a princess, but she wanted a flower crown to really feel like one. Eloise would braid her hair in a crown first, then Kelli and AJ had promised they could weave the flowers through the loops to make the floral arrangement.

She'd started it twice already, because Billie had such fine, cornsilk hair. "This is better," she said. "With the gel."

"I have more right here." Billie lifted up the clear bottle with the bright blue gel inside.

Eloise didn't take it. "I think there's enough. There's none of those little flyaways now." Her emotions rose through her stomach and chest, clogged in her throat and silenced her voice box.

She'd never have a child of her own. Billie and Grace had accepted her in their lives as their maternal figure, and helping the oldest of them get ready for her first real dance and first real date was almost more than Eloise knew how to deal with.

"Look this way," Aaron said, and both Eloise and Billie moved their gazes in the direction of his voice. He snapped a picture, which Eloise was sure would show her looking like a complete wide-eyed doe.

"Dad," Billie complained. "I'm not ready."

"I'm taking pictures of the whole day," he said, grinning at the phone as he pinched and tapped. "I'm thinking of making a video."

"Dad," she said again, clearly disgusted.

Eloise smiled to herself, glad she was working above the teenager. Aaron had been taking a videography class in his spare time—which was a laughable concept for him—and he'd enjoyed putting together still images and video with music.

He'd only been doing it for six weeks, but Eloise could already see the improvement in the videos he'd made recently compared to the ones he'd made in January.

"Dad," Grace called, and Aaron ducked out of the master bathroom to go see what his youngest wanted.

"Let him make this," Eloise said, and she met Billie's eyes in the mirror. "It means a lot to him."

Billie nodded, her eyes wide and sober. "All right."

"He can't do anything else," she said. "We did the dress. My friends are coming to help with makeup and hair."

"He gave me money," Billie said, so open and unassuming.

Eloise smiled and focused on getting the right hair into

the French braid snaking along Billie's hairline. "Money is important, I suppose."

"He said he gets to answer the door."

"That's because he wants to make sure this boy you're going with is respectable."

"He's met him twice now," Billie said, rolling his eyes.

"Boys are still boys," Eloise murmured, her own fears and worries for the night ahead of Billie rearing up.

"I know how to handle boys," Billie said. "I know the safe word. I have all the contacts in my phone. We're going in a group. His dad is driving, for crying out loud."

Eloise allowed another smile onto her face. "It's always best to be prepared in situations like this." She continued braiding, taking out a couple of strands when they didn't lay flat the way she'd like.

Finally, she got all the hair into the braid, and she twisted a ponytail holder around the end of it, pulling it tight right against Billie's head, behind the same ear where the braid started.

She twisted that into a bun, and pulled out a couple of the loops to give it more volume and the appearance of being messy. "Now we just need the flowers."

As if on cue, AJ's voice called, "El? We're coming in."

"Come in," she said, moving away from the chair where Billie sat. The girl came into the bedroom with her to see the flowers, and AJ moved to the side so Kelli could show them the blooms, which currently rested in a bucket.

"These are so gorgeous," Eloise said, reaching for one of the smaller bunches of pure white flowers. "Billie."

"Look at that rose with the pink edges." Billie's voice sounded like it had been touched by angels, and she looked up at Kelli and AJ with wonder. "Thank you so much."

Eloise's gratitude could've been expressed just as genuinely, and she grinned at Kelli. "Tell your mother thank you. And thank you for bringing them."

"Sure," Kelli said easily, her smile easy and casual. "I guess someone else tried to buy these this morning. There was quite the tussle at the Bell Island Market."

"Uh oh," Eloise said, following Kelli into the bathroom. She set the bucket on the counter between the two sinks and turned back as Billie stepped in front of the chair and sat down again.

"Valentine's Day can do that to people," AJ said. "Our Kelli's gotten a little more strong-willed."

Kelli giggled and reached for that pink-petaled rose. "I think this one should go right above the corner of your eye." She tucked it into a thicker part of the braid while AJ put a sack of supplies on the counter too.

"Here's the hair pins," she said, handing one to Kelli. Together, the two of them picked through the blooms and added them to perfectly positioned spots in the crown braid, all the while talking about a couple of boys who'd shown up just as they were leaving the flower shop.

"My mom had the bucket, and she said they followed her out to her car," Kelli said, the words somewhat muffled as she held a pin between her lips. She slipped it around the stem of a flower and eyed her work.

"That's when I showed up," she continued. "I told those

boys they better not even be thinking about asking an old lady for her flowers." She giggled again, and Eloise smiled. Her friends had been so good for her soul, and this was no exception.

"They muttered something about needing flowers for their dates tonight, and I told them they should plan in advance in the future." She shook her head and pointed to an empty spot in the flower crown so AJ could put in the pale pink cherry blossoms she'd been holding for several seconds. "My heart was pounding so hard."

AJ grinned at her and filled the blank space. "But you did it."

"I did it."

The crown complete, the three of them stood back and looked at Billie. "Gorgeous," Kelli said.

"Stunning," AJ added.

"Beautiful." Eloise finally moved aside and let Billie see the crown for the first time. The girl drew in a gasp and stared at herself.

"I look..."

"Older," Eloise said, and Aaron wouldn't be happy about that. "Stay there and let me take a picture for your dad." She'd gotten a couple of other candid shots too, unbeknownst to Billie. Eloise sometimes felt like the middle man between her husband and her step-daughter, because she just wanted the two of them to get along so badly.

"Perfect," Kelli said.

"Don't you let this boy do anything you don't want to

do," AJ said. "Just because you've dressed up and put flowers in your hair doesn't mean it's for him."

"AJ," Eloise said quietly.

"I won't," Billie promised. "I know it's not for him."

"Then who's it for?" Eloise asked, somewhat surprised the words had come out of her mouth. She didn't normally challenge anyone, least of all Billie. She'd worked so hard to get the girl to like her over the past couple of years.

"It's for me," Billie said simply. A wicked smile curved her lips. "Fine. Maybe it's a little bit for Raya Oldson, who told me I wasn't very pretty but that all the boys liked me because I was skinny."

Eloise blinked, sure she hadn't heard Billie properly. AJ snorted and then burst out laughing when she couldn't hold it in, and even Kelli smiled. She drew Billie into a hug and said, "You show that Raya."

"Kelli," Eloise said. "Billie doesn't need to prove anything to anyone."

"Of course she doesn't," Kelli said, but her smile didn't diminish when she stepped back from Billie. "AJ is the master with makeup."

"I learned so much from my days in sportscasting," AJ said, her laughter drying right up. "Less is more, Bills. That's what we're going to do tonight."

The makeup didn't take long, and Eloise marveled at how mature it made Billie look. She was fourteen, but she didn't have hips or much of a chest like some of the other girls yet. Certainly nowhere near the extra roundness Eloise had carried at that age. She was thin, lanky, and tall, and Eloise hoped she loved herself just the way she was.

"All right," she said, leaving the hall and entering the kitchen. "Are you two ready to see her?"

Grace looked up from the tablet in front of her on the table. "Yes," she said, bouncing in her seat. "Yes!"

"Ready," Aaron said, swiping his reading glasses off his face. Eloise secretly loved them, because they made him older, wiser, and sexier. As if that was even possible. The hair that grew in now held more gray than ever, and Eloise sure did like that about him.

"Her date should be here in about five minutes," Eloise said. "So let's take a few pictures." She turned back to the hall, and AJ gave her a thumbs-up. "I give you... your Sweethearts Billie Sherman."

Billie came gliding down the hallway, the dress Jean Shields had sewn for her wafting around her like a caftan in the wind. She was elegant and sophisticated, and Aaron drew in a sharp breath when she arrived fully in the light.

"My goodness," he said, stumbling out of his chair and to his feet. "Is this my little girl?"

"Dad," Billie said in that same dry, *I-can't-believe-I-have-to-put-up-with-him* voice she usually used with him. Her face melted into a smile as he reached her and hugged her, and Eloise snapped a picture while her eyes were closed.

She loved her father, and Aaron loved her. He only wanted the best for her, and Eloise couldn't fault him that.

"You're gorgeous," he said, his voice somewhat choked.

When Aaron showed emotion, that meant things were getting real. He stepped back. "You look so grown-up."

"Thanks, Daddy."

The doorbell rang, and they both perked up to attention, like a deer in the woods who'd just heard a predator.

"I'll get it." Aaron straightened the collar on his shirt and headed for the door.

Eloise gestured Billie closer to her and put her arm around the girl's shoulders. "Two things," she said. "My mom used to say to me whenever I went out." That hadn't been much, admittedly, but Eloise had liked her mom's advice.

"Remember who you are," she said. "And have fun."

"Thanks, El." Billie hugged her too as male voices filtered into the air. They were too low and too far away to make out words, but then Aaron appeared in the doorway that led into the living room.

"This young man seems to think he has a date with Billie tonight." He grinned around at everyone, and Eloise released Billie as she took the first step toward her date, Luke Howard.

"Wow, Billie," he said, his eyes sliding right down to her feet and back to her face. "You look so amazing."

"She *is* so amazing," Aaron said, and Luke's face flushed.

"Pictures," Eloise said, flying into motion. "Come on, Luke. You and Billie in the front room, by the fireplace." She stepped to her husband's side and flashed him a smile. "Get your video going, baby."

He startled as if he'd forgotten, then said, "Right," and dashed over to the kitchen table for his phone.

Ten minutes later, with a very embarrassed Billie towing Luke Howard out the front door, Eloise finally sighed out her breath. "They're going to be fine," she said. "They'll have so much fun." She met her husband's eyes and gave him a big grin. "You did great."

"Did I?"

She ran her hands up his chest. "Yeah. No threats. No firearms."

He chuckled and shook his head. "Those were Billie's two rules."

Eloise leaned into him and kissed him. "Want to watch a movie with me?"

"Always," he whispered, and she looked past him to the table where Kelli sat with AJ and Grace.

"Give me five minutes," she said, and she went to thank her friends and say good-bye to them. "You guys saved me."

"You could've done it, El," AJ said. "It's just a brush." She hugged Eloise tightly, and it still struck Eloise as strange how much AJ had changed since she'd come to the cove for Joel's funeral.

"How's Asher?" she asked.

"Good," AJ said, throwing a look in Kelli's direction. Eloise looked that way too, feeling on the outside of that conversation and friendship. She always had been, and she'd made peace with it long ago. "We'll get out of your hair."

Kelli hugged her too, and Eloise promised she'd try to get away from the inn soon for one of the midweek lunches or a yoga class. She wasn't sure when that would happen, but she wanted it to come to fruition.

Once she'd waved to them and closed the front door, she turned back to Aaron, who'd stayed in the living room. "I want to work less," she said.

"Okay," he said.

She hadn't expected him to argue, but she would like some ideas for how to make that happen. When he didn't add anything, she raised her eyebrows. "Just okay? How do I do that?"

"You hire more people," he said, grinning at her. He received her into his arms. "You take days off. You just do it."

He made it sound so easy, and Eloise wanted it to be. "I need a morning manager and an evening manager. Then I can go in whenever I want—or not." She swayed with him, the light in the evening fading quickly beyond the front windows. "The inn is fully booked through summertime. I have the revenue."

"Do it," he whispered. "Please do it. I'd love to have you home more, or just that when you're home, you're not dead tired or frazzled." He ran his lips down her neck to her collarbone.

Eloise held onto his strong shoulders and thought about her life. Being home more sounded amazing. Not being frazzled was even better.

"Just checking," he whispered, his mouth dangerously close to her earlobe now. "When you said we could watch a movie, you meant in bed, right?"

Eloise grinned and giggled. "Right," she said. "Let's go

make sure Grace is all set up in her room, and then you can even pick the movie."

"Or no movie," he said under his breath, which only made Eloise's smile bigger.

THE FOLLOWING MORNING, BILLIE HAD JUST finished detailing every—last—detail of the dance when Eloise's phone rang. She wasn't sure how much more talking she could handle, but she leapt at the device when she saw her mother's name on the screen.

"Hold that thought, Bills," she said. She swiped on the call. "Mom."

"Hey," her mom said breathlessly. "Are you up at the inn?"

"No," Eloise said, her pulse firing through her body at the urgency in her mom's tone. "Billie had Sweethearts last night, and I wanted all morning to talk to her about it. Even Aaron hasn't gone into the station yet."

"I don't want you to worry," her mother said. "But I'm pretty sure I just saw Zach Watkins. I thought you should know. Aaron too." She pulled in a breath as if she'd been running, and Eloise looked left and right like she could get to her mother and make sure everything was okay right now.

"Zach Watkins?" she asked, turning back to Aaron. He perked up at the name. "Here in the cove?"

Zach had come to the cove a couple of summers ago,

claiming to be Kelli's half-brother. It had been proven he wasn't, and he'd left the cove without a word to anyone.

"I was just at the grocery store," her mom said. "I swear it was him. He didn't see me or anything."

"Okay," Eloise said. "Thanks, Mom. I'll let Aaron know." She hung up and faced the table, the three people she loved best looking back at her. "I guess my mom saw Zach Watkins at the grocery store on Sanctuary."

Aaron got to his feet, his battle face slipping into position. "I'll radio my guys on the island." He had an immediate network he could call on, and as Eloise nodded, she remembered she did too.

She lifted her phone again to send a text to the very same women who'd helped her when Billie had been asked to the Sweethearts Dance. If it were her brother who'd returned to the cove—Eloise shivered simply thinking about seeing him again after all the threats he'd issued—she'd want to know as soon as possible.

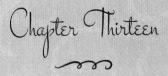

Chapter Thirteen

Alice couldn't think straight, but Arthur kept talking. She didn't hear him.

Her phone had chimed, and she'd glanced at it real quick.

A heads up, Eloise had texted. *My mother just called, and she said she saw Zach Watkins in the grocery store on Sanctuary Island. Unconfirmed, but I thought we should all be on the lookout. I've told Aaron, and he's on it.*

"On it," Alice whispered to herself. She felt so...off it. She'd never confronted Charlie or Ginny about the negative pregnancy test. She'd thrown it away a couple of weeks ago, determined to pretend like she'd never seen it. She hadn't even mentioned it to Arthur.

"What?" her husband asked, and Alice looked up from her phone. Robin would likely be the first to respond to that message, though she had been busy with Mandie, a college campus tour, the Sweethearts Dance—which both of her girls had gone to last-minute—and an extraordinarily full fishing season. She hadn't been to the Wednesday luncheon in a couple of weeks now, and Alice missed her.

"Sorry." Alice gave her husband a smile and put her phone on his desk. She sat in a chair a student might, across from the school counselor she'd married after stopping by this office at Arthur's request. "Eloise just texted something that took me by surprise."

Concern grew in Arthur's eyes. He had been very accommodating for Alice's friendships, and she so appreciated that. "Do you need to go?"

Her phone went off, one chime after another, very much the way it had the first time she'd been in his office. "Maybe." She got to her feet, and he did too. "Sorry."

"It's fine. We finished breakfast, and I have a meeting in ten minutes anyway." Though it was Saturday, he'd volunteered to help clean up after the Sweethearts Dance. She supposed that could be a "meeting," but not the traditional kind she thought of when she heard the word.

He rounded the desk and took her into his arms. "No phones tonight, though, right?" He gazed down at her with love and desire, and Alice grinned up at him.

"No phones tonight," she promised. She kissed him quickly amidst another string of notifications and hustled out of his office. After silencing her phone, she walked to her car, where she started it and got the air blowing so she'd be neither too hot nor too cold. She wasn't sure what about the car made her feel safe and protected, only that it did.

Anyone could see through the many windows. They

could be broken, for crying out loud. And yet, Alice didn't think anything or anyone could get to her while she scrolled back up to Eloise's texts to read the responses.

Is she sure? Robin had asked. *Did your mom ever meet Zach?*

You're kidding had come in from AJ. *Kel? Where are you?*

At the studio, Kelli had said. *I'm fine here.*

Aaron's on it, Eloise said. *She met Zach, yes. She's not sure.*

No sense in freaking out until necessary, Kristen had said, and Alice's pulse settled back into her chest. Zach hadn't been nearly as threatening and dangerous as Garrett Hall, Eloise's brother.

No one had wanted Zach to stick around, that was for sure. Alice had been very wary of him from the beginning, and she'd warned Kelli not to take what he'd said at face-value. For someone so trusting and so good, that had been hard for Kelli.

Kristen's right, Robin had said. *Let's let Aaron handle it.*

"Who else would handle it?" Alice murmured to herself. She looked up and out the windshield. And what would they do? Show up at Zach's door and demand he leave the cove?

We don't own the cove, Kelli said. *He can come here legally.*

I just can't believe he would, AJ said.

I'm on Sanctuary during the week, Laurel finally chimed in. *I can watch for him. We've got two good cops out there today. They'll let us know if something funny is going on.*

Laurel, ever the voice of reason, had been the last to text.

Sorry, in a meeting, Alice said. *I agree with Kristen. Nothing to freak out about yet.*

She put her phone in the cupholder beside her and backed out of the stall. The drive home took ten minutes, and Alice went into the house she'd originally been so proud to live in. She still was, and she took a deep, calming breath in the kitchen.

This house represented so much for her, and she let a balloon of hope and happiness fill her as she made a pot of coffee in the quiet kitchen. There was no fear here. No walls that held things she didn't want the neighbors to know. No judgment, and no one holding their breath just in case a certain person walked into the room.

She didn't have any appointments on the weekend, which was why she and Arthur had arranged their breakfast date in his office while the twins got ready for their day. Charlie had Academic Olympiad practice that morning, and Ginny had gone into the ice cream shop early to learn how to make the cookies they sold.

Alice could putter around her office or the house endlessly, but today, she wanted to relax. After sipping her coffee on the back patio despite the wind trying to make the day gray and cold, she decided she'd call AJ and try for a lunch date.

"I can't," AJ said, plenty of apology in her voice. "I have a tee time with Matt and his parents in half an hour."

"No problem," Alice said cheerfully. Honestly, she could

get something delivered to the house and enjoy it all the same. "I'll call Kristen."

She did, but Kristen had a meeting with Jean that afternoon. Robin was actually on her way to lunch with her mother, which caused Alice's eyebrows to lift toward the sky.

"You could come," Robin said hopefully, but Alice was not getting on that crazy train.

"I can't interrupt that," she said. "But call me back when it's done so I can hear all about it."

Robin hefted a sigh and promised she would.

Laurel was on her way to Nantucket with Paul to meet her parents for lunch, and Alice didn't bother to call Kelli. Whole Soul was busy on the weekends, and she knew exactly what Kelli would say. *I wish I could, Alice...*

Alice wished she could too. She sat on the bottom step, leafing through her options for delivery when the back door opened. Then it slammed, startling her, and footsteps strode inside.

A yell filled the house, and Alice got to her feet quickly. A couple of steps and she rounded the corner to find an aggravated Charlie pacing in the kitchen. "Heya," she said. "What's up?"

She shoved her phone in her pocket as he threw her a dark look. She'd seen one exactly like it so many times on her ex-husband's face.

"I'm going to quit the Olympiad," he growled. He yanked open the fridge, and Alice was honestly surprised the door didn't come off.

"Can you do that?" The competition season literally started in a couple of weeks.

"I don't care."

"What happened?"

Charlie straightened and slammed the fridge. "There was no practice today." His chest heaved, and Alice wanted to transport him back in time to when his life was easier. When he'd been a little boy and gotten angry like this over a toy, she could soothe him. She knew how to help then.

Now, she had no idea what to say or do.

"Oh?" She let her eyebrows go up. "You've been gone an hour." By her estimations, at least. He'd told her the practice started at ten, and it was almost eleven-thirty.

"Sariah just wanted us to be alone in the school." His fists clenched and unclenched. "I broke up with her. It wasn't pretty. I'm the bad guy, of course. And a loser, because I don't want to sleep with her."

All the fight left his body, and his shoulders slumped. Just as fast as that happened, he righted himself again. "I'm done. I don't care if I can quit or not."

Alice didn't want to argue with him. Charlie often thought he existed on the outskirts of popularity at school, but the opposite was true. Just because he didn't conform to certain stereotypes didn't make him an outcast. In the eyes of many, it made him cool.

He had signed a contract with the Academic Olympiad, and Alice remembered some clause about dropping off the team. She chose not to say anything right now and instead, she entered the kitchen and enveloped her beautiful boy into an embrace. "I'm so sorry," she whispered.

"I don't get girls," he said, his voice agonized.

Alice didn't know how to explain the entire female species to him, so she said nothing on that particular subject. "I've been searching for a lunch date. Wanna go with me?" She stepped away, smiling at her son brightly.

"Yeah," he said when she'd expected him to decline. "Let me go change out of this yuppie shirt." He grumbled under his breath as he pulled the blue and white striped polo over his head and went past the dining room table and toward the stairs Alice had just been sitting on.

She followed him, calling, "Bring that trash down from up there, would you?"

"Yeah," he yelled back, and a few minutes later, he came thundering down the stairs with a faded yellow T-shirt on that had a rainbow across the front of it. He carried a big trash bag in one hand—the garbage from his room.

"Did you get the trash in the bathroom?" she asked. "Ginny's room?"

Charlie gave her a death glare, and wow, Alice should've died from the piercing quality of it. "No."

"What did you think I meant?"

He rolled his eyes and then his whole head and went back upstairs. His footsteps echoed overhead, and then he yelled, "Mom!"

"What?" she called.

He appeared at the top of the steps, pure panic in his

face. "You might want to come see this." He darted away from the landing, and Alice started up the steps.

"What is it?" She found him in the bathroom, and he nodded to the counter there. Alice saw the pregnancy test—another blasted pregnancy test—sitting there and sucked in a tight breath. It was like trying to breathe underwater through a stirring straw, and her chest tightened instantly.

"Do you...?" He let the question hang there, and Alice had no idea how to finish it.

"Where did you get this?" she asked.

"It was just sitting in the trash," he said. "Kind of off to the side. When I pulled on the bag on the side there, it shifted, and I saw it." He wore wide eyes and spoke with an edge of terror in his voice. "I don't think Ginny is sleeping with Ray."

"Who else has been over here?" Alice asked, wishing she could tell how recently this had been used.

"The only person who ever comes over here is..." Charlie trailed off, and Alice could see the twin shutters going right over his expression. He knew. He *knew*, and his first instinct was to protect his twin sister.

"Charlie," she said, the mega-power of her Mom-voice employed. When he still didn't speak, Alice's pulse rioted, and she barked, "Charles."

"Emily," he blurted out. "She's been having a ton of problems at home, and she comes over late at night and climbs into Ginny's room. She sleeps there a lot."

"A lot?" Alice pressed one palm to her racing heartbeat. "How long has this been going on?"

Charlie shrugged, his gaze migrating back to the pregnancy test. "Couple of months."

Long enough for Emily to take a test in January and discard it in the same trashcan. Alice picked up the test and put it in the trash, then removed the bag. "Okay," she said, noting that it was negative. She swallowed, so unsure of herself.

Shouldn't she have all the answers by now? At her age?

"What are you going to do?"

"I don't know." She led the way out of the bathroom, her son hot on her heels.

"We should just talk to Ginny."

"And say what?" Alice challenged, ducking into her daughter's room to empty her trashcan too. She wasn't nearly as addicted to Diet Mountain Dew as Charlie, and Ginny barely had anything in her garbage can. She shoved a few crumpled pieces of paper and a full notebook into the bathroom trash bag and looked around Ginny's room. "Where does Emily sleep?"

"Bean bag," Charlie said, indicating it.

Alice instantly saw the very human-like impression on it, as well as the blanket that had been folded and draped over the back. "I think that'll have to stop. What if her parents find out and call the cops in the middle of the night, and then she was found here?"

She shook her head. She understood that families had problems, but she didn't need to get in the middle of them. "Who is Emily dating?"

"No one," Charlie said slowly. "She's not dating anyone. At least that I know of."

Alice's mind went in a dozen directions, none of them good. She took in a long drag of air. "Okay," she said. "Here's what we're going to do. You're going to text Ginny and let her know that I found two pregnancy tests, and I'm a little miffed about it. I think I've seen you use the words 'on the rampage' before. Go with that."

Charlie already had his phone out.

"Twin talk," Alice said. "Let her know she's going to have to explain some things, and that I need to know *all* the details the moment she gets home from work."

Charlie remained silent for several seconds, his phone making all kinds of typing chirps. One last one, and he looked up. "Done."

Alice nodded. "I don't think she's done until three. So." She tied off the garbage bag, as if she could just as easily tie off this situation and the extremely delicate conversation coming up. "Let's you and I go to lunch, and we'll deal with Ginny later."

"You sure?" Charlie asked. "If you're on the rampage, you don't normally take us to lunch."

Alice swatted at her son's chest, frowning at him as he dodged away. "You don't want lunch? Fine by me."

Charlie laughed and ducked out of his sister's bedroom. "I want lunch," he said. "Finally, I'm not the one doing anything wrong. I feel like I'm *owed* lunch."

"Oh, brother," Alice grumbled as she followed him, though she could admit she was relieved Charlie wasn't the one in trouble this time. She hoped Ginny wasn't either, but sometimes it was really easy for people like her daughter— good, caring people who just wanted to help—to get in over their heads.

Thankfully, Alice knew how to help people get out from under the heavy loads and away from the hard situations, and she would do everything she could to help her daughter —and Emily.

Chapter Fourteen

Jean leafed through the scrapbooks Kristen had laid out on the table. The scent in the air in the community center that sat on the government square in downtown Diamond Island reminded Jean of burnt sugar, and she kept glancing toward the door as if the source of it would walk into the room.

Kristen had brought her scrapbooks this morning, and the director over youth programs should be arriving any moment. Cathy Marmelt was a no-nonsense woman who'd intimidated Jean the first time they'd met. Even with a smile on her face, she could've kept any wayward teen in line with a simple look in their direction.

Jean had nodded and said, "Yes, ma'am," about a dozen times before that initial meeting had ended, all the while wishing that Baron Downing hadn't appointed Cathy to oversee the program.

Jean had signed the paperwork necessary to run the

Seafaring Girls program and ran from the room, hoping Miss Marmelt wouldn't need to contact her again.

"I'm so sorry I'm late," a man said, and Jean turned toward the door she'd been watching. Kristen did too, and they both watched as a man in his mid-thirties approached. He carried at least three laptops stacked on top of one another, a to-go cup of coffee perched on top of that, and a ceramic bowl that looked like it had been hand-tossed.

He carried an apple in one hand and took a big bite as he arrived at the table. "This meeting saved me, by the way, so thank you." He put down his laptops like they were made of plastic and unbreakable and then grinned at Kristen with his hands now free. "How are you, Miss Shields?"

Kristen giggled—actually giggled—and Jean stared as her almost eighty-year-old mother-in-law hugged the scruffy-looking gentleman. He sported reddish-brown hair, and a lot of it. It grew on his face in a beard and mustache which hadn't been trimmed in some time, as well as all over his head.

He released Kristen and looked at Jean, the sunbeams in his smile staying as bright as before. "You must be Jean."

"Yes," she said.

Instead of reaching to shake her hand, the man drew her into a hug too. "I'm Ed, and I'm going to build your registration page to your exact specifications."

"Oh, wonderful," Jean said as he stepped back. He'd brought a different kind of energy with him, and the three of them settled down at the table. He opened the trio of computers and got set up behind them like he was CIA intelligence.

"All right," he said. "This is a what-you-see-is-what-you-get builder. Do you have pictures?"

"I emailed them to you," Kristen said. She and Rueben had been up late last night to get the photos scanned and emailed, and Jean gave her an encouraging smile past the cockpit Ed had set up.

"Right," he said. "There they are." He clicked and the mouse moved around on his screen like lightning, and while Jean wasn't a dunce with technology, everything Ed did would've taken her four times as long. "So I think we put one right here. This one is nice." He'd pulled up a picture of a teenage girl from decades ago. "Who's that?"

"Robin," Kristen said with fondness. "Do you remember the Goldens? She's got older brothers, so maybe you're too young."

"Don't know them," Ed said, his fingers flying over the keyboard now. Every tap actually produced a *clack-clack*, and Jean's eyebrows flew toward the ceiling at the speed with which he could get things done, especially because he was only using four fingers—the first two on each hand.

Kristen grinned at her from Ed's other side, and Jean started to relax a little bit. They had the details for the signup page. Once it was approved, it would be sent out to the residents of Five Island Cove for an April start date. They'd decided they didn't need to be gathering in the colder winter months, and for the relaunch of the program, April was soon enough.

"Ed is here," a woman said, and Jean twisted to find Cathy gliding toward them. She wore a dark blue skirt set, complete with a blazer and the whitest of white shirts peeking through at the collar. "Wonderful."

She almost spoke the last word with a British accent, and Jean's heart thrummed out a couple of extra beats. Nervous beats. "Hi, Cathy."

"Jean." The ice smile appeared. "Good to see you again. Kristen."

Kristen lumbered to her feet, and Jean noticed how long it took her. She walked every day, as her condo had a walking trail right along the beach. If she didn't go alone, she went with AJ and Asher, as she'd invited Jean to tag along several times.

Jean hadn't been able to bolster herself enough to do so yet, but she thought she might ask Kristen about it after today's meeting.

"Hello, Cathy." Kristen hugged her too, but Jean opted to shake her hand.

Cathy rounded the table and took a seat opposite the trifecta of computers and said, "You're in good hands with Ed."

He looked over the top of the middle laptop, a winning smile on his face. It was the warmest one Jean had ever seen on a human face, and it still couldn't thaw Cathy Marmelt. Jean wondered what had made her that way, and if she'd once lost the chance to adopt a baby too. Perhaps she hadn't spoken to her mother in a while. Maybe her husband and children had been killed in a terrible car accident, or she'd simply lost them through divorce and distance.

Jean knew better now that every human being—warm smiles or icy exteriors—she came in contact with had a story behind the façade. No one's life was completely perfect, and the human mind had a way of whispering damaging things to a person that were entirely unfair.

She flashed another smile in Cathy's direction and focused on the laptop nearest her, as Ed started typing and the words came up there. He muttered to himself as his fingers moved, the only noise in the room the humming of the furnace and those loud clackety-clacks of the keyboard.

"Fifty dollars?" Ed asked, the typing pausing. "It's only fifty dollars?" He looked at Kristen, then Cathy.

"Per month," Jean said for the both of them. After all, she was running this program, and she couldn't let Kristen answer everything for her. "They'll sign up for a recurring payment with the city."

"Oh, gotcha. Like the dock fee."

"Yes," Jean said, because Five Island Cove charged ten dollars a month to use the docks on the east and west sides of the island, whether someone used their slot a lot or a little.

Ed's fingers got back to work, and he asked a few more questions. Jean answered all of them, reading from her tiny notebook a time or two. Finally, after only about twenty minutes, Ed said, "It's time to work the magic."

He leaned back in his seat and reached out to smack the enter key. The screen on the middle laptop blinked white, and then the sign-up page for the Seafaring Girls loaded.

Right there in living color in front of her eyes, Jean could see the aged picture of Robin that had been scanned in. She stood tall and proud on the bow of a sailboat, one hand holding the mast while the other shaded her eyes as she looked into the sun.

Join the Seafaring Girls sat in big, bold letters to the right of the picture, with all the details of the program beneath it.

They'd decided to run classes on Mondays, Wednesdays, and Saturdays, because then Jean would only have to reschedule her mid-week sewing students. She only had four on Wednesdays, and she could put them on Tuesday or Thursday. It gave her something to do with children five days a week.

Something to occupy her time in the mornings. Someone who was relying on her to show up.

Her chest filled with a breath, and she embraced this new challenge in front of her. A gaping wound in her chest had just been stitched shut, and Jean allowed the happiness and excitement to flow through her.

She'd been seeing her therapist, and she suddenly couldn't wait to meet with Dr. Hill again.

"It's great," she gushed. "Thank you, Ed."

"Come see, Boss," he said to Cathy, who didn't seem amused by his term of endearment. "She's the one who has to approve it." He gave Jean a smile. "She will, though." He lowered his voice as the program director got to her feet. "She'll suggest a different font. Wait and see."

Cathy came around the table and stood between Kristen and Ed. She examined the page and pointed with her finger to tell Ed to pull it down so she could see the bottom of it. "It's great," she said, her voice not nearly as full of appreciation and praise as Jean's had been. "Though I wonder if we could make the font at the top a little more...seaworthy."

Jean stifled her giggles, understanding now why Kristen had reacted to Ed the way she had.

"Seaworthy?" Ed repeated, leaning forward again. "Give me two seconds..." About thirty later, he'd changed the blocky font to something a bit more ropey, and Cathy gave her approval.

"Great." Ed stood and started slamming laptops closed. "Pleasure to see you ladies again." He juggled all the things he'd brought as he walked toward the exit, and once he'd left, the energy in the room simply wasn't the same.

"Is there anything else, Jean?" Cathy asked. "We'll get this out in our weekend email, and it'll go in the bulletin for March and April. We'll have it on the website, and I'll have our social media manager put it out on the Internet."

"That all sounds great," she said, her smile widening no matter how she tried to contain it. She'd warmed to the idea of running the Seafaring Girls over the past few weeks, especially since Kelli had told her what the program had meant for her.

A place to belong. A place where everyone accepted everyone else.

She hoped the girls who signed up would be able to find that for themselves. She needed to teach them about sailing, water safety, and the ocean, but she wanted it to be more than that. She thought of Parker, and how she simply spent time with him, answering his questions and pointing out the fins on the whales when she saw them.

That was what she wanted the Seafaring Girls to be, and she hoped she was strong enough to handle any personality that came to the lighthouse for the program.

"Lunch?" Kristen asked, breaking Jean out of her thoughts. Cathy had gone, and Jean probably hadn't even said goodbye.

"Yes," Jean said, bending to collect her purse. "Let's go to lunch."

AN HOUR LATER, SHE GLANCED UP AS LAUREL SLID into the booth, a long sigh leaking from her lips. "Laurel," she said, plenty of surprise in her name. The cop still wore her uniform, gun belt, and badge. "What are you doing here?"

She glanced to Kristen and Robin, as it had just been the three of them for lunch that day. Alice couldn't get out of a meeting, and their midweek luncheons had dwindled a lot lately. Jean told herself it was just winter. That everyone hibernated in the colder weather, and the wind and rain on Five Island Cove drove everyone indoors.

Eloise was so busy with the inn; Kelli with Whole Soul. Laurel was back on the beat, and AJ had a brand-new baby. Jean hardly came to the Wednesday lunches, and today wasn't Wednesday besides.

"Zach is not on the cove," Laurel said. She looked up as

the waitress arrived. "Diet Coke. A lot of ice. And I'll have the potato skins with extra bacon, please." She waved away a menu and focused on the group as the woman left to put in her order.

"He's not?" Robin asked. "How do you know?"

"We've canvassed Sanctuary from top to bottom," she said, wiping her face. She looked pale and drawn, and Jean couldn't help leaning a little closer to examine her better.

"Are you okay?" she asked, drawing Laurel's attention to her.

Laurel reached across the table and covered Jean's hand with both of hers. "Jean, I'm so sorry about the baby."

Jean took a deep breath, telling herself at least it wasn't a sharp one. The air didn't hook inside her throat and yank anymore. It didn't grab onto every delicate piece of her lungs and grip as tightly as it could.

"The baby would've been born next week," she said, doing what Dr. Hill had told her to do: Talk about the baby. It was okay to talk.

She reached up and brushed her hair back out of her face. "I'm doing okay, actually. Thank you, Laurel."

Laurel's rough, rugged hands squeezed Jean's more delicate ones, and then they slid away. "I'm glad." She turned her attention back to Robin and Kristen on the inside of the booth. "Every cop in the cove has searched their islands. We finally found a manifest on the steamer that leaves Rocky Ridge with his name on it. He left two days ago."

Robin frowned as she picked at the remains of her lobster poutine. "He was here then."

"He was," Laurel confirmed.

"He didn't contact any of us," Kristen said. "Not Eloise's mother. Not Kelli's. Not even her."

Robin lifted her eyes first to Kristen's and then Jean's. "Why was he here then?"

"My partner and I managed to track down someone who'd seen him." She glanced up as her soda arrived. She unwrapped the straw in a hurry and stuck it in the dark, bubbling liquid. She gulped it and let out a long sigh.

Even Robin's eyes widened, and Jean wondered if cops weren't allowed to drink anything on duty.

"The hotel clerk," Laurel said. "She said he booked a boat out to Friendship Island, but there's nothing out there. We followed up with the boat taxi, and yep, he took Zach and a few others out to the island. He goes in the morning. Comes back in the afternoon. Once a day. That's it."

"That's it," Kristen repeated, but she wore a look like that was anything but it.

"Wasn't Clara going out to Friendship Island too?" Jean asked, and Kristen nodded, her eyes down, focused on something on the tabletop.

"Yes," she said. "The inn out there is for sale."

"Do you think Zach could be interested in that?" Robin asked, a measure of shock in her voice. "And how is that inn up for sale? It's one gust of wind away from being blown into the water."

Laurel giggled, but Jean had heard the same thing about Friendship Inn.

"We don't know what Zach is interested in," Kristen

said. "And he's gone now." Her eyes came up, and she wore a look of fierce determination. "It's done."

Jean liked the strength with which she spoke, but she had a feeling nothing was ever really done. Still, she nodded along with Robin and Laurel, and then she sat quietly while Robin quizzed Laurel about why she looked like she hadn't slept in a few nights.

The woman really could interrogate someone in the kindest voice imaginable, and the potato skins with extra bacon had barely arrived before Laurel said, "Fine, I'll tell you, but I'm not ready to make a huge announcement."

Jean's throat tightened, and she knew exactly what Laurel was going to say. She slid to the end of the bench seat and stood, reaching into her pocket for her phone. She pulled it out as she pressed the ringer button to make it chime. "That's Reuben. I'll be right back."

"Jean," Laurel said, but she kept walking. No one had called. Rueben hadn't texted. Jean simply couldn't sit four feet from the beautiful Laurel Lehye and listen to her announce her pregnancy.

Chapter Fifteen

AJ got out of the minivan, thinking for the first time in her life that she should get one. Putting a carseat in the back of Robin's vehicle had been far easier than the sedan AJ drove. "Ready, baby?" she asked as she opened the back door behind the passenger seat.

Asher kicked his little legs, which made AJ smile. She hadn't been able to stop the joy from infusing her face for a couple of days now.

They were finally all getting together for a luncheon. Everyone. Kelli had arrived on Diamond Island a couple of hours ago, and Robin had picked her and AJ up at AJ's cottage after they'd walked through a boutique and bought Kristen and Jean matching bottles of perfume.

"Got him?" Robin asked as if AJ had never lifted her son out of his carseat.

"Yep." AJ flashed her a smile, because Robin had been

mothering people for thirty years and she wasn't about to stop now.

"Alice is here," Robin mused. "She was bringing Kristen. I'm assuming the police cruiser belongs to Laurel..."

"No Eloise?" Kelli asked as she came around the back of the van. AJ looped the strap of her diaper bag over her shoulder and unbuckled Asher. She hipped him and reached to press the button that would make the van door slide closed.

"She hasn't canceled," Robin said.

"It's a Sunday," AJ said. "She's busy on the weekends."

"She's not been going in on the weekends," Kelli said. "At least that's what she told me." Kelli pushed her blonde hair out of her face as the breeze tried to cement it to her eyes. "We've been talking about having a better balance between work and family. Friends."

AJ understood being overwhelmed at work. She'd dedicated her entire heart and soul to her job for a lot of years, and she couldn't even imagine having to deal with Matt and Asher while she traveled, conducted interviews, and wrote articles. She admired Kelli and Eloise for all they did, and she'd watched Robin work herself to the brink of insanity last year in her event planning.

She said nothing, because at least they had dreams and knew how to work to accomplish them. Only hollowness existed inside AJ, and she didn't quite know how to fill it. Kristen had made some suggestions as they took their morning walks, but nothing had struck AJ's heartstrings yet.

"There she is," Robin said as Eloise's sedan pulled into the parking lot at the lighthouse. Jean had invited them all here, but the space wasn't really conducive to hosting eight adults and an infant. Kristen had suggested they set up folding tables and chairs in the cottage that sat down the sidewalk a bit, and everyone had agreed on that.

Eloise parked next to Robin and got out. "I didn't think we were bringing food." She eyed the huge bowl of watermelon in Robin's hands. "I should've known you'd do whatever you wanted." Since Eloise was so kind and she smiled broadly with the statement, Robin only laughed and reached for El.

AJ's emotions swelled as if she were pregnant again and couldn't control them. She hadn't seen Eloise in far too long. Yes, she'd gone over to help Billie with her hair and makeup for the Sweethearts Dance a couple of weeks ago, but she hadn't truly had the chance to sit down and just chat with Eloise.

The two of them bustled off down the sidewalk, leaving AJ with Kelli. Kelli reached for Asher, and AJ let her take him. "Jean said you never asked her to babysit," Kel said.

"Yeah." AJ looked up into the sky. Today, it shone down with blue brilliance, the signal that spring was definitely upon them and summer would arrive soon. "I don't need a babysitter. Matt can come home and sit with him while I go get my hair or nails done."

"That's not really the point," Kel said.

"AJ," Alice said, jogging toward them. Even while

running the woman looked elegant and sophisticated. She wore a pair of white shorts that went to her knee, and she'd paired that with a bright green sleeveless shirt that made her dark hair look like she'd been dipped in midnight. "I want the baby."

She grinned at Kelli and took Asher. "Is that okay?"

"Fine with me," Kelli said. She had been dropping by AJ's more and more, and AJ had even gone out to Bell to attend a yoga class. She'd been terrible at it, and Kelli had told her to try aerobics instead. She had yet to do that, but it was on her schedule for next week.

They followed Alice into the cottage, and the house which had previously been stuffed with papers, bookshelves, and furniture had been cleared out. Kristen had moved last summer, and the cottage had been empty since then.

Jean reached for a roll of paper towels in the center in one of the long, six-foot tables that had been set up, and she grinned at Kelli and AJ as the door closed behind them. "You made it."

"We made it," Kelli confirmed, her smile genuine and perfect. "How are you, Jean?"

"Nervous," she admitted. "They've had the Seafaring Girls signups live for less than a week, and two of the three sessions are full already."

"Wow, that's great," AJ said, her eyes migrating to the kitchen, where Alice held Asher and cooed at him with Laurel and Kristen. The counters held more food than the eight of them could possibly eat, but AJ's mouth watered anyway. She wasn't a big breakfast eater, and it was almost one o'clock and far past her lunchtime.

"All right," Robin called in a loud voice. "Come get something to eat and let's sit down. Be prepared with an update!" Her eyes glittered as if she'd learn the biggest, juiciest gossip in the next few minutes, and AJ could only shake her head and smile.

"What if we don't have an update?" Eloise asked.

"You have about twenty," Robin said with a hint of chastisement. "Everyone has to update. We haven't been all together in months. So think of something. I won't accept that no one has *some*thing to share." An edge entered her eyes, and that only made AJ want to tease her more.

"Relax, Robin," Alice said. "Everyone came knowing there would be a ton of questions and updates."

AJ joined the line with Alice, answering her questions about what baby Asher liked to eat. After several minutes and at least four of them dashing back over to the kitchen to get something they'd forgotten, the eight of them sat at the table, four down each side.

AJ's eyes filled with tears again, and she had no idea what to make of all of these strange emotions inside her. She'd been back on her anti-depressants since Asher had been born, and she definitely felt more even. She simply reacted emotionally to things now that she hadn't in the past.

She decided that wasn't a bad thing, and she embraced her feelings and smiled at Robin, who sat across from her. She must've taken that as some sort of permission to start the announcements, because she took one bite of her spinach quiche and said, "I'll go first, and then we can go around."

"No," Laurel said beside her. "Go around the other way, so I can go last." She glanced at AJ, who would be second if they went the other way.

Robin flicked her eyes in AJ's direction, and she nodded. She could go second. She didn't have a whole lot to say anyway. "Okay," she said. "Mandie and I had an amazing trip to New York and Maryland. She liked NYU the best, and she's going to accept there." Her voice broke on the last word, but Robin didn't take a moment to compose herself.

"I'm a bit of a mess, I'll admit. My oldest living in the big city." She shook her head and sniffled. "It's good. It's the right thing. I have six more months before she leaves." She finished her quiche and looked at AJ, her announcement clearly over.

AJ stuffed another ball of cantaloupe in her mouth to give herself another moment to order her news. No one started a side conversation, and AJ couldn't chew fruit for longer than a few seconds. She swallowed and glanced to Kelli on her left, and then Jean next to her.

"I'm having a hard time adjusting to full-time motherhood," she said, the admission scraping her throat. She couldn't take the words back now, and AJ had never said them in that exact order before. "I haven't left Asher for longer than a couple of hours with anyone but Matt since he's been born."

Her tears pricked her eyes again, and she turned toward her son, who Alice had put in a highchair at the end of the table for her. "Yeah, baby," she said, her voice breaking as she put another chunk of watermelon on Asher's tray.

She looked down the table at everyone, finding the love and support she so desperately needed. It shone in Kelli's eyes, and acceptance radiated from Alice's expression. Even Jean gave her a kind smile, and AJ hated herself in that moment. She had no right to complain about being a mother to someone who desperately wanted to be one.

"I was hoping to ask some of you for help," AJ said, committed now. "I haven't been able to bring myself to do it, though."

"I'd do it," Jean said. "Anytime, AJ, as long as it's in the morning."

Kristen reached across the table and patted Jean's hand, but Jean didn't look away from AJ. She nodded, cleared her throat, and said, "I'm done." She glanced at Kelli and speared a bite of potato. Kristen made the best southwest hashbrowns AJ had ever tasted, and she wasn't going to waste any of her bites.

"I don't have much news," Kelli said. "Things at Whole Soul are going well. El and I are brainstorming ways to work less. Parker is growing up too fast." She gave a quick laugh, but AJ heard the tension behind it. "That's all." She turned to her left. "Alice."

Alice didn't even take a second to breathe before she said, "I've found two pregnancy tests in the twins' bathroom in the past couple of months. Both negative. They belong to Ginny's friend, Emily, but now I have to figure out what to do about that. It's a..." She cleared her throat and shot a glance at Robin. "Delicate situation."

AJ's mind flooded with questions, but El beat her to the first one. "Both negative?"

"Yes," Alice said.

"That's good, I guess," El said.

"What's delicate about it?" Laurel asked.

"Emily's parents are separated, and she's been living with her mom. Or in Ginny's room. I'm not sure what to do about it." Alice flashed a tight smile and brushed her hair back. She picked up a piece of bacon, and the fact that she took a bite spoke loads about how far she'd come in the past couple of years. "I'm not looking for suggestions at this point. That's my announcement."

"Come on," Robin said, but Kelli held up her hand.

"She made her announcement. There were no rules about follow-up questions or clarification." She smiled sweetly at Robin, who blinked at her. AJ hid her smile as she looked down the table to Jean.

Everyone focused on her, and she swallowed, the movement very apparent in her throat.

"It's okay, dear," Kristen said. "It's a no-judgment zone here. Robin forces us all to talk, but it's usually really good."

"I do not *force* you," Robin said. "It's just part of our deal. We haven't been together for a long time." Her voice carried part of a whine, and while AJ usually complained about Robin's rules and pacts and deals, today she hadn't. She wouldn't. She wanted the updates too.

"I've moved all my Wednesday students to Tuesdays or

Thursdays," Jean said. "The Seafaring Girls sign-ups are still going strong, and we only have a few slots left."

"That's great," several people said, including AJ.

Jean looked at Kristen, her update apparently over.

"Nothing much for me," Kristen said. "AJ and I go walking in the morning sometimes. I meet with Robin and Alice for lunch sometimes." She smiled around at everyone. "Life is life."

Life is life. AJ repeated the words in her head, finding them so true. Life *was* life, and it simply marched on, whether AJ wanted it to or not.

Eloise slung her arm around Kristen and grinned at her. "Life *is* life, Kristen." She exhaled as she dropped her arm and picked up a slice of strawberry. "I've hired two new managers at The Cliffside Inn. A morning manager and a night manager. They're going to help me work a normal schedule, keep up with being a mom to teenagers, and spend time with my new husband."

"Whose father is the mayor," Robin said. "And about to launch one of the biggest celebrations in Five Island Cove history."

"There's that too," El said with a grin. "We've got a lot of social engagements coming up, from a balloon launch at the festival and a Mayor's Office pancake breakfast on the official first day of summer."

AJ wasn't sure how El felt about those upcoming social engagements, because she didn't let anything bleed into her voice. She wore a pretty smile, and AJ had been present at Aaron and Eloise's wedding. That man loved her more than anything, and El had the same stars in her eyes for him.

With his father as the new mayor and Aaron as Police Chief, the two of them sure packed a double-punch when they went out in public.

"We'll be at the balloon festival," Kelli said. "It's on Pearl, and Parker's been talking about it for a couple of days already."

"I'm hoping to get the girls out this summer too," Robin said. "Before Mandie leaves."

"Me too," AJ said, chiming in. "My first summer with Asher. He'll want to do all the things, right?" She glanced around at the others who'd raised their children already, and once again found the love and support she needed.

She nodded like she'd plan a new outing or activity every day for Asher this summer, and she better start now though it was only March.

"You're up, Laurel," Robin said without looking at the woman next to her.

"Yeah, I know." Laurel lifted her breakfast sandwich to her lips and took a big bite.

"Oh, brother," Robin said. "Do you want me to tell it?"

"Don't, Robin," Alice said.

"You know?"

"I'm assuming I do, yes," Alice said coolly.

Oh, Robin didn't like that, and AJ once again hid a smile. Robin loved being in-the-know, and she'd always felt the biggest sense of competition with Alice. Listening to the two of them bicker sometimes made Kelli and AJ laugh for days afterward, and she had a feeling this could be one of those times.

Beside her, Asher babbled and banged his palms on the tray. AJ gave him a hunk of sausage about the time Laurel said, "Paul and I are expecting a baby. I'm due at the end of September."

A smile appeared on her face then, though her words had shook coming out of her mouth. More than Robin and Alice knew this news, but Eloise and Kelli both exploded into congratulations with AJ.

Laurel laughed and accepted them all, only one quick glance down to Jean. AJ hadn't heard her voice among the others, but she looked happy enough. Of course, AJ knew what kind of masks a woman put in place to protect herself, because she'd done something similar many times.

When she'd been passed over for another on-air spot. When one of her articles didn't get picked up. When man after man had gone through her life, only to find and marry the very next woman they went out with.

The chatter picked up now that the announcements were finished, and AJ simply basked in the energy of being here with all of these women. She'd missed the Wednesday lunches so much, and she hoped spring and summer really did bring them together again.

In that moment, she realized that the seasons didn't bring people together. If she wanted to get together with her friends, she needed to organize events like this. Jean and Kristen had put this one together, and AJ could easily host everyone at the cottage where she lived.

With that decided, she finished breakfast while chatting with Robin about her sister, Amy, and how they were all getting along.

"This can't be real, can it?"

AJ looked away from Laurel as the both of them looked at Alice. Her voice had cut through the side conversations, filled with shock and disgust as it was. She handed the phone to Laurel, who read the text and then passed the phone to Robin.

"What is it?" Kelli asked.

"It's unbelievable." Robin handed the phone to AJ, as they were apparently going to all get to see it.

Alice, this is Frank. I'm in the cove to look at some property and I'd love to see the twins. Let me know when might be convenient for them and you.

AJ pulled in a breath, looked up with wide eyes, and gave the phone to Kelli.

"He hasn't been to the cove in years," Alice said. "I used to bring the twins alone."

"He doesn't usually ask for when things are convenient for you," Robin said, plenty of bitterness in her voice.

The phone got back to Alice after Eloise had read the text, and AJ had never met Alice's ex-husband. She only knew what Alice and the other women had said about him, and she'd been around a couple of summers ago when Alice had gone through her divorce.

"Ask him what property," Kelli asked. "It sure seems like there's a lot of people coming to the cove to look at property all of a sudden."

"Yes," Robin said as others gave murmurs of assent. "Ask him that."

Alice's fingers flew across the screen, and a moment later, she gasped. She looked up, her dark eyes as big as moons and filled with surprise. "The Friendship Inn," she said.

"What is with that place?" Robin asked. "Who's going to come here to check it out next?"

Chapter Sixteen

Alice smoothed her hands down the front of her blouse, feeling how much flatter it could lay. She pushed the thought out of her head. She didn't have to impress Frank Kelton. Not anymore.

"He's late," she said, though she didn't know why she'd expected any different. Frank had always showed up when it was convenient for him.

Beside her, Arthur slipped his fingers between hers and offered a kind smile. He hadn't met Frank, and he'd admitted he was a little nervous. Alice had told him he had nothing to be worried about, but she understood meeting someone important to her spouse. She'd done it plenty of times over the years she'd been married to Frank, and while he wasn't important to her now for the same reasons he'd been before, he was still the father of her children.

Alice squeezed Arthur's hand and turned to make herself another cup of coffee. As she stirred in a spoonful of sugar, footsteps came flying down the stairs from the second floor.

Charlie arrived in the great room at the back of the house and strode into the kitchen in only a couple of steps.

"Morning, Mama." He grinned at her, and Alice raised her eyebrows.

"What's with you?" For this early on a weekend, Charlie was far too chipper.

"I'm missing a real Olympiad practice for this." He didn't erase his smile as he turned toward the fridge. "Is there any of that brisket leftover from last night?"

"Your dad is taking you to breakfast," Alice said. "He'll be here any second." She hoped, at least. She refused to look at the clock and see how late he was.

"I know." Charlie took out the brisket anyway and stuck it in the microwave. While it rotated around, heating up, he added, "He always takes us to super gross places. Trust me, I need to eat first."

"You haven't seen him for almost two years," Alice said. To her knowledge, Frank had not taken the children out to eat often at all.

Ginny stepped into the house from the back door, and Alice hadn't even known she was out there. Her beautiful daughter looked tired already, and she glanced down the hall toward the front door before looking into the kitchen.

"He's late." Her gaze moved from Arthur to Charlie, barely flickering toward Alice at all. Alice wished she could change that, but they were in the thick of a difficult situation, and that was somewhere Ginny usually didn't find herself.

"Can I have some of that?" Ginny asked. "Did you see that place he suggested?" She made a face of disgust and pulled open the drawer to get out a fork. "I've never even heard of putting meat powder in a smoothie."

Charlie pushed the container of brisket and mashed potatoes closer to his sister. Alice loved them with her whole heart.

"Listen, you two," she said, and that got them both to look at her. "Text or call if you need us to come get you."

"We know how to deal with Dad," Ginny said. "It's okay, Mom."

They'd be adults in only a couple of months, and Alice couldn't rescue them from everything. She wanted to, but she couldn't. "I love you guys." Her voice caught, and she didn't try to hide it behind her mug. Ginny moved first, and then Alice had both twins enveloping her in a hug.

"Love you, Mom," Charlie and Ginny said in tandem, and only three seconds later, the doorbell rang. She held them tightly for one more deep breath and then she released them.

"I'll get it," she said, meeting Arthur's eye. They left the kitchen and went down the hall together, Arthur a warm, solid force behind her as Alice opened the door.

Frank stood on the front porch, filling it with his tall frame and broad shoulders. He gazed up at something on the eaves, a power blonde only a half-step behind him.

He turned his attention to Alice, a smile springing into

place. "Hello, Alice," he said pleasantly, as if they hadn't shared nearly twenty years of their lives together.

"Good morning, Frank." Alice spoke in her professional, Hamptons-inspired voice. "The twins are ready." She switched her gaze to his girlfriend and moved it back to her ex-husband as she inched more into Arthur's side. "This is my husband, Arthur."

Frank reached out to shake Arthur's hand, his dark eyes firing the way Charlie's did when he wasn't exactly thrilled. "Yes, Ginny said you'd gotten remarried."

Alice hadn't needed Frank's permission and she hadn't gone out of her way to tell him about Arthur.

"Arthur, this is Frank Kelton. The twins' father."

"It's a pleasure to meet you," Arthur said smoothly, as he had plenty of practice with dealing with people who weren't excited to see him. "Come on in."

"Is this your place or Alice's?" Frank stepped into the house without introducing the blonde.

"It's ours," Alice said, claustrophobic in the tiny foyer with Arthur and Frank. "Straight back."

Frank eased past her, his smile back in place. Alice looked at the woman remaining on the porch. "I'm Alice," she said. "Frank's ex-wife." She offered the woman a small smile when she really wanted to give her a boatload of advice, starting with, *Turn around and leave now, while you still have some dignity and self-worth left.*

"Betty," she said. "With an I-E."

"Bettie," Alice repeated. "Nice to meet you." Her attention got divided by a round of loud laughter behind her.

Arthur had retreated slightly, and Alice gestured for Bettie to come in too.

She shook her head and stayed on the porch. "Mister Kelton won't be long." She gave Alice a tight smile with those ruby-red-painted lips and stayed put.

Alice left the front door open, because she couldn't close it in Bettie's face, and she went into the kitchen. Ginny, Charlie, and Frank all wore smiles and the evidence of the brisket breakfast was gone.

"All right," Frank said, meeting her eyes. "I can have them for the day?"

"They're all yours," she said.

Frank nodded and waved for the kids to go in front of him. He seemed so...different, and he waited for Ginny and Charlie to go down the hall before he took a single step toward Alice. "Your roof looks a little weathered. Is that normal?"

Alice narrowed her eyes at him. "What are you doing here, Frank? What's Friendship Inn doing on your radar?" If he expected her to give him advice about the property conditions in Five Island Cove, he had another thing coming.

"Expanding my horizons now that I'm not practicing," he said easily, as if he were looking for a ritzy home to retire in.

Alice's eyebrows went up. "You quit the law firm in New York?"

"The twins are here," he said with a shrug. "I thought I might give inn ownership a try."

Alice folded her arms, noting that Frank's gaze swept

down the height of her body, assessing her. "That's a far cry from practicing corporate law," she said. "And both twins are leaving the cove in less than six months."

Confusion crossed his face, and Alice wasn't sure why she was surprised that he didn't even know his own children were graduating from high school in only a few short months.

If they hadn't told him their plans beyond graduation, she didn't have to. "Have fun," she said, a clear indication that he should go now.

"Dad," Charlie said, reappearing beside Arthur. He wore a disgruntled look. "Your *secretary* says we need to go."

Frank's father-of-the-year smile appeared. "Let's go then." He brushed by Alice, shook Arthur's hand again, and followed Charlie out of the house.

The moment the door clicked closed, Alice said, "The roof," and added a scoff. "That man is up to something."

She let Arthur take her into his arms and then out to breakfast. They rode the ferry to go visit her dad and stepmom on Rocky Ridge, where she sipped mocktails and enjoyed the spring breeze over the black sand beach.

But through it all, she couldn't shake Frank and the insane idea of him running Friendship Inn from her mind. It made no sense. There had to be more to the story, and Alice would find out what it was.

ALICE LOOKED ACROSS THE TABLE TO HER daughter as the plate of pasta carbonara got put in front of her. Ginny had loved carbonara from a young age, and it still made her eyes light up and her lips curve into a smile.

Alice liked seeing her daughter happy, and she realized in that moment that she hadn't seen Ginny this bright in a couple of months. Maybe three or four. She glanced to the girl sitting next to her—Emily Pershon, Ginny's best friend.

She too wore a look of wonder at her enormous seafood platter the waiter had just put in front of her. Emily met Alice's eyes. "There's no way I can eat all of this."

"Leftovers," Ginny and Alice said together, and they smiled at one another. Alice's chest trembled, because she needed to turn the conversation in another direction, and it wasn't going to be happy-happy smiley-smiley.

"Thank you," she murmured to the waiter as he put her wedge salad with balsamic glaze, ranch dressing, and a ton of perfectly bite-sized toppings in front of her. Her mouth watered, and she cut into her lettuce, dislodging some bits of bacon, a couple of craisins, and a chunk or two of avocado.

They ate for a couple of minutes. Long enough for Alice to have enough to eat that she wouldn't starve once the conversation started. Long enough for the waiter to check on them and bring drink refills. Long enough for the tension in the secluded booth to skyrocket.

Alice focused on her salad, picking through the tomato and olive for another bite of bacon. "So, Emily, I wanted to talk to you."

The two girls across the table took a breath at the same

time. "Ginny told me," Emily said, her tone full of fear. "I swear, Miss Kelton, I haven't done anything wrong."

"My last name isn't Kelton anymore," Alice said kindly, giving Emily a smile. She'd turned eighteen sometime back in the fall. Maybe winter. The months blurred for Alice. Ginny had gone to her birthday party well into the school year, so it could've been closer to Christmas.

She glanced at Ginny and back to Emily when it was clear her daughter wasn't going to say anything. Alice didn't know what Ginny had told her best friend, so she raised her chin and said, "I've found two pregnancy tests in the bathroom at my house."

Emily's eyes widened and tears filled them on the next breath. She swiped at her face, silent. Alice waited, hoping she'd arranged her face into one of passive non-judgment. Charlie had told her sometimes she could look like she knew better than everyone without meaning to, and she wasn't Emily's mother.

"It's okay," Ginny whispered, and she put her arm around Emily. "You should tell her."

Yes, she should, and Alice picked at her salad again, still waiting.

"It's not my fault," Emily said. "It's..."

"Charlie says you're not dating anyone," Alice said, reaching for another piece of bread. She loved the homemade bread here, and she dipped it in the flavored and peppered oil before taking a bite.

"She's not," Ginny said, her voice louder and stronger. "Mom, it's her step-brother."

That brought Alice's eyes straight up. "What?"

Ginny looked like she might throw up all the pasta she'd just eaten. She looked at Emily, pure desperation streaming from her. "Tell her."

Emily's face crumbled, and she sobbed into Ginny's shoulder. Alice's heart raced through her whole body. She'd been prepared for a secret boyfriend. A lecture about not getting too serious—and possibly using birth control or at least someone else's bathroom for the pregnancy tests.

But this?

Alice had no idea how to deal with *this*. How could she call another mother and tell her that her daughter was... what? Being abused?

She swallowed, her mouth beyond dry. "Emily," she said, all three syllables tearing through her parched throat. "Is he... do you want to have sex with him?"

Emily shook her head as it came up. Her eyes looked around wildly. "No. I've told him no. He just...comes in my room anyway. The first time, he said I'd like it. I didn't like it. I don't like him."

Alice flicked her gaze to Ginny, who wore a look of sympathy mixed with terror. Why hadn't she told Alice? Was she that unapproachable? After all she'd done to be open and honest with her children about intimate things, she couldn't believe Ginny wouldn't *say something*.

She looked at Emily again. "How old is he?"

"He's a senior like us," Ginny volunteered. "Her mom just got remarried a couple of months before you, Mom."

Alice nodded, trying to digest the information quickly

and come up with another question. She didn't want to fire them off, but the girls were talking now, and she didn't want them to stop. "How long has this been happening?"

"Since my birthday," Emily said. "It was like he knew he needed to wait until I was an adult."

"That doesn't make it okay," Ginny said, and it sounded like she'd told Emily that before.

"No, it doesn't," Alice said. "Em, have you told your mom?"

Emily shook her head, tears splashing down her cheeks.

"She went and got birth control from a clinic," Ginny said, squaring her shoulders. "She's been sneaking into my room whenever Randall is there. She takes the pregnancy tests just to make sure, Mom. She's not doing anything wrong."

"We need to report this," Alice said.

"No," Emily said, pure panic in her eyes now. "No. My mom told me to be nice to Randall. He had to move here from Rhode Island, and he has no friends, and..." She looked at Ginny. "She's just so happy that we get along, and she's been so unhappy for so long..."

Alice couldn't believe what she was hearing. "Emily," she said. "He has no right to come into your room and force himself on you. That's not how you welcome someone to the cove."

"Mom," Ginny said harshly.

"What?" Alice demanded. "And you should've told me the moment you knew. You could've spared her plenty of grief. She wouldn't have been assaulted again, at the very least."

"You don't know what it's like at school," Ginny said.

"Thank God for that," Alice said, fire filling her. "I don't care what it's like there. No one deserves to be assaulted, no matter what. The end." She took the napkin off her lap and reached for her purse. "So now that we all know, we need a plan of action."

"Mom," Ginny said again. "You can't fix this."

"I'm not letting her go home to get traumatized again." Alice's lawyerly side wouldn't let this go. "And I *can* fix this. I can tell her mother. I can offer her a safe place to come, where she won't have to be afraid of who's going to come through the door. I can make sure the authorities know there's a predator out there."

She scooted to the end of the bench and stood. As she rifled through her purse to find her debit card, both Ginny and Emily just sat there. Alice looked at the two of them, her heart bleeding for them. "I know you don't know what to do," she said in a much gentler voice. "I don't know exactly either, but this is why you come to an adult and tell them. We have more resources, and we're better equipped. And we don't worry about what's going on at the high school."

She pulled in a breath, wishing she hadn't said that last part. "You two won't even be in high school in three more months. This won't matter then."

Emily nodded, and that gave Alice the permission and courage she needed. "I'm going to go up front to pay. You two take a couple of minutes."

"Then what?" Ginny asked.

"Then..." Alice had no idea. "Then we'll get dessert and figure out how to keep Emily safe." She nodded like she alone could harness the wind, the clouds, the sky, and pull them all to their knees. She walked away from the table, her pulse beating, beating, beating through her whole body.

She didn't find someone to pay her bill. She went outside and she did the first thing that came into her mind.

She called Laurel.

Chapter Seventeen

E loise looked up from the desk in the office where she'd been working on the schedule for next week. A uniformed officer stood there, and it took her a couple of blinks to recognize Laurel. "Hey," she said, leaning back in her chair and smiling. "What are you doing up here?"

"Aaron said he tried to call you a few times."

"Shoot." Eloise flew toward her phone, which she'd left on the edge of the desk. "I turned off my phone while the pool repairman was here."

"That's exactly what he was worried about," Laurel said with a grin. "You sneaking off with the pool guy."

Eloise burst out laughing, glad when Laurel did too. She pressed the power button on her phone to get it to turn back on. "My phone needs a new battery, so I turn it off to conserve."

"Again, I heard that." Laurel sighed as she sat down in front of Eloise, taking a chair an employee usually did. Or

Billie, as the girl often did her homework in El's office after school.

Eloise looked up from her powering-on device. "I don't like the sound of that sigh."

"Just...life," Laurel said with a tired smile.

"Where's Daniel?"

"Getting cookies from Rhonda." Laurel grinned and glanced over her shoulder. "I think he likes her."

Eloise's eyebrows went up. "Yeah? Should I mention that she should go out with him?" A frown pulled at her eyebrows. "She's going through a hard time right now. Bad break-up."

"No wonder she's baking so much."

Eloise wondered what Laurel would do if she had to go through something hard. Probably run. And stay silent. That was what she'd done last year after making a huge drug bust in the cove that had touched all of their lives.

"I feel like this spring has been so weird," Eloise said, glancing at her phone as it finally brightened. Several messages from Aaron popped up, but there were too many for her to read so quickly. She looked back to Laurel, who nodded.

"Definitely strange," she said. "It's like there's something in the air, and it's bringing all these people to the cove we've never seen before."

"Like that guy you and Daniel had to arrest for only wearing the American flag?" Eloise teased.

"And he's just one of them," Laurel said, her smile slipping.

"At least Zach and Frank didn't cause any problems. Well." El shrugged. "Not too many."

"Frank did stay longer than Alice would've liked," Laurel said. "The kids only saw him the one time, which she found a bit odd."

Eloise sent a quick message to her husband—*sorry, just turned my phone on. More in a minute. Laurel's here.* She looked up and decided to focus on this conversation first. "Did she find anything as she started digging into why he quit at the firm?"

Laurel's eyes brightened the way Eloise imagined Robin's would with a juicy piece of gossip. "He didn't quit. He was put on administrative leave pending a sexual harassment investigation."

Eloise's eyes widened. "You're kidding."

"It wasn't his first. Alice suspects they gave him the choice to leave or be fired, and he chose to leave."

"He's not really going to buy Friendship Inn, is he?" Eloise had already checked the real estate listings that morning, something she'd started doing since hearing Clara Tanner had come to the cove and looked at the property. It was still for sale, no offers. So Frank Kelton hadn't made a move yet. Clara hadn't. No one had.

"I doubt it," Laurel said. "Alice thinks it was one of his mind games. She also thinks he had no idea how old his kids were, and once she told him they'd be graduating in a few months, the idea of moving to the cove lost its appeal."

Eloise simply shook her head. She couldn't fathom not knowing how old her children were and being involved in the minutia of their daily lives. She thought about Aaron's ex-wife, and how she'd up and left Five Island Cove—and her two daughters—one day. She'd never come back, and she'd never looked back. Even when Aaron had given her the opportunity to be in her daughters' lives, she hadn't taken it.

"Have you thought any more about buying Friendship Inn?" Laurel asked.

Eloise saw no point in denying it. "I mean, I've thought about it," she said. "It's right here off Sanctuary. I know how to operate an inn." She left the thought there, because she didn't want to expand further.

In every sense, she didn't want to expand further, and Friendship Inn was a massive, huge hotel. It wasn't a house with five or six guest rooms. It was a big hotel, on an island by itself. The listing said it had one hundred and fifteen rooms, and Eloise had no idea what running that looked like.

What it felt like was complete exhaustion and upheaval in her life, right when she needed to be working less. Right when Billie and Grace and Aaron needed her. Right when she was trying to scale back.

"Maybe it's not the right time," Laurel said.

"Laurel," a man said, and both she and Eloise looked toward Daniel. Laurel's partner filled the doorway and he held up a red plastic cup, his grin the kind little boys wore on Christmas morning. "Look what Rhonda gave me."

"A cup of cookies," Laurel said, standing. "I'm sure she told you to share with me."

"She did," Rhonda said for Daniel, squeezing into the

space in the doorway with him. She grinned at him and then Laurel, and Eloise got to her feet too.

"We better head out," Daniel said, backing out of the office. "The Chief won't want us to sit here forever."

"He sent us," Laurel said. "He knows I'm going to visit with his wife when he does that." She followed him out of the office, calling, "Bye, El. Good to see you, Rhonda."

"Yeah, bye, Rhonda," Daniel called.

Eloise arrived at Rhonda's side as the two cops disappeared around the corner, and she sighed. "He didn't say good-bye to me."

"I'm not going out with him," Rhonda said.

"Why not?" Eloise looked at her. "You gave him a *cup* of *cookies*, Rhonda. You're already dating."

They both laughed, and Rhonda shook her head. "I've got to get back to the chowders."

"Right," El said. "Chowder bar tonight." She stayed in the doorway as her chef and night manager left. Rhonda also lived in the on-site apartment attached to the inn. Eloise had hired another evening manager to help with guests, and Diane was probably out by the pool. She'd been going through their towel inventory, and she'd go over all of the repairs with the serviceman who'd come that day.

Eloise had also hired a morning supervisor, and Paige came into work at six a.m. to help with breakfast, check-out, and guest relations. Since hiring the two of them, a great burden had been lifted from Eloise's shoulders.

She turned away from the hallway as her phone rang, and she hurried to get to Aaron's call before it went to voicemail. She'd set his notifications and ringtone to an old-fashioned police siren so she'd know if it was him or an employee when her phone made noise.

"Hey, baby," she said, collapsing into her chair and letting it spin toward the window. "I didn't have time to read any of your messages."

A heavy sigh came through the line. "I was afraid of that. I shouldn't have sent Laurel."

Eloise put her toe down to stop her chair from turning. "Why?" She gazed out at the warm sunshine that had started to flood the cove as March grew closer to becoming April. "What's happened?"

It took Aaron a long time to answer, and Eloise couldn't look away from the greening grass and the brilliant, blue sky. A chill ran down her spine, at complete odds with the heat she'd find outside. It was funny how she could be so close to the picturesque scene in front of her, only separated by a thin pane of glass, and yet be in a completely different mental space.

"I talked to Carol this morning," Aaron said, the words grinding through his throat. He cleared it but didn't say anything else.

"Carol?" Eloise asked as if she didn't know who the woman was. She did. Aaron's ex-wife she'd never met. The woman she'd literally thought about several minutes ago. The woman who'd left her husband and young girls without a second thought.

"Yeah." Aaron exhaled again. "El, she's, well, she wants to see the girls."

Eloise's mind blanked. Carol had never wanted to see the girls before. She hadn't even contacted them since she'd left. El's protective streak reared, and her first instinct was to say no. She and Aaron had been working hard for over a year to build their family. The four of them.

Carol wasn't included.

She'd *chosen* not to be included.

"I don't know how to tell her no," Aaron said, his words warbling in Eloise's ears. He said a couple more things, and then added, "She's their mother."

"No," Eloise said, the word almost a shot out of her mouth. "She's not, Aaron. A mother is more than just someone who birthed a baby."

Silence rained through the line, and Eloise regretted her words. They made her sound jealous and petty, insecure and small.

"I'm sorry," she said, at the same time Aaron said, "I know, El."

She pressed her eyes closed, the bright blue sky still burning into her retinas. Blueness covered everything in her life, as if she'd been plunged into icy water and couldn't claw her way to the top.

Eloise struggled to breathe through the water and air and expectations. She wanted to tell him to do what he thought was right. She wanted to suggest they ask the girls what they thought about seeing their mother after so many years of silence.

"It's been how long?" she managed to ask, and her throat only burned slightly.

"I don't know." But he did. Eloise knew he did. He'd told her that Carol had left right when Billie had started kindergarten. The girl was fourteen years old now. Her biological mother had been gone for almost a decade.

"Can we talk about it tonight?" Aaron asked.

"I think that's a great idea," Eloise said. "See what the girls think." Grace had to have been three years old; she might not even remember her mother. What would Carol do with them? Take them to lunch? Sit on the beach with them?

Despite the blue sky, it wasn't exactly warm on the beach in the cove right now.

"I know what they'll think," Aaron said, another sigh coming from his mouth. It was his Police-Chief-sigh, one that carried the weight of the entire cove with it, the lives of the thirteen thousand people who called these five islands in the ocean home.

Eloise hated the Police-Chief-sigh when it was about work, but she loved it when it made an appearance in their family. Aaron was an action-oriented man. He was a doer. He wanted to fix the problems he saw before him, the ones his cops and detectives brought to him, and the personal issues in his life.

He'd want to fix this. He'd want to make sure everyone —himself, Eloise, Billie, Grace, and even Carol—could get what they wanted. He'd want them all to be happy, and Eloise didn't have the heart to tell him that in some situations, not everyone could leave happy.

"What did you tell Carol?"

"I told her I'd need to think about it," he said. "Talk to you and the girls. The whole conversation was about three minutes."

"Did she say why she's coming back?"

"She said she's lost her job, and she's looking at a lot of prospects. She said she thought now might be a good time to visit the girls, and I quote, 'poke around the cove.'"

Fear pierced Eloise right behind the heart. She didn't want to vocalize the question screaming through her mind. *Is she going to come back to the cove permanently?*

Plenty of people had to share their kids. The children went back and forth between biological parents' homes; they learned how to deal with step-parents. That simply hadn't been Eloise's experience, and she didn't know how to deal with this violent interruption in her life.

She reminded herself that people from coast to coast and all over the world dealt with interruptions. Health scares, deaths in the family, divorce, and more. She could do this, and she would make it as easy for Aaron, Billie, and Grace as she could.

"Okay," she said. "I'll ask Billie where she wants to stop on the way home, and we'll bring dinner." She turned around to face her office instead of the front yard of the inn. "How does that sound?"

"It sounds like you're the most wonderful woman in the world."

Eloise shook her head, no smile on her face and no response for that. If she'd spoken what was really in her heart and soul, Aaron wouldn't think that. "See you tonight."

"I love you, El."

"Love you too, Aaron."

The call ended, and El looked at her computer and then the desk calendar where she wrote down all of her employees' requests for time off. She had no idea where she'd been in the scheduling process, and her brain cells refused to focus on any one thing long enough for her to pick up where she'd left off.

First Clara had come to the cove. Then Zach. Then Frank.

Now Carol?

Yes, it had been a strange spring indeed, and Eloise could only hope and pray that the outcome for her, Aaron, and the girls would be as benign as it had been for her other friends.

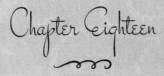

Chapter Eighteen

Laurel peered at the front door of Alice's house, a place she'd been many times. She rode shotgun, with Paul behind the wheel. "The last time I wore my uniform here," she said as she watched the window in Alice's office for flutters of movement. "My partner and I were asking Arthur and the kids about drugs at the high school."

"Mm." Paul reached across the junky console of his police car and took Laurel's hand in hers. "We could turn this over to our sex-crimes division."

"Alice would never speak to me again," Laurel said. "I already clawed my way back from that once."

"We shouldn't even be wearing our uniforms then," Paul said, and Laurel couldn't disagree with him. She could barely get hers on anymore, and she hadn't been to the uniform department to request maternity clothes. For some reason, she didn't want to admit she needed them.

Her baby definitely bumped out in the front now, and

she loved the infant with everything inside her. She wasn't trying to hide it from anyone, as they'd told her parents, Paul's, Aaron, and all of her friends. Chief Sherman's secretary was even throwing her a baby shower in another couple of months.

Laurel simply wanted to hold onto the simplicity of life for this one moment. Really fist her fingers around it and refuse to let go. The moment she opened the door, the world would crack, and all the darkness she'd been able to keep at bay would come pouring in.

The front door opened, and Alice came out onto the porch. Laurel was out of time, and her fingers ached anyway.

She uncurled them and reached for the door handle. Paul met her at the hood of the car, and he slipped his arm along her back and around her waist. "We might have to involve sex-crimes whether we want to or not," he murmured.

"I know," Laurel said, her eyes trained on Alice's. "I told her that." She went up the steps first and embraced her very best friend in the whole world. "Hey."

"Thank you," Alice whispered. "Emily's mother is here, and she is having a very hard time understanding what I'm telling her."

Laurel stepped back, catching the anxiety and unrest on Alice's face. She swept her fingers along her forehead. "You look like you haven't been sleeping."

"Would you be?" She looked at Paul, her face dissolving into a kind smile. "Thank you for coming, Paul." She hugged him too, and watching her tall, tough, cop-husband close his eyes and smile into Alice's embrace warmed Laurel's whole body.

Alice retreated and opened the door, her game face slipping back into position. "Okay," she said. "Let's see how you guys do with her." She led them down the hall and into the kitchen, where Ginny sat at the kitchen table with Emily and another woman Laurel had never met.

Her skin seemed to echo the alabaster paint on the kitchen cabinets, while her eyes could suck at a person the way a black hole pulled on everything that got too close. She jumped to her feet when she saw Paul and Laurel, both of them dressed in their police uniforms.

"You called the cops?" She looked around frantically, and Laurel tensed as if she were a criminal and might start sprinting at any second.

"No," Alice said quickly. "Melinda, they're friends of mine. I told you they were coming." Alice indicated the two chairs on the end of the table, and Paul pulled one out for Laurel.

They sat, and Melinda Murphy perched on the edge of her chair, her eyes wide and filled with fright. "I don't know what's happening."

Alice looked at Laurel, who took a moment to center her thoughts. "Ma'am," she said. "My name is Laurel Lehye. I'm a domestic abuse survivor, and I can help your daughter through some of the trauma she's experienced at home."

Melinda glanced at Emily. "Randall says the relationship is consensual."

"And your daughter is telling you it's not," Laurel said,

holding up her hand as Alice opened her mouth. Sometimes the lawyer in Alice could have a forked tongue, and the last thing they needed was for her to slice through the little progress she'd made with Melinda. "So it doesn't really matter what Randall is saying."

She cleared her throat and glanced at Paul. "I was married to my abuser. Trust me, it wasn't consensual, despite what people might think."

Melinda put her head in her hands, and Laurel knew this level of devastation. She knew what it felt like to be so completely trapped that she couldn't see a way out of the predicament she found herself in. So she got up every day. She made coffee. She let her husband do whatever he wanted. If she played along, she might not get as badly hurt.

Until she did anyway. No amount of placating or playing along could've satisfied her ex-husband.

"Ma'am," Laurel said again, as gently as possible. "Perhaps if you're unwilling to do anything about the situation with Randall and Emily, she could be moved somewhere safer for her."

Melinda jerked her head up. "You want to take her away too."

"Your daughter is a legal adult," Laurel said. "She can move out without your permission." Laurel flicked a glance in Alice's direction. "I know Mrs. Rice has offered your daughter a place here in her home. She won't be kept from you. Emily is an adult, and she can come see you and her step-father any time she wants."

Laurel finally let herself look at Emily, but she couldn't

focus on the girl's face for too long. The pain, the fear, the rigidity in the way she sat straight up, her arms clenched across her midsection was still too real for Laurel. She thought she'd healed completely from her abuse and trauma, and in a lot of ways she had.

In this one—being able to look another victim in the face and not see herself—she hadn't. She reached across the space between her and Emily and touched her arm. "She can heal completely from this. I can help her with a good counselor, and she has amazing friends and support right here in the room with her."

"I didn't know," Melinda said, tears streaming down her face. "I just married Stephen. Am I supposed to break-up with him over something his son did?" She wore agony in her expression as she looked around at the people seated at the table, obviously desperate for someone to tell her what to do.

Alice wept too, and strength filled Laurel. She wasn't as close to the situation as the other two women seated at the table, and Laurel took a breath and kept her emotions dormant. The cop inside her emerged and helped a lot in this situation.

"This isn't going to be pretty or easy or fast," Laurel said. "We have to take it one step at a time. I think the first step is to make sure Emily is safe. To do that, I think she should get a few things from home and stay here with Alice and Ginny."

Melinda nodded, her sniffles as intense as ever. "Is that okay with you, Em?"

"It's fine, Mom."

"Alice?" Laurel prompted.

"We have a bed ready," Alice said, nodding. "I am not taking her from you, Melinda."

"I know." Melinda stood and wiped her hand down her face. "I need a minute." She turned and strode away, going past the fridge and out the door that led into the garage. The resulting slam made Laurel startle though she'd expected it.

She drew another breath. "Okay," she said. "Emily, do you need me to go with you to get anything from your house?"

Emily looked at Laurel, and Laurel found she could gaze back at her steadily now. "No," she said. "Thank you, Miss Lehye."

"It's Laurel," Laurel said with a smile. "You can call me any time, day or night. I know what you're going through." She plucked her police card from her pocket and slid it across the table to Emily. "There's nothing you'll go through that I haven't experienced myself."

She got to her feet. "I think you should be seeing a counselor." She nodded to Alice as Paul put his hand on Laurel's lower back. "I can text Alice the information for the one I see. She's fabulous for abuse survivors."

Alice nodded and got up too. "Lunch is almost here," she said. "I'll be right back." She gestured for Laurel and Paul to go toward the front door, so Laurel did. Her heart fluttered in her chest, moving down to her stomach and up to her throat. It had wings again, and she didn't want to clip them.

"Thank you," Alice said, drawing both Paul and Laurel into a hug. "That went so much better the moment you showed up."

"I thought she might fly," Paul said. "But that wasn't bad."

"Sometimes there's sunshine before the storm," Laurel said, though she didn't want to be a doomsayer. "It really could get messier."

"I understand." Alice stepped back and wiped her face. "But for now, Emily will be safe."

"That's important," Laurel said. "Watch her the first few nights. It's hard to be out of the situation, even when you've been trying to get out of the situation." That made no sense, but to Laurel, it sure did. She still remembered clearly the first few nights at her parents' house on Nantucket, lying in a still room, a single bed. It was so quiet, and Laurel didn't know how to deal with the quiet in her soul.

She looked at Paul, and he seemed to be able to read her thoughts. He wrapped his arm around her and drew her close, right where she needed to be. He made her feel safe each and every night, and she loved him in a way she'd never loved anyone before. Paul pressed a kiss to her forehead and said, "Good luck, Alice. Do let us know if we can help some more."

Then he led Laurel away from the little white house that had also been a safe haven for Laurel in the past. Back in the cruiser, he drew a deep breath as he buckled his seat belt. "What do you think about finding a quiet stretch of beach and just holding my hand for a while?"

"I think you just mapped out the rest of our afternoon," Laurel said with a grin.

A FEW DAYS LATER, LAUREL ROLLED OVER IN BED and tried to sit up. She couldn't do it, and while her eyes had definitely been glued together by trolls in the night, they suddenly snapped open. Her hand flew to her stomach, and she looked down.

The bump could barely be categorized as such anymore. She was easily out of the first trimester now, and at her last doctor's appointment, she'd learned she should be able to feel the baby move any day now.

She pressed against her body, trying to feel through skin and muscle to the life within her. It pulsed through her as loudly as the breath in her ears and the instincts she'd had on some of her cases.

A smile crossed her face, and Laurel enjoyed the still, silent morning moment between her and her baby. On the other side of the bed, Paul breathed in softly, and then out. Comfort and joy like Laurel had never known infused her soul, and she didn't want to move for fear of cracking the feelings and then having to experience them flee from her.

Something bumped against her palm, and Laurel gasped. That had definitely been her baby, nosing her hand as if letting her know he was there, alive and well.

She twisted, her stomach swooping. Not knowing if that was the baby or nerves, Laurel pressed against her belly again. "Paul," she said, trying to keep her voice low but loud enough to wake her husband. She hated doing that, because he'd had such a hard time falling asleep lately. He'd have to get up in a half-hour for work anyway, and as he shifted, she said his name again.

"Mm?" Paul's eyes opened, and he blinked.

"The baby's moving," Laurel said, her voice more animated now. "Come feel. The baby's moving." Her grin widened of its own accord, and she turned to be sitting straight, both hands on her belly now.

The bed behind her moved as Paul rolled and then knelt up on the bed, coming toward her. "Really?"

"Really."

His hand snaked around her and covered hers, and Laurel slipped hers out from underneath so he could be right against the baby. She looked over her shoulder to him, basking in his joy of this pregnancy. Her body had been changing, and Laurel had been sick for the first several weeks. Her exhaustion had been new and hard to deal with. She'd had some cravings, but nothing she couldn't handle.

But Paul hadn't gotten to experience much of the pregnancy, other than allowing Laurel to stop and get French fries for dinner whenever she called and said she needed something salty. He'd cleaned the bathroom after her morning sickness many times, and he'd stopped making scrambled eggs when she'd learned the very sight of them made her nauseous.

The baby didn't move, and Laurel held very still. The weight of Paul's hand against her belly drove her desperation for him to feel their child, because she wanted him to experience this pregnancy with her.

"I don't feel him," Paul whispered.

"Just wait." Laurel pressed on her stomach on the left side, thinking, *Come on, baby. Move for your daddy.*

"It's okay," Paul said, and the moment he finished talking, the baby moved. Laurel snapped her head up as Paul sucked in a breath. "Oh, wow." His voice only held awe, and his smile suddenly matched hers.

"That's your baby," she whispered, tilting her head slightly to kiss him. He kept his hand pressed against her stomach, and the baby tapped against his palm again.

"Our baby," he said, breaking their kiss. "This is amazing, Laurel."

Laurel looked down at her hand on the left, and his on the right, and yes, it was pretty amazing. More than amazing. She wanted to take a snapshot of this moment, and she curled her fingers around his, her lighter skin layering over his darker coloring.

She couldn't wait to meet their baby, and she couldn't wait to become a mother. "I love you, Paul," she said, meaning it now today more than she ever had. She marveled that life continued to provide spectacular moments for her, each new one more wonderful than the last.

"Love you too, sweetheart."

Chapter Nineteen

K elli looked up from the notebook where she and Jean had been keeping track of which girl went into which class. The voices coming down the steps brought a smile to her face, and she grinned at Robin and Kristen as they arrived on the bottom level of the lighthouse, grocery sacks in tow.

"Thank goodness," Jean said, getting to her feet. She removed her reading glasses and dropped them on the folders she'd been studying. She and Kelli had been going over the profiles submitted for the girls, and they'd made their three groups—one for Monday, one for Wednesday, and one for Saturday.

Then, they'd mixed them all up and started again. When Robin had texted that she was on her way over, Jean had asked her to stop for reinforcements.

The candy came out and got piled on the kitchen counter while Jean laughed at the enormity of all Robin had brought. Kelli abandoned the notebook for now and went to join her friends in the kitchen.

"This is the whole candy aisle," Jean said, ripping open a package of M&M's. "Wow."

"You'll need it," Robin said. "Teenagers aren't to be trifled with. If you have a bad day—or they're having one—candy." She lifted a mega peanut butter cup and started to open it.

"The house hunting must not be going well," Jean said. "You look like a professional unwrapping that." She watched Robin, and sure enough, the other woman's weariness shone in her eyes.

"We've looked at a few places," Robin said around a bite of chocolate and peanut butter. "None of them feel...right."

"You just need to keep looking until you find that Dream House." Kristen set a six-pack of Diet Coke on the counter, and Jean dang near swooned.

"Thank you," she said around a mouthful of melt-in-your-mouth-not-your-hand chocolate. "This is going to make the organization so much better."

"It'll go faster too," Kelli said. She'd volunteered to help Jean make preliminary lists, because she knew Jean needed the support. She didn't want to ask Kristen for everything, and she wanted to do more than simply observe and passively learn.

Kelli had dropped Parker off at Shad's office a couple of hours ago, and the two of them would come pick her up once they were ready to go home.

She snagged a candy bar with pretzels, caramel, and

peanut butter while Jean started removing the bottles of cola from the plastic rings. "Who wants one?" she asked, passing the first one to Robin.

"Diet Coke all around," Jean said, and she seemed so very happy. Kelli's heart took flight at the sight of her, because only a couple of months ago, she'd been a shell of the woman she was now. The Seafaring Girls program didn't start for two more weeks, but Jean wanted to make personalized welcome cards for each girl with their assigned day and time.

Some of them had requested specific days; others had said any of them would work. Kelli didn't know all the surnames around the cove anymore, and she actually thought that was a good thing. No one deserved to be judged before they even showed up.

"All right." Robin twisted the lid on her soda, and the hiss of the carbonation filled the air. "Let's see what you guys have done."

Jean turned back to the table, which looked like a bomb filled with blue ink and confetti had gone off. "We've organized and re-organized," she said. "I think we're almost there." She moved over to the table with Robin, but Kelli stayed in the kitchen with Kristen. "Jamie is in the Wednesday group."

"How are you, dear?" Kristen asked. She hadn't picked up any candy, nor taken a soda. She wore a pair of black cotton pants with big, rubber gardening boots that went to her knee, almost like Robin had found her outside, puttering around in the flowerbeds. Her navy blue top had big, splashy stars all over it, and they brought Kelli a blip of happiness.

"Good," Kelli said. "Really good."

"Not too overwhelmed at the studio?" Kristen watched her with kind eyes, her gaze only flitting over to Jean and Robin for a moment.

Kelli blew out her breath. "I mean, yeah, it's busy there." She looked away from the table and back to Kristen. "But I'm managing."

"You always do." Kristen put her arm around her. "Nothing happened with Zach." The statement was actually meant as a question, but Kelli didn't know what exactly Kristen wanted to know.

"No," she said, her mind whirring. "Nothing happened with him. I don't think he'll contact me or my mom again." She couldn't live her life in fear over running into him again. He could come to the cove. She'd have to deal with it.

The best part was, she was now equipped to deal with things like running into the man who'd pretended to be her half-brother. She hadn't known until Zach Watkins how very much she'd wanted to be connected to her family, to her past. So much had happened since then, and Kelli had the relationships and connections she craved now.

Running into Zach? It wouldn't break her. She wouldn't freak out and start to cry. She wouldn't need to call the police and have someone else handle the situation. She was strong enough and smart enough to do that herself.

She gave Kristen a smile and asked, "How is the new condo? First spring there."

"Yes." Kristen dropped her arm and stepped a couple of inches away. "There's a lot of trash that blows up from the beach. It'll be interesting to see when the people start coming." She returned Kelli's smile, and together, they went over to the table.

Since the lighthouse was so small, the table was built for and only held two people. The four of them crowded around it anyway, and Jean continued to outline the girls in each group. "So the Wednesday group will be the largest one," she said. "With nine girls. Saturday has eight. Monday seven. Twenty-four girls."

"Twenty-four," Kristen said. "That's a lot, Jean."

"How many did you manage?" Robin asked.

"About that many," Kristen said, but Kelli had the feeling she wasn't being truthful. She simply didn't want Jean to feel anything but one hundred percent confident going into her first week of meetings.

"I thought you ran sessions four days a week," Robin said, never one to let things go.

"I did," Kristen said. "But if you'll remember, you girls on Wednesdays were it. Five of you." Her message somehow got across to Robin, who simply nodded and looked at the names Jean had typed into her computer and then printed out.

"I think it looks good, Jean."

"The curriculum is coming along too," she said. "Kelli's been helping me with that." Jean glanced at Kelli, who nodded.

"A little," she said. "Nothing major. The manual is right there."

Kristen had brought over her old Seafaring Girls manuals, as the city didn't even own one anymore. She'd marked them up with pen and pencil, and Kelli had spent the first twenty minutes at the lighthouse today leafing through one, thinking of Kristen sitting right here in this room, many years ago, preparing for the lessons that had meant so much to Kelli.

They'd been a lifeline to her then, and her friendships with the same people—and more—had saved her again in the very recent past.

A bell rang, and Kelli hurried to clap her hands over her ears. Robin's eyes bugged nearly out of her head, but Jean and Kristen didn't even flinch. Well, maybe Kristen did a little bit.

With the echoes of clanging still hanging in the air, Jean said, "Someone's here. I'll go get it." She turned and headed for the steps.

"Was that the doorbell?" Kelli asked.

"Yes," Kristen said as Jean disappeared up the first flight of steps. "Why doesn't she use the intercom?"

"Would you?" Robin challenged.

Kristen blinked at her. "I would. Then I wouldn't have to go upstairs. It could be for Rueben. That's why the bell is so loud. So it can be heard up top."

"Jean is...old-fashioned," Kelli said, meeting Robin's eye. Really, Jean didn't want to use the intercom, because Clara had installed it. "She finds the buzzer so...non-lighthouse-like." That much was true. Jean appreciated the silent stillness out here on the edge of Diamond Island, and she'd told Kelli that a buzzer simply didn't belong.

"I suppose I'm just old and lazy," Kristen said, moving into the living room. She collapsed onto the couch with a sigh. "I'm ready for a nap."

"We haven't even started dinner yet," Robin said. "No naps." She marched over to Kristen and extended her hand toward her to pull her back to her feet. "You're helping in the kitchen tonight, young lady."

Kelli giggled at the Mom-tone, turning as footsteps sounded on the stairs. She knew those too, and she wasn't surprised to see Parker jump down the last couple of steps and make his arrival in the basement.

"Hey, baby," Kelli said. She went toward him and hugged him. "How was the office?"

"Great," Parker said. "Shad had a brand-new package of white board markers."

"Oh, he did, did he?" Kelli grinned over the top of her son's head as her husband came into the room. He only had eyes for her, and he sandwiched Parker between them as he kissed her.

"Hey," he said. "If you're not done, we can wait. Parker's convinced the wind is just right for a cliffside kite to fly."

"He's probably right," Jean said. "It's not as stiff of a breeze as usual."

"We didn't bring your kite," Kelli said. "Sorry, bud."

"Rueben has one in the shed," Parker said. "You're not done, are you, Mom?" He looked up at her with pleading in his eyes. Kelli had always wanted to give him the world, and that hadn't changed since her divorce and move to Five Island Cove.

She smoothed his hair back, her stomach grumbling at her. It sounded like Robin and Kristen were going to make dinner together, and Jean had a pork roast in the slow cooker. "I am done, bud," she said. "We've got a long ride back to Pearl."

"We could just stay for a little bit," he whined.

"Once you get that kite up, you'll want to fly it forever," Kelli said. "You can fly it on Pearl. We have one at home."

"The cliffs aren't as good." Parker pouted and stepped away from her. Kelli couldn't give him everything he wanted, especially when he could go outside and explore the cliffs for hours. He had done that, and she didn't want to do that tonight.

"Sorry," she said, and she meant it. She wasn't going to change her mind, but she didn't like disappointing her son. She met Shad's gaze, who'd stayed out of the conversation. She liked that he seemed to sense when she wanted him to step in and when she didn't.

Parker was a good boy, and he hadn't given Kelli or Shad too many problems in the months since they'd been married.

"Maybe we can stop and get some of that chocolate-covered fruit you like," Shad said, and Kelli nodded, sensing what he was up to.

"They're always out of the bananas," she said. "And they're my favorite."

"I like the raspberries the best," Parker said, his countenance lighting up again. "Do you really think we can stop? Before the ferry or on Pearl?"

Shad put his arm around Kelli, his eyes still searching hers. "I think before," he said. "I can tell your mom is getting hangry." He chuckled, pressed a kiss to Kelli's temple, and they faced Parker together. "Raspberries for you. Bananas for your mother. Strawberries for me."

"All right," Robin said. "It's looking good, Jean. You're going to do amazing at this." She engulfed the woman in a hug, and then stepped out of the way so Kristen could too. "We have to get going. Kristen promised me she'd teach me how to make her famous macaroni salad, and Duke'll be back off the docks soon."

Her brilliant smile whipped around the room, and she herded Kristen toward the steps, saying, "If he's late, could you come look at the house with me?"

"We're going to go too," Kelli said. "You really are ready, Jean." She hugged the woman too, feeling the strength with which Jean gripped her back.

"Thank you for coming this afternoon," Jean said. "You could eat here with me and Reuben."

"No," Kelli said. "Shad's like, this gourmet chef, and I'm sure he has something awesome planned for dinner tonight."

Shad burst out laughing, which didn't really jive with what Kelli had just said. She grinned with him though, her happiness galloping through her like wild horses. "Gourmet chef," he said between chuckles. "I think I'm going to grill tonight. It'll hardly be gourmet."

"But it'll be good," Kelli said. Simple. And Kelli only wanted good and simple in her life.

"After the fruit, though, right?" Parker asked. "You said we could get it here, before the ferry."

"I know what I said," Shad said, rolling his eyes the moment the ten-year-old had his back turned.

Kelli giggled and pushed Parker's hair out of his eyes. "It's funny how you can't remember to put your math homework in your backpack, but if I told you we could get frozen fruit six months from now, you'd remember that."

"Mom," he said, half whining and half chastising her. "The fruit stands close soon. Can we go?"

"Give Miss Jean a hug first." Kelli stepped out of the way so Parker could do that, and then she started up the steps with her family behind her. As she exited the lighthouse to a blue-gray sky and a plethora of wind, Kelli paused and took a deep breath of the cove.

Some of the best times of her life had happened right here. Some of the worst too. Kelli wouldn't trade her experiences—good or bad—for anything, and she took Shad's hand in hers and put her free hand on Parker's back as they walked down the sidewalk together.

She held the door for Parker to get in the car Shad paid to park in the lot here on Diamond. Then she stepped into her husband's arms and took a deep, deep breath of his cologne, his skin, his very soul. She caught something else in there too, and it smelled very much like...a dog.

"Thanks for entertaining him this afternoon."

"You should see my whiteboard," Shad said with a

chuckle. "Real quick, I wanted to ask you if you'd thought any more about what we've been talking about."

Kelli stepped out of his arms and looked up into his eyes. Kind, dark eyes that only wanted her to be happy. "I have," she said slowly.

"And?" Shad reached for her door, but he only curled his fingers around the handle without opening it.

"And...I think if you can find the right dog, we can have a puppy."

Shad's face split into a grin, and he took her face in both of his hands. "You're going to make two boys very happy."

Kelli grinned and shook her head. "Yeah, I think you spoke true on that one." Shad was just a little *boy* in an older man's body.

He opened her door, and she stepped past him. "I'll start looking tonight."

"Mm hm." She got in and buckled her seatbelt in the time it took for him to round the car and get behind the wheel. "I don't think for a second that you haven't been looking all this time."

Shad cut a look toward her out of the corner of his eye. "Maybe."

"Yeah," Kelli said, brushing her hand down the arm of his jacket. The tiniest of dog hairs lifted off. "What breed did you go see this afternoon?"

"We didn't—" Shad started, but Parker said, "It was a basset hound, Mom, and *so* cute. You would've *died*."

Kelli stared at the side of her husband's face, watching it grow redder and redder. "So cute, huh?" she asked without twisting to look in the back seat. "What if I'd said no?"

"I wouldn't get a puppy without making sure you're okay with it," Shad said.

"Yeah," Kelli said dryly. "You better start praying they have the frozen bananas. Because I am hangry, and a hangry Kelli doesn't approve basset hound puppies."

Shad pulled out of the lot at the lighthouse and stomped on the accelerator, really hamming it up to get them to the frozen fruit stand quickly. Kelli laughed, only pausing when her phone buzzed, and she saw the text from Zach Watkins.

Thanks, Kel, but I don't think I'm going to buy Friendship Inn. It's too expensive for what it is. Maybe next time I'm in the cove, we can get together.

Kelli didn't respond, and she quickly tapped and held to delete the text. That done, she slid her phone under her leg and got back to the conversation happening in the car.

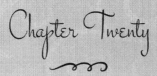

Chapter Twenty

J ean's hands trembled as she held the clipboard and ascended the steps. She couldn't put off going upstairs and outside for another moment, because the girls should be arriving any minute. She'd set up a table that morning and covered it with a bright, cheery, yellow-and-white checkered cloth. She'd baked cookies after that. Made lemonade after lunch.

She had all of the manuals ready for the girls. She had their names memorized.

Janet, Hailey, Paula, Ashley, Ophelia, Joanne, and Adele.

She'd thought about making name tags, but she'd decided against it. They weren't in preschool. She could remember seven names. And if she couldn't, she'd learn and recite until she did.

Pushing open the door, she leaned her weight into the heavy metal structure. It swung open, and Jean probably should've been prepared for the wind to grab hold of it and yank. She normally was, but today, the door got away from her.

She stumbled out of the lighthouse, suddenly without anything to lean into. The pounding of her heart joined the whipping of the tablecloth, which hung on by the plastic clips Jean had used to secure it to the table.

"Are you okay?" a female voice asked. Young.

Jean righted herself just as a dark-haired teen came toward her. "Yes," she said quickly, embarrassment heating her whole body. "I'm not sure how I forgot about the wind out here."

"It comes and goes," the girl said.

Jean focused on her face, noting the wide-set eyes made of dark marble. She had a little bit of acne, but nothing too bad. She probably hated it though, and Jean determined not to stare. "What's your name?" she asked, slipping into the role of check-in hostess as she reached for the pen at the top of her clipboard.

"Adele," she said, and Jean put a check next to her name. She had no idea why, but she told herself that Adele didn't know why either.

Jean looked up and into Adele's eyes and put on the biggest, brightest, best smile she could. "It's great to meet you," she said. "I'm Jean Shields." As she finished with her name, another car pulled up to the curb. Two girls got out, slamming doors and laughing, and Jean kept her grin cemented in place.

These girls wore short shorts despite the still somewhat

cool spring weather, and they linked arms as they came up the sidewalk.

"Hello, girls," Jean said. "Tell me your names. Then there's cookies and lemonade until we're all here."

The two girls moved their eyes to the table and back to Jean as if they had a single brain controlling the four orbs. "Cookies and lemonade?"

Jean raised her chin. "Before I moved into the lighthouse, the woman here always had cookies and lemonade for anyone who wanted it. So yes. Today, while we're checking everyone in, there's cookies and lemonade."

By the end of her speech, she was almost hurling the words at these two teenagers. They would not insult the cookies and lemonade, and a sense of satisfaction moved through Jean as she realized that they knew they shouldn't.

"Okay, thanks," one said.

"Yeah," Adele said. "These look amazing. Did you make these?"

"Yes," Jean said, glancing at her clipboard. "Are you two sisters? Maybe Janet and Joanne?"

Janet, Hailey, Paula, Ashley, Ophelia, Joanne, and Adele, she recited.

Janet and Joanne were twins, though they weren't entirely identical. She couldn't quite place the differences between them though.

"Yes," one said. "I'm Janet. I part my hair on the left. She's Joanne. Hers parts on the right."

"We're mirror twins," Joanne said. "You can call me Jo. Only my nana calls me Joanne."

"Noted," Jean said as she put the two letters next to Joanne's name. She looked up again and smiled at the girls. "Do you two know Adele?" There was only one junior high and one high school in the cove. Everyone went to the same one, at least if they attended public school.

"Sure," Janet said, her voice a touch higher than before. "We know Adele."

"Help yourself to cookies," Jean said, stepping further down the sidewalk to give them more room around the table. She caught sight of a mother walking her daughter toward her, and her pulse leapt into the back of her throat. "Hello," she said from several steps away. "Who is this?"

The mom had her arm around her daughter's back, and it was very clear this teen didn't want to be here. "Tell the woman your name."

"I'm Jean Shields," Jean said. "We've got Adele, Janet, and Jo back there. And so many oatmeal chocolate chip cookies, I think I'll have to make ice cream and turn them into ice cream sandwiches." She beamed at the teenager, who somehow managed not to move her lips at all.

She'd painted them a bright red, and she had a whole Taylor-Swift vibe happening. Blonde hair. Blue eyes. Skinny bird legs. Bright red lipstick. Her clothes were normal enough—shorts and a tee—but it was the deadness in her face that concerned Jean.

"I'm Paula," she said. "Mom, I'm not hanging out with the freaking Farrar twins."

"You're not hanging out, you're right about that," her mother said crisply. She reminded Jean so much of Alice, her eyes flashing dangerous fire at her daughter. "This is a sea-worthy class, and if you want to go out on that boat with that boyfriend of yours, you're going to learn how to be safe doing it."

"Mom."

"It's this or break-up with Dawson. I don't even trust him out there. One of you needs to have some knowledge of sailboats and currents and how to get help." She hissed the last several words, and the tension between the two of them could've filled stadiums.

Paula cocked her hip and said, "Fine."

"Fine." Her mom removed her arm from Paula's back and shook Jean's hand. "I'm Brenda. If she's not paying attention, call me. If she gives you or any of the girls any trouble, call me." She glared at her daughter. "I'm quite certain she won't." With that, she turned on her heel—she actually wore two-inch heels with her navy slacks—and marched back to her car.

Jean called, "Okay," to her and then looked at Paula. Her tongue felt thick and clumsy in her mouth. "I almost didn't come to the cove at all," she said. "I hated it here. I couldn't imagine living beneath the ground in a lighthouse."

Paula's eyes lit up with every word Jean said. "You live in the lighthouse?"

"Bottom two levels," Jean said. "There are no windows, and for a soul that craves light, it was a very hard change for me."

"Why'd you do it?"

Jean gestured to the tall, white, proud lighthouse.

"Because the man I love wanted to come here and run this place. So I came with him." She met Paula's eyes again. "Don't worry about the other girls right now. I can help you learn how to sail, be safe on the water, and then maybe you'll get to follow your boyfriend wherever his dreams take him."

Paula grinned then, her bright red lips curving up and making her face oh-so-beautiful. "All right."

"All right," Jean said, putting a check next to her name. "Now, go get a cookie until the rest of the girls get here."

"I JUST CAN'T BELIEVE IT," JEAN GUSHED AS SHE put two plates on the table. Rueben stood in the kitchen, washing his hands in steaming water. "No one fought. I mean, I could tell they weren't all like, best friends or anything, but they didn't fight."

She returned to the kitchen and picked up the pan with the fried potatoes in it. Rueben turned and took a towel from the stove handle. "That's great, babe." He smiled at her with such love, and Jean pressed into him so he could kiss her. "What else? Did they like the cookies?"

"They did," Jean said, a hint of pride in her voice. "Not only that, but two of the moms have already texted me to ask for the recipe." She sighed—a sound of pure bliss, something she wasn't sure she'd ever felt before—as she set the pan on the hot pad between the two plates.

"Wow," Reuben said. "I told you to put together a cook-book. Your dad has contacts in publishing, Jeanie." His hand slid along her waist, and Jean leaned into his strength again. When she'd told Paula that she almost hadn't come to the cove, she hadn't been making anything up.

She missed Long Island and her parents from time to time, but with every passing day here in Five Island Cove, Jean grew stronger. Her relationship with Reuben did too, and in the end, she'd decided that he was more important than where they lived. Than if they had windows or not. Than if her parents lived just around the corner and would feed them whenever they wanted.

"Remember when we got that bird feeder?" she asked. "In the first house we owned?"

"Yes," Rueben said, his voice low and husky. "You loved that thing. You cleaned it every day."

"Filled it morning and night," she said. "I wanted the birds to be so happy. I wanted them to come to our feeder, because it was the best one."

"They did too." His arm tightened, and he pulled her closer.

"Those girls...they were kind of like those birds," she said. "I could tell some of them were nervous. They all knew *of* each other, but they didn't *know* each other." She was going to teach them to work together, to rely on one another, and to go to one another when they needed help— at least while on a boat.

"It might take a few times," she said. "For them to realize that my feeder has the best seeds and it's always clean and they always have a place here. But I think they'll realize it."

"I think they will too," Reuben said, placing a kiss on

her cheek. "You're an amazing woman, Jean. I know you were scared to do this, and you did it."

She turned into him and kissed him, glad the fire between them still burned bright and hot. She threaded her fingers through his dark hair and let the joy and love fill her to capacity.

"Maybe dinner could wait," Reuben murmured, his lips sliding down her throat.

"It can," Jean whispered, because she'd just had the most amazing Seafaring Girls lesson that afternoon, and she wanted to top that off with an amazing evening with her husband.

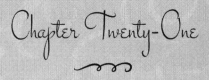

Chapter Twenty-One

R obin pushed her mixer up a notch, really getting the butter to whip. She added dill and the garlic she'd chopped, the scent lifting from the bowl enough to make her mouth water.

She'd already texted everyone on the group string about the house she and Duke had looked at that morning. *This might be the one*, she'd sent. The others had asked to see pictures, and Robin had sent them the overall front view from the listing.

She did like the cute little white cottage, but they'd be giving up some space if they moved there. She told herself Mandie was graduating and moving out soon, and she didn't need three guest bedrooms.

Jean should be finished with her Seafaring Girls lesson in another thirty minutes, and then an hour after that, everyone would be arriving at Robin's for lunch. Giddiness pranced through her, because she hadn't hosted lunch in so long. She'd seen everyone, but sitting down for a big meal wasn't the same as the group text, nor was it the same as going to lunch with a few people here and there.

"I'm coming in," Eloise called, and Robin dashed to the end of the counter to look down the hall.

"Do you need help?"

Eloise came toward her at a rapid pace, a huge box in her arms. "Maybe a little."

Robin could've probably climbed into the box and been mailed to the mainland, and she rushed to help Eloise so she wouldn't drop the produce. "Wow, you got a lot."

"They had everything this morning," El said, and together, they slid the box onto the island in Robin's kitchen. The stand mixer hummed along, and Robin stepped over to flip it off. She turned to wash her hands, feeling grimy from the bottom of that box.

"How are your new managers doing?" Robin asked. "Are they getting along better?"

"I think so?" El sighed as she came to the sink too. She stuck her hands in the water, immediately yanking them back. "Wow, that's hot."

"Sorry." Robin had spent so much time in the kitchen with hot things, she didn't feel the heat as keenly as others. She adjusted the handle so the water would be cooler. "What do you mean you think so?"

"The two managers get along fine," El said, washing now that the water wasn't so scalding. "It's Rhonda who's having a hard time. She thinks Diane and Paige were hired because she wasn't good enough."

"Oh." Robin watched Eloise, the stress of running The Cliffside Inn prevalent on her face.

"I've told her three or four times that I hired Diane and Paige to help her, not hinder her. She works mostly evenings, so it doesn't help that Diane is a little...brusque."

"That's putting it mildly." Robin had called Cliffside to find out about booking in the fall, because she wanted to surprise Duke with a getaway once he returned from Alaska. He was going again this summer for the third time in a row, and he was always utterly exhausted when he returned.

Diane had answered, and she hadn't exactly been Miss Personable when she'd informed Robin that they weren't booking into September yet. When Robin had told El about it, Eloise had gone ahead and booked a room for Robin, saying, "She'll deal with it. Don't worry about it."

Robin hadn't worried about it, but now she wondered if she should. El didn't bring it up, and she only rolled her eyes at Robin's assessment of Diane.

"She gets a lot done," Eloise said. "The guests like her, and our physical facilities are in top notch shape as we near summer." She turned back to the box and started pulling things out of it. "Look at these gorgeous heirloom tomatoes." She put the red, reddish-purple, and orange tomatoes on the counter.

"I could do a tomato salad with those," Robin said.

"Or Caprese," El said. "I know you have basil here."

"Guilty." Robin grinned at her friend, so glad she was here today and not at the inn. "What are Aaron and the girls doing today?"

Eloise dropped the two lemons she'd been removing from the box. "Uh, I'm not sure."

Robin gaped at her, for her friend had just lied to her. Right to her face. "Eloise Hall."

"That's not my last name anymore." El gave her a wicked grin, but it slipped quickly. "Listen, I haven't told anyone, and I don't want to. None of your pacts or games, okay?"

Robin tossed her hair over her shoulder. "I like the pacts and games. They keep us close." At least in Robin's mind, they did. Sometimes Alice held things too close to the vest. If Robin didn't make her say what was going on, she wouldn't.

AJ liked to keep things on the surface, but Robin knew she had a whole mess of things teeming below that. Without the Tell-Alls and the truth games, Robin would never truly know her. Kelli would rather other people speak, though Robin had seen her emerge more and more from her shell, especially since opening her yoga and wellness center—and meeting Shad.

And Eloise...she liked to keep things to herself until they were mostly resolved. Only then would she reveal what had been going on, and by then, Robin couldn't do anything to help. She hated feeling helpless more than anything.

El put her hand over Robin's. "I know they do. I don't really hate them."

"No one does," Robin said. "Everyone just pretends like they do."

El retrieved the lemons and went back into the box to see what else she'd gotten from the fruit and vegetable grab that morning. Robin had said to get whatever she could, and they'd make salads and bowls out of it.

Her stomach tightened as she remembered she'd invited her mother over to help with the food prep. "I need a job for my mom to do when she gets here," Robin said.

Not a breath later, El blurted out, "Aaron's ex-wife wants to come see the girls. She's in the cove, and they might go visit her today."

Robin froze, except for her eyes. They widened. Her heart beat against a cage. She couldn't believe what she'd just heard, and her brain seemed so slow to process the English words.

El reached up and swiped at her right eye. "It's fine. I'm fine."

It obviously wasn't fine, and neither was Eloise.

"Eloise," Robin whispered, all thoughts of fruit and veggies forgotten. "I'm so sorry." She took the kindest, sweetest soul into her arms. "Are you worried?"

"Yes."

"Scared?"

"Terrified."

"Of what?"

"That she'll hurt those girls again," El said, clinging to her. "That she'll somehow get Aaron to fall in love with her again. That she'll, I don't know, and it sounds so ridiculous, but that she'll take away the family I have—that I worked so hard to get."

"That's not going to happen," Robin said firmly. Sometimes the mind didn't work rationally. She'd certainly found herself in that position before. "It's not, El. Aaron loves you. Billie and Grace adore you. They are your family, and someone they haven't seen in who-knows-how-long isn't going to change that."

El nodded and stepped back. She wiped both eyes this time and when she looked at Robin, she wore open vulnerability and fear in those lovely eyes.

"Don't be scared," Robin whispered, wishing she could erase every hard thing for Eloise. "I've seen that man look at you. He loves you. His ex-wife isn't going to change that."

El nodded, another tear leaking down her face. "I know that. I do, intellectually, but I worry about Billie and Grace."

"They're strong, El, because they have *you* to show them how to be."

El nodded again, drew in a deep breath, and looked at the eggplant sitting on the counter. "I have no idea what to do with eggplant."

"Me either," Robin said, a naughty idea forming in her mind.

"Yoo hoo, Robin," her mom sang out, and Eloise spun away from the mouth of the hallway that came into the back of the house, where the living room, dining room, and kitchen sat.

"In the kitchen, Mom." Robin turned to go meet her mother, and she embraced her at the corner where the hall met the kitchen. "Hey, how are you?" If she could give El an extra minute to compose herself, she would.

"Good," her mother said in a somewhat surprised tone.

"Oh, you got the Bountiful Basket. Those have the most amazing things in them."

"They do," Robin agreed, because today, she was going to agree with everything her mother said. There would be no fighting at this luncheon, as Robin mentally told herself one more time. "In fact, I have a job for you." She walked over to the counter and picked up the eggplant. "We have no idea what to do with this."

Jennifer Golden looked at the eggplant, and one eyebrow cocked up. "These are best fried."

"So maybe not with today's menu."

"I don't know," her mom said. "You haven't given me *any* of the details, dear." Mom put her purse on the built-in desk and faced the kitchen. "What protein are we having?"

"Salmon bites," Robin said. "With compound butter. Duke cooked up a batch of lobster tails last night, so I'll get those out. They'll be cold. He's going to put chicken and steak on the grill for me in about a half-hour."

Mom looked at the eggplant. "I don't think we can use this today." She put it on the desk, which only annoyed Robin. She'd be the one picking that up later and putting it where it belonged, and it was almost like her mother wanted to punish her for starting the house-hunting process. "But let's see what else you have."

"I'm going to do a Caprese salad with these tomatoes," Robin said, practically lunging for them. "The girls are at the grocery store right now, getting the stuff we need for the tea and lemonade."

"I'm going to do a warm beet salad with these," Eloise

said, holding up a couple of beets—one purple and one golden. "Do you have feta, Robin?"

"If I don't, I can text Mandie," she said. "Let me look." She opened the fridge and sure enough, found some feta for El. Their eyes met, and plenty was said between them.

Mom kept pulling things out of the box, and when she found a handful of apricots, she said, "Oh, I can caramelize these for dessert." Her eyes lit up, she looked at Robin. "What do you think?"

Robin gave her the best mega-watt smile she possessed. "I think you're on dessert, Mom."

The activity in the kitchen picked up as they each got started on their dishes. Robin loved the scent of the tomatoes as she sliced them. As she layered the slices on a sheet pan, they made a beautiful rainbow of colors, which also brought happiness to her soul.

"Mom," Mandie said, bringing Robin's head up. She glanced over and hurried to push the big Bountiful Basket box out of the way. Mandie heaved the bags of groceries she'd laced over her arms onto the counter with a grunt.

Robin pushed them up farther so she could get the other armful up. "Wow," she said. "You guys got a lot."

"You texted us about fifteen times," Mandie said with a sharp look. "And Dad wants to talk to you."

Robin looked over her daughter's shoulder, but she didn't see or hear Duke. "Okay. Is he in the garage?"

Mandie nodded. "I'll get these unpacked."

"Robin, dear, where's your maple extract?" her mom asked.

"I've got it, Mom," Mandie said. She wore urgency in her expression, and Robin's stomach swooped. She wiped her hands down her apron as she went down the hall toward the front entrance. She detoured out to the garage just before she'd pass the steps, and while she hadn't thought it would be hot, the garage definitely held more heat than the house.

Duke stood at the back of the minivan, handing a gallon of milk to Jamie. They both looked up and toward Robin as she came down the two steps to the floor of the garage.

"Hey," she said brightly, wondering if she'd read Mandie's body language and tone wrong. Nope. Duke's eyes shot darkness and lightning in her direction, and Robin wondered what she'd done wrong. She had texted quite a few times...

"We got everything," he said. "Jamie, take that inside."

Jamie turned away, barely carrying anything from the back of the van, and as Robin glanced at her, she did a double-take. Her youngest daughter was crying. Or had been.

"Hey," she said in a much softer tone, but Jamie just shook her head and kept going.

Robin tucked her hands in the back pockets of her jeans, took slow steps toward her husband, and waited until Jamie had entered the house and the door had closed. "What's going on?"

The darkness in Duke's eyes brightened a little. A long sigh came out of his mouth, and he reached up and ran his hand through his hair. It had started to come in gray, and

Robin found him sexier than ever now that he was aging. "Her boyfriend works at the grocery store."

Robin's eyebrows went up, her neck tightening. "Her boyfriend? Damien Robinson?"

Duke sat at the back of the van, and Robin joined him. "Not Damien Robinson." He curled his fingers around hers when she put her hand on his leg. "Someone else. I didn't get the boy's name. She might have said it, but I wasn't seeing straight after I caught them kissing near the meat counter."

Robin's heart fell all the way to her shoes. "She's fourteen."

"He's fifteen," Duke said. "I got that much. I guess his uncle runs the meat and seafood department, and he has him do clean-up in the back."

"So what happened?"

"We're shopping, and Jamie says she's going to go see if they have any of their seasonal stuff out yet. She wants one of those foam boards this year for the beach. I'm like, fine. You're texting, and Mandie knows where everything is in the store. Off Jamie goes." He gazed out at their driveway, where El had parked to the side. Robin's mother had parked on the street, and nothing else seemed out of the ordinary.

"She didn't come back for such a long time. I don't think Mandie or I noticed how long, until we had nearly everything. It had been at least twenty minutes. So I say I'll go find her, hand Mandie my wallet, and head over to the seasonal aisle. She wasn't there."

Robin heard the beginnings of panic in her own soul, and she'd definitely seen it in Duke's eyes. "So I'm walking around, calling her name, actually yelling in the grocery store for her. I'm thinking I'm going to have to go up front and have her paged, call the cops, I don't know what. She wasn't *anywhere*."

"She's losing her mind. Remember when Mandie acted like this?"

"Fourteen-year-old girls are not my favorite breed of human." Duke squeezed her hand, and they chuckled together. Robin had said that for a solid year after Mandie had turned fourteen. They were hard, and emotional, and Robin hoped they could survive one more. It seemed every age brought challenges, but none were as hard as the year a girl lived through fourteen.

"Anyway, I was just about to head up front when I heard her say, 'I really have to go.' I knew it was her voice, and I jogged toward the meat counter. Right there, this boy had Jamie against the wall, kissing her. I mean, she was kissing him back, don't get me wrong. But I kind of couldn't see straight at that point."

"Duke," Robin warned. "What did you do?"

"I may have pulled them apart and gotten in his face." Duke sighed again and ran his free hand through his hair and down his face. "Jamie was real mad. I was mad. Mandie was mad. We're all mad."

Robin nodded, though having an angry family the day she was hosting a big luncheon at the house wasn't ideal. "Okay, well, take a few minutes to do whatever."

"I'll just putter around in the back yard and get your grill hot," he said. "It's fine. I told her we'd need to have a conversation about this boy, and I wanted to know who he was, how she'd met him, and why he wasn't Damien like I expected him to be."

"What did she say?"

"She said she and Damien are just friends. This kid is in her English class. He's a nice boy—her words, not mine. She bawled the whole way home and said I'd ruined everything." He shook his head. "I gotta say, I don't feel bad about that."

Robin smiled, trying to contain her giggle. She failed, and she laughed as she hugged Duke's arm with both of her hands. "I love you, Duke," she said. "We'll talk to her after the luncheon." She looked at him and pressed a kiss to his cheek. "You didn't get the boy's name?"

"Steven, maybe? Sawyer? It started with an S."

"Mom," Mandie said. "We need the rest of the groceries, and you might want to get in here. Grandma is trying to take over everything."

Robin jumped to her feet, squeezed Duke's hand, and grabbed a couple of grocery bags. "Coming," she said. "Do *not* let her touch my tomatoes."

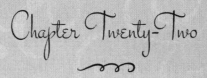

Chapter Twenty-Two

Kristen carried her famous cowboy caviar down the hall at Robin's, the chatter at the back of the house almost overwhelming her already. Behind her, Jean carried no less than five dozen chocolate chip cookies, though there'd probably be so much food in the house that they wouldn't be needed.

The scent of cooking steak had been wafting over the roof outside, and in here, Kristen caught garlic, hot oil, and something fresh. She arrived in the kitchen, Jean right behind her, and they continued toward the island, Kristen looking for an empty place to put her caviar.

Cowboy caviar was a chip dip made with beans, corn, peppers, and other fresh deliciousness. She'd just put the heavy bowl on the counter when Robin said, "Over here, Kristen. This is where all the chips are."

So she hefted the bowl again and took it over to the side counter, as Robin needed to use every available inch of space. "This looks wonderful," Kristen said with her bowl now in the right place. "You ladies have been working hard."

"Thanks." Robin gave her a happy grin. "Jean, the desserts are actually on the table." She indicated the dining room table, which held what looked like an apricot upside-down cake and banana pudding.

Robin moved to help Jean just as Alice and Laurel burst into a round of laughter. El joined them, but Kelli simply smiled and shook her head. Kristen didn't know what they'd been talking about, but she told herself she could step into their circle and they'd welcome her with open arms.

She did just that, and Alice hugged her first. "How are you?" she asked, her mouth right at Kristen's ear. "Doing okay now that someone else is doing the Seafaring Girls?"

Kristen should've known Alice would be the one to pick up on the fact that watching someone else run that program would be hard for her. It shouldn't be. Kristen didn't actually want to be the one in charge of the Seafaring Girls again. She was far too old, and she rather liked her simple, easy-going life of walking in the mornings with a few ladies and then watching her game shows, making lunch, and napping or admiring the beach in the afternoons.

The Seafaring Girls had no place in her life right now. It had been such a huge part of her previous life, and something that had brought her great joy and fulfillment. Of course it would be hard to watch someone else run the program.

She'd done her very best to leave Jean alone to run it. If her daughter-in-law called and asked questions, Kristen answered them. She didn't try to attend any of the meetings she wasn't invited to, and she hadn't called or texted this week to find out how the meetings had gone.

Because Jean was a wonderful woman, she'd initiated the calls and texts after the classes on Monday and Wednesday. Today, Kristen had arrived at the lighthouse mere moments after the lesson had let out, and she'd seen the pure joy on Jean's face. The program had done wonders for bringing the woman out of her shell and reminding her that she had plenty of worth. Not only that, but Jean had so much to offer to the girls who'd come to the lighthouse. She was an excellent seamstress, a good cook, a kind friend, and a smart woman.

"Kristen?" Alice stepped back, her dark eyes probing now. Sometimes she could slip into being a lawyer without knowing it.

"I'm good," Kristen said, putting a smile on her face. "Really, I am." She moved to embrace Kelli, El, and Laurel, and they all turned when the wail of a baby filled the air.

Kelli left the group to go help AJ, who arrived in the kitchen with a red-faced baby about to let loose with another scream. Jean turned toward her too, and she went to assist, actually reaching AJ first. She took Asher into her arms right as he screamed again, and Jean bounced him on her hip and shushed him, taking him back down the hall toward the front door.

"He's cutting a couple of teeth," AJ said. "I had to wake him up to come in." She pushed her hair back off her face, her distress plain as day.

The back door opened, and Mandie, Ginny, and another teen girl about the same age walked in. Kristen assumed she was Emily, Ginny's best friend who was now living with Alice, Arthur, and the twins. Kristen gave the girls a warm smile, though none of them looked her way.

Robin had invited her mother too, and that made surprise and satisfaction flow through Kristen. They'd had a few conversations about Jennifer Golden over the past several months, and Kristen knew how hard it was for Robin to spend time with her mother. The fact that Robin had incorporated her into this luncheon meant something—and it probably cost her something too.

Kristen also loved seeing a younger generation of girls in the group, as Mandie, Ginny, and Emily would be graduating from high school in just a few short months, then they'd be out on their own, the entire world in front of them.

Sometimes life could feel so confined on Five Island Cove. Surrounded by water as it was, Kristen sometimes felt like the rest of the world didn't exist. The people out there didn't know that only twelve miles away, a whole community of human beings lived, worked, loved, and wrestled with the same challenges they did. She had to remind herself from time to time that there was more than the five islands that made up the cove, more to life than just the lighthouse or her condo, and more to humankind than what she knew inside her own sphere of existence.

"All right," Robin called, raising both hands above her head. Some of the conversations stopped, and Jean had somehow calmed Asher, though the boy still sniffled from the corner of the living room. She smiled in their direction, but Jean kept her focus on the child as she rubbed something along his gums he sure seemed to like.

"Everyone," Robin tried again, and Duke whistled, effectively getting Alice and Laurel to stop talking and the teenagers to stop looking at something on Mandie's phone and giggling about it.

"Lunch is ready," Robin said, giving her husband an appreciative glance. "I just want to thank everyone for coming." She pressed one palm to her heart, as if she might recite the Pledge of Allegiance. Her chest rose as she drew a deep breath. "You all mean so much to me, and I love having you here at my house."

Kristen surveyed the group of women, and she sure did love them all too. In her mind's eye, she saw an empty space in the group, a spot next to Kelli where Clara would fit. Shocked at that, Kristen blinked and tried to push the thought away. It would not go, and she had the overwhelming urge to text her daughter and find out what she was doing.

She hadn't said much more about Scott or moving to the cove since she'd come earlier that year, and Kristen had not followed up with her. A slice of guilt moved through her as she realized she should've. Her daughter needed her, and Kristen hadn't felt like that for years.

"...lots of desserts," Robin was saying. "Made by my mother, and she's a fabulous baker." She shot a sunbeamy smile in her mom's direction. "Duke has the steak and chicken outside, and we'll be eating out there, so you can start out there or in here with all the sides or the cold proteins." She looked at Kelli, who took a step away from the island and the spot where Clara would fit.

Her daughter's image faded in Kristen's mind, but she determined not to ignore the prompting she'd just gotten. She'd send her a text while everyone else got their food.

"But first," Kelli said. "Jean's going to tell us how the Seafaring Girls meetings went this week. I think everyone here knows that the main reason we're all here is because five of us were in the same Seafaring Girls group decades ago." Today, she'd left her hair down, and it fell in golden waves over her shoulders. Kristen hadn't realized how long it had gotten, because Kelli normally wore it up, with a visor.

She also wore something besides her leggings and a T-shirt or tank top, her normal attire for teaching aerobics or yoga. Kristen's love for her swelled, because Kelli had really grown into herself as a teenager, and then again in the past couple of years since she'd been reunited with her Seafaring Girls sisters.

"Robin, Alice, Eloise, AJ, and I were all in Kristen's Wednesday group. I wasn't so sure about it at first, and sometimes over the years, I wanted to quit. But really, they were my best friends and biggest supporters. Then...and now." She cleared her throat. "I'm also glad we've found Laurel and Jean, that Kristen still puts up with us and all of our drama, and that we have daughters here with us today."

She hadn't brought her son, and Kristen assumed Parker was off doing something with Shad that day.

Kelli scanned the group, her eyes pausing on Kristen for only a moment. "All right, Jean," she said, twisting toward the woman in the living room. "Give me the baby and tell us how it went."

Jean came forward and started to pass Asher to Kelli as Robin said, "And this is it. I'm not going to do a Tell-All or New Truth or First Rights of Refusal or anything. No revelations today. Just lunch."

"You've got to be kidding," Alice said. "I've been preparing all morning."

Kristen smiled as a couple of others did and as a round of chuckles moved through the women.

"Very funny," Robin said dryly. "You know you love it when I make you all talk. But today, we're just eating." Her bright blue eyes actually got brighter. "Though, if anyone has anything they would like to say, you can go after Jean."

No one volunteered, and Kristen wanted to wrap Robin in a hug when her shoulders fell and her expression dimmed. She also saw Eloise's tension increase, and she wondered what that was about. Laurel too seemed a bit on-edge, despite her smile and the way she relaxed into the corner of the countertop behind her. She had one hand protectively on her belly, and Kristen realized she could feel her baby move.

Happiness popped through her, but she forced herself to focus on Jean as she started to speak.

"I think the lessons went well this week," she said. "The hardest day is going to be my Wednesday group, shockingly." She smiled at the other women who'd been in Kristen's

Wednesday group. "There's some personalities there that don't get along all that well. I have a set of twins on Monday that I'm probably going to have to split up at some point so they get outside their comfort zones. This morning's group was a bit dead, so I'm hoping to liven them up somehow..." Her voice trailed off, and Kristen's mind buzzed with ideas for all of the things she'd said.

She'd labored and agonized over her groups too. How could she make Eloise feel more comfortable around the prettier girls in her group? How could she bring Kelli out of her shell? How could she tame Robin's enthusiasm—and why should she?

She'd never wanted to squash anyone and their innate personality. She only wanted to enhance it, grow it, and help them realize how to use it appropriately.

Robin could be bossy and overbearing, but the same traits also made her a fantastic mother and an excellent event planner. It made her the heart of the group, as she wanted people in her home, surrounding her. She invited people, and she'd absolutely refused to let any of her Seafaring Girls friends miss out on Joel's funeral.

Without her tenacity, Kristen knew they wouldn't be standing there, in her kitchen, today.

Alice was intellectual and proper, but those traits made her a strong woman with a clear sense of morals. She'd had some of the hardest conversations with her children and herself, and she never shied away from a challenge. She reined in Robin, who needed that sometimes, and she complemented Eloise's smarts and showed her that it was okay to use her brain.

Eloise sometimes doubted herself and always wanted to keep the peace. She struggled internally, and to see her open up and ask for help, run a business, and take her life by the horns had been a refreshing reminder for Kristen not to just let life go by. She wanted to live it, the way El did.

AJ had healed the most in the past couple of years, the secrets she'd been hiding for thirty years nearly eating her away inside. She'd been through a lot with men, and these women, and to see her married, with a child, made Kristen's heart glow with gold.

And the fact that Kelli had been an active speaker in the group still surprised Kristen. She'd been so withdrawn, so inclined to keep every eye off of her, so full of fear for so long. She wasn't afraid anymore, and Kristen couldn't be either.

"Anyway," Jean said, and she was another huge example in Kristen's life. She'd moved to the cove when she hadn't wanted to. She'd chosen to stand by her husband and honor their marriage vows, even when it had been very difficult for her to do so. She was a champion in Kristen's eyes—someone who'd lost several fights but got back up every single time to swing again.

"I think it went well," Jean continued. "I'm going to make my dulce de leche rice crispy treats next week, so if the lesson is too boring, at least the treats won't be." She grinned around at everyone and nodded, clearly done speaking.

Kristen had not let a day go by since Jean had come to

the cove without praying for her. When she'd lost the baby, Kristen had worried that Jean would go backward instead of forward, and she thanked the Lord she hadn't.

She pressed her eyes closed and sent up a prayer for all of the women in this kitchen, as well as their husbands, children, and other loved ones. Her eyes came open as the doorbell rang and Robin tried to say, "Let's eat," at the same time.

Kelli quickly said, "I think it's my mom. I'll get it." She bustled off with Asher in her arms to get the door.

Kristen stayed right where she was and started to text Clara while the others around her picked up plates and started taking salads, corn on the cob, and salmon bites.

We're having lunch at Robin's today, Kristen typed out. *I could see you here so easily. How are you? How are things with Scott? I don't need details, but I'm thinking about you and thought I'd ask for an update.*

She read over the text, trying to decide if she was being too nosy—something Clara had accused her of being in the past. Kristen had never thought of herself that way before, and if she'd learned anything from her headstrong and vocal daughter, it was that every person had their own perspective on life. They saw people in their own way. They came at situations differently. They processed at different speeds, and heard things in unique ways.

She'd tried to appreciate that about Clara, but her sharp tongue had left wounds over the years.

I'm good, Mom, Clara responded. *Lena and I are plan-*

ning another trip to the cove, and we'd like to stay with you this time. How doable is that?

Kristen drew in a breath, glad she had time, space, and distance between her and Clara before she had to answer. She'd been relieved when Clara had stayed at the lighthouse, though it had sliced at her too. Emotions could run both ways sometimes, another thing Kristen was still grappling with in her late seventies.

It's doable, she said. *I have an extra bedroom, and I can put up an air mattress in the dining room. It doesn't have a door, but it's a separate room from the rest of the house.*

The dining room branched off the kitchen, and Kristen hardly ever ate in there. She took her meals to the living room, the patio, or ate at the kitchen counter. Sometimes even in bed. She should probably get rid of the small dining table, though she had entertained AJ there for lunch a couple of times.

Great, Clara said. *I'm still working with Lena's therapist about dates. We also need to check with her job. I'll let you know.*

Okay, Kristen said, glancing up as Kelli returned to the kitchen with her mother in tow. Paula had gotten remarried over the Thanksgiving holiday, and Kristen had attended the small wedding. Both of Kelli's sisters had been there, as well as Devon's family. She smiled in Paula's direction, but the enormity of the crowd, which moved and swelled as women lifted spoons and inched around the island, kept their eyes from meeting.

She noted that El had stayed out of the initial fray of

people getting food. Kristen moved to stand by her, and she said, "Girls, go get something to eat," to the three teens standing there. "Mandie, where's your sister?"

Mandie gave her a smile made of plastic and secrets. "She's probably in her room. We can go get her." She looked at her mother, who was directing things from the opposite side of the island, telling someone what all was in the cowboy caviar Kristen had made.

"Come on, guys." The girls moved away, leaving Kristen with El.

"So." Kristen touched El's hand with hers, keeping it out of sight of the others. "What's new with you, Eloise? You look a little troubled about something."

El's eyes landed on Kristen's, and the storm within swirled. "Yeah," she said slowly. "Maybe I could come walking with you one day this week so we can talk."

"I'd love that," Kristen said. "You used to come to the lighthouse and just sit. No talking required."

"And yet," El said with a smile. "You always got something out of me."

"I did," Kristen said, also smiling. "But that was because of you, not me."

El nodded, squeezed Kristen's hand, and said, "Tomorrow, then."

"Sure," Kristen said. "Tomorrow." She'd make her lemon zucchini bread tonight, and maybe they could skip the walk and just watch the sun play with the waves out in the ocean.

Robin turned around and planted both hands on her

hips. "Come on, you two. We're eating. Get over here before all the good stuff is gone."

"That's impossible," El said even as she moved away from Kristen. "Besides, I'm having dessert first." She then proceeded to pick up a paper plate and put one of every dessert on the table on it.

Kristen decided she was going to do the same, and with a busy luncheon and more talking on the horizon, she definitely needed it.

Chapter Twenty-Three

⌒⌒⌒

The scent of lemons hung in the air as Eloise approached Kristen's condo, reminding her that she hadn't eaten breakfast after getting the girls off to school. An emergency had come up at the inn yesterday morning, postponing the walk she'd planned with Kristen.

Honestly, weariness accompanied El everywhere she went lately. To the inn. On the ferry. Into the kitchen to make morning coffee. And down the sidewalk between the two halves of the condo building to Kristen's front door.

She'd dressed in a pair of black leggings and an oversized sweatshirt she certainly didn't need on this April morning. The proper footwear sat on her feet, but El didn't want to take another step. She hoped Kristen had made something lemony, carb-filled, and glazed for breakfast, and perhaps they could simply eat it under the morning sunshine on her patio.

After knocking, she tried the doorknob, the way she'd

done at Kristen's cottage and the lighthouse in the past. The knob turned, and the door opened. "It's me, Kristen," she said.

"Come in, El," Kristen said as she came toward her. "The coffee just finished." She gave El a warm smile, the gesture slipping as she took in Eloise's full appearance. "Oh, dear. You look troubled."

"I'm tired," Eloise admitted as the older woman wrapped her in a hug. "I feel bad I didn't invite my mother to the luncheon on Saturday. I have all these things I need to do, and I don't want to do any of them. Do you think I could just go back to bed?"

"No," Kristen said kindly. "You'll get some bread and some coffee, and we'll find a place to sit and talk. No walking."

"No walking," El agreed as Kristen pulled back. Thankfully, Kristen turned away without scrutinizing El too much. She'd felt so many eyes on her lately, and she didn't like it. Supervisors, guests, the girls, Aaron. She didn't want to let anyone down, but some of the balls she was juggling were made of glass, and El was two seconds away from dropping everything.

Kristen walked into the kitchen, and El followed her. The lemon poppyseed bread had obviously come out of the oven a while ago, because the sugary glaze had already been applied and allowed to get a skin.

Her mouth watered, and she didn't turn down the plate with two slices that Kristen offered her. "Inside or out?" she asked.

"Out," El said, not sure she wanted to talk beneath a ceiling, where plaster and paint could capture her words and echo them back to her. She accepted a mug too, stirred in cream and sugar and headed for the sliding glass doors in the adjacent dining room.

Kristen's patio didn't contain many square feet, but it held two chairs with a small table between them. El stepped past the table to the far chair and set her food and drink on the table as she sat. A great sigh accompanied the movement, and something that had been stuck inside her loosened with the sound and location.

"Tell me what's going on," Kristen said, setting her own plate on the table. She retained her coffee mug and lifted it to her lips as she stood at the railing. She owned a ground-floor condo, with rose bushes on the other side of the waist-high fence. They'd be blooming soon, as evidenced by the tightly wound buds El noticed on the ends of the limbs.

Once they were ready, they'd open and show their brilliance to the world. El felt the same way, like she was still wrapped inside something squeezing-tight. But one day, she'd be ready to show the world how much she'd learned and grown.

"What color will the roses be?" she asked.

"Those are this beautiful, yellow-orange color," she said. "They're called tropical sunset."

El nodded and took a bite of her bread. She chewed as the sugar, lemons, and absolute joy filled her mouth. "I love this stuff," she said around the carbs. She swallowed and smiled at the greening lawn in front of her. "Thank you for making it."

"It's a day old," Kristen said. "Don't be too impressed."

"I'm impressed," El said, shooting her a smile. "Here's the deal." She pinched off a piece of her bread, feeling the sponginess of it. "Aaron's ex-wife is in the cove, and she wants to see the girls."

She let the words settle, glad Kristen gave them time and space and silence to breathe. "They were going to do it on Saturday during the luncheon, but Aaron decided he wanted me to meet her first. He took the girls golfing and to Nantucket instead."

Kristen nodded and sipped her coffee. "Are you nervous?"

"Yes," El admitted. She reached up and started to gather her thick hair into a ponytail. "I don't know why, but I am. It's like, I don't even know what she looks like. I don't want to know. Then I'll see all the differences between her and me, or the similarities, and I know Aaron loved her once." She shook her head, her thoughts inside so jumbled and jangling through her ears. "I don't know."

"I know what she looks like," Kristen said quietly. "You do too, El. When you look at Billie, do you see any of Aaron in her?"

"Only in her bull-headed approach to everything," El said, her chest squeezing so tight. Kristen was beyond right. Billie was white-blonde, thin, blue-eyed, sober. Aaron was about the opposite of that.

Grace at least had hazel eyes, with dirty blonde hair.

Because Billie was the older, more responsible sister, Grace was more bubbly and giggly. She skipped most places she went, and El adored her for her happy-go-lucky approach to life.

"Why is Carol in the cove?"

"Something about how she lost her job, and she thought she'd come see the girls, see if there's any opportunities here." Eloise frowned. "I feel like we've been getting that a lot lately. Zach, Clara, even Frank acted like he'd buy Friendship Inn and open it." She scoffed and shook her head. "Can you imagine?"

"I think Alice would blow a gasket."

El smiled, glad Kristen had said it so she didn't have to. "I just keep thinking—what's in the air this year? The inn is fully booked the moment new dates go up. Why are so many people coming to Five Island Cove?" She looked over to Kristen, whose head moved back and forth slowly as she sipped her coffee.

"There's something," she finally said. "I don't know where it'll end up, that's for sure." She met El's eyes. "But Eloise, I do know one thing: You don't have anything to worry about when it comes to Carol. The cove was not for her fifteen years ago, and it won't be now. Aaron loathes her for walking out on her two babies, and I'm surprised he's talking to her at all."

"Just the one time," El said. At least that she knew of, and a flash of when she'd thought Aaron was cheating on her with Laurel stole through her mind. That situation was a dark stain in her thoughts that El couldn't quite get rid of.

"They've only texted since." She inhaled, wishing the roses had bloomed so she could catch their scent.

"I think he feels like Billie and Grace are her children, and he can't keep them from her, though legally, he could. I had Alice check." She gave Kristen a knowing look. "Aaron checks up on things like that. Why can't I?"

Kristen laughed as she reached over and patted Eloise's hand. "You can, dear. Good for you."

El smiled too, feeling lighter now that she'd been fed delicious, sugary carbs and been reassured once more that Aaron wasn't going to go running back to his ex-wife.

"SHE'S RIGHT THERE," AARON SAID A COUPLE OF nights later. He nodded to the right, across El's body and toward a woman walking down the sidewalk. She and Aaron had been parked in this spot outside the best seafood restaurant in the cove for the past twenty minutes.

Aaron knew how nervous and worried Eloise was about his ex-wife being in town and wanting to spend time with the girls. When he'd finally asked her to tell him how he could help, El hadn't kept quiet.

"I want to meet her first," Eloise had said. That had spawned this mid-week dinner with Carol Byson.

"I think we should talk to her before we tell the girls at all," she'd told him. Aaron had gone along with that, and they hadn't told Billie or Grace that their mother was in the cove yet.

"I want to see her before she sees me," El had told him. Aaron, ever the cop he was, had suggested they arrive early to "scope out the situation." Really, he'd brought a bag of shelled pistachios and an extra phone charger for her car. They'd arrived twenty minutes before the arranged meeting time so El could see Carol before they truly met.

Now, she analyzed the woman, trying to get a sense of her true intentions for returning to the cove.

"I never thought I'd see her again," Aaron said. "Especially here."

"She didn't like the cove," Eloise said, not phrasing it as a question.

"No." Aaron's head moved as Carol drew closer to the restaurant entrance on his side of the car. "She wasn't a small-town person."

"How did you get her to agree to live here then?"

"My stunning good looks?" he teased.

El shook her head, though a smile did grace her face. The blonde—white-blonde, just like Billie—opened the door and went inside.

"She'll text within thirty seconds," Aaron said. "She hates waiting."

Who doesn't? El thought, but she kept the words to herself.

"How she lives in the city is beyond me. The crowds and wait-times here are nothing like Manhattan." He'd told Eloise that was where Carol said she'd been living and working. Twelve miles away—just twelve—from her girls. And no cards. No birthday phone calls. No communication at all for almost ten years.

Her reappearance in the cove made zero sense. "She wants something," El said as the woman's back disappeared behind the heavy oak door.

"I thought so too," Aaron said. "I asked her, El. She simply said she'd like to see the girls, if I'll allow it."

Eloise turned her head from the now-closed door and studied her husband. "Where's your head?"

"You know where it is," he said with a sigh.

"I believe in second chances too," El said. "I just don't know about this. Your girls are doing so well."

"They're your girls too."

But they're not, she wanted to argue. They'd already had this talk, actually. In the end, Aaron wouldn't see things her way, and she'd simply stopped trying to make him. He truly did see her as the maternal figure for his girls, something she was happy to be.

"I'll do what you want, Eloise," he said quietly. "I already committed to that. If you don't feel one-hundred-percent good about her seeing Billie and Grace, then she won't. The end. By law, I don't have to let her."

Eloise nodded and pulled in a cleansing breath. Aaron's phone chimed, and his eyebrows drew down. "That's her," he said. "I'll tell her we're running a couple of minutes late and to get a table for three." He did that while Eloise turned her attention out her passenger window.

She wasn't sure what she expected to see there. Maybe a dark sky with ominous clouds to match the way she felt inside at sitting down to an expensive dinner with a woman she didn't know and didn't want to then compare herself to for the rest of her life.

Only blue sky and a rippling American flag met her eyes. The wind on Five Island Cove seemed about as constant as the waves which crashed against the shores of all five islands, and El drew in another long breath.

"If she says she's looking at Friendship Inn," El said. "You have to send out two cops to see if there's a magic spell on that place or something."

Aaron chuckled and lifted her hand to his lips. He kissed her wrist, then each finger. "Deal, my love," he said. "She's not going to buy and open Friendship Inn."

"She better not," El said.

"Are you still thinking about buying it?"

"I am," El admitted. "I just—it's huge. My supervisors are doing well now, so I'm not working so much, and I don't really want to take on more. I don't *need* to."

"Right, but you could just buy it so no one else can," he said. "Maybe that would stop the spell and all these people who haven't come to Five Island Cove in years will stop coming."

El smiled at him, though neither of them truly believed in magic spells. "It's a thought." She reached for the door handle and opened her door. "Let's do this."

The walk into the restaurant took no time at all. El couldn't even feel the ground beneath her feet. Aaron spoke to the woman at the hostess station, and they were promptly led to a booth, not a table.

Carol was watching for them, because the moment Aaron became visible past the fairy-like hostess, she got to her feet. Thus, El stood side-by-side with her husband while he said, "Hello, Carol." He made no move to kiss her cheek, hug her, or even shake her hand. His fingers in El's held tightly. He indicated her. "This is my wife, Eloise. El, this is Carol."

He gave her no qualifier. No "this is the girls' mother." Not even, "this is my ex-wife." Just "this is Carol."

"Hello," Eloise said, extending her hand for Carol to shake as if she were greeting the queen. She'd learned to treat everyone like royalty at the inn, and before that, at the university's fundraising galas, held twice annually. "It's wonderful to meet you." She smiled at Aaron and back at Carol. "You look so much like Billie, it's crazy."

Carol's eyes widened, as if she'd just now realized that Eloise would know Billie and Grace. "Th-thank you?" It sounded like a question, and Eloise enjoyed having the upper hand for a couple of seconds. The feeling didn't really suit her, and it faded quickly.

Carol pumped her hand once and then pulled her fingers back as if El had sticky stuff on hers. "I hope this booth is okay. I know you like booths."

"I prefer a table," Aaron said, examining the booth like it might turn into a serpent and strike at any moment. "I feel too close to the table in a booth."

"Oh, uh..."

"It's fine," Aaron practically barked. "Though I did say to get a table." He squeezed himself onto the bench first, and

Eloise kept her blinding smile in place as she followed him. She hoped he didn't have plans to make a hasty exit, because he couldn't do that stuffed against the wall as he was.

Carol sat down across from them, and El noted her designer handbag. It went well with her pressed slacks, the silk tank top, and the red-soled heels. Everything about her screamed wealth—and not just money. City money.

Why in the world was she here?

She didn't fit in the cove, not even in the nicest restaurant on Diamond Island. Eloise had worn a black denim skirt and a blouse covered with bright butterflies, all without designer labels. She'd never really cared about clothing anyway, and she could barely name the big brands.

Alice would know, though, and El wondered if she should try to get a picture with Carol. *No way*, she decided. They weren't going to become best buddies and start taking selfies together.

Since she was the observant bystander, she said nothing. She picked up the menu while Carol studied Aaron, and Aaron looked for a waiter. "Have you been here before?" Carol asked.

"Not for a while," Aaron said, finally flagging someone down. "We're in a hurry."

El glanced at him, his unrest outpacing hers now. Finally faced with his ex, El could see how much he didn't like her. She reached under the table and put her hand on his leg. Their eyes met, and in that moment, they were one. Unified in their minds and souls.

She put in her drink and food order while Aaron did the

same without even looking at the menu. Carol fumbled, obviously not expecting to have to order so fast. After asking several questions that fueled Aaron's impatience, she finally told the waiter to pick something for her and handed over her menu.

"What are you doing here?" Eloise asked, reaching to unwrap her silverware. "How long do you plan to stay?" She'd already been in the cove a week, if she'd told Aaron the truth about when she'd arrived.

"Just visiting old friends," Carol said, plenty of walls up around herself. Lots of ice in her voice too. "I've stayed longer than I'd like, hoping to see Billie and Grace." She looked pointedly at Aaron.

"I can't help my schedule," he said. "I'm the Chief of Police."

"I know," Carol said. "You never let me forget."

"You said I'd never go anywhere."

"You haven't," she fired back.

Aaron shook his head, and Eloise hadn't expected to get thrown into a battle between the two of them. No wonder Billie argued with her father and knew exactly how to push his buttons. She'd gotten the confidence and tongue from both sets of DNA that ran through her.

"Okay," El said. "Here's the deal. Billie and Grace are doing so amazingly well. We think your...coming back into their lives will be a disruption for them, and we're not sure that's in their best interest."

Carol fixed her cold, penetrating blue eyes on Eloise. "How long have you known them?"

"Well." El placed her napkin on her lap. "Not long, I'll admit. But for Grace, I think I've known her about four months longer than you have." She looked up and right on back at Carol. "And I've been around her when she can speak and do things for herself. So." She shrugged like she wasn't really comparing, when it was obvious she was.

"I vowed I would protect them," Aaron said. "They're my daughters, and I will do whatever I have to in order to keep them safe."

"I'm their mother."

"Who abandoned them in the middle of the day," Aaron said. "There in the morning. Gone by afternoon. Never to be heard from again...until now." He leaned both elbows on the table. "So be honest, Carol. What are you doing here? What do you want?"

The waiter set glasses of soda and water on the table, and El immediately reached for hers. Carol did too. After a long drink, she looked across the table again, her nerves plain now that she'd been called out.

"I lost my job in the city," she said. "I thought there might be opportunities here. Everyone is talking about the growth Five Island Cove can sustain. I thought there might be...healing. I thought there might be something more for me here than what I have in Manhattan."

"Yeah, something for *you*," Aaron said, tossing his straw wrapper to the table. "This isn't about you, Carol."

She started to nod, and El found her agreement a little odd. "Okay, that's fair."

Aaron deflated, and El thought Carol still knew him pretty well.

"Tell me what you want from me so I can see the girls," Carol said. "And I'll do it."

Eloise opened her mouth. "I don't think you should see them alone. They might be afraid. Grace especially, as she doesn't even remember you." She gestured to herself and then Aaron. "One or both of us should be there."

The stabbing glare returned. "Fine," Carol said through clenched teeth.

"I don't think you should see them unless they agree to see you first," Aaron said. "El and I will talk to them tonight when we get home and see what they say. If they have no interest in spending time with you Carol, I'm not going to make them."

Tears filled Carol's eyes, but she blinked, and they vanished. "Okay."

Aaron nodded like this hostage negotiation was now concluded. "Okay." He looked at Eloise, and she suddenly wished they'd agreed to meet for ice cream cones on the beach. If they had, this would be over and done now.

She looked across the table, because she knew she'd be carrying the conversation for the rest of the meal. "So, Carol," she said. "Tell me what you did in Manhattan."

Chapter Twenty-Four

A lice came out of the master bedroom and went down the short hall to the kitchen. Emily stood there, buttering a couple pieces of toast. "Good morning," she said to the teen. "How was last night?"

She reached for the cupboard door to get a mug, not looking directly at Emily. The girl went to therapy a couple of times each week, and sometimes she came home in distress. She had a lot to work through, and Alice could only hope and pray that she was providing the safest environment for Em to heal.

"It was okay," Emily said, her voice quiet. She lifted her head and looked straight at Alice. Alice paused in what she was doing, the moment between her and this girl she'd only known for a year so powerful. "Alice." Her voice cracked, and her face crumpled.

Alice abandoned her quest for caffeine and drew the girl into her chest. "Hey, it's okay," she said. She wanted to tell

Emily that she never had to go home again. She didn't have to see her step-brother. She didn't have to ever be in a situation where she felt unsafe and got abused. The truth was, Alice couldn't really promise any of those things.

Emily wrapped her arms around Alice and held her tight, and Alice's pulse pounded through her whole body. "Thank you," Emily said, her voice tight and tinny. "Being able to come here means so much to me."

Alice pulled away and stroked the girl's hair off her face. "Have you talked to your mother?"

Em nodded and stepped away completely. "Every day," she said, her tone back to normal. "She's working through a lot too, you know?"

"I'm sure she is."

"And I'll be off to college soon anyway," Emily said. "Out of here. Not in the cove." She spoke with hope and conviction, and Alice knew exactly what that felt like inside a person. She'd felt so much the same way when she'd been about to graduate from high school. Like the whole world lay in front of her, and all she had to do was open her hand and grab what she wanted.

She reached for the coffee pot and began to pour herself a mug full of her favorite brew. "How's the job going? Are you working this afternoon?"

"Yeah," Em said. "Four to ten, so I'll be home after that."

"You like it? Randall isn't stopping by, is he?" Alice cut a look out of the corner of her eye, a tactic she'd used with Charlie to gauge his reaction without studying him. He didn't like that, and Em reminded Alice a lot of her son. She didn't want eyes on her. She didn't want judgments made before facts had been given. She didn't want to be questioned a whole lot.

"No," Em said, shaking her head. "Not after that one time, when my manager then called the police."

Alice nodded and said nothing. "Anything on the housing yet?"

Emily had gotten accepted to the State University of New York at Albany, but she'd missed the on-campus housing deadline. Alice had helped her fill out a late application and submit it anyway, complete with an explanation of why. They'd even gotten her therapist to write a letter of recommendation for Em.

"Nothing yet," Emily said. "They said I might not hear until the end of May, and even through the summer as people cancel. So I don't know."

"We might want to start looking at other housing options," Alice said. "Ginny is only going to be a few hours away, in either Boston or the city. It won't be hard to help you move too."

"Where's Charlie going?"

"He got into Boston University," Alice said, reaching for the sugar bowl. She added a tiny spoonful of the stuff. "But honestly, he's paying the tuition anyway, and I think he might go to NYU if he can get in."

Charlie had just told Alice that he'd like to try NYU a couple of weeks ago, and they'd put in an application for the university in New York City. Frank lived there, and Alice had questioned her son mercilessly about his change of heart.

"I haven't had a change of heart, Mom, jeez." There had been plenty of eye-rolling in the four-minute conversation. In the end, Charlie had simply said, "I'm just not sure I want to go to Boston when Ginny's going to the city."

He'd insisted his father had nothing to do with it, and neither did Mandie Glover, who had committed to NYU, something neither one of Alice's children had done. Alice still wasn't so sure about either of those, but she'd dropped the subject.

Alice's phone chimed at the same time Arthur entered the kitchen and footsteps came down the steps. "Mom," Charlie yelled at the same time Arthur said, "We're okay for dinner tonight, right, babe?" He placed a kiss on the back of Alice's neck that sent shivers scattering across her shoulders, and she leaned into the touch.

"Yes," she said as Charlie rounded the corner. She looked at him and found his chest heaving.

"I did it," he said.

"Did what?" she asked as Arthur turned to face him too.

Charlie broadcasted a mixture of emotions, most of which Alice would identify as happiness-panic. What in the world had he done?

"I got into NYU," he said, breathless. "I just got the email." He held up his phone, his smile showing all those straight teeth Alice had paid for.

Her smile filled her face, even as her heart dropped a tiny bit. She'd actually thought it would be good for the twins to be separated. He'd be too late for housing too, and now Alice had another teenager to coach through how to find somewhere to live after they'd missed deadlines.

"That's great," she said anyway. She stepped out of Arthur's arms to embrace her son.

"And that's not even the best part," he said. "I'm not sure if I'm going to go there or not, but I like that I got in."

"It's great," Alice said. "When are you going to decide? You realize you only have six weeks until graduation."

"I know, Mom." He pulled out of her hug. He took her by the shoulders, his dark eyes flashing with sparks and stars. "The best part is, I posted it on social media. You know, the QuickChat? Anyway, Sariah saw it, and she sent me a private message saying she's decided to go to Georgia Tech." He tipped his head back and laughed.

Alice liked seeing him so happy, but she wasn't sure why this particular thing made him so joyous. He'd told her a couple of months ago when he first broke up with her that he didn't want to hurt her.

"Why is she doing that?" Ginny asked. "She hasn't even spoken to you since you broke up with her."

"We have to talk at Olympiad," Charlie said. He hadn't been able to quit the team, because the boy actually had a conscience. "So that's not true."

"So where are you going to go?" Ginny asked, moving past him and into the kitchen. "Morning, Arthur. You can still give me a ride, right?"

"If you're ready in the next five minutes," he said. "I have a counselor's meeting this morning."

"I'm ready now." Ginny pulled her ready-made lunch out of the fridge and hitched her backpack up on her shoulder. She faced Charlie, her eyebrows up, her question getting asked again, silently this time.

"Where are *you* going?" Charlie threw back at her. "I'm not the only undecided one around here."

Ginny flicked a glance in Alice's direction, and she stood shoulder-to-shoulder with Charlie, because she'd been asking her daughter which college she'd be going to for months. The girl had never been terribly indecisive, but she sure hadn't been able to make any solid decisions about this.

"It feels so final," Ginny had told her one evening, when it was just the two of them out on the patio. "What if I make the wrong choice?"

Alice had told her that lots of people transferred universities all the time. Things changed, and Ginny could change with them.

Ginny raised her chin as Arthur paused at her side. Alice could only see the side of his face, but she saw his mouth move as he said something to her daughter. Ginny looked at him and nodded. "I'm going to NYU. I sent the acceptance last week. Finalized my apartment and everything."

Alice's eyes rounded; her stomach dropped to the soles of her feet. "Why didn't you tell me?"

She looked at Emily, who stood benignly out of the way. "You've been busy, Mom, and I know how to do things."

Alice strode toward her, fire shooting from her core out to her extremities.

"Don't be mad," Ginny said.

"I'm mad," Alice said. "In the garage for two minutes, please."

Ginny turned and went down the hall past the laundry room and out into the garage. "Mom," she said over her shoulder. "I can handle it. Isn't that what I'm going to have to do in New York? Handle things? I'm an adult."

Alice stopped next to Arthur. "What did you say to her?"

"She's been dropping by my office lately," he said. "Running things by me. She didn't want you to know or worry about anything."

Alice wasn't sure how to feel. Something pinched inside her, and she didn't know if she should be relieved that Ginny trusted and liked Arthur enough to go to him, or allow the betrayal to slide through her that her daughter hadn't involved her. She'd never liked being left out, especially when it came to the twins.

They had such a tight bond, and Alice had never been on the inside of it.

"I want to talk to you too," she said.

"I told her you'd react like this." Arthur grinned at her, not worried about their talk at all. "Go easy on her. She's trying to do the right thing."

Alice grunted and continued into the garage. "You have another week until you're an adult," Alice said, letting the door slam behind her. "For your information."

"I know when my birthday is." Ginny cocked her hip and faced Alice head-on. "This isn't a big deal."

"Why would you tell Arthur and not me?" She hooked her thumb over her shoulder. "I'm your mother."

"You've been very busy," Ginny said. "Which I don't blame you for. You always give great advice, and I have told you lots of things. I'm just...feeling my way through making my own decisions and then telling someone who doesn't ask me any questions about them. Just goes, 'Okay, Ginny, sounds good to me. Do you feel good about it?'"

Alice took a breath and let her daughter's words sink into her brain. "Do I ask too many questions?"

"No," Ginny said with a sigh. "Arthur is really good at listening, Mom. That's all. He's neutral. You're not. You try to be, but you're not."

"This doesn't have anything to do with Emily, does it?" Alice asked. "I've been trying to be present for all three of you." Arthur too, but Alice felt stretched thin. She had friends to worry about too, and sometimes there wasn't enough time or energy to go around appropriately.

"You've been doing great," Ginny said, tears appearing in her eyes that made no sense to Alice. "You've been amazing for Emily. She's so different already. She needs you, and I knew I didn't for a little while. Really, Mom. It's not a big deal."

Alice took a few steps and gathered her daughter into a hug. "I love you, Ginny-Girl."

"I love you too, Mom." Ginny's voice broke. "I liked making the decision on my own. It's nice to feel grown-up."

Alice stepped back and examined her face. They smiled simultaneously. "It is, isn't it?"

"Alice," Arthur said as he came out of the house. "Your phone has rung twice. It's Robin." He held up her device, and Alice took it from him. "We have to go, Ginny. We're good?"

"We're good," Ginny said, and Alice watched the two of them get into Arthur's car. He paused as he started to duck down.

"Oh, and your son made a beeline for the front door the first time Robin called. I'm guessing with my counseling degree that he's got something to do with her calling twice —" He cut off and grinned as Alice's phone shrieked again. "Three times in the past three minutes."

Alice sighed and pressed two fingers to her lips for her husband. Then she turned away and answered Robin's call.

"Did you know that Charlie asked Mandie to the prom?" Robin demanded without bothering with a hello.

Alice pressed her eyes closed, her patience and will to push her will onto her children already gone for the day. "No," she said, moving to the mouth of the garage. Arthur and Ginny trundled away, and sure enough, the car the twins shared was gone from the curb in front of the house. "He didn't mention that."

"So you don't know what's going on with them."

"No," Alice said. "I'll be honest, Robin. I'm losing control of everything over here." She leaned against the wall and looked up and down the street at her sleepy neighborhood. She wondered if the other parents who lived in the cove had the same issues with their seniors as she did.

"And I kinda like it," she added, just before she started laughing.

Robin stayed silent on the other end of the line until Alice finished giggling. Then she said, "I'm bringing lunch today. Don't argue with me."

"No argument here," Alice said. She didn't have it inside her anyway. If Robin wanted to bring lunch and talk about why their children couldn't date, Alice would let her. The truth was, Charlie and Ginny were going to be eighteen next week. Mandie already was.

They could do whatever they wanted, and nothing Robin or Alice said was going to change that.

Alice wasn't sure why or how, but she felt a certain... freedom at knowing that she didn't have to control everything anymore. And freedom felt wonderful.

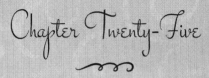

Chapter Twenty-Five

AJ took Asher from her sister, Amy, giving her a smile. "I can take him. He's just not happy right now." She gave her son a kiss, wondering if there was anything else she could do for the boy to help him feel better. "I gave him some of the painkiller already."

Asher settled down and curled himself into AJ's chest. Her heart tore, and she questioned whether she was doing the right thing. She faced the lighthouse, where she and Amy had already arrived.

Before she could back out completely, her sister took the first step up the sidewalk toward the door. *Wait*, AJ said in her head. She hadn't left Asher with anyone but Matt, and she wasn't sure she was ready.

He's nine months old, she told herself. *You're ready. He's ready. It's Jean.* And there was no one better with kids than Jean.

The blue door opened, and Kelli exited, her face brightening when she saw Amy walking toward her. A quick, thick piece of plastic went up between AJ and the other two women, and all she could do was watch while they greeted one another and embraced.

She hadn't realized that having a baby would limit her so much, and AJ hated feeling that way. She pushed the thought away, determined not to feel like that. Asher did not limit her. She loved him, and she adored this new phase of her life. She was still figuring things out, that was all.

"AJ," Kelli said, and the wall between them broke. Kelli had always been exceptionally good at breaking through AJ's dangerous thoughts, and she grinned and took Asher as she started to coo at him.

To AJ's surprise, Asher flailed his arms and laughed at Kelli. Actually laughed. She drew in another big breath and blew another raspberry against Asher's neck. His giggles filled the entire sky, and AJ's heart might burst from his joy.

Kelli turned and went back up the sidewalk without AJ or Amy. Her sister linked her arm through AJ's and they faced the lighthouse and watched as Kelli reached for the doorknob. "He's going to be fine," Amy said. "This is going to be an amazing day for you, AvaJane."

"I know," she murmured, though she didn't. She had faith that Asher would be fine, and she wanted to go shopping and to lunch without a diaper bag or stroller. She didn't want things to be cut short because Asher needed a nap, or she needed to get home and get him new clothes because he'd soiled the ones he was in.

She turned away from the blue door as it closed behind

Kelli and Asher, and AJ walked along the sidewalk toward the end of the parking lot. A flagpole stood there, the red, white, and blue flying proudly in the breeze. Beyond that, only ocean existed, with white spray shooting up every once in a while if a powerful wave crashed against the rocks and cliffs below the lighthouse.

Amy followed her, and the two of them stood on the edge of the world. AJ had felt like this before—hovering on a precipice, with so many horizons in front of her. She'd been headstrong as a child and teenager, and she'd had to grow up so fast after her mother had abandoned them.

"Have you spoken to Ryan?" she asked. "He texted me a couple of days ago. He's bringing his new girlfriend to the cove this summer."

"He mentioned it," Amy said. "Yeah. A couple of days ago. Her name is Lindsey."

"Oh, I didn't get the name." AJ glanced at Amy. "Ryan and I are...still figuring out how we fit."

"You fit with us," Amy assured her. "Me, the girls, Donovan. Ryan too."

"It's a long way to the West Coast," AJ said. "I don't know how to talk to him."

"He needs us," Amy said. "He's never allowed a woman into his life because of the FBI. He *likes* her, AJ. Like, a lot."

AJ nodded. "I'm not even sure what Ryan does for the FBI."

"He's a special investigator out of LA." Amy pushed her hair back and exhaled. "He can't talk about his job, and think about what you and Matt talk about the most."

"The golf course," AJ said with a smile. "His father is getting ready to sign it over to Matt and retire. We think it'll happen in the next couple of months."

"That's great, AJ," Amy said, and when Amy spoke, she meant things. She didn't just give compliments or accolades or congratulations falsely. "I swear, all I talk about are the customers that come into the bank."

"I'm telling you," AJ said. "You should write a book about some of the characters Donovan comes in contact with. Like that woman who went into the vault and cut off a lock of her hair?" AJ grinned at the white-tipped waves steadily approaching the cliffs. "That's a murder-mystery waiting to happen."

Amy laughed, just as AJ had hoped she would. "I'm going to do that, just as soon as I get out of the PTA commitment I've gotten myself into."

"A few more weeks," AJ said, exhaling too. "I can't wait for summer. Everything seems so much easier in the summer."

"It does, doesn't it?"

They both turned when Kelli called them, and AJ raised her hand and said, "Over here, Kel."

Kelli turned toward them and walked along the sidewalk as Amy and AJ put their backs to the ocean. "He adores Jean," she said. "Went to her as if she were the Pied Piper. It helped that she had a plate of pumpkin cookies waiting for him."

"He'll be fine," AJ said, vocalizing what she wanted to have happen, even if she didn't believe it yet.

Kelli's phone buzzed, and she dropped it. The device cracked against the sidewalk and flipped over, the screen facing upward. Kelli groaned and started to bend toward the cellphone. AJ's eyes moved faster than Kelli's body, and she saw the huge name and picture of the ginger-haired man on the screen.

Without thinking, she put her foot over the phone—right over Zach Watkins' face. "Kelli," she said, her voice made mostly of horror and air.

With AJ's foot over the phone, Kelli couldn't pick it up, and she straightened and looked AJ in the eyes. AJ searched, trying to find the reason Zach—a man who had threatened Kelli and her mother in the past—would be *calling* her now.

Kelli was very good at hiding things, and she'd grown stronger in the past couple of years. AJ couldn't read her expression, and she squinted as if that would help. "Why is he calling you?"

Kelli swallowed, her determination and strength shining through her bright blue eyes. "Because I told him to let me know when he had news about his mother."

AJ's mind raced, trying to make pieces line up. "His mother? What do you mean? His mother is dead." She didn't mean to speak harshly, but Zach had told Kelli and the other women in the cove so many lies. Lies they'd uncovered as such, right before Zach had turned dangerous.

"Not technically," Kelli said. "Yes, he told a lot of lies, but we've been texting a little bit."

"I'm picking up this phone," AJ said. She did, managing to keep her eyes on Kelli for most of the bend down. She retrieved the phone and started swiping on it. "It's not even cracked."

Kelli had been doing more than "a little bit" of texting with Zach. The string went on and on, with many texts dating back several weeks.

AJ looked up, having no time or brain space to read them all. "Kelli." She handed the phone back to her best friend, who stuffed it in her back pocket. She didn't have to ask anything else.

"He's not a bad guy," Kelli said. "He's alone in the world, AJ. You know how that feels."

"He's actually not," AJ said, folding her arms. "He has two sisters and an aunt." She cocked her head, wondering if Kelli was really this naïve. "And apparently a mother who's still alive."

"He's apologized for everything. He's been working at a studio in New Hampshire and Vermont. He doesn't ask for money. He doesn't ask for anything."

"You're not related."

"I know that, AJ." Kelli turned away from her and marched down the sidewalk. "Are we still shopping? I have to meet Shad at four."

AJ stared at her retreating back, the fight leaving her. She glanced at Amy, who also wore a look of concern. She knew about Zach Watkins and what had happened a couple of summers ago.

"Four o'clock is like six hours from now," Amy murmured, and somehow that made AJ smile.

"Yeah," she said. "Kelli doesn't want to talk about this,

and I know Kelli. If she doesn't want to talk, no one is going to make her."

"Not even Robin?" Amy asked as the two sisters stepped in tandem. "Maybe we could call her and ask her to meet us for lunch. New Truth or Tell-All or Spill the Beans or whatever you guys call it."

AJ laughed, because calling Robin to get the story out of Kelli struck her funny bone. Kelli turned around, her frown etched between her eyes.

"We're not going to call Robin," AJ said, still smiling. She stepped right into Kelli and hugged her. "If you want to talk to him, fine. But you'll tell me if something goes sideways, won't you?"

"Yes," Kelli said, her arms coming around AJ much slower. They held one another for a couple of seconds, and then AJ moved back. "Thank you, AJ."

"Right," AJ said. "Amy's driving. I'm shotgun, and we're not talking about Zach. Those are the rules for today." She reached past Kelli to open the passenger door. "Oh, and Matt gave me the platinum card, so let's go shopping, ladies." She grinned at her sister and then Kelli, who gave her the most brilliant smile in return.

She could get answers the same as Robin could, just in a different way, and AJ's brain fired at her for possible ways to do that over the next six hours.

A WEEK LATER, AJ BLEW OUT HER HAIR, MAKING IT as straight as possible. She'd put on her professional, reporter-makeup and her nicest summery clothes. After all, it wasn't every weekend that Ryan returned to the cove, and especially not with his "very serious girlfriend."

The summer had come faster for him, apparently, than it reached the cove. Lindsey didn't have any children, and they didn't have to wait for school to get out. Ryan had vacation to take, and it turned out that now was the best time for him to be gone from his field office in California.

AJ didn't mind; she didn't have anything else taking her time, and she was excited to spend time with her dad and both of her siblings, as well as all of their significant others.

She'd been out to Pearl Island plenty of times with Matt, but somehow leaving the house with Asher was harder than she'd anticipated. She communicated with her father regularly, and she expected him to have an entire seafood feast prepared by the time she and Matt arrived at his house.

She switched off the hair dryer and let her hair fall, liking the way it landed like silk over her shoulders. Satisfied with her hair, she moved onto her makeup, then her clothes. She walked out into the kitchen to find Matt dressed in his khaki shorts and bright blue polo, with Asher playing on the floor in his diaper.

"Wow," Matt said, sweeping her into his arms. He swayed with her, the two of them smiling in the small space between them. "Dance with me for a minute."

Beside their feet, Asher banged a plastic measuring cup against the tile, but AJ let her eyes drift closed. She took a deep breath of her husband's cologne, a sense of belonging and love filling her. She tilted her head back, and Matt touched his lips to hers. "You're an amazing woman," he whispered after their initial kiss.

He slid his lips along her neck. "I like this skirt." He slipped his hand in her back pocket of the denim skirt and pulled her flush against him.

"Babe," she said. "We have to leave in ten minutes, and our son isn't dressed."

"Mm." Matt kissed her again, and AJ lost herself to his touch, the heat of their relationship filling her bloodstream with the promise of more to come later.

Then she pulled away, bent to scoop Asher into her arms, and said, "Come on, bud. Let's go get you in your romper so you can meet Uncle Ryan." She gave Matt a look she hoped conveyed that she'd like to pick up this "conversation" later and went back down the hall to get her boy ready for the day.

An hour later, AJ followed Matt, who carried Asher in his arms, up to her father's front porch. Music lifted into the air from behind the closed front door, and an unspoken excitement filled AJ. "Just go in," she told Matt as he raised his hand to knock.

Since he was already in the motion of knocking, he did a couple of times, and then twisted the knob to enter. The music volume went up, and Matt didn't go far into the house. AJ pressed in beside him to see her father dancing with Mary and Darcy, Amy's two girls.

All three of them wore huge smiles, and when her father

looked toward the now-open front door, his face only got brighter. "Hey," he yelled above the music. "Get that, Darce."

The nine-year-old moved over to the retro record player and lifted the needle. The music scratched to a halt, and AJ needed another moment to soak in her father in this new way. He was so different from the man her memory conjured up from the past, and she was still working on replacing the drunk, didn't-care father with this new version of the man who deeply loved his children and grandchildren.

"Heya, Ashy," he said, taking the little boy from Matt. "Good to see you, Matt." Her dad hugged Matt, and then her husband stepped out of the way so AJ could embrace her father. She did, feeling the tension and strength with which her father held her.

"Thanks for coming, AJ."

"Yeah, of course," she said. "Where's Amy and Donovan?"

"Out on the deck," he said. "Ryan texted to say they'd just landed. They'll be on the next ferry." He danced away with his grandson, though the music had been turned off.

"Should I turn it back on, Grandpa?" Darcy asked, and Dad nodded at her. The music blared through the house again, and Matt grabbed onto AJ and they joined the dance party. She laughed and moved in time with her husband, letting the moment fill her entire existence.

Before she knew it, Amy and Donovan had come back inside and squashed the dance party. Food started getting pulled out, and Amy put everyone to work to get the meal on the table at the same time Ryan was set to arrive.

AJ wanted to tell her that maybe their brother would like a moment to introduce his girlfriend, who was practically his fiancée, instead of being thrown right into eating. She said nothing, though, and then the doorbell rang.

Everyone turned toward it at the same time, and Dad had taken two steps toward it, as it was his house, when the door opened. AJ's tall, handsome, happy brother entered, one hand behind him as he brought a woman with him.

Ryan's face broke into a smile and he dropped Lindsey's hand to hug Dad. He wore black slacks and a collared, short-sleeved shirt with blue and white checks on it. Very posh. Very FBI.

Behind him, Lindsey wore a black pencil skirt, ballet flats, and a blouse the color of AJ's blush. Her face contained a smile as she watched Ryan hug Dad, and AJ recognized her adoration of Ryan instantly.

"Oh, boy," Amy whispered as she linked her arm through AJ's. "She's in love with him."

"Yeah." AJ couldn't look away from the woman behind her brother. She obviously had money, and she seemed as polished and ready to meet Ryan's family as AJ was to meet her.

Ryan stepped back from Dad and immediately reached for Lindsey. Oh, he was in love with her too. AJ's heart warmed, and tears pricked her eyes. She sighed, and Amy did too, which meant she'd seen the softness in their usually-stern and very business-like brother.

"This is Lindsey Morford," Ryan said, and AJ started toward him. "My dad, Wayne Proctor." He looked past Dad to AJ and Amy. "My oldest sister, AvaJane. My youngest sister, Amelia." He nodded at them, and AJ moved right past her father and embraced Ryan.

They laughed together, and when he released her to hug Amy, AJ stepped right into Lindsey. "It's so great to meet you. It's a long haul here."

"Yes," Lindsey said. "I told Ryan it was a good thing we stayed in New York last night. I don't think the trip can be made in one day."

"From here to there, it can," Amy said, replacing AJ to hug Lindsey. "But not when you lose three hours of time."

Ryan took Lindsey's hand once all the hugging had ended, and he grinned around at everyone. "Where's my new nephew?" He scanned the house, and Matt wasn't hard to find. Ryan went to introduce Lindsey to Donovan and Matt, Darcy, Mary, and Asher, and AJ wondered whose family she'd fallen into.

She'd never in a million years imagined this scene at the Proctor household. She had the distinct thought that her mother sure was missing out on the best things in life, and that was when AJ realized how very important the concept of family was to her personally. She'd lived so long without that concept as a reality in her life, and now that she had a taste of it, she didn't want to ever be without it again.

"So, what's with Friendship Inn?" Ryan asked, and AJ perked up.

"We're eating first," Amy said. "Talking during lunch."

"Yeah," Lindsey said, grinning at Ryan. "We're starving."

AJ noticed the plural usage of *we*, but she wasn't sure what that was about.

"So I can't ask what's going on with that inn and island while I fill a plate with lobster?" He picked up a plate and put a lobster tail on it. "These look great, Dad, by the way."

"Thanks," Dad said, and Ryan kept on talking.

"I see it's for sale. Have you seen a lot of movement on it?" He looked at AJ, as if she should and would know the commercial real estate market in Five Island Cove.

"I have no idea," AJ said, though she knew several people had come to the cove to look at the property. People who she'd never thought would come to the cove or return to it. "Why? What do you know about it?"

"Nothing," Ryan said, his eyes falling back to the food.

"He's such a liar," Amy said. "You'd think an FBI agent would hide his deceit better."

Ryan laughed and shook his head. It did AJ's heart good to see him so happy, and she suspected that had a lot to do with the blonde woman only a half-step behind him in line, filling her plate with food.

"He looked up the inn at the hotel last night," Lindsey said. "Using his secret search database."

"There's no secret search database," Ryan said, rolling his eyes.

Lindsey cocked her head at him and then tossed a dry look to AJ. They shared a smile, and AJ sure did like her already. "There is. But whatever. He said it's rumored to have—what was it?"

"Treasure," Ryan said. "In one of the one-hundred-and-fifteen rooms." His eyes held delight. "It's a hoax, of course, but there were quite a few stories on it online that I could find."

"Online," Lindsey teased.

AJ giggled too, but her mind spun. If that was true—if there were speculative stories about treasure in one of the rooms at Friendship Inn—that would explain why Zach Watkins had an interest in it. It would explain why Clara had come to the cove and looked at the property.

Frank Kelton, and Carol Byson, Aaron's ex-wife. All of them had come to the cove in the past few months, and they'd all expressed some interest in Friendship Inn.

None of them had bought it though, and AJ didn't know why.

But Kelli was texting Zach. Perhaps she could ask.

Alice could ask Frank, and Aaron could ask Carol. And Clara would be returning to the cove any day now...

AJ filed away this new information as the conversation turned to something else, as she filled her plate with good food, and as she enjoyed her family.

She'd come back to this treasure idea at Friendship Inn later.

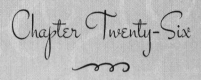

Chapter Twenty-Six

Jean pulled into the parking lot at her mother-in-law's condo, immediately spotting Clara, as well as her niece, Lena. A smile touched her face and her soul, because Lena was a sweet girl with plenty of exuberance and charm.

The moment Jean rose from the car, Lena yelled and started running toward her as quickly as she could move. Jean abandoned her quest to get out the breakfast casserole she'd labored over the previous evening and stepped around the still-open car door to receive Lena.

"Aunt Jean," the girl said, hardly a slur in the words at all. She grabbed onto Jean and squeezed her too tightly. Jean went with it, holding the twenty-year-old as tightly as she could too. She stood a couple of inches shorter than Lena, and she only weighed half as much.

They laughed together all the same, and Jean stepped back and smoothed Lena's hair back. "You colored your hair." She held onto a piece of it, noting how very blonde it was.

"Yeah," Lena said, her smile so contagious. "My mom doesn't like it." She leaned in closer as if she and Jean would share a secret, but she didn't bother to drop her voice. Jean wasn't sure Lena knew how to whisper anyway.

Jean giggled and shook her head. "Where's your grandma?" She looked past Lena to where Clara stood on the lawn, pacing with her phone to her ear. She met Jean's eyes, and something unspoken moved between them.

She looked at Lena again. "How's the grocery store? Is that Todd boy still flirting with you?" With a grin on her face, she turned back to the car to get breakfast.

"Todd, pshaw," Lena said, and Jean was glad she'd gotten out of spitting distance. "He quit anyway."

"He did?" Jean straightened with the half-baked casserole in her hands. "Let's go in and put this in the oven." They started toward the condo, passing Clara, who turned her back toward them as they went by, and Jean kept asking Lena questions about her church group, her job, and what hats she'd been knitting lately.

"Wait till you see," Lena said, almost knocking down the door when she twisted the knob to enter the condo, but didn't quite unlatch it. She got the job done and went inside, and Kristen stepped out of her galley kitchen wearing a bright blue hat on her head.

"Grandma!" Lena shouted, racing toward her. She turned back to Jean, her joy the fullest a person could express. "Look at hers. She's wearing it."

"Yes, I see it," Jean said, returning Lena's enthusiasm. "It's so bright." The loops were only a little loose, because Lena had definitely improved. Part of her occupational therapy was working on something to help her focus her fine-motor skills. Her fingers were fat and clumsy, and the fact that she could hold knitting needles at all was impressive.

She'd been working on winter hats and yarn for a couple of years now, as Clara had been complaining about the yarn scraps and cost for at least that long.

"I have one for you," Lena said, brushing past Kristen and hurrying down the hall.

"Good morning," Jean said, offering a smile to Kristen. "How did things go last night?"

"Easy," Kristen said, though Jean had a suspicion she was lying. She didn't look too exhausted yet, and everyone on the group text had told her to come to their house, day or night, should she need a break from her daughter.

Jean loved Clara, as much as a person could. Clara possessed a special spirit, and she wasn't everyone's cup of tea. Her last visit to the cove had nearly broken Jean, but in the end, Jean actually felt stronger in a lot of ways. She hadn't snapped. She hadn't cried. She'd endured, and she'd learned a lot in the past several months about what that actually meant.

Endurance.

"I just need an oven at three-fifty," she said, slightly lifting the glass casserole dish. "And twenty more minutes. Then breakfast will be ready."

"Thank you so much." The relief in Kristen's voice could've reached mountaintops. "Lena will love it." Her eyes migrated to the sliding glass door and outside, though Clara couldn't be seen. "Clara won't touch it."

"I'm aware of Clara's eating habits." Jean approached Kristen and squeezed past her and into the kitchen. "Did she bring her protein bars and insist she doesn't need anything else?"

"About that, yes," Kristen said. "Then she called in an order at ten-thirty last night."

Jean caught the end of her head shake before she opened the oven and slid the dish inside. The digital display said it was preheated properly, and a flash of love moved through Jean. She faced Kristen, and her first instinct was to step into a hug with the older woman.

She did, glad when Kristen exhaled and held her in return. "Thank you for being such a great support to me," Jean whispered. "These last few months—even the past couple of years—haven't been easy for me. I'm sure I drove you crazy too."

"Not at all, dear," Kristen said, her voice strained.

"It's pink," Lena announced, and Jean opened her eyes to see the girl holding up the hat triumphantly. Though she only stood a few feet away, Jean could see the hat would be far too big.

Still, she beamed as if she'd swallowed four suns and reached for it. "Wow, Lena," she said. "Thank you so much." She pulled the hat onto her hair, tucking all of her dark hair up underneath it and still finding it loose.

"Let me help you," Kristen said. "With this here in the back."

"Is it too big?" Lena asked.

"Only a little," Jean said.

"Not at all," Kristen said, and she pulled the hat tight around Jean's head and pinned it expertly. "See?"

Jean hadn't seen her open a drawer or find a pin, but she'd done something to secure the hat. Lena smiled and smiled, and Jean could only reciprocate the gesture.

"So who else is interesting at work?" Jean asked, adjusting her hat. "And do you have one of these for Uncle Rueben? He's coming out to the island with us, and I know he'll want one."

"His is black," Lena said, her voice so loud in the small space. "I'll get it."

"Leave it for a minute," Jean said, stepping over to Lena and putting her arm around her. "Tell me who's interesting at work. I know there's a new boy there. Tyler? Or was it Teddy?"

"Tyler is *so* cute," Lena said as Jean led her to the couch in the living room. "But don't tell my mom. She doesn't like him."

"Oh?" That made Jean want to find out more about this Tyler boy. "Why not?"

"She thinks he's too old for me." Lena made a scoffing, slurping nose. "He's twenty-six."

"He goes to Lena's church group too," Kristen said, smiling at her granddaughter as she sat in the recliner that faced the couch.

Jean's eyebrows went up. "He does now? That's exciting. Are you going to ask him out?"

"No." Lena rolled her eyes. "Girls don't ask out boys, Aunt Jean."

"Oh, Lena," Jean said with a laugh. "I think they do now. You might want to up your game, or someone else is going to snatch him up."

"Snatch who up?" Clara asked. "You better not be telling Aunt Jean about Tyler." She put her hands on her hips, her dark eyes shooting fire at her daughter.

"I asked her," Jean said, smiling at Clara. "Twenty-six is quite a bit older than twenty."

"Too old," Clara said, her voice lifting up a little in both volume and pitch. She took a seat in the remaining recliner, her sigh the kind legends were born from. "They're expecting us at one-thirty."

"Out on Friendship Island?" Jean asked, her pulse picking up its beat.

Clara closed her eyes and nodded. "She said the price is negotiable."

"Yes, because it's been on the market for five months," Kristen said. "She'll have to budge if she truly wants to sell it."

Jean swallowed and kept her voice silent. She couldn't believe Clara even wanted to purchase the inn. All those rooms. All that responsibility. She worked now but running a dentist's office with a single dentist and a pair of hygienists was hardly the same as taking on a resort-style property with dozens upon dozens of moving parts.

And Lena? What would she do out on Friendship Island? There weren't any grocery stores there. No other restaurants of any kind. There was the inn, period. Jean wasn't even sure Clara would be able to get people to make the journey out there.

Every angle Jean examined told her this move Clara was considering was the wrong one. She'd never say so, however, and she jumped to her feet when the timer went off in the kitchen. "That's the casserole."

"I'm starved," Lena called after her, and Jean promised her she'd bring her some of the eggy, bready, sausagey breakfast casserole the moment she could. The tops of the bread cubes that had been sticking out were brown and crisp, and the egg mixture only jiggled slightly as Jean moved the pan.

She put it on the stovetop and canceled the temperature on the oven. "It's ready," she called. "Kristen? Clara?"

"Yes, please." Kristen came into the kitchen as Clara said, "No, thank you, Jean. I have a protein bar."

She met Kristen's eye, and they both burst into giggles at the same time.

"SHE'S RIGHT THERE," CLARA SAID THE MOMENT she disembarked from the boat that had brought the five of them from Sanctuary Island to Friendship Island. Another woman strode toward them, wearing the brightest, gaudiest red skirt suit that Jean had ever seen. She had no idea manufacturers even made fabric that color, and she'd spent time in

New York City's biggest fabric stores. She'd sewn hundreds of items, and that skirt suit should be burned and the ashes buried immediately.

"Clara," the woman said, her voice one out of New Jersey. Jean had grown up in the East, and she knew a woman from New Jersey when she heard one. Not only that, but the woman had hawk-like eyes that drank in everyone behind Clara—Reuben and Jean, Kristen and Lena —as if she might devour them for dinner.

"Hello, Mimi," Clara said, embracing the woman as if they were high-society friends. She stepped to her side, still facing the long building that was Friendship Inn. With another sigh made of bricks and the disappointments of the world, she turned back to the group. "This is my brother and his wife. Rueben and Jean."

Rueben, ever the cool and non-contentious one, stepped forward with a smile and a handshake for Mimi. Jean did the same as Clara said, "My mother and my daughter, Kristen and Lena." She turned back to the inn as Kristen said hello and prompted Lena to do the same.

"What are we looking at?" Clara asked, and Jean shielded her eyes to see the inn better. At one-thirty in the afternoon, the sun certainly wasn't doing them any favors. A set of scaffolding had been erected on the far end of the inn to Jean's left, and she could easily see what she was looking at.

They were cleaning the inn's exterior. That, or repainting. At the lighthouse, Rueben set up scaffolding like that when he whitewashed the exterior, and the last time they'd done it, he'd only power washed it, no paint needed.

"We're cleaning the exterior," Mimi said. "We've gotten a lot of interest, and a lot of feedback, so we're acting on some of that."

"Like the carpet in the lobby?" Clara asked, her tone filled with sharp points.

"They're considering a carpet allowance, actually," Mimi said. "Come see a few of the improvements."

"Is the owner here?" Clara asked.

"Yes," Mimi said. "But she doesn't want to be in the way. She also doesn't want to meet the potential buyers." She gave Clara a look that told Jean they'd had this conversation before. Clara pursed her lips, obviously unhappy about this news.

"I just want to ask her a few questions."

"That's why you brought your family," Mimi said smoothly. "To help you see things you're overlooking. To help you ask the questions you're not asking." She started back toward the inn, the sidewalk at their feet, which led from the dock right to the entrance of Friendship Inn, a bit crumbly.

The sea water had a way of working its way into every crack and making them bigger. So many things needed to be done, and everywhere Jean looked, she saw work. Just hours and days and weeks of work.

She told herself she didn't have to fix up and operate this inn, and she took Rueben's hand in hers and looked up and into his eyes. "Let's go see what she sees," she said, and Reuben nodded.

He squeezed her hand and bent his head toward hers as

Kristen and Lena followed Clara and Mimi. "I brought a date here once. They used to have Saturday night dances and this great food truck that served waffles day or night."

"Oh?" Jean asked, a smile infusing into her soul again. "I think you tried to impress me with waffles on one of our first dates."

"They've never let me down," Reuben said with a hint of pride in the words.

Jean laughed, glad when Reuben released her hand and tucked her into his side instead. He placed a kiss to her forehead, a silent proclamation of his love for her. She blinked and saw herself crying on the bathroom floor, Reuben telling her she was enough for him.

She was in such a different place now, and she believed him with her whole heart. Nothing could make her want to be without him, and her heart pinched for the situation Clara found herself in.

And her nose wrinkled when she reached the door and smelled the half-sour, half-musty odor rushing out of the inn. Reuben actually coughed, and they both hesitated before they stepped into the jaws of Friendship Inn.

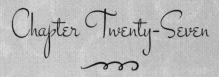
C lara Tanner ran the tip of her thumb down her fourth finger, searching for the thin band of gold she'd worn for so long.

It wasn't there.

Disappointment and unhappiness ran through her, about as strongly as the stench pouring through the lobby of Friendship Inn.

"The smell is worse," she said, flicking a glance in Mimi's direction. She hardly ever looked anyone in the eye. If she did, they might be able to see how very fragile she was. She might accidentally broadcast her insecurities.

Her stomach grumbled about her dietary choices—a single protein bar for breakfast and then a diet cola for lunch. Eating had been terribly difficult since Scott had come home and said he needed to resign.

"Resign?" Clara had asked, truly looking her husband in the eyes. "Why?"

Her husband had actually hung his head and cried. Then the whole story had come out, including how he'd been helping his boss siphon money from clients. The FBI was involved. He had to go in for a deposition.

The interviews had been exhausting and terrifying. She'd watched Scott step in front of Lena and demand police officers leave their home. They'd answered all of their questions in the station, without Lena there. Doing so had been extremely difficult, and Clara couldn't remember the last full night of sleep she'd enjoyed.

Even here, in the cove at her mother's, she hadn't been able to truly find rest. Scott had given all the details he knew, and that alone had saved him from prison. His boss was currently in jail, largely because of Scott's testimony, and Clara pressed her eyes closed and breathed in through her nose.

"Are you okay, dear?" Kristen asked, her hand landing on Clara's forearm.

Her eyes snapped open, eradicating all of the things that had happened in the past six months. Vermont felt so very far away from the cove, and her throat narrowed. Her lips trembled, because she needed to tell her mother the real reason she wanted to come back to Five Island Cove.

"Yes," she said, swallowing back the admission. She'd tell her soon, just not right now.

"Mimi said they're ripping out some of the moldy walls, and that's why the smell has increased." Her mother's eyes shone with emotion, and Clara turned away. Her mom had already seen too much.

She edged up closer to Mimi, the loud, colorful realtor who'd been trying to sell this inn for months. Clara didn't want anything to do with Friendship Inn, but she'd left Monarch Dental a few weeks ago. Neither she nor Scott now had income coming in, and someone needed to make a move.

Everything inside her cinched tight. Without a job, how could she and Scott even hope to qualify for a loan? She pressed her teeth together, thinking about real estate prices in the cove. They'd likely be able to sell their home in Vermont, though the market wasn't exactly booming for sellers. Their property might sit for a few months, and Clara hadn't listed it for sale yet.

Sometimes just making it through the day with all of Montpelier's eyes on her was hard enough. Seeing Scott's picture on the news could send her back to bed for the whole day. Reading another article about "one of the biggest scams in investment history" brought tears to her eyes that would stay all day long.

She breathed in through her nose, which was a huge mistake. She'd spent a while on the phone with Scott this morning, explaining to him that this inn was not worth their time. She pulled out her phone and started snapping pictures so he could see that this place simply needed to be condemned.

"The owner has reduced the price," Mimi said.

Clara turned away from the inner workings of a wall in an inn, not even sure what she'd just taken a picture of.

"It's down to eight-fifty," the realtor said, her smile

trying hard to brighten the room, but in Clara's opinion, nothing could do that. "Should we go up to the rooms again?"

The only reason Clara wanted to do that was to show Scott how the current owner had staged the guest rooms. In her opinion, someone would only stay out on this island, in this inn, if literally every other room on all five islands in the cove were full. And maybe she still wouldn't.

"Sure," she said, and she followed Mimi up the steps as the elevator was currently out of service. Clara had done a little research, and getting an elevator repairman out to the cove would cost thousands.

"Mom, it smells bad," Lena yelled, and Clara wanted to start laughing.

"I know," she said, giving Lena a small nod. "We'll be done soon." Not soon enough, and Clara employed every ounce of patience she currently possessed.

Mimi opened the door to the staged and ready guest room as if she was opening a door to reveal a brand new sports car on a game show. Clara gestured for her mother to go first, and she did. Reuben followed her, a look of mild horror on his face—and he'd only seen the hallway.

Jean looked like she might faint at any moment, as the inn didn't have operational air conditioning at the moment, and May had arrived. She glanced at Clara, their eyes skimming past one another as Jean entered the room.

Clara nudged her daughter to go next, and she entered last. She wanted to show Scott how full the room was with six people in it, and she tapped to take several pictures.

Nothing seemed white, because it wasn't. The sheets, towels, and curtains existed in shades of yellow and beige, and Clara wondered what had been living in them all these years. By the looks on everyone's faces, they were all thinking the same thing.

"Okay," Clara said. "I think I'm done." She couldn't get a proper breath, and she turned and strode out of the room. Her heart pinched along all the edges, because she shouldn't be the first one running out. Shouldn't she at least make sure her mentally disabled daughter got out of this place safely?

Clara couldn't make herself go back, and she raced down the steps to the lobby. Behind her, Reuben called her name, but a scream gathering inside her chest urged her to get outside as quickly as possible. She burst out of the double glass doors and into the sunshine.

Stumbling, she took several more paces away from the inn, until she couldn't smell a mixture of waste, dirt, mold, and murky water. She bent over, panting, and braced her hands against her knees.

"Clara," Reuben said, coming up behind her. He didn't touch her, but she felt him hovering close by. "Are you okay?"

She shook her head, because she couldn't speak.

"Come into the shade," he said, and he guided her over to the side of the building where a breeze cooled the perspiration along her hairline. "Just breathe." Her brother shielded her from everyone else as they arrived outside. "I'll take care of them."

Reuben walked away, and Clara appreciated him so

much in that moment. She knew she wasn't easy to be around. She'd overstayed her welcome in the lighthouse earlier this year. She'd driven Jean to the brink of insanity with the buzzer, and Clara had no idea why she did the things she did.

She turned her back as Reuben reached the group and looked up into the sky. "What am I going to do?" she asked, wishing the clouds, the currents, or the Creator would answer her. No one and nothing did.

She simply knew she couldn't stay in Montpelier. Lena's boss had asked her a few questions, and Lena had gotten upset when she'd thought her father was a "bad man." At the same time, it would be terribly hard for Lena to leave her job at the grocery store and her church group. She also attended group therapy, where she had friends, and she had an excellent occupational therapist who'd taught Lena how to pay her own bills. She'd taught her to set alarms to get to work on time. She'd taught her how to do laundry and clean a toilet.

Leaving all of that behind would be terribly hard for Lena. Clara had looked into the services for the disabled here in Five Island Cove, and they had some great resources. But that all took time to apply for, set up, and get settled into. Lena didn't do particularly well with change.

Clara exhaled her frustrations and all of her feelings of inadequacy into the sky above. She couldn't believe Scott had done this to them for a few extra dollars. She couldn't believe she hadn't known about it.

"Clara."

She turned at the sound of her mother's voice. Her mom had always been exceptional at getting things out of Clara she didn't want to say. She simply waited, letting the silence scream at Clara in unacceptable ways. She wore compassion in her expression, and Clara wished she wouldn't. Then she wouldn't feel so comfortable and so loved and like perhaps her mother could help her fix everything.

"This place is really terrible," she said.

Clara took a breath to agree, but when she let it out, tears streamed down her face. "It really is," she said, her voice choking through her throat.

Her mom gathered her into a hug, and Clara clung to her with every fiber of her strength. "Mom, Scott lost his job. Well, he actually ended up resigning, and the firm was shut down. His boss is in jail, and he almost went to jail as well. If not for the immunity the DA offered him for all of the information he had, he'd be behind bars too."

The words flowed like water over cliffs, and Clara couldn't stop herself. The whole story spilled out in less than a minute, and Clara's chest stung, as if someone had poured bleach down her throat and into her whole body.

"Sh," her mom said, stepping back and smoothing Clara's hair off her face. She looked straight into her eyes, something Clara hadn't allowed in so long. She'd kept everything hidden behind movie-star sunglasses and wide-brimmed hats.

Her mom could see everything now. "It's all a mess," Clara said. "We're going to lose everything, and I just—I can't see the end of this. I can't figure out what to do or where to go next."

She wasn't wearing her wedding ring, and no one had commented on it. She wasn't sure when she'd put it back on, but she knew she would. Sometimes when Scott walked into the room, an inexplicable anger came over her and she had to leave. But she didn't want to go through life without Scott. She didn't want to continue to help Lena live as full of a life as she could by herself.

She also couldn't see herself, Lena, or Scott here, trying to take an inn that had been closed for twenty years and rebuild it. The person who took this on had to be certifiably insane, despite the rumors of treasure in one of the rooms.

Truth be told, that rumor was the main reason Clara had mentioned the inn to Scott. They needed the money, and if she could just find it...

"Let's go get something to eat," her mom said, and Clara's stomach swooped at the very idea of real food.

"Okay," Clara said. She let her mom loop her arm through hers and walk back toward the group. Once they'd arrived back on the boat, Clara stood at the railing and let the wind cleanse her mind, soul, and tears.

Her mother stood next to her, and she only said one thing. "If you and Scott need help to buy Friendship Inn, let me know, dear. I'll do what I can to help you."

Clara nodded, because her mom meant it. "I'll think about it," she said. "Talk to Scott." She hadn't been able to even muster the energy to send Scott the horrible pictures she'd taken. She'd have to do so soon enough, and then that would open a whole new can of worms she'd have to deal with.

She closed her eyes and breathed in the salty air and smiled when cool droplets of water splashed up onto her face. Maybe if she gave herself enough quiet moments like this, she'd know what to do.

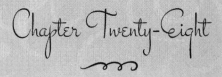

Chapter Twenty-Eight

R obin paced in the kitchen, wishing she'd insisted on Mandie getting ready for the prom at home. She'd wanted to have help with her hair, her makeup, and her dress, and Robin hadn't had the heart to tell her she couldn't go over to Ginny's for all of that.

She spun toward the front door as it opened.

"It's just me," Alice called, entering the house with Arthur right behind her. She wore a look of measured happiness, and Robin strode toward her.

"Are they coming?"

"Charlie left at the same time I did to go pick up Ray and Easton." Alice embraced Robin. "The girls were still upstairs getting ready."

Mandie was going to her senior prom with Charlie Kelton. Robin liked the boy just fine. He'd matured a lot, and he'd never tried to take advantage of Mandie or her kindness. Alice really had done such a great job raising him,

311

and while Robin had experienced some doubts and reservations about the relationship, Mandie had assured her that she liked Charlie too.

She'd never stopped liking him. Robin wasn't sure what boy just flitted from girl to girl, like he needed to sample all the pretty ones before making a decision. At the same time, she knew how troublesome and confusing it was to be a teenager, and she'd let all of her ill feelings for Charlie float away.

Rather, she'd been running five miles on the beach each morning, hoping to pound them into the sand.

She stepped out of Alice's embrace and moved to hug Arthur. "Duke's getting dinner. He said he's got a twenty-minute wait." As she spoke, the garage door lifted, the rumble of it meeting Robin's ears and sending her pulse right up into her throat again.

She backed up a couple of steps and yanked open the garage door to find Mandie easing the mini-van into the space in the garage. Ginny rode in the passenger seat, and Emily behind her. Mandie put the vehicle in park and started to collect her belongings.

By the time the three girls emerged from the van, Robin felt like she was watching fairy princesses descend from their thrones. Ginny's dress hugged her body from the waist up, with wide straps that went over her shoulders and showed off her pale skin. From the waist down, the dress flared and the bright pink fabric sparkled with gems and glitter.

She wore the same sparkly stuff near her eyes, her makeup done in bright blues, yellows, and pinks. Her shoes were the only thing not bedazzled and were in fact a matte white.

"Wow," Robin breathed as Emily stepped to Ginny's side. She wore a black prom dress, made of shiny satin, with a diamond belt right below her bust. The full skirt fell in layer after layer down to the ground, and Emily gathered the fabric into her hands to reveal a pair of ruby slippers.

Mandie came around the front of the van, her backpack in her hands. "Mom, can you take this?" She extended the bag toward Robin, who lunged into motion. She'd gone shopping with her daughter for the prom dress; she knew what it looked like.

Still, seeing the bright blue lace, tulle, and cloth on Mandie's body was completely different. Her hair had been braided up into a topknot, then curled. She'd chosen a much more muted color palette for her makeup, with dark, dramatic swatches of eyeliner and then hardly any eye shadow. Her blush was understated, and her lips looked shiny and nothing else.

Diamonds hung from her ears, courtesy of Alice's jewelry box, and Robin couldn't speak at the sight of her gorgeous daughter.

"You all look so amazing," Alice said, thawing Robin's frozen vocal cords. She stumbled back, gesturing the girls into the house.

"Come on," she said. "Let's take your pictures by the fireplace." She dropped Mandie's backpack behind the steps and held the door for everyone to enter the house. Her eyes flitted everywhere, and Robin let all of the gems, glitter, and glam go by her. Her heart pulsed in her chest and temples, and she told herself to calm down as she pulled her phone out of her back pocket.

"You three are stunning," Arthur said, beaming at the girls.

"By the fireplace," Alice instructed, and Robin stepped to her side, and the two of them held up their phones.

"Where am I looking?" Mandie asked, her eyes glancing toward the front door, though the wall stood in the way and she couldn't possibly see it from her position.

"Right here," Robin said, and all of the girls looked at her.

"Now here." Alice tapped and got a few shots, and the three teens relaxed. Ginny smoothed down her dress and adjusted some of the layers falling to her feet.

Mandie blew out a breath and took a few short steps away from the fireplace.

"Ray is always late," Ginny said. "But I know Easton was already at his house."

"Will you fix up my lipstick now?" Emily asked, and both Ginny and Mandie leapt into action. It took both of them to get Em's lips in the right condition, and Robin scrolled through the pictures she'd taken.

"Remember when this was us?" Alice murmured, her arms crossed over her body.

"My mom almost didn't let me go," Robin said. She looked up and across the room to the girls. Mandie's dress didn't have straps, and Robin's mother would've had a stroke had she seen it. "Remember how my dress didn't have 'appropriate' sleeves?" She rolled her eyes and went back to editing the picture.

The garage door opened again, and Duke walked in with Jamie this time. They both carried a white plastic sack full of food, and Robin moved over to the counter to clear a spot for him.

"You're back early," she said to Duke. "You said there was a wait."

"He thought I was someone else," Duke said with a grin. He glanced at the girls in the living room, nearly tripping over his feet at the sight of them. He wolf-whistled and stumbled the last few steps to the counter to put down the food.

"Wow, Mandie." Duke didn't exude any awkwardness or judgment as he walked over to her. He took her by the shoulders and looked down to her feet, where she'd strapped a pair of sparkly silver sandals. "You look absolutely amazing. This boy is so lucky." He pressed a kiss to Mandie's forehead right as the doorbell rang.

Duke's attention whipped that way, and he said, "That'll be those boys. I'll handle this."

"Dad," Mandie said, but Duke just walked away.

Mandie drew in a big breath and pressed her palms to her stomach. Ginny exhaled as Arthur said, "I'll go with Duke."

"Arthur," Ginny said.

"I'm just going to have a word with the boys," he said. "I deal with a lot of teenage boys; it'll be fine."

Ginny looked like it would be less than fine, and she threw a desperate glance to Alice.

Male voices came down the hall, but no one spoke animatedly enough for Robin to make out any words. She moved to Mandie's side and put her arm around her. "You're lovely," she murmured. "He really is lucky, and I know you feel like you're the lucky one to be with Charlie. But just remember how fantastic *you* are."

"I will, Mom."

Duke and Arthur parted, and Ray stepped between them first. He only had eyes for Ginny, and she stayed perfectly still while he approached. His eyes sparkled like diamonds, and Robin had time to watch him embrace Ginny before Charlie was only a few steps away from Mandie.

"Hey," he said, his eyes glued to Mandie's too. His smile curved his lips, and he really was an extremely attractive boy. Robin's first instinct was to pull her daughter closer to her and never let her leave the house again. Especially not wearing a dress without straps and makeup that made her look ten years older.

Charlie flicked a look in her direction, and Robin moved away, dropping her arm from around Mandie's waist. Charlie inhaled as he embraced her, his eyelids fluttering closed, and Robin saw in that moment how much he liked Mandie.

He'd take good care of her tonight, and Robin didn't need to worry.

They started exchanging flowers, and Duke ended up

helping Mandie pin the boutonniere on Charlie's lapel. Robin and Alice herded the six of them in front of the fireplace again, and more pictures got taken.

Alice took some of just Ginny and Ray. Then just Emily and Easton. Robin snapped several of Charlie and Mandie to go with the candids she'd gotten of the flower pinning.

Then the three couples left, taking all of the energy with them. Robin exhaled as she closed the door behind them, somewhat relieved that she'd survived this pick-up. She went into the kitchen, where Alice was unpacking the Chinese food Duke had brought home.

"Well," she said with a sigh. "They're off." She gave Alice a smile only another mother could understand, and they both nodded at the same time. Mandie had been spending more and more time over at Alice and Arthur's, and Robin had done her very best not to ask for updates or for her best friend to spy on her daughter.

That wasn't the kind of relationship she wanted to have with Mandie.

"Yes," Alice said, handing her a plate. "And we're going to eat and watch that new action thriller."

Robin's hopes for not counting every minute until Mandie returned disappeared. "Great," she said dryly.

Alice gave her an encouraging smile. "Just think, you can text your mom to set up a lunch date and not miss anything." Her look turned pointed. "Or show me the house you got. I want to see all the pictures, not just the one you put on the group text."

Robin looked away and accepted the tongs from Arthur, a double-edged knife moving through her.

Excitement over the house she and Duke had put an offer on brought joy to her. It had been accepted, and now they just had to wait for all of the financing to go through.

But she needed to tell her mother about the house, and she'd told Alice that she wanted to start going to lunch with her mother to try to repair some of the damage that had been done over the years. Try to build a bridge. Robin had done so in the past, and every time, she felt like something happened to tear down all the progress she'd made, as well as blow up part of the structure that hadn't been compromised yet.

She honestly wasn't sure if having a relationship with her mother was feasible at this point. But something in the back of her mind kept nagging at her to try.

After the noodles, she told herself as she put far too much lo mein on her plate.

"IF I'M NOT BACK BY TWO," SHE SAID A COUPLE OF days later. "Call me to give me an out." She stood over Duke, who still lay in their bed. He wasn't wearing a shirt, and while his eyes were closed, Robin could tell he wasn't asleep. She'd slept beside the man for long enough to know.

"Okay," he said, his eyes cracking open. "What time is it now?"

"Almost noon," Robin said, glancing at her phone. "I'm

going to be late." She'd been ready to leave the house an hour ago. She just hadn't done it. She bent down and kissed Duke. "I hope you feel better."

"Mm." His hand slipped along her waist. "If you stay, I'll feel better."

Robin gently stepped away from him. "It's lunch with my mom. I can't cancel." It had taken her over a month just to get this set up. She hadn't expected her mother to agree so quickly the other night, nor to have such an open schedule. She wasn't sure why; her mom didn't work and didn't have a lot pulling at her attention or time. She should be able to go to lunch any day of the week.

Robin straightened her shoulders as she left the house, and she finger-combed her hair at every light she had to stop at on the way to the restaurant. Plenty of cars filled the lot, so Robin didn't waste time looking for her mother's. Inside, she found Jennifer Golden waiting on a bench, and she got to her feet immediately when Robin said, "Mom, hey."

They hugged, and Robin let her eyes close so she could just be in this one moment. This one second of time where she wasn't a failure in her mom's eyes, where a sister-in-law wasn't better, where her mother simply loved her.

"They wouldn't take us until we were both here," Mom said, and Robin nodded. She stood out of the way while her mom went to tell the hostess they were ready, and they didn't have to wait at all, so her mom's passive ire at Robin's few minutes of tardiness was for nothing.

Once settled across from one another in a booth, Robin picked up a menu. She'd lived in the cove her whole life, and she'd eaten at Columbine's plenty of times. She already knew what she wanted, so she took the opportunity to peer over the top of her menu at her mother.

She looked good—strong and healthy. Clean and casual. "So," she said, looking up and meeting Robin's eye. "School is almost out."

"Yes," Robin said. "Mandie's graduation is in a few weeks. Did you get the announcement?"

Mom beamed at her and tucked her graying hair behind her ear. "Yes, I put it on my fridge." She tilted her menu as if trying to see part of it better. "The party is at your house afterward?"

"Yes," Robin said. "Alice and I are combining parties, so she'll be there with the twins and everyone."

"Is Frank coming?" Mom asked.

"I haven't heard yes or no on him," Robin said. "There will be plenty of food. Everyone is invited."

"Everyone?"

Robin's eyebrows went up at the curiosity in her mom's voice. No, that wasn't right. Robin narrowed her eyes at her mother, but the menu suddenly held all of life's little secrets. Her mom wouldn't look away from it. "Yes," Robin said slowly. "Everyone. Kelli is bringing her mom and her new husband. Alice's dad and stepmom will be there, of course. AJ said Amy is going to come with the girls. Donovan has a conference in the city that weekend."

"Mm."

"Mom," Robin said. "Do you have a plus-one?"

That got her mom's bright blue eyes to lift from the

menu. She wore blazes there, not only in fire, but in challenge too. "I can," she said.

Robin let her menu drop to the table. No wonder her mom had agreed so readily to this lunch suggestion. She had *news*.

"Who is it?" she asked.

"Simon Lemming," Mom said, bobbling her head like a doll. "He asked me to dinner a few weeks ago, and I said yes. He's been fun to be around."

"Fun to be around?" Robin blinked rapidly and placed her palms on the table. She wasn't sure how anyone would find her mother fun to be around, but she kept that to herself. "Are you dating him?"

"I suppose that's what it's called."

"What else would it be called?" Robin couldn't tear her eyes from her mom. She didn't want to miss a single reaction.

"Seeing each other?" Mom guessed, a smile touching her face. She laughed lightly and pushed her hair back again. Robin had never seen her touch her hair so much. "I don't know. I haven't dated anyone in such a long time."

Decades and decades, but again, Robin kept that to herself. "Wow, Mom. You didn't say you had news to share."

She just threw Robin another closed-mouth smile and then set her menu aside. "I think you have some news hidden away too."

Robin raised her chin. "Not hidden," she said, twisting to dig through her purse. She didn't have to go far; the envelope sat right on top of her wallet and sunglasses case. She plucked it out and put it on the table. After sliding it toward her mom, she said, "Our last month's rent. We'll be moving into our new home at the beginning of July."

Mom did the rapid-blink thing, though she'd known this day was coming. Robin had told her that she and Duke wanted a house of their own. They were grateful for the help she'd given them all these years, but they had enough now for something only they owned.

She didn't pick up the envelope. In fact, she pushed it back toward Robin. "I don't need that. You keep it."

"I don't want to keep it," Robin said. Her mom had never let her and Duke off the hook for paying rent, not even after the tsunami had destroyed Duke's fishing boat and Robin had started working eighty hours a week.

Of course, her mom had had something to say about that. But rent forgiveness? Nope. Hadn't been offered.

Robin slid the envelope toward her again. "The last month. Cash it. Take your boyfriend to Coney Island or something." She tacked a smile onto the statement. No matter what, she didn't want her mom to be able to hold anything above her head.

"Have you found a house then?" Mom picked up the envelope and tucked it inside her bag.

"Yes," Robin said. "We're just waiting on the appraisal, and then the loan should be in final approval."

"Where is it?"

"It's further north," Robin said. "Here on Diamond, because Duke needs to get to the docks easily." She cleared her throat. "I'm taking my friends this weekend, if you'd like to come. It's empty right now, so the realtor agreed to meet us so I could show everyone."

Their eyes met, and Robin didn't try to hide anything from her mother. Having her come along with all of Robin's friends was hard for her. She felt so much pressure to make sure no one left with a bad taste in their mouth because of something Jennifer Golden had said or done.

"Okay," her mom said. "Just let me know when."

"Saturday morning," Robin said, dropping her gaze to the menu and then letting it rebound to the waiter as he arrived. "Nine-thirty."

Chapter Twenty-Nine

Kristen bent her head to look out the window at the gray house Robin pulled up to. *Wow*, she thought. This was a nice house, in one of the more well-established neighborhoods of Diamond Island.

Robin's new house sat only five minutes from AJ's cottage, and then a seven-minute drive from Kristen's condo, and she'd stopped by and gotten both of them before coming here.

"It's not a new house," Robin said, gripping the wheel with both hands. "They just redid the siding in order to list it. It's been renovated, and it's really nice. But it's not new."

She strangled the wheel like she had something to be nervous about. That honor fell to Kristen, whose phone vibrated in her pocket. She suspected it would be Clara, as they'd been texting a lot since her daughter's return to Vermont. Ever since Clara had confessed to the true reason why she and Scott wanted to move, Kristen had spent hours looking at the national news stories about the "heist" coming out of Montpelier.

Her heart had cracked and broken more times than she could count. Every time she saw her son-in-law's mug shot. Every time she read an article that dragged Clara and Lena into the spotlight. Every time she thought about her daughter giving up everything they'd built and established in Montpelier and coming back to the cove—a place she didn't like all that much.

Kristen missed her daughter, and she was glad Clara had finally told her the truth. She could keep a secret with the best of them, and she hadn't breathed a word of Clara and Scott's troubles to anyone in Five Island Cove.

She had offered to help Clara if she needed it, and the flurry of texts that had started last night had been about a down payment on Friendship Inn. Apparently, Scott knew someone willing to finance the inn so they didn't have to qualify for a loan—something Clara didn't think they could do now that they were both unemployed. But he wanted a fifty-thousand-dollar down payment, and Scott and Clara didn't have it.

Kristen thought of her bank account and Joel's life insurance settlement. If Clara knew that would finance the buying of the inn, she might not take it. Kristen had chosen not to tell her, just as she wasn't sure how to tell Robin about Clara's real reason for returning to the cove, nor how to break the news to Eloise that someone was going to buy the inn and come into the cove as her competition.

Her stomach tightened, but she got out of Robin's

minivan the moment the other woman moved. "The yard is nice," she said. That would make Robin happy, as she enjoyed tending to bushes and daffodils.

"You should see the back," Robin said, and she took the first step toward the front door. "There's a hot tub, and a huge patio."

"Perfect for your entertaining," AJ said with a smile. Behind them, another car pulled up to the curb, and Alice spilled from the car with Kelli and Eloise. The slamming of car doors filled the air, and then the classic *whoop-whoop!* of a police car punctuated it all.

Lauren grinned as she pulled into Robin's new driveway, which would hold four cars across. Seeing as how Duke and Robin just had two cars, Kristen wasn't sure what they would do with so much cement.

Jean got out of the front of Laurel's cruiser, laughing. Kristen sure did enjoy seeing that, and she detoured toward her daughter-in-law. Laurel rounded the front of the car, her belly bumping out slightly against her uniform.

"I have twenty minutes," she said.

"Let's tour fast," Alice said, exchanging a glance with Robin. "Then we can reconvene at my house for mocktails."

"Before noon?" Robin asked, her tone shocked.

"It's a weekend," Alice said. "After a rough week. So yes, I'm planning on spending my day with the sun and a drink to sip." She grinned at Robin and led the way up the steps. "Plus, after you do the second tour with your mom, you'll be begging me for a drink. A real one."

Robin pressed her lips together, neither confirming nor denying Alice's statement.

Alice smiled broadly at the porch. "Nice porch. Big, wide, just the way Robin likes things." She sounded just like a real estate agent, and a couple of the girls twittered.

Robin was not one of them, and she pushed past Alice to enter the code on the lockbox. A key came out, and she let them into the house. The air conditioning pumped, and Kristen took in the vaulted ceilings and light, airy atmosphere.

"There's an office right off the front," she said. "Just like my other house."

"Like Alice's," Laurel said, crowding into the space last.

"Yes." Robin led the way into the great room, which was easily twice as big as the house where she and Duke had lived for so long. The place really had been renovated, and by someone with a lot of money. The hardwood floors shone, and the granite glinted. The windows needed curtains, but Robin would get everything dressed up nice, Kristen was sure of that.

She led them out the double French doors to the back yard, and Kristen did let out of sigh of contentment then. The emerald green grass stretched back to a six-foot vinyl fence, and the hot tub sat right off the deck. A great big deck that would easily hold the picnic tables Robin currently had on her cement pad in her other back yard.

"Oh, this is phenomenal." Kelli beamed around at the trees lining the entire left side of the yard. "I bet those will be excellent shade this summer." She hooked her arm through Robin's. "I can't wait to come here and have you feed me."

They laughed together, but it was obvious that Robin couldn't wait to do that either.

The rest of the house tour went quickly, because it was just bedrooms. This house had four, which was one less than the house where she lived now, but it did have an extra bathroom. Everything here was far done in far nicer materials. New, and nice.

Robin let out an exhale as they left the house and she turned back to lock it up. She glanced over to the three-car garage—one more than they currently had—and faced the group again. "We like it."

"You love it," Eloise said, grinning. "And you should, Robin. You've worked so hard for a house like this."

Robin gave a closed-mouth smile and nodded. "I'm going to have to take on a few clients to keep up with the mortgage." She lifted one shoulder in a shrug. "But I told Duke I'm not doing it until fall." Her eyes lit up as she surveyed the group. "That way, we'll have all summer together before some of our kids leave."

Alice nodded, and so did Kristen. "All right," she said, blowing out a sigh. "Mocktails all around. I'll keep the hard stuff for you, Robin."

Everyone looked toward the road as Duke pulled up in his sedan, Jennifer Golden in the front passenger seat.

"Yeah, you better," Robin said, giving everyone one more smile before she went to meet her husband, mother, and girls.

"I'll drop you, Kristen," Laurel said. "I've got to get back to work."

"I can take her," Alice said, and Kristen stayed out of the way as AJ said she'd go with Laurel and they'd all meet back at Alice's.

She checked her phone, and sure enough, the buzzing from earlier had been from Clara. *Scott and I would love to accept the down payment, Mom. Thank you so much. This is going to be a brand new start for us.*

Kristen agreed with that, but worry still ate a hole in her stomach. Lena would have to be uprooted, and that would be hard on everyone. Not only that, but Friendship Inn wasn't livable right now, and a thought flew into her mind.

Where are you planning to live? she sent to Clara. *Robin just bought a new house, and perhaps her mother would rent to you.*

She looked at the sentence, floored she hadn't thought of this before. Robin had taken her mother to lunch a handful of days ago and told her they'd be moving out at the end of June. Could Jennifer Golden rent the house so fast?

"Robin," she called, hurrying to catch the woman now. Robin twisted back from her conversation with Duke. Kristen told herself to calm down. For all she knew, Clara and Scott had housing plans.

A buzz in her hand had her looking down. For someone her age, she really should concentrate on one thing at a time, something her brain screamed at her as her ankle twisted.

Time slowed.

Robin's eyes widened.

Someone cried out, the sound warbled and coming at Kristen too slow, and then too fast.

Then her phone went skittering across the cement, and she landed on her hands and knees. They smarted with pain shooting up to her elbows. The wind left her lungs.

"Kristen," Robin said, cutting through all the noise in Kristen's head. She arrived in front of Kristen, her purse abandoned as she used both hands to help Kristen. "Are you okay?"

Kristen couldn't get a breath, and she watched as Laurel picked up her phone and Alice rushed at them.

"Yes," she managed to croak out just as Jean and Kelli knelt in front of her too. Each of them wore concern in their eyes, and AJ put her hand under Kristen's arm.

"Let's get her up," she said.

Kristen helped as much as she could, but she was glad for all the strength and support the other women leant her. Laurel handed her the phone, and Kristen looked at the screen. It hadn't been cracked or damaged at all. Clara's text sat there, saying, *That would be great, Mom! If you don't want to ask her, I can call her. Just see if she'll give you her number for me.*

"I'm okay," she said, shoving her phone into her pocket. "I just got excited about something."

"What?" Robin asked, staying right by Kristen's side as the group of them moved together down the sidewalk and over the grass bordering it.

"Clara and Scott are going to be moving here," she said, trying to measure out the words before she said them. "They don't have much money, and they need somewhere to live." Hope filled her as she turned to look at Robin, then further away where Jennifer Golden had stayed with her grand-daughters. "Would your mother rent to them possibly?"

Surprise covered Robin's face, but Kristen wasn't sure which part of what she'd said had caused it.

"I can ask her," Kristen said. "I just wasn't sure if she'd mentioned anything to you about new renters. Maybe she's not even going to re-rent it."

"I don't know her plans," Robin said, glancing away with an edge in her eyes Kristen had seen many times before. "I can ask her too."

"I have her number." Kristen shot her a smile Robin didn't see, and they arrived at Alice's car. Jean didn't leave her side until she was settled and buckled, all the while shooting furtive glances at her, which she ignored.

Robin returned to her family, and she swept both arms toward the house. The girls shrieked, and they all started to cross the front lawn toward that wide, big porch.

Kristen sighed and looked at her hands as Alice eased away from the curb. Yes, she'd have to tell the girls everything soon. She simply didn't want to do it right now.

A WEEK LATER, THE MONEY LEFT HER ACCOUNT and got transferred into Clara's and Scott's. They'd listed their house. They'd talked to Lena, who hadn't taken the news well. Clara texted to say that she cried everyday, and

Kristen had started texting her granddaughter about all the fun things they could do this summer after she moved to the cove.

Jennifer Golden had asked for Clara's number, but Kristen hadn't heard if they'd been able to work out a reasonable price for the house rental. She tried to let her daughter come to her with the information she wanted to share, because the last thing Kristen wanted to do was pry.

The media buzz in Montpelier had not died down, and Clara had started to talk about moving to the cove as soon as possible, before the purchase of Friendship Inn went through, and before they had housing secured. There were extra bedrooms at Kristen's condo, the lighthouse, and an entire cottage sitting unused.

She'd just closed her Internet browser after reading yet another inflammatory article when her doorbell rang. Since she wasn't expecting anyone today, she assumed it would be a package. She loved the art of ordering things online, and she opened the door, her eyes already on the ground.

She found police boots there, and her gaze quickly traveled up the height of Laurel's body. She wore anxiety in her eyes and displeasure in the downturn of her mouth.

Kristen's heart thunked against her ribs. "Laurel," she said, surprised. "What are you doing here?"

Laurel held up her phone. "This is Clara, right?"

The screen showed the horrific mugshot of Kristen's daughter, and the ground beneath her feet shifted. She'd felt like this a few times in her life. Wild, careening through the universe, completely out of control. Once, when Joel had died. Once, when she'd lost a baby many years ago.

And now again today.

She stepped back, keeping a tight grip on the door. "Come in, Laurel. Let's talk."

Laurel stepped into the condo while shoving her phone in her pocket, and Kristen closed the door. Her mind blitzed through her options, and she landed on the only one she found acceptable.

Telling the truth.

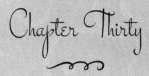

Chapter Thirty

Eloise reached for the saltshaker, wishing it had the everything-bagel seasoning in it. This shrimp salad needed something. It tasted like mayo, soggy noodles, and cold shrimp that might have not been seasoned before they'd been cooked. She added a healthy amount of salt to her bowl as Laurel pushed her veggies around with her fork.

"What's going on?" El asked, glancing from Laurel to the pool. It was the dead time at the inn between check-out and check-in. The wind played peacefully with the leaves on the trees, and the blue sky stretched forever over the patio, the cliffs, and the world.

El loved sitting outside, even in the heat, during this time of day, and Laurel had brought a late lunch. She wasn't wearing her police uniform, but a casual pair of cutoffs and a tank top that bulged over her growing belly.

She looked up at Eloise, then out past the pool, over Sanctuary Island, and toward the mainland. El liked to pretend she could see it sometimes, though she couldn't. Not really. She just liked to feel connected to a bigger land mass from time to time.

Laurel put a spear of broccoli in her mouth and reached for a pita chip to scoop through the hummus. "Did you see that Friendship Inn went under contract?"

The way she spoke in such a measured tone indicated that Laurel had seen it. Eloise had stopped checking on the property a couple of weeks ago, her attitude one of *whatever will be, will be.*

She and Aaron had talked, and she didn't want to purchase the inn. She'd looked. She'd called. She'd asked the realtor about the condition of the inn. Whoever ended up buying it would need at least a full year to renovate—and hundreds of thousands of dollars—and Eloise didn't want that rock on her plate.

It was a boulder. A huge, hulking piece of granite she didn't want to try to carry around and see past.

She gave another shake of the salt and shook her head. "I stopped looking."

"It went under contract," Laurel said. She paused eating altogether and picked up her phone. "I don't want to freak you out. I've already talked to Kristen, and she doesn't know how to tell everyone."

Eloise put down her fork too, her stomach tightening at the way Laurel tapped and slid and arrived at something. El almost didn't want to see it. "What do you mean? Kristen doesn't know how to tell everyone what?"

Laurel turned her phone toward Eloise, but El kept her focus on Laurel's face. "Just tell me."

Laurel sighed and set her phone face-down on the table. She inhaled and held her breath. "Clara and Scott are in some legal trouble in Vermont," she said. "They need to get out of there. They need a fresh start. They bought Friendship Inn."

Eloise's thoughts liquified, and she couldn't grab onto any one of them. They flowed through her synapses like water, rushing, rapid, river water, and she found herself tumbling beneath similar waves, gasping for breath.

Laurel's dark eyes, full of caring and compassion, locked onto Eloise's. "Kristen gave them the down payment. She's terrified you'll be upset with her."

Upset wasn't the right word. El searched for the correct term to describe the feelings pouring through her. Raining and pounding against her skull and the back of her throat.

Betrayal.

She felt betrayed.

"She gave them the money?" The words scraped her throat. "They'll put me out of business."

If they can get the inn up and running, she thought. She seized onto that thought, because it was the one ray of sunshine in her soul at the moment.

Then came the tidal wave of guilt. She didn't want to root against Kristen's daughter, especially if she and her family were in trouble. Clara would need the support in the cove—somewhere she'd never liked living—and Eloise pressed her eyes shut, trying to reason through everything in under a second.

She couldn't, and thankfully, Laurel didn't say anything else. What else could she say? There were no words to make this okay, and Eloise left behind her shrimp salad and the hummus and paced over to the edge of the swimming pool.

In a few hours, it would be filled with laughing, yelling children. Their parents would sit in the provided loungers around the deck, trying to stay out of the heat of the sun but enjoy its rays. Their towel attendant would be busy. The scent of dinner would fill the air.

No one would care that less than two miles away, directly down the hill and across a short swatch of water sat another island. Friendship Island, which housed Friendship Inn.

Would all of her guests go there once Clara and Scott got the building and grounds cleaned up and ready? Could they even do that? Would Eloise be able to help them?

She knew so much more now than she had last year. She had systems for cleaning rooms in a timely fashion, and she had an amazing website, good hosting, and excellent booking software. Clara could probably use her help and expertise... and Eloise didn't want to give it.

Feeling monstrous, she closed her eyes and imagined she could whip through the solar system at the same speed as the Earth. Maybe then she'd be able to cleanse herself of her jealous, awful feelings.

"El," Laurel said, and her eyes jerked open.

The other woman stood right beside her. She towered a

good six inches taller than El, so it was easy for Laurel to put her arm around Eloise's shoulders and bring her against her side. She held her there in such a kind, loving gesture that Eloise's composure slipped.

"Did she ask you to tell me?" El asked.

"I told her I was coming to lunch today," Laurel said. "And that you were my best friend, and I couldn't possibly just pretend like I didn't know."

"How did you find out?"

"Aaron regularly checks the news feeds coming off the mainland," she said. "Particularly Nantucket, New York City, Boston. You know, the big hubs."

El nodded, her chest cavity growing cold. "Are you telling me my husband knew about this?"

"No," Laurel said. "He pulls the reports. He doesn't read all of them. Gill saw it. He showed me, and I went to talk to Kristen. She confirmed that most of what's in the news stories is true."

Eloise leaned into Laurel and put her arm around the other woman's back. "Am I a terrible person for wanting it to fail?"

"Not at all."

"Then I think—she'll need our help. Everyone came here to help me. We should all go down there to help her." Eloise looked up at Laurel, who continued to gaze over the island and into the blue, blue distance.

"Scott's company went bankrupt. His boss had been stealing money from their clients for years. By testifying against him, Scott got immunity."

Eloise wanted to know at the same time she didn't. "I don't need all the details."

"There's more," Laurel said.

Eloise thought of the past couple of years of her life. Everything from her job to her personal life had been upended, blown up, and pieced back together. She had a job and a business she loved. Friends she craved spending time with. A loving, handsome husband, and two girls who walked on water to her.

Her wedding dress had been covered in mud and ash only two days before the I-do. Her biological brother had threatened her and all of her friends. Just last year, Laurel had blown open a huge case in the cove that had everyone pointing fingers and asking questions.

She could handle whatever Laurel said. She could.

"All right," El said, giving Laurel permission to keep talking.

"They're going to rent Robin's house."

El pulled in a breath. "Of course. Sure. They'll need a place." She simply wished it didn't feel like Clara could replace her in the blink of an eye. She'd been so busy with Cliffside in the past few months, and she'd missed a lot of the midweek luncheons. She didn't see her friends nearly as often as she once had, though she still texted with them each day.

Spending time—physical time—with a person was different than texting, and she knew it. That fact seethed down in her stomach, hooking in claws and pulling off pieces of flesh.

"Tell me what you're thinking," Laurel said.

"I don't want to."

"Do it anyway."

"I'm not under arrest, am I?" Eloise smiled, though she still felt stone-cold standing in direct sunlight. June would arrive in only a week or so, and the temperatures had been soaring lately.

Laurel dropped her arm, saying, "No, but I could make that happen." She giggled, and Eloise found herself smiling too.

She wrapped her arms around herself and said, "I'm feeling like she'll replace me. She'll be on Diamond, where all the get-togethers happen. In Robin's house, with that great backyard. She'll need a lot of help with an inn. That all sounds pretty familiar, doesn't it?"

She faced Laurel so she could see her reaction. Laurel didn't try to hide anything. Her eyes blazed with dark fire, and she shook her head. "No one can replace you, El."

"She'll need help, and everyone loves Kristen, even if they don't love Clara. They'll go help."

"Probably." Laurel shrugged one shoulder. "But it doesn't mean they'll love you less. It doesn't mean that if you needed help, we wouldn't come. We would. In a heartbeat."

Deep down, Eloise knew that. She hated feeling left out, though, and she'd lived her whole life on the outskirts of friendships. She'd just started to feel like she was a core member of her group, and now she'd been booted to the fringes again.

Some of that is your choice, she told herself. And it was.

She was comfortable on the outside, as she'd always been there.

She nodded. "I know. I'm going to bring the girls to all the summer activities." She'd lose sleep if she had to. She'd need to run the inn, and summer was a very busy time. But Billie and Grace needed her, and Eloise needed her friends.

She could sleep when she was dead.

"Whether you come or not," Laurel said. "It doesn't change your status in the group, El." She spoke quietly, yet with real power. "I get how you're feeling. I came to your group about thirty years too late. I've never really fit."

"Don't say that," Eloise said. "It's not true. Alice and Robin love you. Kelli and AJ rallied around you." She tucked her hand through Laurel's arm. "You're one of my best friends too."

"I hear how forceful you sound," Laurel said. "Now double that, and that's how Robin would talk to you about your place in our group. And Alice. And AJ and Kelli and Kristen."

El focused on the distant water too, some of her unrest settling back into peaceful waves. "Okay," she said, taking a deep breath. "I just need time to process it all."

"Kristen understands that," Laurel said. "You're the only one who knows. I told her I'd tell you, but she has to woman-up and tell everyone else." The steady strength of Laurel beside her warmed all the icy places inside Eloise's chest.

"Okay." She turned away from the gorgeous view and

started back toward the table. "Let's go see what Rhonda has in the kitchen. This salad is bland."

"Mine wasn't good either," Laurel said, following her and picking up the brown rice bowl. "It just goes to show you, El, not everything that's new on the island is all that great." She gave her a huge grin, and El shook her head as she laughed.

She loved Laurel for her good heart and kind spirit. For the way she tried to reassure Eloise. For being so observant and thoughtful.

In the kitchen, they found chocolate chunk cookies, and while sweets didn't make everything better, they certainly helped.

El's phone rang after her second bite, and she glanced at it to find Kristen's name on the screen. "Did you tell her you told me?" She looked at Laurel, who also peered at El's phone.

"No," Laurel said. "I haven't texted her yet."

El made a quick decision and swiped the call to voicemail. "I need a few more cookies before I talk to her."

"Fair enough," Laurel said with a smile. "But you will talk to her, right? You won't just go silent the way I did?"

"Oh, so you admit that wasn't the best thing to do?" El's eyebrows went up in challenge.

Laurel kept her smile in place as she shook her head. "Definitely not the best thing to do."

El took another bite of her cookie, thinking while she chewed and swallowed. "Fine," she said. "I'll talk to her, but I just don't want to do it right now." She didn't know what she'd say, because her default was *It's okay.* She'd just bury everything under a rug in her soul, and she'd work through her bitter, negative feelings alone.

She'd done so plenty of times in the past—sometimes with Kristen on the upper deck of the lighthouse.

Right now, this didn't feel okay, and El didn't want to talk to Kristen until it did.

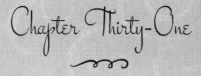

Chapter Thirty-One

Jean really needed to get upstairs and get out the gear for today's sailing activity. But she'd been texting with Kelli for a half-hour, and she couldn't just leave the conversation so open.

I feel bad for Eloise, Kelli said. *Have you spoken with her?*

No, Jean said. *Every text I send goes unanswered.*

She's still talking in the group text, Kelli said. *Maybe I'll just stop by her house. Or the inn.*

The clock at the top of Jean's phone flipped over to the next number, and her heart pinched. She needed to go upstairs to greet the girls. Sabrina didn't even want to be there that day, and Jean had used all of her persuasive powers to get the girl to come.

Her Saturday Seafaring Girls group had dwindled from eight girls to seven, then to six. Sabrina wanted to quit, but her mother wouldn't let her. She claimed to be afraid of the ocean, but she'd handled the smaller boating activities they'd done.

Today, they were sailing all by themselves. Jean would be there, of course, but the girls were handling everything from start to finish. She reminded herself she didn't need to go pull out the equipment and get ready. The girls should be doing that.

Not only that, but she'd hosted the girls in the living room here in the lighthouse, and they'd just come inside when they arrived. No one waited awkwardly outside anymore, and Jean didn't set up tables with lemonade and cookies every week.

Kristen should've talked to El first, Kelli said.

Jean didn't know how to feel about the situation with Eloise, Kristen, and Clara. She wasn't sure she wanted Clara and her family to come to the cove either. She got along with Clara just fine, because she didn't say anything. She could easily do that for a few days, but permanently?

Jean wanted to be herself too. She wanted to have opinions and be able to voice them. Surprised at her own resistance to Clara's move to Five Island Cove, Jean finally put down her phone and pulled on her boots.

When she arrived in the kitchen, she found Reuben there with a cup of coffee and two slices of buttered toast. "Hey, sweetheart." He placed a slick kiss on her forehead that made Jean smile.

"I'm heading out," she said.

"You're not going to eat before you go sailing?" His eyebrows went up, and Jean didn't know how to tell him that the worry and guilt in her gut had filled her right to the brim.

"I'll take a protein bar," she said. "We'll only be gone an hour. It's Seafaring Girls." Their meetings only lasted an hour, though sometimes the girls stayed a bit longer just to chat.

She grabbed the box of protein bars and found two inside. She took the whole thing, as well as a bottle of water, and kissed Rueben again. "I'll see you when I get back."

"I have that lecture I'm going to," he said. "At the library?"

"Oh, right." Jean noted his slacks and polo with blue boats all over it. "Have fun learning about nautical tracking systems."

His grin matched hers. "I will."

Jean dashed up the steps and arrived on the landing leading outside just as someone twisted the doorknob to come in. She dodged out of the way and found Karly entering. "Hey," she said.

"Oh, Jean." Karly pressed her hand to her chest, her eyes flying wide. "I'm sorry. Did I hit you?"

"No, you're fine." Jean indicated she should go back outside. "I was just coming up." They went outside together, and Jean frowned up at the darkening sky. It was mid-morning, almost June, and the weather could dictate things in the ocean.

The wind clawed at Jean's hair, which she hadn't secured back into a ponytail yet. She got that job done while Halle and Tara arrived. "We might need jackets," she said, but the girls waved away her protests.

"The sky over there is blue," Halle said. "We'll be fine once we get out there."

Jean spied the blue sky in the west, and she nodded. "Sabrina is a little worried about today, you guys." She looked at Tara, who was the leader of this group. "Let's be really supportive of her today."

"Yeah, of course," Tara said, glancing at Halle. "Where do you think she'll be the most comfortable?"

"Land," Karly said dryly, and the other girls smiled.

"She's here," Jean said as a minivan pulled into the parking lot. "It's huge that she's even here."

"Her mom won't let her do anything if she doesn't come," Halle said. "Even school."

"School?" Jean looked between the three girls while trying to keep one eye on Sabrina. Behind her came Cheryl and Emmy, who lived next-door to one another. That was everyone, and Jean would be on a boat in less than ten minutes.

She adored boats, and she'd really enjoyed her Monday and Wednesday outings this week. Having the girls work together bonded them in a way that book work, tying knots, and doing shoreline activities simply couldn't.

Sailing brought Jean joy, and she hoped it would do the same for all of her girls.

"Yeah, school," Halle said almost under her breath. "Her mom said she'd home-school Bri if she didn't come to her stuff on the weekends."

"Why?" Jean asked.

"Her mom's brother died in a boating accident," Tara said, stepping away to go greet the girl. "She wants her to know how to survive on water. Hey, Bri." Her voice brightened in volume and pitch as she reached Bri. She hugged her and brought her right into the rest of the group.

Jean offered her a blinding smile too, her phone vibrating a few times in her pocket. She couldn't be distracted with her own personal issues today. She shelved them by pulling out her phone and silencing it, then facing all the girls as Cheryl and Emmy arrived.

"All right," she said. "We're sailing today. We need to get all of the equipment out of the shed, get it on the boat, and get going." She'd given the girls all of the tools they needed to do this, and Tara nodded.

"Let's go," Tara said, and she led the way down the sidewalk to a set of steps that took them to a storage shed. The rocky cliffs gave way to a rockier beach, where the girls had learned paddling, how to put up a sail, knot-tying, water safety, and more.

Today, a glorious, white sailboat had been anchored at the temporary dock, and sunlight filled Jean's soul. "Isn't she so pretty?" she asked, and Cheryl in front of her confirmed that the boat was beautiful.

Jean stayed out of the way while Halle and Tara directed everyone to get life jackets, the ropes they needed, their navigation technology, and their supplies. Jean had taught them never to go out on a boat without water and cellphones. To make sure the radio on the vessel worked, and how to check the boat to make sure she was seaworthy.

Cheryl and Emmy ran through that checklist, while Bri and Karly brought on the water, checked the radio, and slathered on sunscreen. Jean got on the boat when Tara called to her that they were ready, and then Halle, Tara, and Karly launched them away from the dock.

The gentle rocking back and forth of the boat soothed Jean, the way a mother would soothe her crying infant. She smiled with her eyes closed, her face leaning toward the sun. It disappeared, covering Jean's eyelids with a deep navy color that prompted her to open her eyes.

Not a moment later, the boat jerked as the sails caught a huge gust of wind. "Whoa," she said, grabbing onto the pole nearby.

Bri cried out, but she steadied herself, and Tara called out, "It's okay. Just caught big wind there."

She and Halle manned the rudders and the wheel, steering the boat past Sea Lion Beach and around toward the northern tip of Diamond Island. They couldn't quite circumnavigate the whole island in an hour, so Jean had been taking them to the docks where the steamers came in from Nantucket and then back to the east side of the island.

The big commercial docks where the fisherman launched from sat on that side of the island, while the commercial shipping ports resided on the west. Ferry terminals ran out of the north and south ports, and the Nantucket Steamer came in on the northwest corner of Diamond.

Out on the water, Jean always felt so small. The ocean itself felt all-encompassing, and the land only a couple of miles away that was Sanctuary Island loomed in the distance.

"Take a breath, girls," she said. "Feel how free you can be out here. Isn't it great?"

The sun hadn't come out yet, and Jean wished she'd gone back inside to get a jacket. Still, with the cool wind kissing her skin, she felt free. Wild and wonderful and free.

Out here, she didn't need to worry about how Eloise would feel when Clara and Scott opened Friendship Inn. She didn't have to lament the fact that she and Reuben hadn't been chosen as parents since they'd lost the baby a few months ago. She didn't have to feel unworthy inside her own skin.

Out here, the waves treated everyone the exact same. Push and pull. Stop and roll. Come and go.

Something clanged, and then a horrible whistling sound filled the air. They'd just rounded the northeastern side of the island which was made of sheer cliffs, and the rocks echoed the shriek back to them.

Just like that, the sails went limp. The boat started to lilt and drift. They'd lost their power, and they existed inside the shade from the cliffs.

The temperature plummeted, and a spray of water came cresting up over the bow of the boat. Cheryl and Karly cried out as they got soaked, and Cheryl swung back to Tara. "We can't stay here! The waves are too big!"

The boat rocked dangerously now, and Jean scrambled past the cockpit, where Tara and Halle hovered, to the middle part of the boat, where the mast raised up and held the mainsail. The boom swung wildly, and Jean ducked down so she wouldn't be taken out by it.

Around her, girls shouted at one another, and Jean straightened and looked up. Up, up, up into the sky, along the mast.

It had bent, and was very near to breaking.

They were in trouble.

The jib still had some wind in it, but that sail was taking them closer to the cliffs, not further away. "I'm going to release it!" Bri yelled, and she unhooked the connection to the bow, rendering both of their sails obsolete.

A quiet fell over them, the only sound now the lapping of waves against the side of the boat. The wind played an eerie tune as it moved through cracks and crevices in the cliffs, and Jean didn't want to get any closer to them.

"All right," she said. "Halle, we need our mast repair kit here. Tara, get on the radio and let them know we need help." Jean pulled out her phone to check for a signal. She had a weak one, but she couldn't call for help. The radio would alert the right people.

"Cheryl, Bri, get over here and hold this. We need to fix that bend so we don't lose the mast in the water." Jean didn't even want to think about what they'd have to do then.

"We're in neutral. The boat is moving broadside," Halle called. Instantly, the rocking intensified, and Jean's stomach lurched with the more violent movement.

"Karly, you're the smallest. You're going to climb up with the kit." Jean gestured the petite girl over to the mast.

"There's footholds there. We can cleat it on both sides, and we can get the stabilizing rod around it, like you do to straighten a tree."

They'd have to turn back immediately, though Jean considered continuing their trek around these cliffs. If they could just get there, they could make it to the ferry port. At this point, it was probably sixes for what was closer.

"Here's the kit," Halle said.

"Guys," Tara called, enough urgency in her voice to bring every eye to her in the cockpit. She lifted the handheld radio. "There's no signal."

Jean panicked, the feeling welling up from her toes to her knees to her gut. She pushed against the waves of emotion. "What do you mean?"

She left the others standing at the mast and picked her way to Tara in a few seconds. She grabbed the radio from her and pressed the button. "Five Island Cove dock and lighthouse, this is vessel Seafaring-seven-four-eight-one, requesting assistance on the northeast corner cliffs."

Nothing came back. Not even static.

Tara pointed up to the mast, and Jean realized someone had dismantled the boom so it wasn't swinging wildly and causing problems. "The antenna was on the mast." She pointed up to it, the black wire swinging in the wind.

"I'll call for help," Jean said. "Karly, get up the mast and get securing it." She looked at Tara. "Stay here and man the controls. Have them call out to you what they're doing."

She turned her back on the teenager, telling herself she was the adult. She was in charge. It was up to her to ensure their safety and get them back to land immediately. She jabbed at the numbers on her phone, figuring 9-1-1 would be enough to get the right people out to them.

The line rang once, but she couldn't hear anyone on the other end of the line. "We need help," she said anyway. "I've got six teenage girls on a sailboat on the northeast side of the island. Our radio is out, and our mast is broken."

No response.

Jean hung up and willed her fingers to fly faster and faster as she texted the top number on her list.

Kelli.

She watched the circle next to the message go round and round and round, her desperation turning into a sob. She sucked it back in. She would not break down out here with these girls. They hadn't, and she would *not*.

She spun around when a cry lifted into the air. Horror filled her as Karly slipped, tried desperately to grab onto the mast, and missed.

She fell, and Jean screamed. She rushed forward as the girls closed ranks and caught Karly, simultaneous pride and fear striking her behind the heart again, and again, and again.

Karly found her footing, and Jean's chest throbbed as it heaved. "Okay," she said, her voice made mostly of air. "Are you okay?"

"Yes." Karly nodded, though her face was the color of cheery puffy clouds on a clear summer day. Which was not today.

Jean looked around at the five girls around her, then back to Tara. "We're going around the cliffs to the ferry port.

Let's tear down the rigging. Pull in all the lines. We'll stow them in the cockpit lockers. We don't want anything to interfere with the propellers."

She checked her phone as the girls got to work, the circle still spinning, spinning, spinning.

Chapter Thirty-Two

K elli dropped the colored pencil she'd been using to shade the sky in Parker's coloring book.

"Mom," he said, but Kelli's hands trembled as she re-read the text she'd just gotten from Jean.

We're drifting on the northeast corner of Diamond. Lost our mast. Radio wire severed. Need help.

The text had just come in, but Kelli had no idea if Jean had actually just sent it or not.

Her fingers stumbled as she tapped out a message for Jean. *I'll get help. Are you turning around or going toward the ferry station?*

She didn't wait for a response before dialing 9-1-1. She paced away from the table in the corner of Shad's office, where she and Parker had been waiting for him to get done with one of his weekend meetings. Then they had plans to get chicken sandwiches and walk the beaches on Diamond before heading back to their twinhome on Pearl Island.

Summer only lay another week in the future, and Kelli had committed to taking more time away from Whole Soul so she could sunbathe with her friends, take lunch to her husband on a weekday, and make sure Parker got out of the house and did summery things with his friends.

She'd already penciled in helping Robin move into her new house and taking a weekend trip to Nantucket with AJ and Jean. They hadn't invited everyone along yet, though Kelli had told the others that they should.

"Yes, I need Coast Guard or search and rescue to go get a sailboat on the northeast corner of the island. My friend is out there with her Seafaring Girls, and they've lost their mast and their radio."

"Ma'am, all boats have just been called out to an emergency six miles off the coast of New York."

The air left Kelli's lungs. "What?"

"I can probably rustle up a fishing boat that can go." The 9-1-1 operator sounded apologetic. "There's been a multiboat collision that all of our first responders have gone to. Came in fifteen minutes ago."

"I have a friend with a fishing boat," Kelli said. "I'll call him." She didn't wait for the emergency services operator to confirm. She hung up and called Robin. "Robin," she said breathlessly, striding out of the office. "Can Duke get us out to the northeast cliffs? Jean's stranded out there with her girls."

"Duke...what?"

Kelli really didn't want to explain again. Frustration fueled her tongue, and she spoke in rapid-fire words. "Jean's stuck with her girls on a boat with a broken mast and no radio. They need help. All of the Coast Guard boats went to an emergency. I need a boat, and Duke has a boat."

"He's fishing today," Robin said, her voice small and sounding very far away. "Even if I called him back..." She let the words hang there, because he wouldn't make it in time.

Kelli burst out of the downtown buildings where Shad worked, her mind on overdrive. She didn't even realize it had started to rain until the drops hit her skin. "Jean's out in this," she said, her voice choking. "We have to go help her."

"They just suspended ferry service," Robin said. "Due to wind."

"I'm going to the dock," Kelli said. "I'm going to find a boat, and I'm going to go help those girls."

"Kelli—" Robin started, but Kelli ended the call. She ran back inside, yelling to Parker. He came out into the hallway, and she skidded to a stop in front of him, dropping to her knees.

"I have to go help Jean," she said. "You stay right here and color. Shad will be out in twenty minutes."

"Can I go?" he asked.

Kelli smoothed back his hair. "No, baby. You stay here." With that, she rose to her feet again and ran back toward the exit. She called a RideShare, and they were still running, because one pulled up a few minutes later.

By then, she'd texted everyone on their group chat, and responses had come pouring in. She should've thought to call Laurel, as the woman had police department connections. Kelli's mind frayed along the edges, and she barely had the wherewithal to tell the RideShare driver where she wanted to go.

"West dock," she said. "Fast." She trained her eyes on her phone and saw Laurel's text as it came in.

We're on the way, she said. *Sirens going. I'll get you a boat.*

Thank you, Kelli typed out.

She tried another message to Jean, hoping something would go through. Multi-person messages usually sent a different way, but perhaps she'd get a single text from Kelli.

We're coming Jean. Hold on.

TWENTY MINUTES LATER, KELLI CINCHED THE straps securing the lifejacket around her waist and stepped from the dock onto the boat. She hadn't been on a boat besides a ferry in a while, as she wasn't the hugest fan of water vessels. She pushed against her fear and turned back to help Eloise onto the boat.

Alice, Robin, and AJ had all come too, and every one of them insisted on getting on the motorized boat Laurel had managed to secure. She was on-duty and with her partner, so she wouldn't be coming with them. Kristen stood next to her, her hands worrying about one another while she wept.

Kelli didn't know everything that had gone on between Kristen, Jean, Clara, or anyone else. She knew for Eloise to be here was a great sacrifice, and she knew exactly who would take control of this boat.

Alice, just as she had in the past. And when Alice needed a minute to breathe, Robin would take charge. AJ would do whatever anyone told her, and Eloise and Kelli would do what they'd been taught. They'd never really stepped into leadership roles as teens in the Seafaring Girls program, but Kelli felt a new fire inside her as she strode toward the controls of the boat.

Alice stood there, and Kelli joined her. "Let's go," she said. "We're all on." As if punctuating how dangerous this rescue mission was, the wind intensified and drove the rain straight into her face.

Someone came running toward them, waving both hands above his head.

"Now," Kelli said. "Or they're going to ground us."

Alice looked up and saw the man too. His voice shouted on the wind, no words audible.

"Robin?"

The blonde woman heaved in the last of the ropes, and yelled, "Go!"

Alice hit the gas to ease the boat back away from the dock, but she'd punched it. Everyone lurched; cries rang out. Once Kelli had gripped the railing in front of her, she glanced at Alice to find determination in the thin line of her mouth.

"We have to go," she said, as if that explained her violent launch from the dock.

The boat had a big spotlight on the front of it, and Kelli flipped it on as they started north away from the docks. The others crowded in around them, the rain creating a symphony off wood, metal, and plastic.

The scent of rain usually made Kelli smile, but today it just signified dampness and danger.

"Look," AJ said, and Kelli lifted her head. "The lighthouse is on."

The bright beam cut across the water, sweeping left and then right, welcoming and warning all who got close to Diamond Island.

"Rueben is probably beside himself," Robin murmured, and Kelli could only agree.

"It's okay," she said. "They're going to be fine. We'll get to them, and they'll be fine." Perhaps if she thought so, it would become true.

The trek past the lighthouse, past Sea Lion Beach, and toward the curve in the cliffs seemed to take forever. Kelli had breathed a thousand times. Her whole life had laid flat in front of her, and it could not include any harm to Jean Shields.

She loved the woman like a sister, and she had to help her. Kelli moved out of the cockpit and toward the bow of the boat, taking care to hold onto ropes and handholds in the railing. If she stood up here, she could position the light and start to search for the boat.

With frozen fingers, she swept the light left and right, steady and slowly the way the lighthouse bulb moved. She couldn't see anything.

Then, all at once, the light caught on something shiny and white. She stilled the spotlight right on the sailboat.

It drifted in the choppy water, dark slashes of waves against the whiteness of the boat. The mast had been broken straight in half, and no other sails, riggings, or equipment could be seen.

"There," she called over her shoulder. "Bring the rescue ropes up!" Kelli climbed up on the lower railing and cupped her hands around her mouth. "Jean!" she screamed into the wind. "Jean!"

Why couldn't she see anyone on-board. Had they fallen overboard? Panic gripped Kelli's vocal cords, and she hurried back to the spotlight to start sweeping the water surrounding the boat. If they'd fallen in, those cliffs would make mincemeat out of them.

She saw nothing in the water, and when she refocused the light on the sailboat again, a woman stood there.

Jean.

No coat. Short sleeves. Hair plastered to her head and face. She waved one hand above her body as one, two, four, six girls crowded in around her.

"Dear Lord," Robin said right out loud. "Please hold off on the really bad weather for just twenty more minutes."

"Get us closer!" AJ called to Alice, who still manned the controls of the boat. Kelli joined her best friend on the rails again, this time with a rope in her hand. If she could get the drifting sailboat attached to this trawler, they could stabilize it enough to get the girls over here.

Alice inched them nearer and nearer, at a pace that made Kelli want to rage into the storm. The sky lightened and then darkened, and the wind picked up right as she tossed her rope.

One of the girls on the sailboat lunged for it and grabbed it. She quickly tied it to their boat, and Kelli pulled them closer, closer, closer.

Finally, the hull of the trawler nudged the sailboat. Jean pushed a girl forward, and the petite teenager started the journey across railings and a two-foot gap of ocean from one boat to the next.

Robin received her with a blanket and hustled her off toward the sheltered part of the trawler. Girl after girl arrived, until only Jean stood with one girl. They appeared to be arguing, and the remaining teen sobbed and sobbed.

"She's afraid of water!" Jean yelled to them. "I can't leave her here."

Kelli looked at AJ, who stared steadily on back. Without another thought, she went over the railing, the gap, and another steel railing to the sailboat. "What's your name?" she asked, her lungs tangled in her tongue.

"Sabrina," Jean supplied for the dark-haired girl.

"I'm Kelli," Kelli said. "I did Seafaring Girls when I was your age. I hated it."

Sabrina looked up at her with wide, frightened eyes. "You did?"

"I didn't like the program, but I loved my friends. I was so scared of the water. Once, we went out to Friendship Island, and we lost sight of the land. We were just out in all this water." She put on the bravest smile she could. "I couldn't give up. I couldn't let my friends down. I rowed and rowed and rowed."

She gestured to the boat behind her. "No rowing over there. You just need to get over there so we can get back home."

"You can do it!" someone yelled, and Kelli turned back to find the teens had returned to the railing.

One girl gestured at them. "Come on, Bri! It's just a few steps."

They continued to offer her their encouragement, and Kelli's heart swelled with love for this terrified girl, for those trying to buoy her up, and for the four women who'd come into the belly of an ocean storm with her without question.

"Come on," Kelli said. "I did it, and I hate the ocean. You can do it."

"I hate the ocean too," Bri said, her lips trembling.

"Then we'll go together." She put her hand in Bri's and guided her fingers to where to hold. "Step there. Grab the rope. Then the railing. Go. Now."

Bri did, scampering across the space and into the arms of her Seafaring Girls.

Kelli looked at AJ again, this time with boat railings and water, rain and wind, between them. She bridged the gap easily and turned back to help Jean should she need it.

Once Jean had arrived on board, Robin yelled, "Back up, Alice! Take us back!"

Only then did Kelli look up and see how close the cliffs had gotten during their rescue. They towered above her, no sky showing for how close Kelli stood to them.

Terror gripped her heart, but Alice used the powerful motor on the trawler to get the boat away from the cliffs and out of danger.

Only then did Kelli take a full breath and face her friends. Eloise was the first to step forward and hug her, saying, "You did it. You saved them."

Robin piled onto the hug, as did AJ, and then Alice.

"No," Kelli said. "We all did it. Together." While her arms were full, she managed to open them a little wider, an indication for Jean to join them. She did, and so did all of her Seafaring Girls.

"Seafaring Girls forever," Kelli whispered, and Robin repeated it. Then Alice, until everyone was chanting it together, in time with the pounding rain on the deck.

Chapter Thirty-Three

A J left the bathroom, a sigh moving through her body. Heat and light filled the cottage, and AJ had only been so thankful to be safe, dry, and warm on a couple of other occasions.

The chatter out in the kitchen area of Kristen's former cottage told her that the coffee had finished and people had started to thaw. She paused in the doorway that led back to the two bedrooms and single bath, noting that all the girls had been picked up. That had likely contributed to the looser, more relaxed tongues too.

Kelli met her eye, and they had an entire conversation. AJ had not seen Kelli as determined and as fierce as she had on the dock and then the trawler in a long time. Maybe ever. She migrated over to the other woman and slipped her arm around her.

"Did Shad take Parker home?"

"They're getting the chicken sandwiches and coming here," she said. "We might just stay on Diamond. The wind is still kicking up out there, and ferries are getting blown around." Kel leaned into AJ, the tension finally leaving her body. "I can't believe I went over those railings."

AJ grinned at Jean and Robin as they talked. She noted that Eloise stayed out of the kitchen and over by Rueben, Aaron, and Laurel. In fact, the three of them made a wall between her and Kristen, who'd been cornered in the kitchen with Alice and Arthur.

"It was amazing to watch," AJ said. "Matt's on his way too. I guess the golf course was going to wait out the storm, but when it reaches a certain amount of rain, the ground is too wet. They don't want people's cleats ripping up the green."

"Makes sense."

AJ thought so too, and she'd told him that she'd left Asher with their neighbor so she could come be with her friends. Jean's conversation with Robin wrapped, and they both turned toward Kelli and AJ.

Jean had gone home to shower, and she now wore a sweatsuit with a matching top and bottom in a bright, fluffy blue. "Thank you, Kelli." She wrapped Kelli in a hug and held on, her eyes clenching shut too. "I don't know what we would've done had you not gotten my text."

"You'd have made it to the ferry station," Kelli said without hesitation. "You'd have been fine."

AJ wasn't sure about that, and she took a turn hugging

Jean too. Her eyes met Kristen's as she pulled away, and she instantly swung back around to Eloise. She disliked the tension in the group, while previously, she'd thrived on it.

AJ had loved competition and sports, and she didn't mind being in the thick of contention. Motherhood had changed her, and she just wanted everyone to get along. Maybe she could handle it professionally and not personally anymore. She wasn't sure.

What she knew was that she wanted Kristen and El to get along. She wanted Eloise to know how much she was loved, and she needed Kristen to know she could make her own decisions and be supported.

She nodded at Eloise to come over, but she gave AJ a quick shake of her head. Helplessness filled AJ, and she accepted a warm mug of coffee from Alice.

"I see something brewing in you," Alice murmured.

"I hate that they won't talk through this," AJ said, frowning at the sugar bowl. She added a teaspoon and started to stir, watching the dark liquid swirl and gobble up the granules. "This cottage feels the way my house did for years. Suffocating."

AJ just wanted to *breathe*.

She moved away from Alice and pulled out one of the two chairs at the small dining room table. She might be forty-six years old, but she'd gotten married and given birth in the past year. She'd often been the talk around the cove. She'd stood on a chair in front of her friends before.

Maybe not this many—with the Chief of Police, Laurel,

and Jean present—but her memories flowed thick as she put one foot on the chair seat and boosted herself up. "Okay," she called, and all conversations stopped.

"AvaJane," Kristen said quietly, but AJ ignored her just as she had over thirty years ago when Kristen had tried to coax her off the chair.

"This is stupid," AJ said, starting her speech the same way now as she had then. "Remember that time when everyone was mad at me because I'd started going out with Wes Gregory? Robin wouldn't talk to me, because she'd already expressed interest in him. Alice sided with Robin. Laurel wasn't around, but she'd have looked at me with that cop-look in her eyes, questioning my sanity."

She smiled at Laurel, whose face broke into a grin too. "I didn't sleep with him, though everyone thought I had. Kel knew I hadn't, and Eloise—in proper Eloise fashion—stayed out of it. But it made an impact at our Seafaring Girls meetings. I could tell Robin was mad at me, but back then, I didn't know how to talk. I didn't know how to apologize."

Her words clogged in her throat, but AJ pressed forward. Her one saving grace was that Matt wasn't here yet to hear all of this.

"Eloise, I love you with my whole soul. I don't want to pick sides, and I know Kristen doesn't want to either. You are an amazing person, and I know you feel like your future now rests on rocky ground, but I don't think it does."

Eloise simply blinked at her, and AJ turned toward Kristen. "Kristen, I know you carry guilt for your daughter and that she doesn't like the cove. I've read several articles about her and Scott's situation, and I'd want to rescue them too."

"I'm not rescuing them," Kristen said, her voice powerful but quiet.

"You're helping them," AJ said. "I would do the same for my child. Now that I'm a mother, I understand this deep, bottomless need to make sure my son has what he needs. I can't imagine that dries up as they age."

Alice stepped to AJ's side, and that move told AJ that Alice would be up on this chair, saying all the same things if she could.

"I want this summer to be amazing," AJ said. "I want us to get together and not have El park down on one end, silent. Or Kristen choose to stay in her condo when she could be with us. I want to welcome Clara back to the cove the way you guys welcomed me back. I'm going to be the most amazing Godmother to Laurel's baby, and I...can't." Her voice broke. "I can't do it alone. Please. Please, let's just talk."

Robin came to stand next to Alice, facing Eloise. Laurel left her husband's side and joined them, then Jean. Kelli joined the ranks, and she and Jean faced Kristen.

"Mom," Reuben said, and that was the male version of everything AJ had just said.

Kristen moved to the mouth of the kitchen, her eyes on her son. They switched to the women standing in the middle of the cottage, a united front, then to Eloise.

Aaron bent his head toward hers and said something, and Eloise nodded. She took a step toward Kristen, then another, and on the third one, she broke into a jog. With the small size of the cottage, she didn't have many more steps to reach the older woman, and they embraced.

"I'm sorry, dear," Kristen whispered, holding fiercely onto Eloise. "I do not want to hurt you."

"I know." Eloise kept her eyes closed. "They'll be two different types of places. It's not me or her."

"Exactly," Laurel said. "One is a completely different type of experience than the other."

"Clara is hard to swallow," Jean said. "We're going to need each other when she moves here."

"A safe place to fall for sure," Robin added.

"Just like we always are for one another," Alice said.

AJ's eyes burned, and she reached for Kelli's hand so she could get off this chair without killing herself. When she had both feet solidly on the ground again, she stepped into Kristen and Eloise and hugged them both too.

This time, no one started chanting *Seafaring Girls forever*, but AJ felt the chorus way down in her very being. Every fiber vibrated with love and acceptance for the people in this cottage. They gave her the same thing—a place to belong, a safe spot for her to get up on chairs and speak her mind, a feeling of love that couldn't be revoked.

Woman after woman joined the hug in the middle of the cottage, so many arms around AJ. Every hand patting her on the back, whispering, *We love you. You've got this thing called life. You're not alone.*

The door opened, and AJ caught Matt's eye as he froze,

their son in his arms. He took in the scene and looked at Aaron. "What did I walk in on?"

Aaron started to laugh, and so did Eloise, right in the middle of the group hug. AJ giggled too, but she quickly wiped her eyes as the group broke up. Then she made a beeline for the man who'd always been the eye of life's hurricane for AJ.

"Hey, my love," he whispered, his big hand landing on her back. "Say hi to Mommy, bud."

"Ma-ma-ma-ma," Asher babbled, and AJ pulled away, surprise running through her. Her son had been vocalizing for weeks now, but usually B-sounds, or "da-da-da."

Matt beamed at her, and then Asher. "That's right, bud. Mama." Matt kissed AJ, and everything shifted in her life again. This time, all the pieces moved into the right places, and she turned back to the group to find Eloise hugging Jean, and Reuben embracing his mother.

Seafaring Girls forever, AJ thought, turning as someone else entered the cottage. This time, it was Mandie, and she carried a huge tray of sandwiches.

"Food's here," AJ called, moving to help Robin's daughters carry in the fresh fruit, veggie tray, and drinks.

"Wow," Eloise said, arriving to help too. "I thought this was for your graduation party," she said, glancing at Mandie.

"That's not until next week," the girl said with a grin. "Mom called and said get food, and Jamie and I ran to the grocery store."

"Ginny and I went too," Charlie said, ducking under the eaves and entering the house ahead of his twin. He smiled at

Mandie and glanced at her tray. "Looks like you got the food, and we brought the desserts."

"Don't stop in the doorway," Ginny griped, and everyone moved out of the way so she and Emily could bring in the mint brownies.

Chapter Thirty-Four

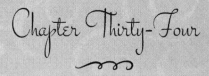

Jean stood on Robin's doorstep, the huge barrel of ice cream sitting at her feet. Mandie herself opened the door, and Jean gave her a caring smile. "You're answering the door at your own party?"

Mandie returned the grin and reached for the plastic bag in Jean's hand. "I knew it was you, and that you'd have the ice cream."

"Reuben is getting the rest," Jean said, checking over her shoulder. "He'll have the smaller bucket with him."

Mandie ducked out onto the front porch. "Great, then we can sneak a bite before we go in."

Jean didn't argue with her, and when Reuben arrived with a five-gallon container of the banana chocolate chip ice cream, Mandie took it from him and told him he could put the bigger barrel in the chest freezer in the garage. Then she sat on the top step and rummaged around inside the bag to get out a plastic spoon.

Mandie offered one to Jean, who joined her on the steps with a sigh. "All graduated," Jean said, gazing across the street. This neighborhood sat in peace and quiet, and Jean did enjoy the quaintness of it. When Robin moved, she'd be in an equally quiet and pristine neighborhood, one a little newer than this.

"Yeah," Mandie said, cracking the lid on the ice cream container.

"Are you excited to go to the city?" Jean asked. Her mouth watered at the sight of the creamy, off-white ice cream, with specks of chocolate throughout.

"I am." Mandie dug out a chunk of ice cream and handed the bucket to Jean. "It's a little scary, but my mom never really left the cove, and I want to get away from here... at least for a little while."

"You'll love the city," Jean said, taking her own bite of ice cream. The banana flavor melted in her mouth, and she bit down on the chocolate chip and got the burst of sugar. "It's different, for sure, but that's what you want, right? Different."

"Definitely," Mandie said.

"Is your mom giving you grief about Charlie?" Jean passed the ice cream back to the teen.

"Not anymore," Mandie said. "I think she's accepted that I'm an adult, and I'm not a total idiot." She gave Jean a wry smile, and Jean shook her head and giggled.

"You're definitely not an idiot."

Behind them, the door opened, and Robin said, "There you are." A beat passed as she came outside and Mandie and

Jean twisted back to her. She surveyed the scene, her expression changing quickly. "What is going on here?"

"Just an ice cream appetizer," Mandie said, getting to her feet. She gave the ice cream container to her mother, along with her spoon. "Try it. Jean's a genius with cream and sugar." She continued into the house, leaving Jean on the steps and Robin holding the treats.

Robin exhaled as she settled onto the cement. She took a bite of the ice cream, a moan starting down in her throat. "She's right. Genius."

Jean smiled and capped the container. "Come on. You don't have time to sit out here and eat ice cream."

"I know, but I don't want to go back in."

"Of course you do. You love parties."

"I like parties celebrating happy things," Robin clarified. "And this is my oldest daughter leaving home."

"Which is a good thing," Jean said. "She's ready, Robin, and she's smart."

"As everyone has been telling me for weeks." Robin smiled and licked her spoon clean. "All right. Help me up so I can go check on the grill and make sure Arthur hasn't distracted Duke to the point of charring something."

Jean stood and extended her hand toward Robin, helping her stand. A pause happened, and Jean gave Robin an encouraging look. "I know this is hard, but you're handling it like a pro." She drew Robin into a hug, surprised that the power blonde sank into the gesture.

Jean had always regarded Robin as the woman who had everything together. She had the answer to every problem.

She didn't fear anything. In that moment, she realized how human Robin Grover was, and how much she loved her for being real.

"You're one of my heroes," Jean whispered. "She's not leaving forever. She's just going twelve miles away, and she has a phone with video capability."

"Right," Robin said, pulling away. She looked Jean straight in the eyes. "You are one of my heroes too, Jean."

The door opened again and an angry Alice stood there. "What are you two doing out here? Things are imploding in here."

"Imploding?" Robin repeated at the same time Jean started to laugh. She couldn't even hear chatter and laughter coming from inside.

Alice's face dissolved into a smile as she backed up and gestured for Jean and Robin to follow her inside. They did, and the closer Jean came to the kitchen, the louder the crowd became.

Jean had left this only a few minutes ago, but she saw everyone with new eyes now. Alice stepped over to Kristen and AJ, who had a large cutting board covered with chunks of watermelon. She merged herself right into the conversation as if she'd never left it, and Jean knew she could also step over to Kelli and Parker, Shad and Jamie, who were laying out pieces of cheese on a tray that already held lettuce leaves and tomato slices and join them too.

She didn't know Alice's father and step-mother well, but AJ's sister seemed to be entertaining them just fine, and Jean wouldn't be afraid to make small talk with anyone here.

Eloise came in the back door, empty-handed. "Duke says the hot dogs and hamburgers are ready," she called. "Buns are outside."

Robin entered the fray, as it was her house and a lot of her party. Jean found the teens huddled together on the couch, Charlie between Ginny and Mandie. Billie had squished in on one side of them, with Emily on the other, all of them peering at something on Charlie's phone.

"Everyone, let's go outside," Robin yelled. "If there are condiments sitting on the counter, pick them up and take them with you."

The teens burst into laughter in the lull in conversation, which drew all the eyes of the adults and others prepping the food. Alice moved forward, frowning at her kids. "Charlie, put that away. The party is starting."

He stood, which got all the girls to get to their feet too. "Yeah, sure." He pocketed his phone easily, his smile wide and sticking to his face despite his mother's displeasure. In fact, he slung his arm around her and kept on grinning.

Alice caved under his charm, and Robin lifted both hands above her head. "Mom, grab that watermelon. AJ and Kelli, all the bottles, please. Plates and utensils are already out here. Toppings and buns. Duke will serve the meat right from the grill."

Robin paused and looked around at everyone, from Arthur to her mother to Matt Hymas to Rueben to Alice's father. Tears filled her eyes as she paused on Eloise, Alice, AJ, Kelli, and Kristen.

She wiped at her face as she smiled at Jean, and one

more voice entered the fray. "Sorry, we're late," Laurel called, and she hurried down the hall, her husband Paul right behind her. They both wore expressions of anxiety that melted away when they saw that the party hadn't really started yet.

"Thank you for coming," Robin said. "This feels like a good way to celebrate Mandie, Charlie, Ginny, and Emily as they finish something long and hard, and an amazing way to start summer."

Alice lifted her mocktail, a bright red concoction with two lime wedges in it. "To Mandie, Charlie, Ginny, and Emily."

"To summer," Eloise added, lifting her Diet Coke can.

Jean didn't have anything to drink, but she added her voice to those offering congratulations and good wishes, and then Duke poked his head into the house. "Everything's getting too hot or too cold. Let's eat."

Robin grinned at him and then everyone else one more time. "Yes, let's eat."

A WEEK LATER, JEAN GAZED AT THE BRAND-NEW sailboat at the dock. "It'll be great," she said to Rueben, who stood at her side.

"No Seafaring Girls for a while, though, right?"

"Just June," Jean said. She needed a break. They needed one. Several of the girls and their families were taking vacations. They'd lost their boat. It felt like a few weeks off would reset everyone, and Jean couldn't wait to meet with her girls again.

She also couldn't wait to show her friends the new boat. She lifted her phone and snapped another picture. She'd see them all later today at their first beach afternoon of the summer. Even Chief Sherman would be there, and Jean had already called dibs on taking Asher into the ocean for the first time this season.

Still, neither she nor Rueben moved from the rocky beach, the lighthouse up the sidewalk and behind them. This dock was private, and Jean wanted to come here whenever she needed to dip her toes in the water and think.

"You're going to come to the beach this afternoon, right?" she asked.

"Yeah," Rueben said. "I don't think there'll be any emergencies today." The sky stretched into blueness above them, without a single skiff of white for a cloud. Down here, Jean couldn't feel a breeze, but the boat rocked gently with the waves as they came ashore.

The day wasn't too hot yet, but as the sun continued to warm the islands, her feet would burn on the white sand on the other side of Diamond Island later.

"Let me just send this to everyone, and then we can go start packing lunch."

"Mm." Rueben placed a kiss against Jean's cheekbone. "I'm so glad you're mine, Jean."

She looked up from her phone, surprised at his statement. Reuben was very good at showing how much he loved Jean. She'd never doubted him. He was less vocal about it, though he'd definitely told her he loved her. He'd said he didn't need anyone but her.

Their eyes met, and Jean tipped her head back to receive his kiss. "I'm glad you're mine too," she whispered. No, they didn't have a baby. Jean wasn't sure if they'd ever get one. Their adoption profile was still active, but they hadn't been chosen for parenthood in the past six months since losing the baby.

Jean had been checking the website and her email for the adoption agency less and less. She loved her Seafaring Girls. She loved her friends. She loved her husband.

Life had knocked her down a time or two, but she'd always gotten back up. Just a week or so ago, she'd been stranded on a boat, getting pushed toward cliffs. She'd been rescued; she'd survived.

She tucked herself into her husband's chest and faced the new boat. Not only had she survived, but she'd get out on that sailboat again. She wasn't going to let the storms of life scare her or bar her from what she wanted.

Her husband needed her to be strong. She had two dogs to take care of, and sewing lessons, and all those girls to educate about the sea and boats.

Kelli would need support this summer too, as Parker was once again going to New Jersey to be with his father. Alice was losing both of her children in a few short months. Robin was moving. Laurel was due with her first baby at the end of the summer.

Kristen's daughter was moving here, and Eloise had tasks to do with her family and the inn up to her eyeballs.

Jean could—and would—help them all.

Her phone chimed, and Jean removed it from her pocket. "Oh, boy," she said, tilting the device so Reuben could see it.

He exhaled and looked out across the water. "What are you going to tell her?"

Jean re-read the message from her mother. She did miss her, and it had been very hard for her to leave her family in Long Island and move to Five Island Cove.

"I'll tell her to come anytime," Jean said, deciding on the spot. "After all, I won't have to be alone to entertain her this summer."

"True," Reuben said. "Just don't let her try to convince you to go back to Long Island."

"I think she knows who I've chosen," Jean said, sending the message to her mom and putting her phone back in her pocket. She turned toward Reuben. "That's you, in case that wasn't clear."

He grinned down at her, touched his lips to hers, and said, "Yeah, if your friends aren't doing anything more fun than watching waves."

She giggled and cradled his face in her hands. "You're glad I have friends, though, right?"

"Of course," Reuben said. "I'm thrilled about that. You've...come alive in the past six months, Jean, and you've barely been to therapy. I'm absolutely glad you have your friends."

Jean nodded and pressed her eyes closed as she tapped

her forehead against her husband's. "Me too," she said. "But you're still my very best friend."

"I'm glad about that too." Reuben kissed her again, and Jean enjoyed the slow comfort he offered in his touch. He pulled away and said, "All right. Let's go pack lunch for today."

As they went back up the sidewalk to the lighthouse, Jean said, "This summer should be interesting, what with Clara and Scott moving here."

"I hope we all survive it," Reuben said seriously, and Jean added her hopes and prayers to that sentiment too.

She thought of Robin, Alice, AJ, Kelli, and Eloise. She thought of her mother-in-law, and Laurel. With the seven women in her mind, Jean knew they'd more than survive this summer.

They'd make the absolute best of it.

Read on for the first couple chapters of **Rebuilding Friendship Inn** for more great friendship and sisterhood fiction that brings women together and celebrates the female relationship.

Rebuilding Friendship Inn Chapter One:

C lara Tanner knelt in front of her daughter, pressing the busyness of the airport out of her peripheral vision. "Lena," she said. "Look at Mom."

The twenty-year-old clutched her stuffed elephant, her eyes blitzing all over the place. This man. That woman. The television screen with the news playing on silent, the captions running along the bottom.

Everywhere but at Clara.

"Lena."

Her daughter had been born with Down Syndrome. She possessed the chubbier cheeks classic of those with the mutated gene, and she was lovable, bright, and still very much a child. So much of her world had been upended in the past couple of weeks, and Clara reached way down deep for her extra reserve of patience.

"Lena, we have to get on the plane soon. I need you to look at me."

Lena finally brought her hazel eyes to meet Clara's dark brown ones. She gave her daughter a kind smile and reached up to brush her bangs back off her forehead. "It's like going to see Grandma. Uncle Rueben and Aunt Jean will be at the airport to meet us."

"Dad's coming," Lena said, and Clara nodded encouragingly.

She refused to make her voice higher pitched. She'd never talked to Lena like she was an infant. She had a disability; she wasn't stupid. "Yes," she said. "Dad's getting the pretzels you asked for. He's coming this time too."

Their whole family was making the move from Montpelier to Five Island Cove. Clara had arranged with Jennifer Golden to rent a house on the island. It waited in a sleepy, old neighborhood that Jean told herself would be perfect for all of them. It would be away from the news crews, the cameras, and the rumors. The house would offer them far more than protection; the new location, with a new address, would give them anonymity.

Neither she nor Scott would be looking for a new job. They'd managed to get the sale of Friendship Inn to go through with her mother's generous donation for the down payment. Scott's only remaining friend in Vermont had financed the loan. Otherwise, they never would've been able to do it.

As it was, he was probably putting their soft pretzels on a credit card right now. She'd have to figure out how to pay them off later.

Later.

The word ran through Clara's mind, as it had been one she'd been seizing onto for a while now. She'd be able to pick up the pieces of her life later, once she figured out where she'd be living.

She'd be able to provide a sense of safety and normalcy for Lena later, once they'd left Vermont and settled in the cove.

She'd be able to find a way to forgive her husband later, once all the dust had finally settled from the indictments, the bankruptcy, and the nervous looks from friends and neighbors.

"Here you go, Lena-Lou," Scott said.

Clara looked up at her husband and got to her feet, a pinch in her back telling her she was getting too old to crouch down. Her knees testified of it too.

Scott still made her world light up, and Clara turned away from him physically, almost wishing he didn't. His light hair made her think of California, and his blue eyes had spoken to her soul the first time she'd met him.

She clenched her arms across her midsection, feeling how much weight she'd lost recently. Only fifteen pounds or so, but it was enough to make her clothes baggy and her ribs a bit more pronounced.

Since she didn't have money to buy new blouses and shorts, she wore her old ones, the belt loop just one or two tighter than before.

Clara was a master at cinching everything tight. Life hadn't been horrible to her; she felt like she'd taken the good with the bad, rolled with the punches, and survived some of the worst storms. She'd been able to do so, because of the man at her side.

Scott Tanner had always given Clara strength. He was rational when she was emotional, and when he needed to vent, their roles reversed. He'd been kind and attentive to both Clara and Lena as the girl grew up, and heaven knew how many challenges the three of them had faced as they dealt with counselors, therapists, and doctors.

Lena's disability would challenge anyone, but when Clara had found out about the Down Syndrome, her first reaction had been peace. It would be okay. She and Scott could dedicate their lives to their daughter—who'd turned out to be their only child.

She'd felt like that *because* of Scott. The man had a larger-than-life personality, which had attracted Clara as well. From small-town Five Island Cove, where everyone knew everyone else, she'd been looking for excitement and adventure once she'd finally gotten out from underneath her father's thumb.

Scott had provided that. She'd fallen in love with him so fast, and she still loved him now, as she sat down in a hard airport seat a couple away from Lena. Their carryon luggage took up the space between them, and Scott sat to her immediate right, holding the cup of soft pretzel bites for their daughter.

Clara's thumb moved to her ring finger, where her wedding band should be sitting. She still hadn't put it back on. She wondered how she could learn to forgive faster. She puzzled through how to feel betrayed and broken and still in love with the man who'd done that to her.

She riddled through when she'd put the band back on, and how she'd feel when she finally did.

A FEW HOURS LATER, CLARA'S WELL OF PATIENCE had dried up. They couldn't fly a car over from Montpelier. Couches and beds, all the Christmas decorations, the treadmill, even dishes had remained in Vermont.

Clara had the clothes, toiletries, and essential papers in her carryon, with more shoes, clothing, and other necessities in her checked bag.

Times three, that's what the Tanner family currently possessed. The rest of their stuff would arrive on a ship in four to six weeks, and that was only if Clara managed to find the funds to pay for it.

She couldn't look through couch cushions or strategically move money from one account to another. Not anymore. She had no couch, and the federal government had seized and frozen all of their bank accounts.

They'd gotten one back after the first couple of months, and without the help of a few kind souls in Montpelier who'd been Clara and Scott's closest friends, along with Scott's father, they'd survived.

Her phone chimed several times as Reuben maneuvered the SUV into the parking lot at the beachside condo where their mother lived.

The house which Scott and Clara had rented wouldn't be ready for another three weeks, and they'd been forced to ask for more help. A weight of exhaustion pressed against the back of Clara's skull, sending shockwaves of pain through her brain to her eyes.

She told herself over and over that it was okay. Everyone needed help at some point in their lives. She'd been there with meals, babysitting, and money for others over the years. Service brought her joy, and she needed to seize onto that word instead of the one that had been rotating through her mind lately.

"All right," Reuben said, pulling into an uncovered parking space. "This is as close as I can get you." He smiled at Scott in the front seat, his eyes moving to the rearview mirror to flash a grin in Clara's direction too.

She didn't want to seem ungrateful for the free ride, so she quickly curved her lips up. The cost to do so took the minute amount of energy she had left, so she moved just as rapidly to open the back door.

"Lena," she said across Jean, who sat in the middle. "Please come to the back and help with your bag."

The girl wouldn't, and Scott would have to ask her again. Jean would probably be the one to get Lena to do what she'd been asked to do, because Jean was gentle and powerful at the same time.

Clara glanced at her before she slid out, and she found the stress around her sister-in-law's eyes. Compassion filled her, making tears flood her eyes.

She couldn't hide them, so she simply let them fall down her face as she stood and faced her brother.

"Oh, come on," he said, his voice infused with kindness. He took her into a hug, and Clara clung to her big brother now as a forty-two-year-old the same way she had as a child.

"It's not so bad here," he said. "Especially in the summer."

They shifted out of the way as Jean exited the car, and Clara nodded as she stepped away from Reuben. "It's not that." She grabbed onto Jean and hugged her too. "Thank you guys for helping us. It means so much to me. To all of us."

She couldn't see what was happening on the other side of the SUV, and it didn't matter. Clara didn't say thank you enough, and she needed to do better at that. Heck, simply the fact that Reuben thought she'd been crying about being back in the cove told her what her brother thought of her.

She told herself it wasn't a crime to be strong. She was allowed to have her own opinions, *and* to voice them. It wasn't her job to make anyone else feel good about their choices, though she could lend a listening ear.

"You're welcome," Jean said. "If you're dying here, come to the lighthouse."

"Or we'll help pay for a hotel room," Reuben said, his dark eyes filled with concern. He flicked a glance toward the back of the vehicle as the hatch opened.

"Mom," Lena said at the same time Clara wiped her face.

"Thank you," she said again. "We'll be okay. I'm okay."

She took a deep breath, willing the oxygen to make the okay-ness she wanted simply appear.

She wasn't sure if it did or not, but she was able to step to the back of the car to help Lena and Scott with the bags. Reuben and Jean came too, and the five of them towed their six pieces of luggage across the lot and down the sidewalk.

"I'm sure Kristen will have coffee waiting," Jean said.

"She's been cooking for a couple of days, I know that," Reuben added.

A hot meal sounded like a slice of heaven to Clara, but she said nothing. What she really wanted was a room where she could be alone. Where she could cry as much as she wanted. Where she could scream until her throat ripped and all of the negativity inside her fled.

Then, she'd be able to rejoin her family with a better atti-tude and without tears.

They went past the dog park, where a couple of pooches played with one another while a man watched, and on to her mom's building.

She wasn't sure she could take another step, and then she did. One after the other, she did.

Reuben reached the door first, and he twisted the knob. Or tried to. "Huh." He looked down and then over to Clara. "It's locked."

He reached to ring the doorbell, and the *cling-clang-clong* of it reverberated through the condo, loud enough for everyone to hear outside on her porch.

She didn't come to the door. No one called from inside.

Reuben's eyebrows furrowed at the same time Clara's

panic rose. "Where is she? She knew we were coming. I texted her."

Clara leaned closer to the door, trying to edge past a huge bag they'd checked. "Mom?" she called.

No answer.

Frustration piled on top of Clara's already frayed nerves, and the scream she needed to let loose migrated up her throat.

"I'll check the patio," Jean said, leaving behind the luggage she'd been carrying.

Reuben leaned toward the door too. "Mom?" He tried the doorknob again. "It's Reuben and Clara. Are you okay? We can't get in."

Clara dropped her carryon, her shoulder aching. Tears slipped down her face again, the thought of not having her mother for support as she transitioned her family from life in Vermont to life in Five Island Cove completely over-whelming.

And also selfish, she thought. But that didn't erase the fact that they couldn't get in the condo.

There was no relief from the heavy baggage and hot sun.

Her mother wasn't there, so that only left one question in her mind—and which she found in Reuben's eyes— where was their mom?

Rebuilding Friendship Inn Chapter Two:

～◦～

Kristen Shields pressed the square of tissue she'd found in her pocket to the scrape on her knee. She hissed through her teeth, angry at herself for not watching the ground as intently as she should've.

Her and her bleeding heart—and now her knee. She'd just finished the appetizer tray for her children's arrival that evening when she'd seen the feral cat she'd been slowly taming over the past couple of months.

She'd grabbed the chicken cubes she'd cut up for her and dashed outside. Cats could move like ninjas, but with a little persistence and a lot of chicken, she'd managed to find the gray and white cat hiding out in the bushes lining the picnic area of the condo association, where Kristen lived.

She'd lured the cat down the decorative rocks to the beach and fed her the rest of the chicken. She'd even managed to give the cat a stroke or two before the feline had gotten startled and scampered off.

She hadn't been able to go through with getting the puppy she'd once said she'd take. She really was more of a cat person, and she'd been leaning feline for the past few months.

"Are you okay?" The male voice startled Kristen, and she very nearly stumbled again.

She looked up and away from her simple scrape—right into the navy eyes of Theodore Sands.

He lived in her community, and she'd seen him at a couple of the activities she'd managed to attend. She'd never spoken to him much, though sometimes their morning walks had her going out to the beach as he came in.

A nod. A hello. She knew him.

"Yes," she said with a sigh. "I was just feeding this cat, and my foot got caught in the rocks." As if a testament to what had happened, Kristen's ankle sent a spike of pain up her calf.

"I twisted my ankle and just went down on the one knee." She'd gotten up by herself too. No one had seen her, she was fairly certain of that.

Her chest heated, and she certainly hoped Theo had not seen.

Why? she asked herself. *Why does it matter if he saw you fall?*

Confused, she looked up at him. He was a handsome man, Kristen could admit that. The moment she did, her heartbeat stuttered in her chest.

"Let me help you back to your place," he said, extending

his hand toward her. Feeling dumb, Kristen put her hand out too. That was what one did when offered help, wasn't it?

His fingers slid along hers, and he froze. She did too, not sure why her blood had started popping and fizzing and bubbling.

She quickly pulled her hand away. "I'm okay," she said. "My kids will be here any minute. I was just trying to stop the bleeding, so I didn't have it dripping down my leg while I walked."

Theo's eyes slipped down to her knee. "I think it looks okay now."

"Yes," Kristen said. "I'm okay." She straightened and wadded up the bloody tissue, quickly stuffing it back into her pocket. She offered Theo a wide smile, hoping that would let him know he could move along.

He gestured for her to go first up the steps that led back to the picnic area. Kristen couldn't think of a reason why she wouldn't go that way, so she went. His footsteps came behind her, a fact that sent her pulse into a whirlwind.

"It's Kristen, right?" he asked once they'd both reached the top of the steps. He gave her a smile that seemed genuine and kind.

"Yes," she said. "And you're Theo." She glanced over at him, finding him ducking his head as he smiled.

"Yes." They walked down the sidewalk together, and Kristen found herself taking in the glorious June evening. Somewhere in the distance, a dog barked, probably at the dog park on the other side of her building.

"Listen," Theo said. "I notice you go walking on the beach, same as me."

"Sometimes," Kristen said. Sometimes she went walking with AJ in the morning. Jean had been joining them this summer, as had Alice. Robin punished herself by running, and far too early for Kristen's liking. The older she'd gotten, the more sleep she'd needed. Especially since Joel's death, Kristen felt far older than she ever had previously.

"Maybe we could synchronize our walking schedule," he said, his silver eyebrows going up.

Kristen's mind screamed at her to say yes. Of course she wanted to go walking with Theo. He seemed interesting, and he was handsome, and she hadn't reacted to a man like this in a long, long time.

"There you are," someone said, and Kristen turned away from Theo, realizing she'd stopped walking. So had he.

Her son rushed toward her, pure panic on his face. He scooped her right into his arms, saying, "The door is locked, and we thought maybe you'd fallen inside." He stepped back and held onto Kristen's upper arms, his eyes searching for injuries. "Are you okay?"

"Yes," Kristen said, somewhat surprised at his worry. Clara, Scott, and Jean came around the corner too, and Kristen's embarrassment doubled. "I just...saw that feral cat." She threw a look at Theo. "I'm fine."

He smiled, and his teeth certainly looked real. He ticked all the boxes for Kristen, especially as he kept her secret about twisting her ankle and scraping her knee. It was what toddlers did, and she really was fine.

"Clara's exhausted," Reuben said. "Do you have the key? I'll get the house unlocked and everyone settled." He focused on Theo for longer this time, his eyes harboring questions when he looked at Kristen again. "Then you can finish your conversation."

"We're finished," Theo said. "No intrusion." He waved his hand like Kristen's children's worry over her was nothing, but it sent a hot poker of embarrassment through her once again.

"I don't have my key," Kristen said slowly. Theo paused in his exit, and Rueben's eyebrows bushed over his eyes again.

"The door's locked," her son said. "The sliding door too."

"We'll have to call the front office," Kristen said. "I must've hit the lock in my haste to find the cat."

Reuben looked like he had something to say about her chasing down feral cats, but he held his tongue. Thankfully. Kristen didn't want to get into anything with him in front of Theo, and she had no idea what that meant.

"I've got a key," Theo said, sending shock through her.

"You do?"

He started walking again, and she practically leapt to get to his side again. "Yeah," he said. "I work in the front office sometimes. I have can get in and get you a spare." He gifted her with another brilliant smile, and Kristen swore her muscles melted right off her bones.

"Mom?" Clara asked as they approached one another.

"Hello, dear." Kristen set aside her hormones, a bit

surprised they worked after all these years. "I'm sorry about this. How was the flight?" She put one hand on Clara's shoulder while the other brushed the hair off her daughter's forehead. She looked one breath away from a complete break-down, and Kristen found Scott hovering back near the corner.

"It went well enough," Clara said.

"I'll only be a few minutes, Kristen," Theo said, touching her forearm. "Be right back."

"Thank you, Theo," Kristen said, and she watched him walk away for a few steps before she looked at her daughter again.

Everyone had gone silent, and a charge rode in the air she hadn't felt in a while. Her gaze moved from Clara's narrowed eyes to Rueben's, which held a calculating look. Jean wore a bright smile on her face, and it looked like she might start laughing at any moment.

"What?" she asked just as Clara opened her mouth.

She stopped, breathed again, and asked, "Who was that, Mother?"

"Theo," she said.

"He's running off to get your spare key." Clara made it sound like a scandalous thing to do.

"He said he works in the front office," Kristen said, stepping past her. She couldn't look at Reuben, so she focused on Scott and Lena. "Hello, my family. Sorry I locked us out."

"The door is locked," Lena said, her voice loud and blunt.

Kristen grinned at her. "Yes," she said. "It sure is. Is that a new backpack?"

"Mom bought it for the plane." Lena looked down at the bright purple straps. She adored anything with purple and glitter, and Kristen wished she hadn't locked the sticker book she'd bought for her granddaughter in the condo.

"Are you dating him?" Clara demanded, to which Jean burst out laughing.

Kristen almost twisted her compromised ankle, but thankfully, it held her. She gave Clara the best withering look she could. "No," she said. "Of course not."

"Grandma," Lena said, whose attention had wandered somewhere else. "Come look at this gray cat."

LATER THAT NIGHT, KRISTEN FINALLY ENTERED her bedroom, the light off. She didn't reach to flip it on, because she needed the dark, quiet space. She closed the door behind her, glad everyone had found an acceptable place to sleep.

Scott had ended up going to the lighthouse with Reuben and Jean. They had an extra room on the second floor, and everyone could feel and see that Clara and Scott weren't really getting along.

That wasn't right. It wasn't that they argued or fought. They simply didn't speak to one another. Clara spoke *about* Scott, never truly looking him in the eye. Scott would say,

"Clara has all of our important documents," and smile at her while she refused to look at him.

Kristen didn't know all the details and having Rueben and Jean living in the cove had taught her a boundary she couldn't cross when it came to her children's relationships. Scott and Clara got to decide how things functioned inside their marriage, and Kristen wasn't going to say anything about it.

Lena had taken the second bedroom, just on the other side of the wall from Kristen's, and Clara was once again sleeping on an air mattress in the formal dining room. Kristen had commissioned a barn door to section that room off from the rest of the condo to give her daughter some privacy, and it would be here in a couple of days.

Clara said she didn't mind. Kristen had seen so many changes in her already, and while she'd thoroughly enjoyed this evening, their dinner, the conversations, and presenting Lena with the sticker book, her emotions had been through a woodchipper.

She sighed as she sank onto the bed and removed her shoes. Theo had been fairly quick in getting the spare key to her condo, and she'd thanked him. He'd left without another word about synchronizing their walking schedules, but the thought hadn't left Kristen's mind, not even for a minute.

Her phone lit up the room, and Kristen looked at it. She'd put it on silent a while ago, and she hadn't bothered to check it. The only people who texted her were her Seafaring Girls—and any others they'd adopted into the group.

Jean was on the string, and Kristen had it on her list of things to do to ask the girls if she could add Clara. Her daughter would need the support this summer, and so many of Kristen's girls had been through hard things in the past several years.

Marriages, babies, divorces, new relationships, children graduating. The list went on and on.

She found over one hundred messages in the group thread from her girls, and she sighed as she tapped to read them. The arrow shot her back up to the last unread message, and she sucked in a breath as the words entered her brain.

Kristen was seen flirting with a very handsome older man outside her condo.

"Jean," Kristen murmured, stunned her daughter-in-law had tattled on her.

The thread had exploded from there, with everyone chiming in to know who it was, what was said, done, the whole nine yards.

"My goodness," she said, reading something she wished she could scrub from her eyeballs. "Alice."

Her thumbs started flying across her screen. *None of this is true. Yes, a man helped me after I twisted my ankle on the beach. It was and remains nothing.*

She sent the message and pressed her fingers against the corner of her phone to take off the case. There, a slip of paper fluttered to her thigh, and she shined her phone on it, the blue light illuminating the numbers there.

The name.

Theo.

She'd spoken true—she had twisted her ankle on the beach. A man had helped her. It was nothing, and it remained nothing.

At least until she got up the nerve to text him to let him know what time she liked to go walking on the beach.

Another message came in, and Kristen started typing again. This text would settle things once and for all, and nervous excitement fluttered through her stomach.

Rebuilding Friendship Inn is now available! Will these women in Five Island Cove rally around one another as they've been doing? Or will this finally be the thing that breaks them? **Find out today!**

Books in the Five Island Cove series

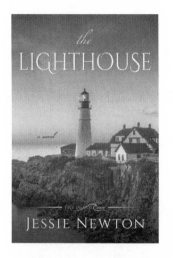

The Lighthouse, Book 1: As these 5 best friends work together to find the truth, they learn to let go of what doesn't matter and cling to what does: faith, family, and most of all, friendship.

Secrets, safety, and sisterhood...it all happens at the lighthouse on Five Island Cove.

The Summer Sand Pact, Book 2: These five best friends made a Summer Sand Pact as teens and have only kept it once or twice—until they reunite decades later and renew their agreement to meet in Five Island Cove every summer.

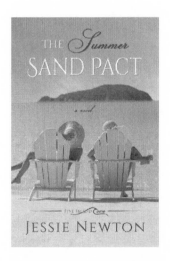

Books in the Five Island Cove series

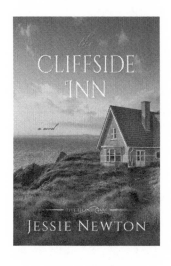

The Cliffside Inn, Book 3: Spend another month in Five Island Cove and experience an amazing adventure between five best friends, the challenges they face, the secrets threatening to come between them, and their undying support of each other.

Christmas at the Cove, Book 4: Secrets are never discovered during the holidays, right? That's what these five best friends are banking on as they gather once again to Five Island Cove for what they hope will be a Christmas to remember.

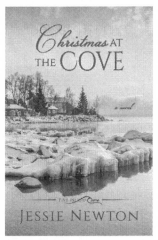

Books in the Five Island Cove series

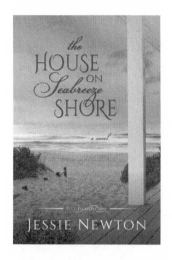

The House on Seabreeze Shore, Book 5: Your next trip to Five Island Cove...this time to face a fresh future and leave all the secrets and fears in the past. Join best friends, old and new, as they learn about themselves, strengthen their bonds of friendship, and learn what it truly means to thrive.

Four Weddings and a Baby, Book 6: When disaster strikes, whose wedding will be postponed? Whose dreams will be underwater?

And there's a baby coming too... Best friends, old and new, must learn to work together to clean up after a natural disaster that leaves bouquets and altars, bassinets and baby blankets, in a soggy heap.

Books in the Five Island Cove series

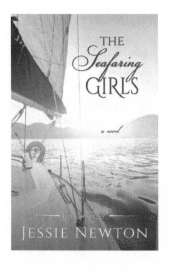

The Seafaring Girls, Book 7:
Journey to Five Island Cove for a roaring good time with friends old and new, their sons and daughters, and all their new husbands as they navigate the heartaches and celebrations of life and love.

But when someone returns to the Cove that no one ever expected to see again, old wounds open just as they'd started to heal. This group of women will be tested again, both on land and at sea, just as they once were as teens.

Rebuilding Friendship Inn, Book 8:
Clara Tanner has lost it all. Her husband is accused in one of the biggest heists on the East Coast, and she relocates her family to Five Island Cove—the hometown she hates.

Clara needs all of their help and support in order to rebuild Friendship Inn, and as all the women pitch in, there's so much more getting fixed up, put in place, and restored.

Then a single phone call changes everything.

Will these women in Five Island Cove rally around one

another as they've been doing? Or will this finally be the thing that breaks them?

Books in the Five Island Cove series

The Glass Dolphin, Book 9:
With new friends in Five Island
Cove, has the group grown too
big? Is there room for all the
different personalities, their
problems, and their expanding
population?

**The Bicycle Book Club, Book
10:** Summer is upon Five Island
Cove, and that means beach days
with
friends and family, an explosion of
tourism, and summer reading
programs! When Tessa decides to
look into the past to help shape the
future, what she finds in the Five
Island Cove library archives could
bring them closer together...or
splinter them forever.

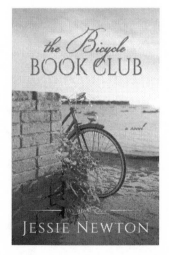

Books in the Nantucket Point series

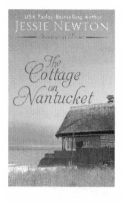

The Cottage on Nantucket, Book 1:
When two sisters arrive at the cottage on Nantucket after their mother's death, they begin down a road filled with the ghosts of their past. And when Tessa finds a final letter addressed only to her in a locked desk drawer, the two sisters will uncover secret after secret that exposes them to danger at their Nantucket cottage.

The Lighthouse Inn, Book 2: The Nantucket Historical Society pairs two women together to begin running a defunct inn, not knowing that they're bitter enemies. When they come face-to-face, Julia and Madelynne are horrified and dumbstruck—and bound together by their future commitment and their obstacles in their pasts...

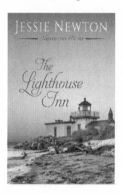

Books in the Nantucket Point series

The Seashell Promise, Book 3: When two sisters arrive at the cottage on Nantucket after their mother's death, they begin down a road filled with the ghosts of their past. And when Tessa finds a final letter addressed only to her in a locked desk drawer, the two sisters will uncover secret after secret that exposes them to danger at their Nantucket cottage.

About Jessie

Jessie Newton is a saleswoman during the day and escapes into romance and women's fiction in the evening, usually with a cat and a cup of tea nearby. The Lighthouse is her first women's fiction novel, but she writes as Elana Johnson and Liz Isaacson as well, with over 200 books to all of her names. Find out more at www.feelgoodfictionbooks.com.

Made in the USA
Middletown, DE
22 February 2024